Birgit's Consequences

A Morally Reprehensible Woman...

G M GAUDIO

Copyright © 2021 G M Gaudio

The moral right of the author has been asserted.

Apart from any fair dealing for the purposes of research or private study, or criticism or review, as permitted under the Copyright, Designs and Patents Act 1988, this publication may only be reproduced, stored or transmitted, in any form or by any means, with the prior permission in writing of the publishers, or in the case of reprographic reproduction in accordance with the terms of licences issued by the Copyright Licensing Agency. Enquiries concerning reproduction outside those terms should be sent to the publishers.

This book is a work of historical fiction. While some characters are genuine and out of history, others , if any resemblance to real people or incidents are purely coincidental.

Matador
9 Priory Business Park,
Wistow Road, Kibworth Beauchamp,
Leicestershire. LE8 0RX
Tel: 0116 279 2299
Email: books@troubador.co.uk
Web: www.troubador.co.uk/matador
Twitter: @matadorbooks

ISBN 978 1800463 288

British Library Cataloguing in Publication Data.
A catalogue record for this book is available from the British Library.

Printed and bound in Great Britain by 4edge Limited
Typeset in 11pt Adobe Garamond pro by Troubador Publishing Ltd, Leicester, UK

Matador is an imprint of Troubador Publishing Ltd

This novel is dedicated to Dr. Bryan Gaudio, my son,
for being my inspiration

and to Elisa J. Stadelmann for being my salvation.

Contents

BOOK 1

1	An Inconceivable Act	3
2	Disposing of the Corpse	20
3	The Early Inquiries	33
4	Police Involvement	46
5	Preparations for the Journey	59
6	Secret Meeting with Annalisa	68
7	Progress of Police Investigation	86
8	Lorenzo's Trip to America	94
9	Inspector Delves Deeper	104
10	Naples Central Station	120
11	The Orphanage	132
12	On the Ocean Liner	137
13	Day to Day at the Orphanage	147

14	Making Difficult Decisions	163
15	Matteo's Funeral	175
16	Giacomo's Quest for Control	191
17	Lorenzo's Horoscope	209

BOOK II

18	In the Beginning	221
19	Who is Birgit Karlsen?	241
20	Time Spent Recovering	256
21	The Affair	266
22	The Gardener's Folly and the Administrator's Problem	276
23	The Lieutenant's Transfer to Aker Hospital	293
24	Closing Astergarden and Birgit's Visit to Aker Hospital	301
25	Birgit's Pregnancy and Turbulent Times	320
26	Lieutenant Kuhlemann on Leave	325
27	Birgit at the *Lebensborn* Home	333
28	A Child is Born	342
29	Trying to Pick Up the Pieces	349

| | Epilogue | 355 |

BOOK I

Chapter 1

An Inconceivable Act

She had always been considered a beautiful woman, at least since her fourteenth birthday when everyone could see that nature had been kind to her. Francesca Benedetta was, as her surname implied, blessed. During Sunday morning mass her natural attributes stirred passion in young men, envy in middle-aged women and often brought a blush to the face of the forty-five-year-old parish priest when he greeted her, and the rest of his flock, at the church's gate.

But as life would have it, her God-given endowments were a blessing on one hand and a curse on the other. Within a few short years of puberty, while Francesca's peers were still in school attempting to cope with the awkward years or daydreaming about their future, Francesca's childhood was forfeited. Her parents said it was a "beneficial arrangement" with her second cousin Matteo. So, at fifteen she did what was expected of her and withdrew from school. At sixteen she was married. At seventeen, twenty-three hours after her own birthday, she became defined as baby Lorenzo's *Mama*. And when she was absurdly addressed as Signora Benedetta, she coyly smiled. Still, and in due course, the newlywed's relationship had grown from a marriage of convenience to one of true love.

Fast forward two decades and circumstances had dramatically changed. Matteo had been sick for several years and Francesca had seen whatever savings they had struggled to accumulate on their farm largely depleted, yet she still managed to eke out a living with the help of her son. Her husband required medical treatments in Rome every month to deal with a viral infection that increasingly compromised his lung function and then inexorably moved on to damage his heart and other vital organs. During the last treatment the doctor at the Rome Polyclinic had been reluctant to tell Matteo the truth about his prognosis. But after Matteo's insistence, the hospital director was called in and together they gave Matteo the unpleasant news. He had three to six months to live before his body would succumb to the pernicious onslaught of the disease. It took him about ten days to digest this news and for tears to stop rolling down his cheeks. After that, he developed a sense of resignation followed with a certain equanimity. Then he did what people do when hope begins to fade. He threw himself at the mercy of the Lord.

Now, as Francesca made her way down the narrow, winding dirt path to the old barn several hundred yards from the main house, she carried a straw basket on her arm. Inside the basket were two kitchen towels and a small bag of seeds. The towels were to cushion the fragile contents she expected to carry on her way back home. The seed was to lure away the chickens from their eggs. She was momentarily lost in reverie, thinking how quickly her life was passing. It was the early 1970s, and after so much time living and toiling on the farm, giving birth to her oldest child, Lorenzo, and to Gabriella five years later, she felt that she still had her spirit and her grace but wasn't so sure about her looks. However, any reasonable observer would disagree because her delicate narrow face and glowing skin still reminded them of the pretty Madonna on the church frescos. She wore her dark brown hair the same way she always had, slightly past her shoulders and tied back with a hair clip that complemented her five-feet ten-inch statuesque figure. She wore a loose-fitting, one piece cotton dress, camel-colored, frayed around the side pockets, and with a thin belt around her waist.

As she walked, Francesca looked admiringly at the large track of vineyards to her left. The scraggly vines grew down the mountain slope, beginning some twenty paces east of their loggia and all the way down to the side of her neighbors' farmhouse. Further east, beyond the vineyards and at eleven o'clock, she had a partial view of the dark blue, almost turquoise Tyrrhenian Sea. In the same general direction, but southerly, were their second-closest neighbors, the Salvaggis. They were a stone's throw away from the water and approximately a quarter mile from the Benedettas'. On her right side, and as far as the eye could see, was a lush valley, green and teeming with chestnut, beech and pine trees. The chestnut trees extended beyond the main house and to the upper reaches of the mountain where cactus plants took over and at sunset seemed to stand guard like ancient Roman warriors. Several miles beyond the valley on the adjacent mountainside was St Biaze, an archipelago of homes and small farms arranged in such fashion as if an artist had splattered his paint in a moment of rage. The small farmhouses were dressed in either lavish stucco or painted in warm Mediterranean colors with tin roofs or orange-colored ceramic tiles capping the structures. To get down to the closest town, a seaside community called Longobardi Marina, or to reach Cosenza, the nearest city, one had to travel about an eighth of a mile down the Benedettas' dirt driveway and get on the narrow, winding public roads for some twenty minutes by truck. Then one would reach relatively flat terrain, travel on that for another five minutes and finally merge with a state road.

As she looked up, Francesca saw angry, dark clouds shifting across the late October sky. They were being swept furiously, chaotically, by the westerly winds blowing from the sea and across the southern Italian Peninsula. Little animals burrowed under leaves and dead branches. Birds hid and squirrels scurried in the trees. The crows gave off loud shrieks that could be heard echoing in the valley. And the noise of the rustling leaves in the trees synchronized with the cicadas' crescendo. Francesca knew that a thunderstorm and heavy rains were imminent. No sooner had she made the observation than a streak of lightning seemed to tear apart the very fabric of the heavens. The blazing sky was followed by stupendous rolling thunder that seemed to shake the earth's core. Frightened, she clutched the medallion of St Francis round her neck. Then Francesca felt cold droplets of rain on her skin and saw larger droplets pounding the dusty path ahead of her.

Her thoughts shifted to Lorenzo and she wondered if he had gotten back from his uncle's house and whether he had been at the barn to feed the animals. She hoped that he wouldn't get caught in the deluge. The last thing she wanted was for him to get sick. During early breakfast he had mentioned going to his uncle's house to drop off some animal feed, but she knew better. It was probably to see their newborn calf. Newly born animals had always fascinated her son. She didn't know where Lorenzo had acquired this love of animals. It wasn't anything in her nature or in Matteo's character, not like his dark hair that he acquired from her husband, or his disarming wide smile and defined facial features that made him look strikingly handsome. Then her thoughts flashed back to her task at hand. Once she had collected the eggs from the chicken coop, she would hurry home to start dinner, give Matteo his medications, change his soiled clothes and make the beds.

Walking around the exterior of the old barn, she noticed that the chicken coop on the opposite side seemed to be empty of its feathery occupants. Whoever said chickens were stupid was wrong, she thought. The hens had an instinct to recognize changing weather conditions and had probably made their way inside the barn for shelter via a small porthole. As she came face to face with the double barn doors, she dropped her basket to the ground in order to unlatch the metal bolt and swing open the heavy door, but suddenly realized that the door was unlocked and slightly ajar. Perhaps Lorenzo had been there to feed the animals and forgotten to latch the door on the way out. She made a mental note to bring it to his attention. Now that it was getting dark, she regretted not bringing the lantern, and the thought of going back home to get one crossed her mind but was ruled out just as quickly. She didn't want to trudge back and forth in this nasty weather, and settled on the fact that there was still some faint natural light coming in from the open door and the upper barn window. From the entrance she could still make out the bales of hay in the loft. The younger of the two cows heard her and gave off a low mooing sound as she picked up her basket. Her eyes adjusted quickly to the dim interior light. She could see that some of the chickens had managed to fly up and take temporary shelter in the hayloft where they were probably laying most of their eggs.

"*Enzo, sei qua?* (Enzo, are you here?)" She called for her son several times while her eyes roamed around the barn. There was no answer. Another wave of thunder rolled in, followed by a flash of lighting that again lit up the sky. This prompted some of the chickens to cackle excitedly while others, unfazed, stayed in their warm nesting position or pecked at each other. Francesca saw the wooden ladder leaning against the interior wall, several feet from the entrance. A pile of dried firewood was stacked next to the ladder; behind the ladder were several shovels and a pitchfork. She dragged the ladder across the width of the barn and leaned it against the edge of the loft. After adjusting the legs for balance and convincing herself that the ladder was secure on the ground, she started to climb. On the second rung she stopped abruptly and listened to what seemed to her to be a thumping noise coming from behind the half partition.

"*Chi che?* (Who's there?)" she cried. "*Enzo, sei qua?* (Enzo, are you here?)" No response. She waited and listened; nothing. She convinced herself that it was probably a field mouse scampering around and continued her climb. With the straw basket in her left hand she grasped the side of the ladder while her right hand stretched to reach the next rung.

When she was almost at the top, she could see that the hens were agitated and were flapping their wings. One made a screeching noise. Without warning a second bird got pecked by another and flew erratically towards Francesca's face. Instinctively, she threw up her hand for cover as her body tensed and the ladder slipped away from under her. She had enough presence of mind to try and grab a plank protruding from the edge of the loft but her grasp slipped. And like in a bad dream, she was overwhelmed by the panic of uncontrolled falling as she plunged helplessly backwards.

The last thing Francesca remembered was a thud as the back of her head struck something hard. Then everything went blank. The ladder came to rest at her side and her body was sprawled out in the center of the barn floor. For seconds and then minutes it was remarkably quiet, as if the unfortunate accident was frozen in time. Then a large figure slowly rose from a crouched position behind a partition and cautiously emerged into the open. It made its way in the darkness lit only by the sporadic illumination of flashing light coming through the small loft window. The figure came to stand several feet from Francesca where his six-feet four-inch frame towered over her. He stared at her and saw her head resting perpendicularly on a wedge of firewood, her arms and legs splayed open on scattered hay. While gawking at her, he began shaking his head in seeming disapproval of what he was witnessing. This distressed him and as the level of distress intensified, he started pacing back and forth anxiously, like a wild animal trapped in a cage. Then while more lightning flashed and thunder roared outside, the brawny figure clasped his ears with both hands and squeezed his eyes shut, desperately trying to drown out the noises. He wanted nothing more than for the scene to go away; for the wind to stop howling and for the rain to stop pounding overhead on the barn's tin roof.

The large man became more and more agitated as the noises resonated in his head. He was breathing heavily and almost uncontrollably, as if millimeters away from a panic attack. A sprinkle of perspiration formed on his forehead and the back of his neck was moist. His initial reaction was to run away but there was nowhere to run from the clamor. He stood there with his eyes and ears shut until it got quieter and then images came streaming into his head, all sorts of images, jumbled and disjointed. His eyes returned to the woman on the ground and still she wasn't moving. The unpleasant scene didn't make sense to him. She was always nice and smiling at him. Why wasn't she smiling now? Why wasn't she moving? What could he do to help her, to make her feel better?

In the erratic flashes of light, she reminded him of a black and white photograph. This elicited other images in his head, particularly ones he had seen at the construction yard. There, on the office walls, were lots of pictures of smiling families plastered about that he often looked at. But there were also "special pictures" that Tariq, the Albanian, had shown him. He remembered Tariq laughing and telling him that he should stop looking at those silly family pictures in the office hallway, and instead pay attention to the ones he was holding which showed happy men and women. Then Tariq displayed them to other co-workers in the yard who milled about and while slapping a page with the back of his hand, told them emphatically: "*Cosi fa una donna contenta* (This is how you make a woman happy)." After staring at the photos in his magazine, the construction workers nodded their heads in approval as they walked away, some laughing, some joking and making hand gestures, while a younger man with broken teeth excitedly grabbed his crotch. As he recalled, the magazines showed women, naked women in all sorts of positions with men, some lying on a bed or sprawled on a haystack, "*frecando* (fucking)", is what Tariq had called it.

Now, in the scrambled synapses of the man's mind electrical impulses were randomly and chaotically firing away. He wanted to make the nice lady smile again and talk to him; he wanted to make her happy, just like those pictures where none of the women were sad or unresponsive.

As his mind seized on Tariq's advice, he became less agitated and his breathing slowly came under control until he finally stopped pacing. Then he took a few steps toward Francesca, and, with a swoop of his hand, he thrust the ladder aside and knelt next to her. His head was turned away from her. His left hand covered his eyes, like a visor shielding bright sunlight, all because he was embarrassed at being so close to her. But after several moments he collected himself and lowered his hand along his temple until his gaze settled on her brown hair; slowly he came to focus on her face. She was so beautiful and her beauty seemed to mesmerize him until his thoughts switched back to the glossy photo pages. It was then that he gently lifted her head in the palm of his hand and slowly removed the block of wood from underneath. And while holding one hand behind her neck the other hand softly brushed back the straggly hair resting over Francesca's eyes and cheekbone. Then with the back of his thick fingers he caressed her several times from the back of her neck to her porcelain chin before placing her head on the ground. He stared at her for a while, then, lowering his torso closer, like a hyena extending its neck, his face was next to hers. He inhaled deeply the scent of her perfume. And grazed his cheek against her soft skin. This gave him a strange but warm sensation all over that seemed to intensify even more when he clumsily brushed his lips against hers. He repeated the act several times, but slower. At first the warm feeling seemed to concentrate in his belly, but then, like wildfire, it spread up his legs to his loins. He had seen men and women kissing and they always seemed happy, but the pretty lady was not yet speaking, moving or smiling.

Could he be doing something wrong? His mind, again, seized on the images in the centerfold of the magazine. He placed his right hand over her dress and started fondling her left breast. Within moments he had repositioned himself beside Francesca's limp body to more easily cup her breasts. Even over her thin cotton dress she felt so soft, so warm and inviting. Her skin was silky smooth. It reminded him of the baby chicks he loved to pet in the hen house where they would scurry about and hide behind crates. He became bolder, his hands explored under the cloth, he felt the roundness and warmth of her breasts. Her nipples were large and firm, and he was startled at the sudden tightening in his breeches. At first, he was scared and pulled his hands away from her chest like an infant from a hot stove, but only to have some irresistible force take hold of him, dominate him, excite him uncontrollably. And like a child not yet satisfied with the wonders of a new toy, he reached for the thin straps of Francesca's dress. He pulled them down from her shoulders, and again began stroking her breasts and nipples in a circular motion. The bulge between his legs grew increasingly uncomfortable as it pressed against the thick fabric of his trousers.

His eyes soon came to rest on the hem of Francesca's dress. From the fall, it had slid above her hip. Her thighs were exposed as well as her white underwear. Curious to feel the softness of her inner thigh, he moved his right hand from her breast to her upper knee. It was at this instance that fear and desire clashed in his mind. But desire overpowered any capability of reason and, awkwardly, he pulled down her underwear. The sight of her genitals sent an unexpected current through his body that was expressed as an inhuman guttural moan. It sounded like an excited and starved animal about to rip into the soft underbelly of its prey. He placed his open hand over her pelvic bone. He was fascinated by the supple texture of her pubic hair and began to stroke it. Then, he grabbed both her knees and spread her legs wide apart. And hesitatingly, but uncontrollably drawn, touched her vagina. With intensified excitement, he began exploring with his fingers.

Again, many glossy images interposed themselves in his mind and he felt the heat of those images commingle with the sweet scent of the naked woman lying beneath him.

With one hand he continued to fondle Francesca's genitals and with the other he reached for his suspenders. Though his large hand and thick fingers frustrated his dexterity, he fumbled with the straps.

When he finally freed himself from the suspenders, he tried to undo the buttons on his overalls. The struggle with the buttons proved even more challenging. But in order to satisfy nature's demand for expediency, he ripped off the second button.

His swollen, pulsating organ never felt so hard and so huge as he held it in his hand. Then he leaned over the naked woman and with both hands he gripped her waist and slid his hands under her fleshy buttocks. When Francesca's body was properly inclined, he pulled her legs closer and over his thick muscular thighs. Then he spread her legs further apart and with a groan plunged his throbbing manhood into her warm, soft cave. His strong arms pulled her enveloping flesh closer to his loins. He thrust into her, again and again, as if she were a rag doll and no longer human.

At a point, his desire became so manifest, so uncontainable, so insatiable that he grabbed her shoulders with both hands and repeatedly slammed his engorged organ even deeper. The lust was primitive and encoded in his genes. It was autonomic and unquenchable. No thought was required, none was possible, short of pursuing unrestrained gratification. Francesca stirred and moaned but not of pleasure, only of pain. Still, she didn't regain consciousness. Her moan only intensified his desire. His blood surged higher and coursed faster and faster through his veins. He felt an earthquake starting to rumble in his lower abdomen. And like an impending storm, energy gathered between his thighs until muscular contractions took control. A volcanic eruption followed where everything was gained, yet, everything was lost. The massive man's body quivered spasmodically with ecstasy and pain; life and death clashed at the crossroads.

At first, the huge figure teetered and then dropped to the ground like a sack of cement. His left hand still clutching onto Francesca Benedetta's buttock. His right hand still clinging to the shaft of his penis. On the ground, his body contorted involuntarily for several minutes, semen still spilling out of him and blood oozing from the blow he had just received. His head was partially decapitated. The impact of the sharp blow sent a section of the man's skull bouncing off the barn wall, traces of blood mixed with brain tissue visible on the piles of hay.

A lanky figure held a shovel in his hand and stood behind the still quivering body. His young face reflected both agony and rage as he tossed the bloody shovel to the ground. He took a closer look at the partially undressed corpse; the contortions had left him in a fetal position. The lanky figure recognized him, but made no attempt to help. The man on the ground had greenish-blue eyes, wide open, almost in a religious trance. From what was left of his skull, he could see the young man's blond hair, receding and parted to the right. He had a big face, very tanned, and a square chin. His large muscular arms and torso were covered with a disheveled brown corduroy shirt, rolled up to his elbows, tails out of his pants.

The lanky figure walked around the huge body, cautiously, anticipating that he might still be attacked. His face was contorted in disgust from what he had just seen. His hands were trembling. Lorenzo wasn't sure if the feeling of disgust was from the brutal attack against the woman on the ground – his mother – or from what he had done to the attacker; maybe both. Then he kneeled next to Francesca, and to his great relief, he discovered that she was still breathing. Lorenzo looked around, stood up and unhooked a mule blanket from the wall. The blanket was old and worn, and used only to protect the mule's hide from developing friction sores during long rides, particularly when the animal was overloaded. He folded the blanket several times and placed it under his mother's head, only to discover a gash behind her skull that needed to be attended to. Gently, he brushed back her hair, then pulled up her underwear and pulled down her cotton dress until the hem came to cover her knees.

Lorenzo was numb. He didn't want to think of the internal injuries she may have suffered. This was his mother; he should not have seen what he saw; it was impossible to conceive of something more horrible happening to his mother.

He decided that he must get her home before she awoke. He could see outside, past the open barn doors. The rain had subsided to a drizzle but it was much darker. The clouds, like a giant umbrella, blocked the moonlight. The torrential downpour had filled in a dip just outside the doors and left a large puddle. Birds could be heard chirping and complaining deep in the woods while the previously excited barn animals had now settled down. Everything seemed almost normal, but he knew that nothing would ever be normal again.

Gently, Lorenzo lifted his mother's limp body off the ground, all 120 pounds of her. Her head leaned against his chest like a helpless child. He readjusted his arms around her to get a better grip. She moaned in pain but didn't open her eyes. Lorenzo saw the dead man in his path and felt the gorge rise within him. He wanted to kick the bastard in the face, but instead, stepped around him as he headed for the door. Mama didn't feel as heavy as he initially thought but getting up the hill was another matter. Even though Lorenzo was used to doing hard physical labor on the farm, carrying his mother's dead weight was more difficult than lifting bundles of hay.

By the time Lorenzo had carried Francesca some fifty feet he noticed that the fresh air and fine drizzle were helping her regain consciousness. When she started to come around, he lowered her on the wet grass.

"*Mama, como ti senti?* (Mama, how are you feeling?)" She opened her eyes. She took a few seconds to orient herself before responding.

"*Enzo! Cosa e successo?* (What happened to me?) I feel sore all over," she murmured in a very low voice.

"You must've fallen off the ladder and hit your head. When I got to the barn you were out cold until now. Stay still, Mama, I'm taking you home," he responded.

"Aaaaahhhh," she exclaimed as she raised her hand to touch the back of her head.

"It's a nasty gash," he said, not sparing her the seriousness of the injury. "Do you remember anything?" he asked, deliberately probing.

"The last thing I remember was climbing the ladder and reaching for something and then losing my balance and falling backwards. I must've hit my head against a post." Again, she reached behind her head and felt a bump and dampness. Her hair was matted from the congealing blood. She pulled her hand back and saw blood on her fingertips.

"Can you walk a little if I support you?" asked Lorenzo.

"I'll try, Enzo," she said, almost incoherently, followed by a deep sigh.

Lorenzo helped her up as she placed her arm around her son's shoulder. They walked some twenty feet when her foot slipped on wet grass and mud. She landed on her knees with Lorenzo holding her under her arms and trying to support her. Her knees and the front of her dress were splattered with muddy water.

The two struggled up the incline towards the house. When they reached flatter ground, Lorenzo wasn't sure whether he should tell his mother anything more. Then decided to wait until she felt better, perhaps tomorrow. She had more than enough to deal with, especially with Papa on his deathbed. He remembered the local doctor telling his Uncle Dominick and his mother that Papa had limited time. When pressed, he said it was a matter of several months at best.

With all this going on, how could he possibly tell his mother that their retarded neighbor, Andreas Salvaggi, had just raped her? He wasn't sure how she would react. He had heard crazy stories of women being traumatized so deeply and feeling so distraught that they threw themselves off cliffs or drowned themselves. Even knowing that his mother was stronger than that, how could he in good conscience inflict her with more pain?

His sister, Gabriella, hearing them outside, came down to open the front door. Lorenzo told her that Mama had taken a bad fall and needed to wash and that her head wound needed cleansing and bandaging. They guided her to the kitchen and Lorenzo pulled out a kitchen chair for her. When she sat down, she gave out a sharp cry. Gabriella shifted her mother's hair to one side and both looked at the wound. It had stopped oozing but was swollen. They decided that they should wash the cut, treat it with antiseptic and bandage it. Gabriella ran upstairs to get the antiseptic and was back in an instant, also carrying a pillow and a blanket. After they made her a little more comfortable, Gabriella went to prepare her for a bath.

Francesca was resting her head on a pillow on the table, a blanket wrapped around her shoulders. At times, Lorenzo could hear her quietly groaning in discomfort when she exhaled. Not knowing what else to do he put a pot of water on the fire to make her some chamomile tea. Angry thoughts crossed his mind: that retarded son of a bitch, what could have possessed him to attack his mother? What could he have been doing in the barn: stealing eggs, taking shelter, petting the animals? He must've gone crazy since he had always behaved respectfully towards Francesca. His mother was a strong woman in many ways but she had a kind heart and a soft spot for this imbecile neighbor. She would often give him a dozen eggs or a loaf of fresh-baked bread when she saw him around, and in turn, he would help Francesca with some chores. He was, generally, very mellow and peaceful. What Andreas did was totally out of character for him, not just to hurt his mother, but to defile her.

Lorenzo could not even imagine that Andreas would conceive of attacking any woman let alone a neighbor that he liked. Could he have been drunk on wine? Was he looking to steal something from the barn? Lorenzo unclenched his fists; he could not let Mama see him so upset, she had enough to worry about.

Lorenzo searched his mind. The only instance of violence he could remember was five years earlier when Andreas was walking home from his family's construction business. It must've been about six in the evening when Andreas got into a fight with a sheepherder. The sheepherder had called him a "retarded bastard" after Andreas was found in a ditch petting a baby lamb. It all started when the lamb's mother had stopped and refused to move along with the herd. She kept looking back and baying in an attempt to call her baby, like a human mother calling her wayward child. The commotion attracted the sheepherder's attention. He went to investigate and found Andreas in a gully with the young animal. After yanking the animal from Andreas' arms and calling him various unflattering names a shoving match ensued. At some point, the sheepherder's dog got involved in the fracas and attacked Andreas. But as the German Shepherd jumped up to bite his arm, Andreas grabbed the dog by its collar, lifted the dog four feet off the ground and was literally strangling the dog in mid-air. When the dog's body went limp and offered no further resistance Andreas dropped the animal. The dog survived that experience, but thereafter, whenever the dog saw Andreas or whenever he passed near his home the dog would circle at a distance.

Lorenzo also reflected on the various rumors about Andreas. That he could not be left alone with young girls. But there was no real proof that he ever did anything wrong except for people having a general distaste for having a retarded man around.

Now, Lorenzo had to deal with the events of this nightmare, a surreal night.

He could hear the rain outside quickening its tempo after the previous lull. But despite the rain he had to set things right, or, at least, he had to hide all signs that Andreas had been at the farm. He knew that it was a matter of time before questions would have to be answered.

He also knew that going to the police was an impossible choice. He had no money to defend himself because his father's medical expenses had depleted all their savings. Andreas' stepbrother, Giacomo Salvaggi, would press for the maximum penalty and he would probably prevail. Everybody knew that he was in cahoots with the captain of the municipal police. Also, it was not unlike him to seek personal revenge and Lorenzo could find himself with a bullet in his head. Equally tormenting was the possibility of jeopardizing his upcoming trip to America, where his Uncle Pietro had promised to sponsor him for a good paying job in the construction industry. This was the opportunity of a lifetime and Lorenzo felt that he owed it to his family to jump at the chance, especially now that his family was in financial straits due to his father's illness.

Lorenzo analyzed his predicament very carefully. He would probably be in jail until a trial, or, at the very least, they would seize his passport and order him not to travel. Even if he assumed the best outcome for himself it was his mother who would suffer intolerable shame for having been violated. Her life would be destroyed, as they both knew it. People would inevitably ask why she could not control a half-wit who was a simple, gentle creature from what they knew. They would torture the facts to reach the conclusion that she had seduced the local retard.

He had to devise a plan to quickly get rid of the corpse. But how? Should he dispose of the body at sea? Just put the corpse in a dinghy, tie some rocks around the torso and drop him a mile out in the open waters? The problem was his size and weight; lifting him on the truck and then dragging his body from the road to the boat would be almost impossible. Chances of being seen were too great, even in bad weather. He considered pouring kerosene on the body and throwing it on a pile of wood to be consumed by flames. Farmers burned garbage all the time. But then he would have to sift through the ashes for teeth and any body parts that weren't totally immolated. The police forensics were advanced in these types of cases, especially with someone like Andreas who had been adopted from abroad; records and information existed with multiple agencies which could assist in identification. The idea of the fire was further complicated by the fact that it was raining and everything was wet. He didn't have the luxury of waiting for the rain to stop. Lorenzo's thoughts shifted between different plans as beads of perspiration collected on his forehead. He knew that a third alternative had to be found, and found quickly, before the dead man's family became concerned and started looking for him.

While Gabriella was helping her mother with her bath, he found himself pacing back and forth between the kitchen and dining room. He even went upstairs to his father's room, perhaps in a subconscious attempt to get some advice, but it wasn't to be, his father was completely unconscious. Then when his sister came upstairs to get some towels, he told her that he would be going back to the barn to feed the animals and finish some other chores. No sooner had he said that than he found himself walking down the hill totally consumed by a new idea floating in his head and taking control. He was fixated on this idea.

He thought that the best place to hide something of value was in the most obvious place, accessible and in an almost visible location. Don't design an elaborate plan; don't complicate the plot; don't search for remote solutions since police investigators burned most of their energy unraveling what they thought to be complex entanglements. Lorenzo gave this theory more buoyancy by recalling what his father told him once: that the best place to hide a precious jewel from thieves was on your dining room table, under a doily with a few pieces of junk mail over it. This strategy was akin to playing chess; too often players focused on second and third dimensional moves, when to the opponent's chagrin, checkmate resulted on the first tier. The vignette appealed to him; it contained the key to his quandary and it spurred him to action.

Chapter 2

Disposing of the Corpse

When he reached the entrance to the barn there wasn't a dry spot on his body. His clothes were soaked down to his underwear and clung to his skin like the casing on a sausage link. He pulled open the left side of the barn door and struck a match against a rusted farm implement leaning against the inner wall. Then he lit the kerosene lantern and held it up to eye level. He looked around the entire barn and moved closer to the corpse, studying the enormous form on the ground. The stench of blood and bodily waste wafted up to his nostrils. Andreas had fouled himself in the final moment of terror, something everyone is presumed to do when they die. He saw the man's blue overalls around his ankles, worn and frayed in various spots. His ankle-high boots were made of rawhide. The grooved soles were caked with mud and the right heel was worn unevenly down to the sole. A pool of blood flowing from his head had formed an elliptical shape on the ground and carried off clumps of hay to its outer perimeter. There, the straws, like a beaver's dam, had collected and enclosed the dark red liquid.

Lorenzo knew that the barn had to be immaculately cleaned after the body was disposed of, and all was to happen before the night was over. He had no other choice but to erase the events of the last hour. Grabbing a pitchfork, an old rolled-up tarp and the blood-smeared shovel that had sliced open Andreas' skull like a knife through gelatin, he made his way back outside. Some twenty yards down to the southeasterly side of the barn he stopped. There, he stood under an enormous beech tree that had been there before Romulus and Remus and served as shade. Underneath the tree was a weathered gray picnic table his father had made of natural hard timber. The table was used for preparing bread and baking Sicilian pizzas, trays of pork sausages that were made within a day or two after a slaughter, and Easter bread during Lent or special occasions. A short distance from the table stood the adobe-style, wood-fired, brick oven that took forever to warm up, and each time its doors opened, smoke and soot would cover your face, redden your eyeballs and more often than not singe your eyebrows. But these family cookout events had become rare the last two or three years since Matteo took ill.

Decayed firewood, exfoliated tree bark, fallen branches and rotting leaves had collected around the tree trunk. And especially around the legs of the table where foliage had found refuge and piled up during many windstorms. Lorenzo put the shovel and pitchfork down to the side and then shifted the wooden table from side to side until he felt he had enough clearance for his purpose. He then carefully unrolled the piece of canvas on the ground, far enough from where he would be working, and placed a rock on each corner to hold it open. Then he used the pitchfork to carefully haul up the slimy decomposing leaves, spade by spade, and placed them on the canvas. Like a jigsaw puzzle, he strove to maintain the integrity of their natural formations. Lorenzo was mindful not to excessively disturb the order of the decaying leaves and to remember how to recreate the scene in a logical manner.

The rain had saturated the soil, making it relatively easy to dig. With the tip of the shovel he drew a rectangular outline of where he wanted to dig. After making the mark he started shoveling dirt with a crazed determination, carefully placing the excavated dirt in the cleared area. When the hole was about three feet deep, he looked up the hill towards the house. He could barely see through the fog and drizzle a light shining in his father's bedroom and a dimmer light in Gabriella's room. He thought his father must be awake and Gabriella was probably trying to feed him some soup. The last few weeks Papa had been eating very little and the lack of sustenance accounted for his extreme weight loss.

Lorenzo wiped his forehead with his shirtsleeve and felt a burning sensation in his eyes. He didn't know if it was dirt, sweat or a combination of the two mixed with rainwater. He took a deep breath and with added determination plowed deeper into the soil. In less than an hour he had reached a depth of five or six feet. The length of the hole was now about seven feet and its width about three feet. He had tried to limit the width of the hole to no more than the space his shoulders and arms required to maneuver the shovel in flinging soil over the top. He wondered what burial regulations were at the local cemetery and whether the regulations had ever changed as people got consistently taller in modern times. While catching his breath and pondering these seemingly ridiculous thoughts he leaned too hard against a side wall and a partial cave-in resulted. "*Vaffanculo!* (Fuck!)" he cursed out loud, then caught himself, afraid that someone might have heard him, but with the wind howling and the fine rain whipping his face he realized that there wasn't a soul around except Andreas' dead body.

Lorenzo worked frantically but cautiously in removing the collapsed soil. Then, careful so as not to risk another mishap, he climbed out of the hole from a firmer side. He looked around, inspected the prospective grave with satisfaction and headed towards the barn. Once inside he grabbed a leather strap from a hook on the wall, next to where other farm tools hung. He also snatched the mule blanket that was still folded on the floor and had served as a pillow for his mother. Then Lorenzo walked up to the dead man, squatted down and, with hand trembling, closed his eyelids. He wrapped the blanket around Andreas' head and worked the strap around the man's massive neck. He buckled it tightly to prevent more blood from spilling out as he moved the corpse and to avoid looking at the man's face. Having finished that task, he grabbed the dead man's wrists that were connected to calloused hands and oversized arms. No doubt the hands had performed many years of manual labor. Andreas' job had been to load and unload masonry and lumber supplies on and off trucks, and when not doing this sort of backbreaking work he would install marble flooring and exterior pavers. Andreas' brother, Giacomo, having realized the extent of Andreas' abilities, would hire him to neighbors for various building projects. And as long as he had some supervision, he was able to repeat the same pattern over and over without too much confusion or unwarranted anxiety by the homeowner where the work was being done.

With a firm grip on the dead man's wrists and being careful to avoid spreading the pool of blood, Lorenzo jerked the heavy body sideways and began dragging it. As he pulled the corpse towards the door, he realized that Andreas' pants and underwear were sliding down to his shins, effectively exposing him. The scene disturbed and disgusted Lorenzo on seeing the prodigious genitalia that had violated his mother, so he pulled up the dead man's pants and decided to reverse his grip. Instead of dragging the corpse from the wrists he would drag it from the ankles. But pulling the corpse from his legs required spinning the body around, which was another ordeal. Several times he paused to rearrange the hay on the ground with his foot so as not to have the body drag it. Then outside the barn doors he stopped again and removed the man's shoes. He placed them on the side and bemoaned the fact that heaving 240 pounds of dead weight was a challenging task. Still, between the barn and the tree he was forced to stop only once, to wipe his slippery hands on a dry corner of the blanket.

He positioned the body parallel to the grave, mindful of another possible collapse of the soil. He arranged Andreas' arms and legs close to the body and then it crossed his mind to tie each set of limbs together. But, on second thoughts, it was too much bother and he decided to quickly roll the body into the hole. The corpse landed face down with a thud and an avalanche of dirt followed. He stood there for a moment and thought about this simple-minded idiot's life and the journey coming to an end at this very spot. If one purpose of life was to seek joy, as his priest had once told him, Andreas probably never found it, at least not from Lorenzo's perspective. Maybe he was better off now. Lorenzo couldn't help wonder if those like Andreas, the fragile, were put on Earth to suffer. The physically and mentally disabled, the uneducated, the poor had always been relegated to the bottom of the social pyramid. Everyone that came in contact with these poor souls used them to some advantage: for cheap labor, to expiate guilt with token assistance, to buttress their ego in comparison, etc. Whether at school or work these misfits were always targets of bad jokes and insults. Even when they elicited a feeling of compassion in the observer it made this individual feel better to think how fortunate he or she was in not being like them. Suddenly, and seemingly from nowhere, tears rolled down Lorenzo's face, whether for Andreas, himself, or the pathetic human condition he could not say.

Once the corpse was in the grave, Lorenzo felt a sense of relief in knowing that the hard part was over. He picked up the shovel and started backfilling until he remembered that part of the man's skull that was severed was still lying on the ground inside the barn. He hurried back inside and found it embedded in dirt. He used the tip of the shovel to scoop it up and saw spongy brain matter still clinging to the bone like spider webs clinging to dingy basement corners. Then he walked it to the grave and, as if letting go of a poisonous scorpion, he flung it into the hole to join the rest of the body.

Lorenzo, with adrenaline still coursing through his body, worked feverishly in completely filling the opening. Then he leveled the ground and tamped down the soil by walking over it. Having packed it tightly he graded it again, this time a little higher than the surrounding ground to allow for some settling. Lastly, he replaced the soggy piles of leaves exactly as they were originally sequenced, a precise jigsaw puzzle. Now, he had to deal with the big outdoor table; with catty-corner movements he meticulously repositioned the table over the grave so that the four legs straddled the width of what he had dug and rested on hard, undisturbed soil. He looked around to see if all was in order and rearranged other rotten debris and dead branches where they had naturally fallen, exactly as he had found them. Now, nothing looked disturbed or out of place.

He looked around and found a tree branch with leaves still clinging to it and used it to sweep side to side, back and forth to cover up his footprints and the drag marks from the corpse. Then with some rags he found in a corner of the barn he meticulously cleaned inside until everything was in its proper place. Finally, confident that there was no trace that Andreas had ever been present inside or outside the barn, he felt satisfied with his work. Then, even though some animals were already asleep, he gave them some feed. On the way out he held the lantern at arm's length from his face and took an overview of the place. Again, he nodded with satisfaction and picked up the bunch of dirty rags he had used to scrub clean and sanitize. He buried them several feet deep behind the barn and covered the spot with some loose bricks lying about. When he finished, he went back inside the barn to return the shovel and the pitchfork to their proper place, stepped out again and shut the double doors.

As he walked away from the barn he glanced towards the house and the old tree and then towards the eastern sky that was still gray and dark. His clothes were wet and streaked with mud. He felt a deep penetrating sensation rising from his lower abdomen and creeping through his bowels to his belly. In that instance the immensity of his deed finally hit him like a sledgehammer. First his hands began to tremble and then his legs. He felt an immense weight forcing him to the ground. He realized that the rest of his life would be affected by this singular act. His mind conjured up biblical images of Cain and Abel. Had he become Cain's heir? The parallels were certainly there. In a metaphorical sense, Andreas was the innocent younger brother who had been sacrificed. Andreas was the victim and Lorenzo the murderous farmer, the older and more knowledgeable brother. Would God favor Andreas, like He had favored Abel by perpetually tormenting his killer? Or could it be that he, Lorenzo, had been an instrument of God and delivered this defective, simple-minded human being from his heinous existence? For Lorenzo it was unthinkable to be banished from the Lord's presence. If so, how long would he be condemned with this stain on his soul? Would he ever experience redemption? But what else could he have done? This simple-minded man-child had raped his mother; he had witnessed the heinous act. Should he have saved him even though he had done irreparable damage to his mother? Or, take action as he had done, saved his mother and destroyed the ravenous beast? *What else could I have done?*

Dio mio (My God). What have I done? What have I done? Over and over he repeated the question in his mind.

On his knees, hands outstretched, eyes to the heavens, again and again he uttered: "*Perdonami, Dio, perdonami, Dio, o fatto un peccato* (Forgive me, Lord, forgive me, Lord, for I have sinned)." As he started reciting, "Our father who art in heaven…" he felt bile rising from the pit of his belly. His body acted spasmodically and without command. Several minutes passed and putrid, bitter vomit flowed out of his system until the retching stopped and he was totally empty.

He felt that his nightmare wasn't over yet, but despite this, he forced himself up. It took him a while to reassemble himself. Then he began walking across the field to the end of his family's property. He carried a package wrapped in burlap. Arriving at his destination, he turned along a dirt road and meandered his way for nearly half a mile until he stood on a grassy mount along a municipal road.

From here Lorenzo could see the extent of the cove and the turbulent water slapping against the gray sand and dark gray pebbles. Beyond that, as far as he could see, the white caps were riding the powerful waves, like an invading army on horseback, racing towards the coast. This municipal road, perpetually under construction, stood between where he was and the narrow strip of beach. He could also see boulders and rocks of various sizes and shapes adorning both ends of the cove. Several tree trunks lay haphazardly towards the center, used as benches by bathers. At one end of the cove a narrow tunnel ran from the north side of the street to the south connecting with the beach area. The tunnel allowed bathers from the private homes, condos and a couple of small hotels to safely walk to the water. A number of small fishing boats and dinghies were anchored securely near the shore while others were tied down firmly to metal spikes further inland so as to be able to weather most storms. He recognized a good number of these boats, even ones without names, and personally knew many of the owners.

Lorenzo's position gave him an extensive view of the entire area. He looked around carefully to make sure no one was present and no one was following him; not a soul anywhere. People sought shelter on a night like this. What lunatic would be out and about? With the limited moonlight making its way through some dark clouds that were breaking apart he could make out the outline of a blue and white dinghy tied to a metal anchor protruding from a slab of concrete. He sat down on the edge of the grassy mount and quickly unwrapped the burlap package he was carrying under his arm. Now he was holding the dead man's boots by the tongue and placed them at his side. He removed his own shoes and put them behind a shrub. Then, without untying them, he slipped his feet into Andreas' large shoes. Slowly, he made his way to the base of the mount, crossed the road and climbed down the boulders to a rocky area in the direction of Andreas' blue and white dinghy. As he got closer to the boat the pebbles gave way to coarse sand and then finer sand. He looked back.

Evidence of Andreas' footprints was being left in the fine, wet sand, exactly as he had planned.

The small boat was turned upside down but was unmistakably Andreas'. He looked it over a bit before untying it. Then he turned the dinghy right side up. He found two paddles, a broken fishing rod and two empty soda cans. He placed the items inside the boat and dragged the boat to the water's edge. Then he pushed it in and saw that he was leaving behind even deeper footprints in the wet sand. When he was waist deep in the turbulent water, he used every ounce of strength to thrust the small boat further out as the waves were retreating. It bobbed up and down in the rough waters a few times before the sea embraced it. Minutes later Lorenzo was straining to see it through the mist.

Careful not to leave tracks in the wrong place and in the wrong direction he sprang over the rocks, from boulder to boulder. Then Lorenzo made his way across the road and back up to the grassy mound. His own shoes were still under the shrub where he had left them. After putting them back on his feet he took the dead man's shoes and flung them, one by one, as far into the water as his strength would allow. He knew from swimming in this area that the underwater currents formed a very uneven topography, with sudden drop-offs. Thus, he hoped that Andreas' boots would find their permanent resting place in a very deep spot.

As he started walking back up the narrow footpath that would eventually lead him to the wider dirt road, exhaustion overwhelmed him and he became momentarily oblivious to any cars traveling on the state road. Then suddenly, upon hearing the whirring of a car engine his ears perked up. By its roar he knew that it was moving quickly. Crouching low, he hoped that no one had seen his silhouette. He listened intently. The sound seemed to diminish, and with a rush of relief he concluded that the vehicle was traveling in the opposite direction, away from him. When he finally raised his head and was about to stand straight he saw lights coming around the bend in the road. Quickly, he dropped down to the ground, again, and crouched there motionless. His heart was pounding in his chest as if he had just finished a marathon. He knew that the driver would see him when the car came around the curve. And to be seen at this hour, at this location and in this manner was the last thing in the world he wanted.

He had seconds and his options were limited. Standing and running was not a choice. He couldn't go forward. He couldn't stay where he was. His only and best chance was to crawl further out to the edge of an escarpment and then slide down the slope to the shoulder of the road where some half-dozen large sewer pipes were stacked. Maybe, just maybe, he could crawl inside one of those pipes. This would put him so close to the oncoming vehicle that sweat from fear began forming down his body. Short of this evasive move he might as well stand up and wave to the oncoming vehicle. As his body slid over the grassy embankment he felt like an undulating snake that sensed a hawk above ready to swoop down and clench him in its claws. Just then he began rolling downwards without control. He tried to grasp at something, anything, fearing that if his momentum didn't slow down, he would wind up in the middle of the road and not only be seen but be run over. Midway down his hand found something to grab – a small scraggly pine tree. It wasn't strong enough to stop his roll but sufficient to slow his momentum before it was uprooted. When he came to a full stop, he found himself next to one of the sewer pipes. The oncoming car was now directly in front and seemed to be unmistakably gunning for him. Quick as a chipmunk, feet first, he slid inside the pipe. Lorenzo gave a heavy sigh as his chest absorbed more blows from the pounding sledgehammer that was his heart.

From inside the pipe he could see the car slowing down some fifty feet beyond where he was. It was a black Audi, 8 series. There weren't too many of this imported model in these parts but he had seen this car before. Lorenzo was momentarily terrified with fear when, like an emergency police raid, the car doors flew open almost simultaneously.

At first, he thought they must've seen him and they were coming for him, with guns drawn. The low-lying fog made the men's faces difficult to discern but their voices were distinct, unmistakable. One was that of Andreas' father and the other of his brother. The older man, Bruno Salvaggi, was in his mid-fifties, very robust and very capable of defending himself. Lorenzo knew this because he had seen Bruno flinging hundred-pound bags of concrete onto his truck. His upper torso had also been sculpted from years of backbreaking work as a migrant laborer on the German rail system. The younger man was his son, Giacomo, and he was about thirty. He owned a building supply warehouse where lumber and masonry products were his stock in trade. The warehouse was located between the resort town of Paola, a beachfront community that looked towards the future by catering to north European tourism, and Cosenza, one of the oldest, grimiest cities in these parts, which was inescapably entwined with the past. The younger man, Giacomo Salvaggi, was known to have "*una grande presenza* (an imposing presence)" in these parts. Not only did he own the warehouse with a separate house on the site, where he conducted much of his business, but he also did some selective building of luxury villas. And because of his connections, he obtained lucrative municipal contracts. Rumor had it that he had other assorted businesses which people didn't feel comfortable talking about. But between family members, and people you trusted even more than family members, the conversation revolved around one word and that word was only said in a whisper: 'Ndrangheta – a secret society known for its viciousness and the unlimited reach of its tentacles.

As the two men scanned the beach area, the older man was pointing in the direction where Andreas' boat would be tied. Giacomo was stroking his goatee as if weighing up everything his father said. However, his thoughts were actually racing towards his own conclusions. Then the two men left the car running and made their way down the side of the road towards the moored boats. This left a perfect opportunity for Lorenzo to make his getaway up the embankment while the two men's line of vision was blocked. He crawled out of the tube, crouching low like a cat prowling in the bushes, and made his way up the hill to the dirt path. From that point he could not see either man. In fact, he could barely see the beach area. But he had another immediate concern: if the Salvaggis poked around more, they could discover the uprooted pine tree and the freshly eroded soil on the side of the embankment. Should they discover that location they probably would not believe his carefully crafted "lost at sea" alibi and start looking elsewhere for an explanation of Andreas' disappearance.

Lorenzo finally got home about 10pm. He must've been several hundred feet from the porch when he spotted the only light in the house; it was coming from Gabriella's room. She was probably finished with Papa's dinner and had changed his bedding. He must already be sleeping, Lorenzo thought. Since his last trip from the clinic in Rome, Papa seemed to be doing a lot of sleeping. He wondered if his mother was also in bed or if his sister was still tending to her. It had been several hours since he had left the house. The front door was unlocked and he let himself in without turning on the light. Inside, he found his way to his sister's room. He pushed her door open, slowly, and their eyes met. His mother was lying on Gabriella's bed with a wet cloth over her forehead. She appeared to be sleeping. Gabriella was sitting next to her by the bed.

"How's she doing?" he whispered.

Gabriella stared directly at Lorenzo, put her index finger across her lips and led her brother out of the room into the hallway.

"She fell asleep about half an hour ago."

"Was she complaining much about her head?"

"After I helped her with her bath, she was still alert for a while but complained about a splitting headache and of her insides hurting. She refused to eat, took two aspirins and fell asleep," Gabriella said. "And what happened to you? You were gone for quite a while."

"I fed the animals and cleaned the barn some. Did she say anything else?" he asked, needing to search but not wanting to seem to be.

"Something about the blasted chickens being frightened and one of them flying in her face," she answered.

"She deserves a good rest," added Lorenzo. "She had a very difficult night," he said, being cautious not to disclose anything further to his sister.

"I think she was also having nightmares," said Gabriella. "The noises she was making brought me back from the kitchen when I was making you some dinner. She sounded tormented or anxious about something." She paused. "I wanted to call the doctor but she became really upset and told me that she was fine, just a little bruised. You know how Mama is. Do you think she should be checked out?"

"I think we need to let Mama decide for herself. As for me, I don't want any dinner, I'm too tired. I'm going to change and go straight to bed," Lorenzo responded.

Then he walked down to the end of the hall and looked into his father's room. He couldn't see anything but heard his heavy breathing. The pungent smell of medication always assaulted Lorenzo's nostrils. He pulled the door partially closed and made his way across the hall to his small room, completely and totally drained. As he sat on his bed and pulled off his shoes, he thought about tonight's events; everything seemed to be surreal. He wasn't sure if what he remembered really happened. It seemed like a cover story of a sensational magazine, stuff that happens to other people. But one thing was for sure: he was too exhausted to make sense of anything. Right now, he needed sleep. Tomorrow, with a clear head, he would make sense of it all.

Chapter 3

The Early Inquiries

That night Lorenzo dreamed that he was working in the field during the harvest, cutting and bundling grain. As he came to an area where the grain was trampled flat, he tried to figure out what happened until he saw two large serpents coiled together like a helix. They were intertwined in an upright position seemingly absorbed in each other like two lovers. As he threw stones at them, hoping to separate them and nudge them away, they snapped their heads in his direction. Yellowish-black eyes transfixed on him. Then faster than angry hornets attacking someone who poked at their hive, the snakes uncoiled, dropped to the ground and slithered in his direction. With the curved blade of his scythe he scooped up the first snake and catapulted it into a clearing, far behind where he was standing. Undeterred by Lorenzo's action, the second reptile slithered near his feet, ready to inflict its venom. Lorenzo stepped aside and, this time, caught the head of the creature under the blade of his scythe. He pressed down with all his might and then applied the weight of his foot. His right hand pulled a knife from his belt strap and slashed away at the writhing reptile. Lorenzo was terrified, goose bumps forming on his arms and down his back as he hacked the animal into six pieces. As the six parts were still wriggling away in different directions, he stomped on the head of the beast with the heel of his boot. Satisfied that this snake would never bother anyone again, he looked to see if the first creature had scurried away. He didn't see it; it was gone. Reassured, he resumed the task of collecting and bundling the grain until he heard some rustling behind him. He turned around and was stunned to see that the six hacked parts of the snake had regenerated into six separate reptiles. They seemed to follow the larger snake he had flung afar. Lorenzo woke up in a cold sweat wildly flailing his arms and legs.

As he sat up in bed gasping in fear, the sheets and blankets were tangled around him. He shook his head, like a dog shakes off rain, to compose himself. His eyes went to the light coming through the window, where the morning sunlight was making its way through the slits of the wooden shutters. As his senses sharpened, he heard voices downstairs by the front door. He bounced out of bed, ran to the window and peeked through the slits. Bruno and Giacomo Salvaggi were speaking with his mother on the porch. The older man was wearing a blue jacket and gray corduroy pants. Giacomo, standing a little to the side and just behind his father, appeared to be listening intently, wearing a white shirt, black leather jacket and blue jeans. The older man kept gesturing with his hands. Lorenzo strained to hear what was being said through the barely open window.

"He never got home last night," he heard Bruno say in disbelief. "It's not like him to stay out all night," he added, while scratching his head.

"We've been searching for him since before midnight," Giacomo said.

"Maybe, because of the bad weather, he stayed at the job site where he was working," replied Francesca, trying to offer assurance that he would be found.

Giacomo stared at Francesca, almost incredulous at her naïveté.

"Did Lorenzo run into him yesterday?" asked Bruno.

"No," she answered truthfully. "But I will tell him what happened and ask him if he saw Andreas or heard anything when he gets up."

"Andreas' fishing boat is also missing," Giacomo said.

"You think he could have taken the boat out before the storm?" Francesca asked. "The storm and the high tide could've also loosened the boat and taken it out to sea. It's not the first time that boats have broken away from their moorings."

"Well, if he doesn't turn up in the next few hours, I think the police should be notified," Bruno said.

"Pop, we're not going to find him by staying here any longer," Giacomo added. He impatiently fingered the car keys in his left hand and started to walk across the porch to the side of the house where his Audi was parked.

"Didn't mean to bother you this early, Francesca," the older man said as he turned and took a step towards the waiting car.

"No bother. I just hope everything turns out okay," she replied as her hand went to the bandage on her head.

"Me too," said Bruno. Then he stopped and, thrusting his chin in the direction of her injury, asked, "What happened to your head?"

"I fell off a ladder," she said.

"*Le cose brutte accadono quando meno te le aspetti* (Bad things happen when you least expect them)."

After the Audi left her driveway, Francesca turned to go back in the house but couldn't help wondering if Andreas had really taken his boat out to go fishing just before the storm. It had come in quickly and violently. His dinghy may have overturned in the water, and since he was a poor swimmer, he may have never made it back to shore. On the other hand, some foul play could have also taken place. She knew as well as anyone else in these parts that Giacomo was involved in shady business deals. There was no end to rumors that his reach was far and wide and included not only questionable business practices but outright illegitimate activities. Thus,

Giacomo's enemies might have taken revenge indirectly by striking at his disabled brother. She grew sad because Andreas had always been very helpful and kind in the past. She remembered the times he helped her husband out during harvest. She also remembered when Matteo was involved in large projects, he would hire Andreas by the day and that the young man always did the work of two people. Francesca felt even worse to think that some individuals were capable of causing harm to such simple-minded and innocent human beings, especially Andreas, to whom providence had dealt such a poor hand of cards from his birth, in a faraway land, and under such difficult circumstances.

Lorenzo was washed and dressed when he came into the kitchen. His mother was sipping some chamomile tea and Gabriella was frying up some fresh pork strips. He found the aroma of the bacon irresistible and believed it to be one of the most seductive of all food smells. He was famished from having skipped supper the night before. As he came through the kitchen door his eyes met his mother's.

"How are you feeling this morning, Mama?" he asked, bending over to give his mother a kiss on the cheek.

"Sore and bruised everywhere, Enzo. It's my own fault for being so careless," she responded.

Lorenzo, feeling uncomfortable with the conversation, turned away from his mother and changed the topic. "I didn't hear Papa last night, did he sleep alright?"

"I think so. Gabriella and I gave him his medication early this morning and he was a bit more like himself. He even asked for a little toast with marmalade," answered Francesca.

"By the way, I saw Mr. Salvaggi and Giacomo from the window, what did they want?"

"They were looking for Andreas. They said that he went missing last night and were wondering if you might have seen him anytime yesterday."

"No, I didn't speak to him," Lorenzo answered truthfully.

"They were also telling me that his boat was missing. I wouldn't be surprised if he took it out before the storm and got swept out to sea. It wouldn't be the first time it has happened to people."

"Right, the undertows can get nasty, especially during a storm and high tide."

Their conversation turned to his upcoming trip to America. Francesca wanted to know if he was having second thoughts about it.

"I think I should go," Lorenzo said. "It's a once-in-a-lifetime opportunity. I'll be able to send you money to keep the farm going, and Uncle Pietro and Grandpa said they would try to fill the void. As for Papa, he could be in this condition for some time, according to his doctors."

"I know this trip was discussed before your dad took ill, and arrangements had been made, but I wondered if you had any second thoughts."

"I did. At times I did, but now I feel compelled to go," Lorenzo said, again, truthfully and as a matter of fact.

*

Giacomo had dropped his father off at his parents' house where his mother, Antonia, and his sister, Annalisa, were talking to neighbors. The neighbors knew about Andreas' disappearance since they had been approached earlier in the morning by the father and son. Antonia Salvaggi was making the sign of the cross while wrapped up in conversation. She was known to be extremely religious. She was a tough, diminutive woman with a small, pointy face and coarse dark hair which she wore in a bun pulled tight to her skull. Giacomo waved to them from the driver's window. Bruno got out of the car. And, without wasting any more time, Giacomo pulled away and headed for the supply house where he could do more to search for his adopted brother than to talk to chattering neighbors. He also had another urgent business matter to resolve.

His Audi rolled into the yard in less than fifteen minutes. It was still early Sunday morning and very quiet. Few people were on the roads. The sun was coming up in its full glory and burning through the few residual clouds from the night before. While everything was still wet from last night's downpour, the air felt crisp, cool and invigorating. The only people in the yard were the foreman and his assistant, Tariq, the Albanian. Unlike other business days, when employees would be busy loading and unloading truckloads of supplies, and forklifts would be whizzing around with palettes of masonry materials to be sorted for deliveries or pickups. The two men were talking and smoking.

Giacomo knew that his warehouse and yard was the largest in the province. It was spread over four acres and had three substantial buildings. The front cottage was used as the office for ordering, shipping, dispatching and accounting. On the far left of the main entrance was a huge warehouse, jam-packed with building lumber piled up to the rafters. Also, inside could be found finishing and specialty woods for moldings, doors and windows. The interior of the building was like a ribcage, constructed of metal girders, rafters, posts and supports. From the exterior a green skin of galvanized metal covered everything. And stacked adjacent to the exterior wall was CCA-treated lumber, able to withstand all forces of nature. To the right side of the main entrance and far back was Giacomo's office and on the second floor were his living quarters, well fortified. To anyone visiting the yard for the first time the place looked immense. The customer could find every imaginable type of masonry product stacked high on palettes. Beyond that were mountains of sand, gravel, blue-stone, crushed marble, etc., some piled two and three stories high. It was not just a supply warehouse, it was Giacomo's fortress.

There was not one private construction project of significant size whose owner or project manager didn't come through Giacomo's gates at one time or another. This gave him a direct opportunity to be aware of any substantial development being undertaken. In most cases he knew of a project before blueprints were filed for approval with the local municipality. And when it came to public works, he had firm arrangements with influential government officials. As for the voters, if there were questions, the public officials could always hold up the estimates and invoices showing slashed price cuts, daring anyone to find them cheaper. This was a good arrangement. It fueled the elected officials' desire to deal with "Signor Giaco," as he was affectionately called, at least in public. Going to Signor Giaco was almost a given as soon as a public project was approved. In case this tactic wasn't enough to cement his bids, Giacomo would also wine and dine the local politicians, contribute heavily during election time and send his crew, *gratis*, to remodel their homes at a mere intimation that a new roof, a swimming pool or an extension was needed.

Giacomo's house was modest and stood to the right of the main entrance, way back. It had a brick façade, five wide slate steps, and a porch extending the full width of the house. The other three sides of the structure were finished with white stucco. The white was not so white anymore since maintaining it was not one of Giacomo's priorities. The lack of attention could also be seen around the upper windows where rainwater flowed off the eaves, bounced off the window ledge and resulted in noticeable brown stains. The porch had huge pots of roses on one end, rambling along a trellis anchored to the building. A wooden bench stood between the rose bushes and the front door. On the other side stood several chipped and discolored ceramic pots filled with geraniums, giving a first-time visitor the impression that they had seen their glory days.

Depending on a visitor's line of vision a rectangular building seemed connected to the house, but it was not. This smaller single-level building was, in fact, separated from the main house by a six-foot breezeway. The smaller structure stood on the south side and was constructed years after the main house where Giacomo currently lived. The smaller building was where he had a gym and sauna and conducted his other business dealings.

As he eased his car into the "reserved" car stall, a few feet from the front door, he realized that his two trusted *confederati* had not arrived with his "guests." He glanced at the clock on his dashboard. It was still early. There was time for him to put on a pot of espresso since he felt tired and irritable from lack of sleep the night before. As the door swung open into the smaller rectangular building one could see that it was modestly furnished: a large living room to one side and a desk at the opposite end with two chairs directly in front, like the layout of a lawyer's office. The wall behind his desk was decorated with a large blueprint, pre-construction, of a shopping center on the outskirts of the city and next to it was a photo of the same project finished and juxtaposed like Goya's *Majas*. On the other walls he had an aerial view of the province of Calabria and a mural of the strait of Messina which linked the southern tip of the peninsula with the island of Sicily. The landscape showed peak activity, cargo ships and ferries heading to various destinations.

On the wall closest to the door, not even noticeable upon entering but visually inescapable upon leaving, was a 2x4-feet rectangular poster of a Norwegian fjord depicting the deep and natural carvings of rock by eons of erosion. Its high cliffs, clear waters and lush greenery were captured with uncharacteristic intensity. The scenery had particular meaning for Giacomo.

The building was also equipped with a bathroom, a kitchenette off to the corner, the gym and a small room with a metal door where Giacomo kept his safe, his files and his firearms. He was the only one with a key.

Twenty minutes had elapsed since he entered. A pot of espresso coffee was sitting at the corner of his desk and he was starting his second cup while opening mail when he heard the knock on the door. Gregorio and Attila were always punctual and reliable. Related through his oldest uncle on his mother's side, he knew he could trust them implicitly and that there was nothing they would not do for him. All that he ever expected from them was respect, unquestioning loyalty and silence, and he got it all.

In turn, he made sure they were well treated. They made good money. He had set them up in nice homes. There wasn't a birthday in their families or a holiday that he ever forgot and often they would receive generous bonuses. To Giacomo they were trusted confidants and "facilitators" who would lay their lives on the line for him. They made sure that when any problems developed a solution was found. These solutions were for problems not only within his organization but also outside. Gregorio was the ideas man and often came up with diplomatic solutions. His way was always tried first. Attila, on the other hand, preferred to resolve situations with a more direct approach. He saw diplomacy as having limited benefits. The two were a good counter-balance and worked well and earned their keep.

"*Entra* (Come in)," Giacomo responded to the second knock on the door.

Gregorio entered first without speaking a word, followed by Paolo Pucci and Fiorella Azunis. Attila was behind.

"*Buon giorno, Don Giaco*," Paulo said upon seeing him. He took a few steps in from the door.

"*Buon giorno*," repeated Fiorella, demurely.

Attila closed the door behind them and stood there with his hands behind his back. Gregorio walked halfway around the room, checked the bathroom and then took a seat on the couch and crossed his legs.

Giacomo didn't acknowledge Paolo and Fiorella's salutations but waved them closer to his desk, his hand gesturing towards the two chairs facing his desk.

"Please sit down," he said.

"*Grazie*," said Paulo as both followed his cue.

Giacomo took the stack of mail on his blotter that he had been working on and moved it to the side of his desk, folded his hands and leaned forward, looking at them eyeball to eyeball.

"Do you know why you're here?" he asked softly.

"Something to do with the club?" said Paulo, criss-crossing his legs and looking a bit uncomfortable.

"Business has been a little slow recently," chimed in Fiorella.

"Recently, it's been a little slow?" repeated Giacomo, his mood noticeably changing and his voice rising.

"I think, perhaps, it has to do with the opening of that new club on the other side of town," ventured Paulo, his voice quivering.

"Really. Well let me tell you something, that fucking rat hole doesn't compare to mine, and it just opened three weeks ago. My receipts have been going down for over three months." Giacomo's tone hardened and his face got red.

Fiorella tried to interject, but Giacomo put his index finger over his lips, cutting her off.

"Let me give you my take on it," he said. "I'm ninety-nine percent sure you're fucking with me. You're stealing my money! I have plenty of reasons to believe that. But even if you're not pocketing my money then you're not putting effort into running my business. Maybe you're putting your time and effort into screwing each other at my expense or you're just incompetent. The bottom line is, very quickly, you're both becoming useless to me."

"It's just a temporary setback, Mr. Giaco. Give us another chance. Please. We'll make it right. I promise we'll redouble our efforts and make the club more profitable than it's ever been," pleaded Paulo. Beads of sweat dripped from his armpits down his sides, leaving a widening stain on his crisp tailored shirt.

"Yes. That goes for me too, Mr. Giaco, we'll redouble our efforts," interjected Fiorella, her face flustered as her four fingers on her left hand squeezed hard round her thumb.

Giacomo straightened up against his chair and pushed it back, eyes never leaving their pale faces. He opened the top desk drawer and pulled out a silver revolver with a polished wooden grip. He placed it in the middle of the blotter on his desk, closed the drawer and pulled his chair to its original position.

Paolo and Fiorella swallowed hard. Their eyes widened and their bodies stiffened.

"Please. Please, Mr. Giaco, I swear on my mother's grave, on everything holy that you'll never have a problem again. You'll see the business improve immediately." As Paulo rambled, his right hand was visibly shaking. Fiorella seemed not able to speak.

Giacomo took the revolver in his left hand, held it vertically pointing to the ceiling and with his right hand opened the chamber. Six bullets slid out onto the desk. Then, with everyone's attention focused on the weapon he picked up a single bullet, placed it in one of the six empty chamber slots, spun the chamber and quickly snapped it shut. Finally, he placed the pistol on the corner of his desk. He looked at them with a cold smile.

Fiorella squirmed nervously in her chair and Paolo Pucci's face glistened with greasy wetness. Gregorio bolted from the couch and suddenly was behind Paolo. He put a bath towel over Paolo's head, wrapped the ends tightly in his left hand and tilted Paolo's chair back.

Gregorio had him exactly where he wanted: totally disoriented, sightless, without balance and panicked. The club manager flailed his hands like a drowning swimmer. Then Gregorio reached for the revolver on the desk and pressed the barrel in Paolo's right ear then, he heard the click of the trigger.

Fiorella was stunned. She had no time to even let out a cry. She felt Attila grab her hair and jerk her head backward against the chair. His right hand squeezed her throat. From the corner of her eye she saw him whip out a sharp, skinny blade from his breast pocket, next she felt the tip pressed against her windpipe. A drop of blood started rolling down her throat. The whites of her eyes bulging out, she started gagging.

With a wave of his hand Giacomo called off his attack dogs. Gregorio and Attila moved back to where they were earlier.

As Paolo's chair came crashing down to an upright position, he frantically pulled the towel off his head, revealing an ashen face. As his senses gradually came back, he felt a warm wetness between his legs. Fiorella coughed and tried to catch her breath as she clawed at her throat with her fingertips. When she pulled them back to look, they were smeared with blood. She fumbled for her pocket, pulled out a tissue and held it against her neck. Her teeth were chattering and her eyes were wide with fear when she looked at Giacomo.

Giacomo was leaning back on his chair quietly, studying them. When he felt that they were composed he spoke to them, but only looked at Paulo.

"This time the odds were in your favor. Next time, if there is a next time, neither of you will be so lucky."

"*Grazie, grazie, mille grazie*," Paolo and Fiorella echoed each other.

"I swear, Mr. Giaco, there won't be a next time. Business will be better than ever," Paolo muttered with a level of conviction and assurance in his voice that seemed unquestionably genuine.

"I'm granting you a chance to redeem yourselves. But if you fuck with me or anything that belongs to me again, ANYTHING…!" Giacomo's chair suddenly snapped forward. His index finger was pointing at them, like God castigating Adam and Eve after their fall. "I swear that I'll cut you up, piece by piece, put you through a meat grinder, and feed you to your families."

Giacomo knew that Paolo and Fiorella would never again stray from considering his interest paramount to all else. They had been with him seven years and had been useful throughout until now. They had grown complacent, lazy and overconfident and forgotten their place. He was satisfied that the lesson had been learned. His club's bottom line would never fall in the red again, even if they had to take money out of their pockets and deny their families food. Giacomo felt that he had made the right decision by being practical. Why waste the experience and knowledge of the business Paolo and Fiorella had garnered the last seven years? And the goodwill of the clientele, the johns that Fiorella had cultivated, were invaluable.

As Giacomo reflected on what had just happened, a famous prince from the north came to mind: Niccolò Machiavelli. He had keenly and accurately observed human nature and had offered a blueprint for ruling and controlling vassals. To control your subjects, he said, you could rule them by love or by fear, but the latter was by far more effective. With Pucci and Azunis he had tried the former. Today, it was time for the latter.

As Attila was shuffling the two reformed employees out of the office, Giacomo told Gregorio to remain. He wanted to tell Gregorio of Andreas' disappearance and to ask him to get a group of men together to search the woods for any sign of Andreas. They were to also search the coastal area for any evidence that may have washed up. Finally, if nothing turned up he wanted them to comb the surrounding hamlets and, if necessary, Cosenza. He wanted results by the next day, Monday morning. He was not enthusiastic about getting the police involved twenty-four hours later, particularly if special units from outside the province had to be called in.

Chapter 4

Police Involvement

Monday morning at 9am, Giacomo Salvaggi's men had come up empty-handed in their search for Andreas. Gregorio, who had organized a team of eight men, including the older Salvaggi, had split them up. Three were given the task of searching the woods, operating under the assumption that Andreas may have seen an animal and followed it into the forest, then got lost. Andreas would often lose his focus if he saw a deer or even a rabbit, much like a tracking hound that picks up a new scent and then becomes oblivious to its master's objective.

They had started the search by following the roads and pathways he habitually used to walk home and, presumably, at strategic locations where he might have veered into the forest. The second group also consisted of three men; they were told to canvas the four local hamlets and some nearby farms under the suspicion that Andreas may have been given a ride by a passerby. Then he was either given shelter or fell asleep in some shed or barn during the pending storm. The final team consisted of two men who were assigned to comb the coastal area for any personal items, or even a body, that may have washed ashore. One of these two men was Bruno Salvaggi, the father. They were pursuing a conviction that maybe, just maybe, his adopted son may have taken his boat out fishing and then gotten caught in the violent storm; the choppy waters and strong undertows could have dragged his dinghy out to open sea. Once out there, in the midst of the dark, frigid, choppy waters, God only knew; even lightning could have been a factor.

Giacomo had his own theory. He believed more likely that his disabled brother may have been the victim of foul play. Foul play directed at him through his family and possibly conceived and carried out by business rivals. Despite the surface pleasantries he shared at meetings with rivals he knew that turf competition, resentment and jealousy were always brewing below the surface. This was most prevalent in Naples where shifting alliances were a constant. Especially when a capo died or was arrested and a power vacuum was created and the next in line always had to prove himself. This power play did not bode well for him and his friend, who had started a joint venture smuggling drugs from Turkey and Afghanistan and distributing them in the ghettos of Naples. But, despite Giacomo's assumption of foul play, his mind didn't stop there; it considered every other possible scenario.

The fact that he and his father, Bruno, had discovered a freshly uprooted bush, sloughed earth along the embankment, some footprints by the drainage pipes and a fairly dry burlap cloth both troubled and intrigued him. All these signs seemed to lead up to the old dirt road towards Mount Cucuzu, where a handful of families resided. Like metal shavings dropping near a magnet Giacomo's mind kept returning to the set of circumstances making it a local matter. But if it was a local matter, it would lessen his suspicions that competing 'Ndrangheta families were behind it. But if his rivals were not behind it, what was the motive? Aside from a gold chain his brother wore since he was a child, he had nothing else on his person of any value; perhaps a few lira to buy *gelati* when the opportunity presented itself. He also carried around an old watch that skipped time, which didn't really matter since Andreas couldn't tell the time. It was just an accessory that had made him happy and made him feel important.

Giacomo was hoping for another day for his men to exhaust the search and to follow other suspected leads, but because his family was in tears, and his mother was also in despair, he relented. By ten o'clock Monday morning he stopped the search and called in the Provincial Police. He had explained the circumstances and the family's efforts in believing, since late Saturday night and into Sunday, that Andreas was lost and in a matter of time would show up or be found. When he didn't show up by Sunday night their worst fears surfaced.

*

It was a quarter to twelve noon when Inspector Gustavo Bellin arrived at Bruno and Antonia Salvaggi's home. The police car was a 1965 Fiat with a blue and white stripe along the sides and a small cherry on the roof. No sirens, no lights, no fanfare. The car rolled onto the cobblestone driveway behind the parked white Renault and came to a slow stop. Inspector Bellin was accompanied by his assistant, Sebastiano Calvi, and a policeman in uniform who was behind the wheel. Bellin was seated in the passenger side looking over some papers on a clipboard. Calvi sat in the back, directly behind the driver. As the engine stopped, Calvi swung open his car door and walked around to Bellin's window where his superior mumbled something, held up the clipboard and directed Calvi's attention to some printed matter that was underlined. His assistant paused to read it, nodded approval and then opened his superior's door.

Bruno Salvaggi was already standing on his porch with his arms crossed; next to him stood a statuette of the Virgin Mary holding baby Jesus. He observed the police car and the interaction of the officers. Giacomo was not in the house. He had decided to wait for the inspector at the yard where Bellin would stop by after the home visit. He had spoken to the inspector earlier that morning and knew him from previous social functions, but only casually. Giacomo then informed his father that the inspector would arrive before noon and told him a little about police procedure. Still, the older Salvaggi was surprised to see three officials in his driveway. His peasant instinct told him that Bellin was a veteran who had witnessed the most sordid affairs of human nature. The evidence was landscaped on his face. He had been fighting life's battles for more than half a century and society's cancers, probably, for some three decades. He had an unnaturally long face made more pronounced by an overly extended chin, deep horizontal furrows on his forehead and deeper still, vertical grooves on his cheeks. Bellin's face was closely shaven but clearly showed the outline of a dark, bluish beard ready to sprout. Despite the first impression, his looks were partially redeemed by a full head of black curly hair with a hint of gray, a tanned face and a burly physique. His dark blue suit, while inexpensive, appeared well fitted and meticulously ironed. One could truly take him for a southerner, *un Siciliano,* whose family went back hundreds, if not thousands, of years in Sicily. Perhaps he had Saracen blood coursing through his veins that went back to the seventh century when his Muslim ilk overran the island, navigated across the Strait of Messina and ruled these lands, in some form or other, for some 400 years.

His younger associate was a study in contrasts. He was probably about half Bellin's age and, at five-nine, a bit shorter. He had reddish hair and freckles, as if someone had plucked him out of Ireland and dropped him here in Calabria. He was a reminder to the astute student of history that the Normans had also been here for several centuries, that during their rule they had intermarried or defiled many local women.

The authority of his ancestors was now conspicuously displayed by a 38-caliber, state-issued Beretta, positioned in his chest holster. Calvi's thin frame was draped with a white turtleneck, gray blazer and gray slacks. He was not as neat as Bellin. However, his speech pattern and clear enunciation announced that he was a university graduate. He was a scout for his generation in this profession and represented things to come in law enforcement.

"*Buon giorno, Inspectore,*" greeted Bruno Salvaggi as he dropped his hands to his sides.

"*Buon giorno.*" The inspector, followed by Calvi, climbed the porch steps towards Bruno who had extended his hand. The uniformed officer stayed in the police vehicle speaking on his radio. Bruno introduced them to his wife, Antonia, and their daughter, Annalisa. They were escorted to the kitchen where they were offered a cup of espresso.

Pleasantries above emotional turmoil, the inspector thought. But the officers accepted the offer appreciatively.

After some small talk, Annalisa said: "I have the photo you had requested."

Then she produced a 3x5 black and white picture of Andreas from a scrapbook.

"Good," said Bellin as he took it and studied it for a moment, thinking that her brother didn't look as disabled as he was purported to be. The picture showed only his upper torso. He was smiling while sporting a white shirt with a small gold medallion of St Francis, the local patron saint, around his neck. *A big "boy,"* thought Bellin. Then he handed the picture to his assistant.

"When was this taken?" asked Calvi, not taking his eyes off the photo.

"Last year on his birthday, when he turned thirty-three," answered Antonia, as she brought a tray to the table.

Antonia's eyes welled up as she set out some homemade *biscotti* and then poured the coffee.

"Exactly how long has he been missing?" asked the inspector.

"Well, he didn't come home for dinner on Saturday night. We waited thinking that he might have taken shelter somewhere because of the storm and would probably get home in an hour or so, but when he wasn't back by ten o'clock Giacomo and I went searching for him," Bruno said. "We searched for him during the night and Giacomo had some of his men from the yard expand the search on Sunday morning. When no solid leads turned up, we felt it was high time we contacted your police department."

"Did he ever go missing before?" asked Calvi, holding a half-eaten *biscotti*.

"No, not for this long, only once he got lost in the woods and slept there half the night before he was found huddled up in a pile of leaves. That was about three years ago," Antonia said.

"How well can he take care of himself?" The inspector put down his cup of *demitasse*.

"He functions with the mind of an eight-year-old and the innocence of an infant," Antonia said, making the sign of the cross. She sniffled, but held back tears.

The inspector pressed on. "Can you think of anyone that would want to bring harm to him?"

"No!" said Annalisa as she pushed herself away from the kitchen counter and took a step closer to the table where her parents and the officers were sitting. "Everybody loved him around here. He was always very respectful and helpful to neighbors. Whenever he helped with construction jobs the customers were happy with the result. They treated him with the utmost gentleness. He was often treated better than all his other co-workers." Her voice cracked mid-sentence as if she realized she was using the past tense; as if her brother's death was a *fait accompli*.

Inspector Bellin knew that the two women could start wailing hysterically with his next question, but he asked anyway.

"Giacomo informed me that your son's boat was missing from the cove, is that right?" Almost on cue, the older woman first made the sign of the cross and then tears started rolling down her face.

"Saturday night, during a lull in the storm, we drove along the beach looking for Andreas, that's when we discovered that his dinghy was missing," Bruno said. "We saw his footprints in the area but couldn't tell whether he had taken the boat out before the storm or if the boat was released by the wind and high tide."

"We'll be looking at that area this afternoon," said the inspector. Then he looked at Calvi, paused, as if considering the weight of the evidence, and said, "The Coast Guard may want to get involved."

"For now, is there anything else you want to tell us that might help us with the investigation?" asked Calvi as he put his pen and notepad down and picked up his empty cup of coffee and placed it in the tray.

"You do know that my brother was adopted?" Annalisa asked.

"Yes, Giacomo told us," said the inspector. "Was there ever any contact or attempted contact by the biological parents or anyone else?"

"None," said Bruno. "Except that the orphanage in Germany had communicated with us on two occasions the first year we took him home. They gave us various letters and a journal from his dead father. From what I was told he was killed in the war."

"Wait," said the inspector, putting his hand up like a school crossing guard. "Andreas was *not* adopted within Italy?"

"No," said Bruno. "He was adopted near Munich where I was a *gastarbeiter* (an early guest worker), after the war."

"Well, we may need to get into that. First, let's see where the preliminary investigation takes us," said Bellin. "In the meantime, would you mind showing us his room?"

Bruno took the officers upstairs to Andreas' room. Annalisa hugged her mother in an attempt to console her.

The officers found his room sparsely furnished. It had one window with shutters. His bed was on one side of the room. A bureau was on the opposite side with a family picture on top. Andreas was shown standing between his father and brother and modeling a broad smile for the photographer. A chair was in the corner next to the dresser.

Behind the chair was a fairly new fishing rod leaning against the wall. Calvi looked through his closet that was half-filled with clothes, with several pairs of work boots and one pair of polished shoes for very special occasions. A few feet over his headboard hung a wooden crucifix with a ceramic Jesus whose toes were missing. On the left side of the cross was a small Italian flag and on the other side a picture of the Italian soccer team. The bedspread was designed with prints of classical cars. The pillowcase was white. The bed was neatly made.

The officers made some comments among themselves about the dismal performance of the current soccer team. Then Bellin asked Bruno, who had been standing in the hallway, if Andreas would often go fishing alone. Bruno told them that he and Giacomo had been out with him many times when he was younger and that eventually, after Andreas learned to swim, he was allowed to row the dinghy out, but no further than beyond the piers.

Downstairs, the officers proceeded straight to the front door. They assured the family they would do everything possible to find their missing son. The inspector intimated that he might want to know more about Andreas' background, depending on the direction of the preliminary investigation. Finally, he thanked Antonia for the coffee, shook hands with Bruno and said that they would be in further contact with them and Giacomo. When the uniformed officer saw the two investigators come out onto the porch, he put down his magazine and promptly started the police car.

As they drove on state route 89 Bellin looked at his watch. It was a quarter after two. The time prompted him to ask Calvi and the uniformed officer if they wanted to stop for lunch. Calvi had worked with Bellin long enough to know that if the question was posed as an alternative, what his superior really wanted was to forget lunch and to stay focused on the case. If eating was truly on his mind he would have asked if they wanted to stop at Umberto's or Rescolini's Sea Side Café.

"I'm not hungry," said Calvi.

The uniformed officer took this as a cue and said he wasn't hungry either. He lied. In fact, he could feel his stomach growling. But he couldn't help wondering if his two passengers had been fed something during the almost two hours they had been in the house.

In less than twenty minutes they had arrived at Giacomo's masonry and lumber yard.

At the front gate one of the workers directed them towards the flat rectangular building in the far rear. As the cruiser navigated around the front office and around forklifts carrying skids and several trucks loading materials, they saw an Audi parked near the small rectangular building.

"When is our department going to upgrade our Fiat for something like that?" Calvi asked.

"Don't hold your breath," snorted the uniformed officer.

Two other cars were parked a short distance from the Audi but closer to the main house. Calvi and Bellin proceeded up the few steps and before Calvi could knock on the door, it swung open.

"I saw you pulling up," said Giacomo as he stood there with a slight smile, looking at the inspector and extending his right hand.

"Good to see you, Giacomo," responded the inspector. "Too bad it couldn't be under better circumstances."

"It's been a little over a year since we last saw each other at the Mayor's dedication," Giacomo reminded him.

Looking from Giacomo to Calvi standing at his side, Bellin said, "This is my assistant, Detective Sebastiano Calvi." The two shook hands.

"Please come in." Giacomo walked towards the two sofas positioned facing each other and with two upholstered chairs on each side. He gestured for them to take a seat.

"*Per favore* (Please)," he said.

"*Grazie*," Calvi replied. Bellin didn't say anything; he sat on the recliner while Calvi sat on the couch.

"Can I get you some coffee or a bottle of mineral water?" asked Giacomo.

"No, but thank you," responded the inspector. "Your mother indulged us less than half an hour ago."

Giacomo sat on the other lounger facing both men. At that point the inspector pulled on the knees of his pants and leaned forward, arms resting on his lap. This indicated a discussion of a more serious nature.

"Bruno told us that you had some of your men search the woods and the surrounding areas yesterday, only to find little or nothing."

"Yes." Giacomo relayed all that his men had done. "When he didn't come home for over twenty-four hours and we had no solid clues, we felt it best not to wait and contacted your department," explained Giacomo.

"We've also been informed that his boat is missing, is that right?" Calvi added.

"Yes, that was the only half-assed lead we got. The boat was discovered missing just before ten o'clock, Saturday night, when Pop and I took my car and went looking for him. We found footprints that appeared to be his where the boat was supposed to be tied. I suppose it's conceivable that he took the dinghy out just before the storm, not being aware that bad weather was coming. This was not unusual for him to do. He would row the boat out but was well aware not to go beyond the jetty, to stay close to shore. We knew that if he ever got into trouble, he was able to swim back that short a distance."

"Alright, this is what we're going to do," said Bellin. "First, we want to see where his rowboat was anchored. Second, we want a list of all your employees that Andreas frequently worked with. Third, we want the names of all the customers he worked for during the last three months."

"Of course! My family and I want to do everything possible to find my brother," said Giacomo, while thinking to himself that this was precisely why he didn't want the idiot police involved in the first place. Their fucking probing, snooping, questioning was repugnant to him. He felt that the whole police matter might spill into his private business dealings and potentially compromise some of his clients and his more lucrative activities. At the very least, he would have to waste his time and energy staying ahead of the inspector. He didn't need this *merda* (shit), especially now, when his international operations were about to expand up north. These bureaucrats were as useful as bad bottles of wine at a picnic!

"The sooner we get started at the coast the better," said Bellin as he stood up.

Giacomo and Calvi, showing equal resolve, snapped out of their seats.

"I'll take you to the spot where the rowboat is usually anchored," volunteered Giacomo.

A short time later they reached the cove. Giacomo parked his car on the opposite side of the road, against traffic, since there was no shoulder on the south side. The uniformed officer parked the police vehicle just behind him. The late afternoon sun was glowing, yet not warming up the cool, crisp air blowing in from the sea. The water was a little more turbulent than normal but not wild enough to keep several fishermen from casting their lines. A couple could also be seen in the distance, walking hand in hand, near the water's edge. No one else was around. As Giacomo made his way to the edge of the road, he could see the entire span of the coast. Bellin and Calvi followed behind. The uniformed officer was outside the radio car, leaning against the roof and looking at the horizon where the sky met the sea, puffing on a cigarette.

"That's where Andreas kept his rowboat," Giacomo told the two officers, while pointing to the left and in the general direction of the rockiest part of the shoreline. On the inner side of the promontory several small boats were anchored. Then the three took a few steps closer to the precipice and looked for the best route down. Giacomo told them to make their way toward the large dark boulder.

*

The uniformed officer walked the length of the car, puffed on his cigarette and stood on a small ledge. He observed every step the inspector took until he reached the bottom of the rock pile. There he saw his boss stop and make a quick entry in his journal. As they approached their destination, Bellin and Calvi separated. The uniformed officer saw them making various observations, pushing debris with their shoe, bending to pick up something or other of possible interest. Then he saw them walk to the furthest point of the wet sand, where the water had crested. It was there that Calvi discovered what appeared to be a boot partially buried in sand. The uniformed officer could barely see Calvi tug at the upper leather ridge with one hand. It seemed heavy from being laden with sand and water. Using two hands he scooped away some of the surrounding sand and managed to pull the shoe out. Then, holding it from the top, he called to his superior.

"I found something here," shouted Calvi, holding up the shoe. Bellin and Giacomo walked over.

"Recognize it?" asked Calvi, while looking at Giacomo, who took the shoe for a closer inspection.

"It looks like one of a pair of work boots I gave Andreas for his birthday last year." Then he flipped back the shoe's tongue and read: *Manufatura Silvestri-Mancini, Milano.*

"This is the brand and his size," said Giacomo.

Then he handed the shoe back to Calvi, who pulled out a plastic bag from the pocket of his blazer and placed the boot inside.

Bellin focused on the distinctive pattern on the sole of the boot and started looking around in the sand, but couldn't match them to any footprints evident in the area. Calvi walked back to the spot where he found the evidence. He was hoping to find the second shoe near some rocks where the current had washed up all sorts of debris. He saw crushed cans, beer bottles and plastic bags bobbing up and down between the rock crevices.

"Whatever footprints were here Saturday night have been washed clean," said Giacomo. He inspected the rusty hook protruding from the concrete block that had held the dinghy in place during previous storms. Then he pulled on the metal protrusion to see if it was loose but it was intact.

After exhausting the area near where the dinghy had been for clues, and the shoreline, Inspector Bellin told Giacomo that there was nothing more they could do here. The found boot, the identified missing boat and the previously seen footprints leading to the shore reported by the family warranted a request for a Coast Guard search.

He wanted them here as soon as possible. Realistically, the earliest would be sometime in the morning. He told Giacomo that if his family had any more news, they should call him immediately. He jotted down his personal number on the back of his card and handed it to Giacomo. Then they walked back up to the road, bid goodbye and drove away in their respective vehicles.

Chapter 5

Preparations for the Journey

It was a quarter after five on Wednesday morning, the autumn of 1972. Lorenzo was awakened by the crow of the rooster. Soon after, the cows started mooing like sequenced instruments in an orchestra. Lying in bed looking through the partially opened shutters he could see the leaves of the beech tree tickled by the morning breeze. The splendor of the morning sun was beckoning life's spirit to stir. He stood up in bed scratching away the irritation from the wool undershirt his mother had knitted and listened to a muffled noise that seemed to be coming from one of the rooms down the hallway. Quickly, he spun himself around to the edge of the bed and bounced off, slipped his pants on and gently tiptoed across the room. He opened his bedroom door cautiously so as not to make the hinges squeak. Gabriella's door across the hall was closed and quiet. The subdued laughter was coming from his father's room whose door was cracked open, allowing Lorenzo to peek in and see his mother, in her nightgown, sitting on the side of his father's bed holding his hand. He thought he overheard his father say something that struck him as mildly humorous regarding Andreas' disappearance.

"...maybe he got fed up with them and decided to go back to Germany to search for his real parents."

"Ssshhh, *mi amore, non dire questo* (Don't say that, it's unkind)," Francesca gently admonished. "Bruno and Antonia adore that boy."

Lorenzo, for a long time, hadn't heard his father's voice sound as lucid as it sounded today. But even though his mornings differed in degrees of clarity, what seemed consistent was how progressively worse he got by the end of the day. His energy level dissipated and he became disoriented. By early evening he looked less like the corpulent man in the picture on the armoire and more like a corpse. Which is what made today's behavior a rarity since he was propped up in bed with pillows on each side. He must've been sharing some special moments with Francesca because they were laughing, almost giggling.

Lorenzo noticed that his mother had removed the bandages on her scalp. Over the visible outline of a vertical red gash, a scab had formed. Francesca turned partially around to put down a medicine bottle on the nightstand when she saw him from the corner of her eye. With a quick hand motion, she waved him in. As he entered, he saw the hot water basin, soap brush, soap tray and a straight-edge razor, closed, resting on a towel next to the water basin. His father smiled at him as Lorenzo went over and kissed him on the cheek. Today his face was smooth; the graying wiry stubble was gone. The smell of perfumed soap and talcum powder were also a welcome relief from the pungent medicinal aromas that would normally assault his senses.

"You look good, Papa. Did you sleep well?" he asked, returning a smile.

"I feel good. It must've been your mother's chicken soup from last night," he said, while looking at Francesca amorously with a broad grin on his face. She gently brushed his hair back with her fingers.

"I was about to ask your mother if she could help me to that chair, by the window. I miss not seeing the sun rise in the morning."

"Are you sure you are strong enough, Matteo? Do not overtax yourself," Francesca said, with little worry lines forming on her face.

"This morning I am strong enough for anything," Matteo said, giving his wife a meaningful look.

"I guess it would be okay," said his wife with a small smile, "but as soon as you get tired, you're coming right back to bed, promise?" Matteo nodded his head in acquiescence while meeting Francesca's eyes.

Francesca rolled back his bed covers and Lorenzo steadied his father's back and shoulders while the fragile man rotated his legs to the edge of the bed, then they each grabbed him under his arms and slowly walked the fifteen feet to the window where they sat him in a chair. Lorenzo tucked a pillow on the inside of the arm of the chair, and shifted the chair slightly to give Papa the best view of the eastern sky and what promised to be a glorious sunrise.

"This is perfect," Matteo said as they looked out and saw a gentle breeze stirring the multitude of colors on the trees, the dew on the plants and the sun's radiance announcing life to a world awakening from the night's slumber.

"What an incredible day."

"We deserve it," Francesca sighed deeply, "after what we went through with that storm on the weekend."

"You've both been killing yourselves working," Matteo said, "especially this time of the year. I'm so sorry I haven't been there to help you," he continued, his voice saddened with regret and guilt.

"We're all part of this family and we all do what we can," said Francesca.

Matteo turned to his son. "Do you have any new thoughts about the trip?"

"There hasn't been a day I haven't thought about it," said Lorenzo. "I'll miss everybody, but I've decided that I should go. Uncle Pietro bought me the ocean liner tickets to America months ago; I still have them in my drawer. It's the chance of a lifetime. I could always come back if things don't work out by the spring. But assuming all goes well, I'll be able to send money home so that Mama or Uncle Dominick could hire some local help when necessary. Uncle Dominick also said that he wouldn't mind picking up some slack, particularly the next four months of winter, when not much is happening. He understands that people around here go to work abroad all the time. They would kill for the opportunity to go to America instead of Germany or Australia."

Lorenzo saw anguish flash across the faces of his parents but knew that they wouldn't oppose his decision. His mother, grasping the back of his father's chair with white knuckles, gave a deep sigh. His father looked far into the distance. He knew that his parents couldn't blame him for trying to escape from eking out a living on a small family farm on the side of a mountain. He was going to turn eighteen in a few weeks and if he didn't do it now, when? Once he was married with children, life would get more complicated and opportunities would vanish.

Lorenzo still had three days before departure. But he considered leaving for Naples tomorrow and spending one night in the city. The ocean liner was scheduled to depart at 2pm Friday so he was fearful of some glitch in his travel plans, due to constant railroad delays between Paola and Naples. There was no end to threatened work stoppages and strikes were becoming a way of life. He just wanted to make sure he was on time to board the ship.

Lorenzo also felt that the sooner he departed the better, so as not to get entangled with Andreas Salvaggi's investigation. Should the police get hot on his trail, his recurring concern was that they would probably take away his passport and prevent him from traveling anywhere.

"*Buon giorno*," his sister greeted him as she walked in wearing her mother's hand-me-down nightgown. She came over by the window and kissed Papa on the cheek, followed with a hug. Then she kissed her mother and jokingly shoved her brother with her shoulder.

"Did I miss anything?" Gabriella said. "You weren't talking about me while I was sleeping, were you?" she asked with a smile on her face.

"You're always the subject of our conversations!" her brother teased. "Especially when you're not around."

Their mother brought the subject back to a more serious matter.

"We were talking about your brother's upcoming trip to America."

"Then it's okay! Talk all you want, as long as I get his room when he leaves," she said, not yet finished jousting with him.

Lorenzo turned to his mother. "Now you know why I'm anxious to get going as soon as possible," he said, frowning at his sister.

"Stop! Both of you," Francesca commanded sharply.

"Right, Mama, let's move on to things of greater interest," Gabriella said, trying to sound more sophisticated than her age suggested.

"Fine, shut up! And I'll tell you what one of our neighbors, Mr. Rossini, told me at the minimarket. I saw him while purchasing a few last-minute items for the trip. Since he works at Giacomo's warehouse, he hears everything. On Monday, he said, Giacomo called the police to investigate Andreas' disappearance. Shortly after, the police found a shoe near the water. It belonged to Andreas. So, the police called the *Guardia Costiera* (Coast Guard) to search five miles out. They even had divers looking for his body." Gabriella and Lorenzo's parents were listening attentively.

"Did they find anything?" said Matteo as he turned his head away from the window, facing Lorenzo with great concern.

"He did say they found Andreas' row boat, a few miles from the coast and half filled with water. Nothing was in the boat except a broken fishing rod. But at one point in the afternoon, the divers hoped that they had discovered his body some forty or fifty feet down, in an area that was deep and murky. It turned out to be a small burned-out log with seaweed and coral wrapped around it."

"So, the police must've concluded it was a drowning?" asked his sister.

"He didn't say," said Lorenzo, "but I think they're still looking into other aspects of the case. According to Rossini, Giacomo had to furnish the police with a list of names of people that Andreas worked with, and worked for, during the last few months."

"For what purpose?" asked Francesca.

"Possibly to see if there were disgruntled employees or customers and if anyone had a grudge against any member of the family," offered Matteo.

"Mr. Rossini said, unfortunately, he is also in the middle of this inquiry," continued Lorenzo.

"What can Mr. Rossini really know?" asked Gabriella.

'Well, Rossini is a foreman at Giacomo's yard. Two weeks ago, he was assigned to a job in Amandea. He was to demolish an old stoop and stairs and build a new and larger one in its place. Now, guess who else worked on that project?" Lorenzo, himself, appeared surprised.

"It was Andreas!" blurted out Gabriella.

"Sometimes, you're smarter than you look," quipped Lorenzo.

"Well, this gets a little crazy, but stay with me. I'll see if I can remember what Rossini told me." Lorenzo was focused on his parents.

"Mr. Rossini, Andreas and another employee called Dante worked on the project. They were to finish in two days. At the start of the day, the foreman had the other two men load the masonry truck from a list of materials needed at the job site. Rossini said he was careful and meticulous with all the materials because if he has to go back and forth to the yard it's such a waste of time. Also, he's reluctant to leave his workers alone. He said from past experience, the possibility of things going bad was unending." Lorenzo paused, trying to recollect.

"Enzo, are Mr. Rossini's work habits really that important to the story?" she asked.

'Yes! They are very important. You need to know the background to appreciate what's coming."

"Okay, go on," said Francesca.

"The morning of the first day of work was uneventful. The three men ripped down the old stoop, stairs and cleared everything out.

But the afternoon was very different. After Dante had a hefty lunch with a couple of beers, he was using a miter saw to cut wood for framing out the stairs. Mr. Rossini and Andreas were on the opposite side of the house busy mixing concrete for the walkway. It was then that they heard Dante screaming and cursing at the top of his lungs like it was the end of the world. Rossini dropped everything and rushed over to see what was going on. Coming around the corner of the house, he saw Dante squeezing his left wrist with his right hand. As he got closer, Rossini saw that the tips of Dante's index finger and middle finger were on the ground. And part of his ring finger was hanging from his hand suspended only by a piece of skin.

"Ohhh, nasty! I'm going to vomit," said Gabriella.

"Well, yeah! Rossini even said he was aghast from what he saw. But he didn't panic. He reacted quickly. He tied a handkerchief around the injured man's wrist to stop the blood flow; got a towel from the truck and wrapped it around Dante's hand. He picked up the tips of Dante's fingers and put them in a cup and rushed the victim to the hospital. But before he drove off, he gave Andreas orders to shovel the mixed concrete into the framed walkway, before it hardened. Also, to level it off. He said Andreas nodded and seemed to understand these simple directions. He had done the same work many times. Once finished, Andreas was told to sit down and wait for Rossini to come back. He would be back in an hour, then he'd drive Andreas home." Lorenzo stopped talking and went over to his dad to reposition him on the chair.

"I hope the best part is coming, it's turning out to be a long story," said Gabriella.

"Well, what's coming is not meant for children. So maybe you should leave the room." Lorenzo having said this, Gabriella quickly perked up.

"Mr. Rossini did come back in just over an hour. From a distance, he saw Andreas and some boys in the middle of a melee. He accelerated down the street, honking his horn. The group's leader dropped a board he was ready to clobber Andreas with and took off with the others," Lorenzo said as he was trying to recall exactly what he was told.

"Was Andreas hurt?" asked his mother.

"I'm getting to that," said Lorenzo. "Rossini heard the leader yell at Andreas: 'This isn't over, retard.' Later, on the way home, Mr. Rossini asked Andreas what happened. And Andreas told him, still shaking, stammering and with much difficulty, that he did exactly what he was told. He filled the forms with concrete and leveled them with a trowel. It was very smooth and looked perfect. Andreas said that it would make Mr. Rossini happy."

"You didn't answer Mama's question, was Andreas hurt?" asked Gabriella.

"He was more shaken than hurt," said Lorenzo as he picked up the story again. "Andreas continued to tell Mr. Rossini what happened before he came back with the truck. That he was sitting on a rock near a pile of bricks when four boys, with school books, came walking up the street joking and clowning around. They were some twenty feet away from Andreas when the leader whispered something to the others. They grouped together around the freshly setting concrete. Andreas was looking at them thinking that they were admiring his work. Instead, the leader unzipped his pants and peed on the fresh cement. He tried to carve his initials with the stream of his urine. This is what he saw on the fresh concrete."

"Andreas didn't do anything?" Matteo asked.

"Well, this is the gist of the dialogue between Andreas and the boys," said Lorenzo.

"'Hey, stop that,' Andreas shouted at the leader.

"'What are you gonna do?' said the boy as he zipped his pants.

"'Stop that,' Andreas repeated several more times.

"'*Vaffanculo*, weirdo!'

"Then he told Mr. Rossini they called him some other very, very bad words he couldn't repeat. Mr. Rossini realized that the boys thought that Andreas was either scared or retarded in his slow response since he was stuttering and repeating himself. So, the boys didn't feel threatened when they stomped on the fresh cement. At that point, Andreas grabbed a brick from the pile next to him and threw it at them. The brick hit the leader's thigh and the boy took a few steps back limping and screaming.

"'It's not over. I'm going to kill you. Mother f…!'" Lorenzo repeated the boy's last words.

"I suppose the police inspector will want to follow up on that story," said Francesca.

"It's probably one of many leads that the inspector is pursuing," added Matteo, appearing troubled by the whole Andreas incident.

Finally, Lorenzo said, "I'm going to milk the cows." He kissed his father, who was already beginning to look very tired, his short burst of energy having waned for the day. Lorenzo's anxiety today was not so much about the direction the investigation was taking, as it was about his afternoon appointment.

Chapter 6

Secret Meeting with Annalisa

Ever since tensions had developed between the Benedetta and Salvaggi families, Lorenzo and Annalisa were not permitted to see each other. But they saw each other less often and in secrecy. Today, at three o'clock, they would rendezvous at the old slate quarry near the top of Mount Cucuzu. Both would lie to their parents or distort the truth as to their whereabouts. Annalisa would say that she visited with her girlfriend from school to study together. Her girlfriend, Laura, was the perfect cover and knew exactly what to say if confronted with questions by Annalisa's family. In most cases Annalisa would make a quick stopover at Laura's house. This would further support her story, if called on it, and not make her into an outright liar. Lorenzo, on the other hand, would say that he was going into the woods to gather some more wild chestnuts for the hogs since stock was running low. At times he would carry a full sack of chestnuts from the barn, cross the field unseen, hide the sack of chestnuts in some brambles and walk up the mountain to his tryst with Annalisa. On the way back, to lend credence to his story, he would often stop back at the house to make sure someone saw him with the chestnut sack on his back.

They had an appointed spot where they would leave a message on a certain day if they needed to see each other for whatever reason. The message was often short and sweet:

"Need to see you, 3pm, same spot. Al."

"Al" wasn't a closing name nor was it a deliberate attempt to throw off anyone that might find the note. It was just a special term of endearment and devotion to each other. This was Lorenzo's idea from two years prior when he visited a gift shop in Paola that catered mostly to tourists from the north. In the store he had noticed a small jewelry box on the counter. It contained various oval-shaped stones and small silver charms with different script writings carved in them: love, trust, peace, harmony, etc. One amulet, in particular, had caught his eye. It was heart-shaped and the last one of its kind in the box. Inscribed on it with fancy lettering was the word, "Always." He bought it without a second thought. Later he purchased a beautiful silver chain from a jewelry shop and he gave both items to Annalisa for her sixteenth birthday. And from that moment on, "Al" came to mean to them, "Always in my heart."

A message from Lorenzo would mostly be left on Wednesdays because it was the most convenient day for both. This was their routine; he would leave the note early Wednesday morning and she would get it on Wednesday afternoon, just after her high school classes were over. On the other hand, Annalisa would leave her note on Tuesday for Lorenzo's pickup on Wednesday morning. At first it seemed complicated but then it quickly became a habit. The small folded note would be left inside a stone wall that was on the public pathway leading to Mount Cucuzu. This was also the path they could take to reach their respective homes. At the rear of the stone wall and just about a foot from the uppermost corner was a loose rock which they removed and replaced on numerous occasions, perhaps too numerous to count. If it were a note from Annalisa it would be on perfumed stationery and embossed with tiny flowers around its four corners. Lorenzo would take the folded note and hold it close to his face; he would shut his eyes and inhale deeply as if taking in her very essence. Then he would read it. If it were a note from Lorenzo it would be on plain white paper but would either have a drawn flower or a smiley face. Today she found no drawing and no smiley face. Instead, she found a real red rose lying behind the wall, on the ground, next to the loose rock. To Annalisa a smiley face was interpreted as a joint soul. They were thinking of each other. They were feeling each other. And the world was left on the sideline. On the other hand, a rose was recognized as love, but the world was somehow intruding. There was a problem. To them the rose was delicate, beautiful, fragrant and yet, its thorns could make you bleed.

The world had previously intruded on their lives when their parents had forbidden them from seeing each other. It had started with a squabble between the two families. The difficulties broke out during a long and parched summer when a small stream virtually dried up. The small stream of water originated at the top of the mountain and flowed down through the Benedettas' property and continued on to their neighbors, the Salvaggis' property.

In the normal course of events, the Benedettas would fill up their cistern and their pond for personal use and then would free the stream for their neighbors' use below. Unfortunately, the exceptionally hot summer not only triggered forest fires but resulted in a water flow that was almost a trickle. This was barely enough for the Benedetta family, particularly since Matteo had expanded his vineyards earlier that year, requiring more water for irrigation. The Salvaggis immediately complained that they were being denied their normal share of water. They felt that it should be shared no matter what the circumstances. Matteo felt that they were being very careful in not wasting water. He offered to give them some large containers for personal home use and suggested that they build a well. The Salvaggis felt that because of Matteo's extended farming it was his fault that their crop burned up. So, they sold their few animals, stopped growing crops and were forced to make trips to the municipal pump every other day to fill up jugs of water for their personal use. After that period, they never went back to farming or raising animals.

Giacomo thought that this slight from the Benedettas, in denying them water, was the reason his family had to alter their lifestyle. He never forgave them. He became sullen and even his attitude towards his father changed. He did not disrespect his father nor did he show him any great respect because he saw a mark of weakness in his character. From that day forward Giacomo showed the same singleness of purpose as his mother, although his purpose was not religious. Giacomo vowed that neither he nor his family would ever be denied anything or be taken advantage of again. He would be respected and listened to, period!

A few years later, when his business was profitable, he had a water well built for his family at considerable cost and time because the drilling company had to go some sixty feet below through hard rock to find water. It was about the time of the drought that the children of the two families were forbidden from seeing each other, even though they had been brought up together and had attended the same elementary and middle schools since they were children.

Annalisa had attended primary school under the roof of the Benedettas' house since it was one of the few houses in the mountain community of La Pera that met state requirements. It had taken the Benedettas almost two years to gain certification after putting in an application to the state and making some modifications to the house. After Matteo added another entrance to the rear, converted two storage rooms and built another outhouse, the state finally rented the large room on the first floor and allowed Matteo and Francesca a stipend to pay for desks, a blackboard and a few furnishings. The second room that served as living quarters for the teacher was above the classroom. It was rented, and paid for, by the instructor herself, directly to the owners. At the end of it all, some seventeen students from the immediate area either walked or cycled, up and down or across the mountains each morning and each afternoon when class was let out.

The method of teaching was known as Montessori and its technique was originally intended for children with physical and mental disabilities but later became more broadly accepted, particularly in rural areas. The teacher dealt with various grades in the same classroom so it wasn't uncommon for students to range in age from six through twelve, level one through five. The methodology favored an emphasis on a hands-on approach and independent learning by the child. The instructor made materials available from the real world using plants, animals, rocks, lumber, etc. so as to teach skills. Often the older children became assistant teachers by sharing what they had learned with younger students while the instructor's role was one of a "silent presence." Grades and testing were discouraged in favor of moving on to other more advanced skills when the child was ready.

Annalisa and Lorenzo were in Signorina Vitulli's class. The teacher was a plump unmarried woman. She was pleasant to the parents and rigorous with her students. Matteo and Francesca were so fond of her that they invited her for dinner every other night and treated her genuinely as a family member. The "*Professoresa*," as her students called her, was in her early thirties and everyone considered her a spinster at such a late age. Some locals even felt sorry for her. Years later, when she had moved on to bigger and better things, Francesca still kept a picture of her on the wall. The photo was taken in a field covered with snow; Signorina Vitulli, Francesca and two other women were depicted laughing up a storm. She wore a full-length coat and had a snowball in her hand as if ready to hit the photographer.

The two children sat together because they were at the same level and of the same age, merely months apart. They had known each other virtually since they popped out of their mothers' wombs. Often, when Lorenzo was called on to recite the multiplication table, if he stumbled or seemed unsure, Annalisa became flustered for him. Lorenzo would look at her for salvation during these stressful moments. Annalisa would then dip her pen into the inkwell and write down the answer on a scrap of paper that he would see and, after making believe that he was counting on his fingers, recite the answer she had written. During lunch they would sit under a tree, in their usual shady spot or by a little pond, where they would pitch pebbles in an attempt to hit frogs that were swimming or ones that were sunbathing on a branch or large leaf. Whenever they hit the mark, the frog would give out a croaking sound that made them laugh hysterically.

However, Annalisa would get angry with him when he went along with the pranks and cruelty of other boys. Sometimes they would catch a bullfrog and tie it by its hind legs with a string. Then they would tie the other ends of the string to a tree or a bush on opposite sides of the street and waited for a truck to pass by and run over the helpless creature. The poor thing always struggled to hop away but always landed in the same spot. The big thrill was when a truck came by and the little animal popped under the tire like a firecracker on the fourth of July. Annalisa did give Enzo credit for trying to convince some of their schoolmates not to do "the cat swing." They both realized that this was very cruel. Basically, the kids would catch a feral cat, tie a loose noose around its head and hang it from a tree branch. In its struggle to get free it swung from side to side and clawed wildly in mid air. If the cat survived for five minutes they would reward its effort and tenacity by releasing it. Freeing the cat gave them an even bigger rush because the cat became disoriented from lack of oxygen to its brain and would often wobble like a drunken sailor and run around in circles. At times, it would hop away like a bunny or instead of running in a straight line it would hop away sideways.

In hindsight, Lorenzo couldn't believe what he did in those days. He was glad that those childhood pranks were over. He knew that

Annalisa forgave him for many of those transgressions. But wondered if she could ever forgive him now, for what he did to her disabled brother. And would she believe what he did was to protect his mother from being raped by Andreas, a man with the innocence of a child? Lorenzo had an inordinate desire to confide in someone. And she was the closest person in his life. But what would be her reaction? And if she did believe him, she would inevitably ask: why did you have to kill him? Would she understand that when he struck that fatal blow it was dark and he didn't recognize Andreas? And if she had doubts, would she be quiet about all these strange events that still appeared imaginary?

He let out a deep breath; if she didn't turn her back to him or run away as if he were a monster, she would insist that he confess to the authorities. And if he didn't confess and she didn't go to the police, would she betray Lorenzo and tell her family so as to lessen their anguish?

One thing was certain. Annalisa knew that he had tickets to travel to America and that his trip to America was imminent. But she didn't know that Lorenzo was planning on staying there. He had wrestled with that decision and was tormented by it for some time. Only the events of the last few days had made his resolve unshakable. Lorenzo also knew that the decision he had made, and the actions he had taken recently, would permanently change their relationship. Even if he begged for her forgiveness and she did forgive him, the closeness and the harmony they shared would forever be diminished. It was unavoidable. The act was more unimaginable and shocking than having been caught in an affair or having breached any type of trust. Those events could be granted absolution, this was something else and Annalisa would find it unforgivable.

The events of Saturday night superimposed themselves again on Lorenzo's mind like a recurrent boil. He contemplated not only his current predicament but also the impact on his future and the loss that would follow. He knew better than anyone that his life would be forever, irrevocably changed. His life as he had known it was also buried with Andreas.

He hurried through his farm chores and arrived at the quarry some fifteen minutes earlier than their appointed time. Since Saturday, he had developed a total revulsion in being anywhere close to the barn. He was alone with this unspeakable secret that Andreas' corpse was yards away, in the cold earth and without even a casket. His family could never properly bury and mourn their son, and he would continue to be consumed with anguish. Lorenzo visualized vermin devouring the remains. He felt that Andreas' spirit would probably haunt that barn for years to come; maybe until after it ceased to exist. Even the feeling of joy he got from being around animals was now like a flickering candle about to be extinguished. He tried not to focus on any aspect of that night, but the harder he tried to forget the more his mind became obsessed by it. No matter where he was, what he was doing or what he was thinking, his mind circled back to that tomb; Andreas' grave was Lorenzo's personal abyss. Nights were no better. He felt like a hamster perpetually running on a metal wheel. He hoped that going to America, the distance and change in environment, would bring some peace of mind.

Lorenzo wiped the sweat and hair from his forehead and looked at his watch. Annalisa was late. Could she know somehow? There were instances when they were far from each other and yet they seemed capable of reading each other's thoughts. It wasn't just coincidence because the occasions were too numerous. He would pick up a holiday card for her; and she would select the exact same card for him amidst hundreds. He would call her randomly and then find that her line was busy because she was calling him at that instant. At one time they were both in Paola with their respective mothers but at opposite ends of the city. When it was time for lunch Lorenzo had entered this quaint little restaurant that he had never visited before. He was enjoying the ambience and wondering how nice it would be if Annalisa was there. Then midway into lunch

Annalisa and her mother walked in. She swore that she had never been to that restaurant before and didn't know that it even existed. There was an inexplicable energy, a connecting force, like an invisible thread, between them that they could sense but not explain. Lorenzo remembered reading somewhere that researchers believed it could be a primitive power that might have been lost or become sublimated eons ago during an evolutionary shift. But some animals still had it. They were able to communicate using pheromones or chemical signals, at some frequency and at great distances from each other. If it was an irresistible chemical attraction between them, it didn't matter to him why or what it was, what mattered was that they were definitely soul mates.

While leaning against the rocks near the quarry Lorenzo could see a few homes in the distance clinging to the side of the mountains. He observed that all the homeowners had constructed their front doors to face the sea. He would miss these views, especially looking out from the small plateau where he was standing. Here, there was no fear of height. Even the deepest parts of the valley seemed less unsettling since the arrangement of boulders gave one the feeling that they were stepping stones to the sea. The clusters of sheltering pine trees to his left, where he and Annalisa had lost their innocence, also gave him a sense of security. These trees were shedding many of their lower needles at this time of the year. The deciduous trees, on the other hand, were naked on top while the lower branches held tenaciously to their foliage like mothers to their children. The gentle wind cajoled them, ruffled them, swayed them side to side, but made no headway in defoliating them. Occasionally, one or several leaves would spiral down to the earth but the others were hell-bent on remaining attached to the branches. As for those on the ground, the wind teased and nudged them until they sought refuge between rocks and tall dry grasses.

Lorenzo remembered everything of that day they had been together. They rode their bikes down to the town where they bought a long loaf of bread that was still warm from the oven, several different cheeses, some prosciutto, melon and a bottle of local wine. It had been a mild day in September and they, at first, decided to spend a little time at the beach and have lunch there but after ten minutes they changed their minds because it was too chilly. Instead of going home they had decided to bike up the mountain, taking a shortcut that required zigzagging up some rocky cliffs. More often than not, they found themselves walking their bikes. When they had arrived at the slate quarry they had to catch their breath. It wasn't the first time that they had pedaled to this place but that day was the first time they spread a beach towel under the pine trees, had lunch and enjoyed the panoramic view while sipping glasses of wine. The location gave them a sense of peace and security, like eagles in the middle of their nest. They were away from everybody and yet sheltered and nestled amid the trees and the heaps of slate behind, the grove of pines on one side and a sprinkling of huge rocks embedded in the earth and slanting precipitously towards the bottom of the valley, opposite the evergreens.

When they had finished setting out lunch and opened the bottle of wine, Lorenzo had stretched out with his hands behind his neck. It was moments later when Annalisa placed her wine glass on the side of the beach towel and leaned over while his eyes were momentarily closed. She started teasing Lorenzo by brushing a stalk of dry grass along his exposed skin. He was smiling broadly and they laughed together. Annalisa sighed sweetly and deeply as she lay down next to him on the small blanket and closed her eyes as well, enjoying the sun and slight breeze. Their hands and hips touched. She wriggled away a small distance as propriety would dictate and Lorenzo felt a sense of loss but resisted the urge to move closer out of respect. Then, unexpectedly, she softly kissed his lips. His body and soul reacted like kerosene pouring over dormant cinders and trembling excitement came over him. He felt a sudden, irrepressible desire growing. He opened his eyes and saw Annalisa's face close above him. Her crystal blue eyes united with his. Lorenzo felt her desire equally palpable and irrepressible.

The wine blunted their inhibitions and enhanced their yearning. Lorenzo sat up. He continued looking at her with such insatiable hunger that could not be described or conveyed in words. The feeling transcended the physical needs, the carnal. Their desire was at a place inhabited by their souls. He kissed her, timidly at first, then again and again, on her mouth, on her face, on her neck. Annalisa rolled closer to him and placed her thigh across his legs. Never looking away from him, both of them trapped so sweetly and urgently in that moment, she straddled him. He put his arms around her and pulled her closer. Their lips met again. He could feel her firm swollen nipples pressing against his chest. Their hearts, like drums, were beating wildly, rhythmically with delight. He remembered her unbuttoning his shirt, kissing him on every inch of his skin. He felt like someone who had been lost in the desert. But he did not thirst for water, his thirst was unquenchable for her being. He removed her blouse, pulled her closer and their essence became one as their lips, their hands, their fingertips glided uncontrollably, exploring the richness and beauty of the other's strong, young, innocent and unmapped territory. They became one; they moved in a singular existence. Time stopped. Life's concerns were cast aside; before them was an ocean of bliss. They made love with primal lust. After, they kissed and clung to each other. Their bodies separated but their souls still joined.

That afternoon, from the top of the world, they had made promises to each other as only those in the blush of first love will. No matter what, they would love one another until their last breath. They discussed their future. She wanted to be a doctor and pursue studies in pulmonary medicine. She would be the one to find a cure for the illnesses of the world. He wanted to be a civil engineer, and with a beaming smile, told her he wanted to put his name on a plaque, on both sides of the Strait of Messina. The plaque would proclaim that Lorenzo Benedetta was the visionary behind the project: a suspension bridge linking the island of Sicily with the southern tip of the peninsula. This would improve the economy and bring the dreams of many people to fruition.

They assured one another that they would not lose each other in the chaos and unpredictability of life, and that the pursuit of their goals or even attaining them was inconsequential to what they felt for each other. They talked about the other's wishes, not if they got married but when they got married. The type of home the future engineer would build, where they would live, how many children they would have and even what their names would be. For a girl, they both agreed it was to be Laura. If a boy, she wanted a Micheluzzi; teasingly, he said he wanted a Citroluzzu. Then he had asked if their parents would be offended if they did not honor them with their name. Annalisa responded that her aunt, who had seven children, had given them all exotic names and no one in her family felt offended. She even suggested that her aunt could help in deciding the appropriate names. At that point, Lorenzo suggested that they postpone the decision for future consideration. They lay in each other's arms, and dozed in the sunshine, with the confidence of the very young that love alone would be enough.

Lorenzo's reverie ended when he heard the wheels of a bike behind him. He turned around to see that Annalisa had finally arrived. He beamed with a pure, unaffected smile. She smiled back as she came to a full stop and tried to catch her breath. Her bike dropped to the ground. Lorenzo walked up to her. Her hair was braided. Her dark hair and rosy cheeks were a stark contrast with her fair complexion. She wore jeans, a denim jacket with a new beige blouse he had never seen before. She walked into his arms and kissed him with absolute enthusiasm.

"Sorry I'm late," she said, "couldn't get away any faster." She always expressed herself with an overflowing abundance of vitality. Her exuberance wasn't about seeing life as a half-empty glass or a half-full glass but as a glass whose contents were always spilling over the top. She was talking rapidly and using hand gestures. She had a way of drawing you into her world not only by sucking up the oxygen around but by pushing your senses to their pinnacle. Whether at a party, a school function or family gathering all would know when Annalisa walked through the door or what corner of the room she occupied.

"That's alright. I haven't been waiting long but I was beginning to get a little worried. Is everything alright?" Lorenzo inquired.

"That Inspector Bellin stopped over again, asking more questions," she responded, a little annoyed. Lorenzo wondered if the annoyance was due to the inspector's unexpected visit or due to the progress of the investigation.

"Any new developments?" he asked, with a hint of reservation as to what she might say.

"Well, you might have heard or read in the papers that the police divers were called in. They searched underwater for a full day and came up with nothing. However, they did find the dinghy some five miles out at sea and one of my brother's shoes on shore. Mom and Dad think that Andreas may have been caught in turbulent waters stirred up by the storm, then got swept further out and couldn't swim back. They're acting as if he's already dead!"

"What do you and Giacomo think?" he asked, feeling a bit apprehensive about her answer.

"I think seeing my brother's disappearance as an accident makes it easier for them to accept it and gives them some closure," she responded, with sadness in her voice. Then, almost as an afterthought, added: "Giacomo and I are on a different page from them."

"*Amore mia, mi dispiace moltissimo* (I'm very sorry, my love)." He said this with perceptible sincerity but felt dejected and miserable while putting his arms around her. As he looked into her eyes, he saw her pain. At that moment, he wanted to fall to his knees. He wanted more than ever to tell her everything, to confess to her, to ask for forgiveness, to share the unbearable burden. He wanted to tell her the whole story but wasn't sure if she could live with the truth. How could he inflict more pain on her or expect her to share his burden? He had to rally his nerves and contain himself. How could he expect her to keep the secret? He would be asking her to choose between him and her family. Sooner or later she'd crack under the stress and the truth would come out. First her mother would know, then Bruno and Giacomo. Before the day was over the police would be knocking on his door and taking him away in handcuffs. Worse, Giacomo could deliver a bullet to his head. Then the papers would plaster his face on the front page. The "*scandolo* (scandal)" would kill his mother. The trip to America would be aborted. And the publicity would exacerbate his father's failing health, destroying him. He searched for answers, alternatives. Could he ever prove what actually happened?

She saw his genuine concern and hugged him.

"It's not your fault," she said slowly and softly as she continued. "Maybe there's another explanation. It's possible that he may still be alive. Inspector Bellin has requested more information from my parents about my brother's adoption and all the events leading up to the adoption. Maybe he suspects abduction or something else," she said, almost wishfully.

Hand in hand they walked several paces to a small boulder that had scratched carvings on its surface and leaned against it. The scribbles memorialized what seemed, at that particular time, the most important event for the authors. He and Annalisa had done the same but on a tree. They had carved their initials on a pine tree close to where they had first made sweet love and experienced intimations of paradise.

They sat next to each other on the large sun-warmed rock. Annalisa fumbled with her jacket and finally peeled back her left pocket to pull out a small square box, gift-wrapped with yellow paper and tied with a pretty rainbow ribbon.

"This is for you," she said, smiling. "It's a going away present," she said as she handed it to him.

"You shouldn't have done this, really," said Lorenzo, examining the box and shaking it.

"I wanted to; after you gave me the necklace, I wanted to get you something practical, permanent and memorable. Until I saw this I couldn't decide," she responded.

Lorenzo untied the ribbon and unwrapped the yellow paper from the box while she was talking. Then he lifted the top of the small box and his eyes lit up.

"Wow!" he exclaimed. "Couldn't come at a better time. The one I have is broken. This is the one we saw in Paola, isn't it?" he asked with a broad smile.

"Yes. It's the 'engineer's watch,' the one we saw at the jewelry store. The one you couldn't put down," she explained, smiling, as Lorenzo kept looking at it and studying it.

She continued, "As I told you: practical to tell time, permanent because it's waterproof, and unbreakable if dropped. And the memorable part is when you take the point of a pen and press into that tiny circle on the side. Here," she pointed to the spot, "something happens." Then she pulled out a pen from her pocket and handed it to him.

Lorenzo inserted the tip of the pen where she had indicated and a thin circular plate on the bottom of the watch rotated out to reveal their photo. Lorenzo was intrigued. He studied the photo. The close-up picture had been taken in town to celebrate their first anniversary together. It was taken right after last New Year's Day. They were leaning into each other and their faces were beaming with happiness. Then he gently pushed the plate back to the original position and it clicked as it locked. He ran his index finger along the curvature, which was almost imperceptible as a separate compartment, and stared at it.

"This is crazy! It's crazy-beautiful," he said, flashing a broad smile. "I never saw anything like this."

"I got the idea from an old pocket watch my grandfather had. I figured if they could do it with a pocket watch seventy-five years ago, why couldn't they do it on a smaller scale with a wristwatch? And, PRESTO! See, you're not the only one with engineering ideas," she said jokingly.

"I promise that wherever I go I will always keep it with me." He hugged her.

"Yeah, and promise not to forget me," she added softly.

"And I promise not to *ever* forget you. How could I, *carina* (dearest)?" he repeated, looking deeply into her eyes.

"And that you'll be back before the year is over," she continued, with sudden moisture in her luminous eyes.

"I promise to do everything possible to be back before the year is over," he said, echoing her.

She took a deep sigh. "God, it's going to be rough around here, with my brother's disappearance, you being away, and with my medical school entrance exams coming up. How can I possibly concentrate?"

"I'm sorry to contribute to your anxiety," he added, "but I know everything will be resolved. Remember what Father Campisi always says: 'God doesn't send us any more problems than we can handle.'"

"I just don't know how much longer my family can handle this ordeal of Andreas missing," she confided. "Giacomo thinks differently from our parents. He seems to have his own theories about the disappearance."

"How so?" he asked, trying not to feel jolted.

"Well, if I overheard correctly last night while in my room studying, he told Pop that the inspector may be barking up the wrong tree. Giacomo's got this notion that someone up in this mountain might be involved with Andreas' disappearance. Aside from our own families there are another seven up here, on this side of the mountain. One of them might know something. The way he figures it, Andreas left work on Saturday a little after 5pm. If he went fishing, he would've been in his boat by about six. The storm blew in between seven and eight that night. If Andreas had been on the boat that early, then how do you explain his fresh footprints at about ten o'clock when Giacomo and Pop searched the coast?" She paused.

"Obviously, Andreas would not have gone out during the storm when it was dark. Also, he claims to have found a burlap cloth, a small tree uprooted and other footprints, which were fairly fresh. This was all on the path leading up the mountain. The only thing he's not sure about is motivation. Why would anyone want to harm Andreas? It couldn't have been for money since my brother never carried more than a few lira in his pocket."

Lorenzo felt a cold chill down his back. He was terrified by Giacomo's analytical ability. Not only was he smart and observant but also brutally efficient. Now, not tomorrow, was when he wanted to be on the train bound for Naples and on his way to New York.

"Has he shared these ideas with the inspector?" asked Lorenzo.

"I think he wants to be completely certain before he relates anything else to the police," she guessed. "Besides, the inspector is exploring various other theories."

"Isn't it possible that Andreas could have brought harm to himself somehow?" he asked. He instantly regretted having said that.

Lorenzo felt like someone standing at the edge of a very high precipice and who almost lost his balance. Then he walked away a few feet and picked up a twig, and snapped it in half, turning back to face Annalisa.

"What kind of question is that?" she asked. "Causing harm to oneself is not criminal and the police would not be investigating him as a victim of a crime," she shot back with a puzzled look, then added, "Andreas wasn't capable of premeditating any wrongdoing like that, and he wasn't like that by nature, you know that."

"Well, with all due respect to your brother, I think that all children, even some with developmental disabilities, are capable of wrongdoing. At other times, misunderstanding of an event can lead to consequences, even if the action lacked bad intent," Lorenzo said.

"Who will ever understand them, Lorenzo?" she shot back,

raising her voice almost in anger. "Who will understand and accept and forgive the Andreas' of the world, those who are deficient in some way, or even orphaned. Why are they always to be blamed for their deficits?"

"I don't have the answer," said Lorenzo. "Perhaps it takes personal tragedy, like yours, to make people truly compassionate and force them to see that each and every one of us matters. We're all a vital thread in another person's tapestry; our lives are all woven together, and all are very precious."

These last words seemed to console her and make her believe that she had no real reason to snap at Lorenzo as she had. She took a step closer to him. Without saying anything, they held each other tightly for a long time and finally kissed. Soon after, he walked her down to the fork in the road and held her closer. Before they parted, she made him promise to write from time to time and reminded him to address the letters to her girlfriend using a secret code on the envelope. He watched her ride away from him for what would be the last time, although she did not know that yet. He felt an emptiness that he didn't think possible. He felt more afraid than he ever had. But he had to leave this place and he had to leave now before Giacomo put all the pieces together.

Chapter 7

Progress of Police Investigation

The police had been working feverishly on the Salvaggi case since Giacomo's call on Monday. It had been four days from the time the case landed on the inspector's desk and almost two days prior to that since the alleged victim went missing and still no substantial breakthroughs. Sure, there were numerous theories about his disappearance but none of the ones they had explored stood up to close scrutiny. Bellin was mindful that time was of the utmost importance in cases like the Salvaggi kid, perhaps even more crucial in his case because he was disabled. If he was kidnapped, he couldn't conceive of an escape or some means of contacting the authorities. If he was lost in the woods or anywhere else, he didn't have any primitive skills to survive. Also, if the police didn't resolve the matter within the next few days, evidence would disappear, eyewitness accounts would get murky, and media interest would fade just like the wall posters of other victims that were plastered in the piazzas in Cosenza and surrounding towns.

But Bellin saw the worst problem to be internal time. His superiors could pull him off the case at any time or hand him another file, on top of the dozens that were active. But despite his department being under a pressure cooker he was tired of his requests for more funding being denied. They wouldn't even allow the bare minimum, hiring two more detectives. His superiors and the politicians who held the purse strings gave him the same litany: "Resources are scarce, therefore we have to do more with less or limit the time on cases." Well, the inspector had reached his own limits and had been counting down the months to his retirement. "Burnout" was an understatement. He had found it harder and harder some days to get up, prepare himself mentally and drive to the office. Lately, it had become a battle; like the manic-depressive trying to accomplish his daily chores, the smallest activity required a monumental effort. Still, he told himself to suck it up until the pension kicked in. In the meantime, he was giving serious thought to what his sister had suggested, that he move to Sardinia near her residence and buy a condo at the shore.

With the current case, he and Calvi had set up a perimeter, very much like the epicenter of an earthquake that radiated out for five miles. The launch point was the yard where the victim was last seen and spread out from there. This effort encompassed the mountain area where Andreas lived and the nine or so families that inhabited that general region. There wasn't a house, a barn, a shed or cave in the mountains they hadn't searched. They had briefly interviewed all the inhabitants on the mountains. Calvi had even searched Benedettas' farm and high-tailed it out of there as fast as possible. One of his uniformed officers had even opened the outside oven door, next to the barn, unknowingly putting him a spit away from the decomposing body. They had found nothing but a putrid smell coming from the chicken coop. The stench of animal feces mixed with animal urine wafted up to Calvi's nostrils like fresh ammonia. While holding a handkerchief to his nose, Calvi had to do everything in his power not to retch up his lunch. In fact, he still held the handkerchief to his nose after they were some distance from the animals and the barn.

The entire episode had given him a headache as well, which lasted for several hours. He chucked the entire revolting experience to Matteo Benedetta's illness and his inability to do his farm chores.

Earlier, he had talked to Francesca and her two children while they were having an early dinner. This was so that Matteo didn't have to be awakened for the night when he fell asleep before dusk. Francesca had managed to tell Calvi about her husband's illness and how difficult it was to keep the farm going without his help. Calvi was even permitted to look in Matteo's room and around their home. The young officer had left the house feeling a certain pity for the family and believing that they had enough agony within the family that he could not in good conscience burden them with further questions regarding an external police matter. Then on his way back, after inspecting the barn, he decided to knock on Francesca's door to say goodnight, thank her and excuse himself for the intrusion. Meanwhile, the two officers who had accompanied him were walking around the loggia smoking and bantering while heading for their vehicle. No doubt this was at Calvi's expense, for having such a sensitive stomach and not being able to handle a little animal shit.

While being driven back to the police station the assistant inspector reviewed the notes he had made while canvassing La Pera. He consulted his map. He thought it was strange that this mountain community was not even on his map. But the fourth family they had approached and questioned had given him something that his boss would find interesting. Bellin had speculated early on in this case that in many adoption situations there was something he had called "the biological mother's remorse syndrome." Calvi wasn't sure if this was a bona fide, generally accepted, psychological diagnosis or whether it was the inspector's own way of explaining what he thought. He didn't remember coming across the term in his criminal studies classes at the university. Either way, his notes would lend some credence to his boss's speculation that abduction by Andreas' biological mother wasn't to be ruled out. The fact that decades had gone by, according to Bellin, didn't preclude a kidnapping, especially in this instance when dealing with a person who had the IQ of an eight- to ten-year-old. It wouldn't take much to entice him to her car, especially if she had some understanding of his likes and dislikes, like a child's favorite candy. Sometimes candy alone could lure a child and neutralize whatever suspicion he harbored of strangers.

Calvi also thought about other things the inspector had alluded to: that the natural parent, usually the mother, would have an awakening often triggered by some life-changing experience. In some situations, the inability to have other children, simple loneliness, a growing fixation or even just curiosity to see their offspring. This compulsion would consume them until they located the child. Sometimes it would take years. Then they would spend an inordinate number of days studying the child's movements and planning the best time and best way of approaching them, often under some pretense of asking directions.

When Calvi learned that a Volvo was seen parked in front of the *negozio di alimentari* (minimarket) on the road to St Biaze, his curiosity intensified. With his inquiries came answers from the local residents. It wasn't a late-model vehicle. It didn't have a distinctive color or features that attracted attention. One and only one factor made it unique. That was the unusual color of the vehicle's plates; they were of German registry. Mr. Alpino, the fourth door they had knocked on, also said that inside the store were a handful of people whose faces he had never seen before. They walked up and down the aisles with groceries in hand. He couldn't say more about the vehicle's owner or even if one of the customers in the store was the owner of the Volvo. He remembered grabbing a can of coffee off the shelf, paying for it and leaving promptly. Calvi also knew that stacked against this bit of ear-perking information was the fact that a number of locals worked in Germany, and, at times, drove down to visit their relatives in the summer months. But this was almost

November and things didn't mesh. Calvi wondered if Bellin would glean more information from Mr. Alpino's account.

While the assistant inspector had been canvassing the mountain area and interviewing locals and searching the caves in the woods, Bellin had managed to track down the four schoolboys who had the altercation with Andreas. This had been simpler than expected. Mr. Rossini had provided a rough description of a couple of the boys and Bellin had visited the principal at the local secondary school. From his office window the principal pointed out a group of boys in the playground that hung around together. They often got into trouble together. And they fit the description noted on the inspector's pad. He had even provided Bellin with their address. The woman who answered the door at the address furnished by the principal tearfully admitted that her boy had taken up with three others who were a bad influence on him. She pleaded with Bellin to scare the leader of the group and to help extricate her son from his control. She was convinced that sooner or later her boy would be pressured into some serious crime. Then without being asked, she confided to the police officer that her son's father had taken up with a younger woman two years earlier and was living in Rome. According to her, this lack of fatherly supervision was one reason for her son's waywardness. She worked full time and raised him alone. But as the child got older things were spinning out of control. Bellin promised her that he would meet with the group leader's parents and impress on them that their son was on the wrong track and that they needed to be more involved with his life. He would also have a "talking" with the boy.

It turned out that the leader of the group was not as rotten as the picture painted. He was just acting up and showing off with his friends. Even the parents were surprised at his uncharacteristic behavior. They had been very apologetic to the inspector. The offender, who had been questioned by Bellin in the presence of his father and mother, was visibly shaken. The inspector couldn't determine if his hands were trembling because of the police presence or because his father was scowling at him. When the inspector left, a beating was guaranteed. Bellin concluded that the boy did not have the mean-spiritedness and strength of character to carry through whatever threat he was heard making against Andreas.

On his way back to the office Bellin wondered if Calvi had had better luck searching the caves in the woods and with the interviews of the locals in La Pera. He went over and over in his mind the bits and pieces of information his investigation had uncovered so far. The coastal search still didn't tie neatly Andreas' disappearance to an accident at sea. Something about this bothered him. There were numerous factors still unexplained and he wasn't prepared to close the file yet by declaring it an accident. The employees at the various work sites had nothing but praise for Andreas' work. None of the homeowners who had contracted for work projects were disgruntled, with the exception of one who complained about the cost. In fact, the majority remembered Andreas, they had felt sorry for his disability, and even went out of their way to say something nice about his hard work and his sweet temperament.

There were still two other possible avenues that needed to be explored. One concerned Giacomo's business rivals, who may have wanted to send him a message by doing harm to his disabled brother. Since Giacomo owned or had some interest in multiple enterprises and could have angered other heavyweights, this was a real possibility. It was generally known that he owned several bars and clubs in Cosenza and another in Sorrento; rumors were constantly circulating about prostitution at these clubs. He also owned, or was involved in, not only the building supply house but also two fairly large construction companies. But the real concern was the talk among his peers, not totally unfounded in Bellin's opinion, that he had become the head of the *'Ndrangheta* families. If that was the case, he would be looking to expand his empire into other sordid areas, including drugs. And because his rise to power had supposedly occurred recently, Bellin couldn't help thinking that there might be a link to the missing brother. His suspicion had been aroused sufficiently that he had assigned two investigators from a special unit to look into Giacomo's business dealings. The second hypothesis Bellin was working on was about a possible abduction. Not by someone who wanted to slow Giacomo's rise to power and was motivated by jealousy and hatred but someone who was consumed by love, a maternal instinct that perversely manifested itself over a long period.

During the last meeting with Bruno and Antonia Salvaggi he had expressed the need to know, at some point, all the circumstances surrounding the adoption. They seemed to be compliant with his request so long as it might shed some light on their son's disappearance. Desperation would force them to tell all. Interestingly, Antonia Salvaggi had referred to her intellectually handicapped son as "*l'amore della mia vita* (the love of my life)." She said he had suffered so much and traveled so far in his tender years that he had earned an abundance of love. Then the husband chimed in to say that she had affectionately shortened the phrase to "*Vita*" to illustrate the central role this child played in their lives. And when asked by neighbors how things were going with the boy she would say: "Vita is the sunshine of our existence." For years, the other members of the family went along with the nickname until he was in his twenties, when they had gotten rid of the farm animals, due to the drought, and he started working at his brother's warehouse. There he had been introduced to the other employees by his birth name, Andreas. Thus, his birth name was resuscitated and popularized to the point that, if his mother made reference to him as "Vita," most people would look at her bewildered.

Antonia and Bruno certainly had overwhelming love to give this man-child. The inspector was unsure if all this was pure love stemming from their inability to have a second child of their own for some time, or if part of this love's equation was really a feeling of sorrow for the child's travails and the unfortunate circumstances with which providence had burdened him. For Antonia, faith seemed to have fueled her life as if she had received a sign from the Almighty and had focused that faith on her son "Vita." Regardless, the inspector had to admit to himself that aside from the police investigation, personal curiosity was a driving force for him to delve deeper into Andreas' background.

Chapter 8

Lorenzo's Trip to America

The nights were too tormenting for Lorenzo to sleep. He lay in bed, hands behind his head, eyes closed, unable to let go of the physical world. So many questions popped into his mind: would this be a permanent goodbye to his father? Would Giacomo or the police inspector be knocking on his front door any second? Would he and Annalisa get to share the life they dreamed of, or was this the end, despite all the plans and the promises made? What was he to expect on this journey to America? And when he reached it, if he ever reached it, what then? How would his mother and sister cope after his dad passed on? These concerns would flow in and out of Lorenzo's head. The more he tried to dismiss them the more persistent they became and his mind always found some link to Andreas, his face or his voice or his grave. He pictured himself lying next to him, his body cold, and skin gray and decomposing. He wondered if vermin sensed blood like sharks. If they did, they would gather like ants around a sugar cube. They would crawl inside his hacked-off skull, in and out of every other cavity, feasting in every imaginable place. What really frightened him about these images was a crazy belief that he could not shake. What if Andreas felt his body being devoured and was unable to do anything about it, like a silent spectator observing the molecules that defined his physical space in the universe being disassembled.

By 4am Lorenzo was up. It was still dark outside. He pulled on the ceiling chain and a small 20-watt bulb lit the room. His one suitcase was open on the floor by the back wall. He had packed all his essentials the day before. Aside from his travel documents and some personal toiletries he felt confident he had everything he needed. He scanned his room – the furniture, the wide uneven planks on the floor, the picture of his family on the dresser – and reminisced about the eighteen years of his life here. But from this day forward, time and space would change everything.

His train was scheduled to leave the station at 10am. Arrangements had been made with his Uncle Dominick to drive him there. He would probably arrive at the house about 8.30am. Lorenzo looked at his watch. He still had about four hours. Then apprehension and dread set in as he imagined the inspector or Giacomo showing up at the last minute and unraveling his plans. A rush of blood came to his face.

Gabriella told Lorenzo that she had decided to miss another day of school. And she could watch over Papa until their mom and uncle got back from the station. He also knew that his mother was torn between accompanying him to the train and leaving her husband alone. Sensing Mama's difficult decision, Gabriella promised to stay by Papa's side for as long as necessary. Lorenzo had even dragged a heavy chair close to his father's bed while his sister piled some books on the floor next to the chair with the intention of studying while he slept.

Lorenzo felt groggy and tired from lack of sleep but dressed quickly and tiptoed downstairs without shaving or washing his face. At the stair landing he combed his fingers through his hair. He looked forward to a large cup of strong coffee and his favorite breakfast, a couple of eggs with fried pork strips and chunks of crusty bread tossed in. He concluded that his unusual hunger pangs were due to lack of sleep. He had observed a strong correlation: if his body lacked rest, it compensated by calling for extra fuel.

He heard no sounds anywhere in the house; everyone was still in bed. After breakfast he planned on doing his morning chores, as usual; he couldn't believe this was to be the last time he would tend to the animals. He had stocked the barn and the shed with enough animal feed to last throughout the winter so that his mother had one less thing to worry about. He had also chopped more than four cords of firewood for the fireplace. He stacked these under a tarp on the side of the house. By the time supplies ran out it would be spring. Then he would be able to send some money from America; his mother would be able to hire a farm hand to help with some of the chores.

Halfway into his breakfast he heard footsteps on the staircase. It was his mother, still in her nightgown. She smiled and walked around the table where he was sitting, put her arm around his shoulder, bent over and held him close to her. Then she kissed him on his left cheek.

"Good morning. I see somebody is hungry. Couldn't sleep, huh?" she asked.

"Not a bit. I was up all night," he sighed. "It's so hard going away and leaving Papa in his condition and you and Gabriella alone with the farm."

"Don't worry about anything, Enzo. We'll manage. We've discussed this before and have help available if we need it." She patted his hand on the table. "Don't get me wrong. We'll miss you. I'll miss you very much. My baby bird is flying the coop."

"I'll miss everyone too, Mama. It's going to be weird. I keep thinking I'll be different and I won't fit in." He frowned. "Just to think you guys are not going to be with me, my friends are not going to be around. Even the animals are going to be a thing of the past. My routines and habits will be changed; everything will be so new and strange."

"With your Uncle Pietro you won't be alone," his mother said. "He'll make sure of that. And you'll make new friends quickly, you always do. As for your family, don't be concerned, we'll always be here and you'll be in our hearts every single day," she told him as her eyes welled up with tears.

By 8.30am the sun was coming up but it was still a crisp and cold November morning. Lorenzo's bag was packed and sitting by the front door. Gabriella was up and moping. She followed him around the house like a puppy waiting for a scrap of food. When he hugged his father goodbye, Lorenzo felt his stubble pinching his face. This reminded him how he would brace for a similar moment when he was a child. Now he realized that this might be the last time he would feel that comforting embrace, that they probably would never see each other again. He knew that his father knew this as well. It was palpable in their embrace. Slow, unexpected tears started flowing down his face. He promised his father that he would write every week and make every effort to come back to visit in six months. But as they looked into each other's eyes they knew the truth. This was the last time on this side of eternity they would see each other. Lorenzo quickly rose from the bedside and pretended that neither of them had tears in their eyes or down their cheeks. He cleared his throat and said, "Take good care of Mama and Gabriella, Papa. I'll be back before you know it."

"And when you get back you'd better be ready to outwork me in the field, Enzo, *figlio mio* (my son)," he said with a break in his voice.

Uncle Dominick, with his little red Fiat, had pulled up to the house at just about a quarter to nine. Gabriella let him in and after planting a kiss on her forehead he proceeded to his younger brother's room. He saw Francesca next to his bedside and gave her a hug. Lorenzo always found his presence a relief, particularly the distraction he created during agonizing moments. He went to his room to compose himself. Always jovial and goodhearted, his uncle had the ability to assess the moment and turn it around.

"How's my little brother doing? Ready to go chop some wood?"

Matteo smiled and responded sarcastically with a circular motion of his hand as if to say: stop the nonsense.

Dominick placed his hand on the patient's forehead and gazed at Francesca as Lorenzo came back into the room. "No fever. His color looks good." Then he shifted his gaze back to Matteo saying, "It must be the excellent care and attention you're getting here."

Francesca ignored the attempt at joviality.

"Care for some coffee?" she asked instead.

"Thanks, I just had two cups. I'm wired for the rest of the day." He kissed his brother on the forehead and stepped away from the bed. "So, are you both ready?" he asked, looking at the mother and son.

"Yeah, we better get going before the train takes off without me." Lorenzo moved towards the door.

"I left the car running so that it'd be nice and warm," his uncle said. "Earlier this morning it was unbelievably cold."

"We should be back in a couple of hours," Francesca said to Gabriella. "Make your father some breakfast in a little while and keep him company, okay?"

Gabriella nodded as she grabbed her father's hand.

By 9.30am, the three of them were standing on the station platform and talking. Two trains had arrived on the opposite track, almost back to back, one from as far north as Turin and the other from Rome. Very few tourists were traveling this time of year; most were locals and commuters from nearby cities. Neither train was very crowded. The contrast of the passengers was remarkable in the manner of dress and demeanor. The locals were dressed in shabby clothing, carrying bags and small valises, speaking a detectable dialect and dragging their children by the hand. Then you had the business and professional class, distinguishable not just by their manner of clothing but in demeanor and attitude as well. They could be seen conversing with equals or reading the daily paper and financial journals fastidiously, ignoring the locals. A good percentage of the passengers would probably go as far as Reggio Calabria or Palermo, the country's large southern cities.

Dominick recognized a few people and nodded as they passed by on the platform. The three of them were now standing next to a bench with Lorenzo's suitcase resting on it. He asked his mother and uncle if they wanted anything from the little concession stand and restaurant at the far end of the station. They declined.

"Watch my bag, I'll be right back," he said to his mother.

"Don't take forever, your train should be arriving in five minutes," she said, and continued the conversation with her brother-in-law.

Lorenzo walked briskly towards the little store selling *panini*, newspapers, soft drinks and an assortment of pastries. Two tables were set up by the front door and a couple were having coffee with pastries. It was obvious that the woman didn't care for her pastry since it was broken into several pieces, pushed to the corner of her plate and on it was a snuffed-out cigarette. Several other travelers were either making purchases or seemed to be having a difficult time deciding what they wanted. Lorenzo passed them by and went to the bathroom. On the way out he picked up *La Stampa,* the morning paper, and a bottle of *San Pellegrino* mineral water, and got in line to pay. The attendant greeted him robotically at first, as he had the other customers, but then paused a bit longer as if studying his face and trying to place him. Lorenzo handed him the money and walked out. He did not see either the flash of recognition on the cashier's face or the telephone receiver in the man's hand.

On the platform, the lights were flashing, indicating his train's imminent arrival. He quickened his pace. By the time he had embraced his uncle, kissed his mother and grabbed his baggage, some passengers had disembarked and others were getting on to take their warm seats.

Within five minutes the train's whistle blew as it rolled out of the station. He waved to his mother from the train window as she dabbed her eyes with a handkerchief. But his mind was on the store attendant and the looking-over he had given him. Where did he know him from? By the time the train moved on to the next stop Lorenzo's subconscious had made the correct association and the answer percolated to his consciousness.

"Giacomo!" He should have known immediately. The attendant was one of Giacomo's relatives. He had met the man at a Christmas party at the Salvaggis' home. At the time he was introduced to the store attendant it was a more propitious time, before the incident with the water shortage. Then, the two families were as close as neighbors could be. Lorenzo also remembered something the man mentioned about being connected with the railroad but he couldn't remember in what capacity. He couldn't even remember the man's name but was certain it was him since he had the same odd birthmark at the base of his neck.

About two hours had lapsed since he boarded at the Cosenza station. The train had already made several stops. One of the train's assistant conductors was a burly man. The "I'll do my job but don't fuck with me" type of guy, sporting a wiry-corkscrew beard, had already collected Lorenzo's ticket. The train had been moving at a fast clip for a while when the conductor announced over a muffled loudspeaker that the next station was Salerno; arrival was in approximately thirty minutes. Lorenzo looked around in his compartment and saw a handful of passengers. Not a heavy travel day, he thought. A few passengers, including the mother of three obnoxious kids, had already gotten off. The train would probably refill during the next stop at Sorrento, a very busy station. So, instead of fighting the lines later, he thought this was the perfect opportunity to relieve his bladder. He checked for "WC" signs. At the end of his compartment was the women's toilet. That meant that he had to cross into the next rail car and walk to the other end to reach the men's facilities.

He stood up from his seat and walked forward a few feet, staggering as the train lurched on the track. He looked back at his overhead luggage, trying to impress on his mind the location of his seat. At the end of his compartment he pulled the door open and then shut it behind. As he took one or two small steps on the outside platform, he felt the shifting and swaying of the cars, giving him the impression that the train was accelerating. The door latch on the next car was busted and the door was sliding back and forth on its own. He pushed the door slide to the left and walked in without bothering to turn around to lock it. Even fewer people were in this compartment. An older gentleman was eating his bagged sandwich and caught his eye as he passed by. Two women were sitting towards the middle and a young man with a knapsack sat on the seat just behind them reading some travel maps. Even before opening the rear compartment door he had seen the sign through the glass, "*Toilette*," with the international blue man symbol. The restroom was on the left side, wedged close to the two carriages. A white light illuminated a small rectangular sign announcing the word "*Vacante*." Slightly to the left of the toilette was a small exit door leading down three steps to the platform. It was wide open and he wondered if it was deliberately left open so as to ventilate the area. As Lorenzo unlatched the door to the bathroom, he heard someone approaching from behind.

 Reflexively, he turned his head forty-five degrees and could make out the shape of a tall, beefy man with a black leather jacket. Because the man was standing right behind him, he couldn't see his face. For a second he thought the man was having an emergency and needed the restroom. Then he heard a rapid clicking noise like a sequence of bedsprings snapping from the frame and saw a flash of light reflected off the metallic wall. He was about to turn around when he felt a needle-like object pressing against the small of his back. The man's powerful hand hooked around his neck. Lorenzo's heart jolted forward like a race car driver pulling out of the emergency pit. He could feel adrenaline shooting into his bloodstream and goose bumps erupting on his skin.

"Where's the retarded kid?" demanded a gruff, no-nonsense voice in his ear, while the hand tightened around his trachea. Lorenzo's body jerked forward when the sharp object pressed deeper into the small of his back to emphasize the point.

"I don't know what you're talking about," answered Lorenzo apprehensively.

"*Ascolta, piccolo cazzo* (Listen, you little fucker), I'm going to fillet you right here unless you give me the right answer." To underscore his impatience the man removed his hand from around Lorenzo's throat and slammed his head against the toilet door. The door flew open from the impact. In that instance it dawned on Lorenzo to run inside and shut the door but the room was slightly larger than a telephone booth and it would be impossible to hold the door against a man twice his size. Besides, if the man followed him inside the small room, he would have all the privacy in the world to practice his filleting skills, unencumbered.

"Okay! Okay!" answered Lorenzo, trembling.

Just as the man loosened his grip on his skull and stepped back, a train conductor rolled open the compartment door between the carriages. He looked at the two of them and saw that the younger man's face was pale and wet with perspiration.

"Is everything alright here?" asked the conductor.

"Fine, my nephew wasn't feeling well all morning and the train ride is making him feel nauseous," answered the gruff voice, partly facing the train attendant and his right hand seemingly supporting Lorenzo.

"Well, hang in there, in twenty minutes we'll be in Salerno," said the train attendant as he proceeded to the next wagon.

The interrogator again turned towards his victim; Lorenzo shifted his body and pulled his right knee up and crashed it into the man's crotch. The brute doubled over but didn't go down. His face contorted. He took a deep breath, his left hand consoling his agonizing testicles. Still, he tried to straighten up, his face grimacing from pain or anger, or both. It was then that Lorenzo heard that sound again, a springing noise, metal sliding against metal, when a needle-tipped stiletto shot out from under the man's right sleeve. Before the attacker had a chance to thrust his blade into Lorenzo's torso, he pushed the man with all his might down two steps and in the direction of the open door. The train picked up momentum. It was approaching an embankment, just before heading into a tunnel. The attacker lost his balance and rolled further back onto the third step, teetering inches from the open door. But, with the agility of a panther, his left hand grabbed the vertical metal bar on the side of the door. He tried to reel in the rest of his body. Lorenzo, with equal swiftness, stepped forward and stomped on the hand holding the bar while avoiding the man's other hand which was ready to thrust the knife into his groin. Lorenzo's shoe, again, slammed directly on the man's knuckles. Now, he had a clear view of the attacker's suntanned and very weathered face but couldn't tell if he was expressing panic or loathing as his body went spinning backwards, out of control, and rolled down the embankment with only seconds to spare before the train slipped into the tunnel.

Chapter 9

Inspector Delves Deeper

It was late Friday afternoon when Inspector Bellin arrived at the Salvaggis' home. Bruno and Antonia Salvaggi expected him. They had very cordially invited him to dinner. At first, he had declined, telling them that perhaps the situation was still too raw and too painful for them to have guests. But after Antonia's insistence, saying that they had to eat anyway, and then Bruno getting on the phone and reminding him that reconstructing Andreas' past might help find his son, the inspector relented. Had it not been for their insistence he would've cancelled. The last few days he had been working overtime and felt exhausted. He had been picking up the slack left by Calvi who had requested several days off due to his wife's pregnancy. She was expected to give birth the following week but her doctor had ordered her to the hospital earlier, suspecting possible complications.

In addition to his languorous condition, the inspector felt a cold coming on. He had the usual sniffles and his nose was sore and red from blowing it repeatedly during the day. The only place he wanted to be was in bed with a hot water bag under his feet, some hot chamomile on his nightstand and, perhaps, a good book on his lap until he fell asleep.

The weather didn't help his condition either. It had been, and continued to be, an ugly day, with alternating rain in the morning that lessened only to drizzle in the afternoon. As the inspector drove, crosswinds whipped the fine rain against his windshield. The gray, misty sky had been the one constant during the day, but that had now changed for the worse; poor visibility and downed wet leaves on the road added to slippery and dangerous driving conditions. Thick mountain fog was a known curse on these narrow roads. On such days, when negotiating a mountain curve, drivers were in the habit of blowing their horns, as a warning to oncoming vehicles to slow down and veer to the right side. That was precisely what he did as he came around the last turn on the public road before seeing his host's home.

The inspector drove his personal vehicle, a seven-year-old, 1966, mid-sized, gray Renault. He pulled into the driveway, turned off the fog lights, rolled up the window that was open about two inches and killed the ignition. He reached over to the passenger side, opened the glove compartment and retrieved a notepad with a black pen separating old notes from clean pages. He inserted the notepad and pen in the inner pocket of his black raincoat, grabbed a bag off the seat and got out of the vehicle.

Inspector Bellin believed in what was often repeated in police training classes, that new discoveries favored a prepared mind, and to that end, he wanted to know the background of what appeared to be a very unusual adoption of this missing "man-child." Intellectually, Andreas was a child indeed. The inspector had been told that his functional ability was at the level of an elementary school child. But chronologically, at the age of thirty-three, he was a full-grown man and his work ethic seemed to be better than most adults'. He hoped that the parents could give him that fortuitous piece of information that would break the case. Chance occurrences happened in different spheres of life more often than people realized. When you least expected a discovery was precisely when you stumbled on something that turned out to be a watershed moment for humanity, and no one ever imagined its social ramifications.

The inspector, who thought of himself as a science buff, ruminated about "accidental occurrences" in science. The phenomena were not relegated to one particular group or culture. Galvani was awed by the discovery of electric current in Italy. Daguerre couldn't pull his eyes away when he discovered strange images that later became known as practical photography in France. And Roentgen's X-ray discovery in Germany and Fleming's penicillin promise in England were some other amazing, fortuitous moments. Chance, pure circumstantial chance, brought about the monumental breakthroughs which proved to be enormously beneficial for humanity. Perhaps in each instance, when the conscious mind was relaxed and uninvolved, did that spark of light reveal itself. And in that flitting millisecond when the mind was stirred, that individual seized the opportunity and took the novel phenomena in a rational direction. The inspector analogized the timing to a prize fight. After a lucky punch sends the opponent teetering against the ropes, without a moment to spare and instinctually, the pugilist rushes forward with fervor to exploit his good fortune and win. Similarly, Bellin hoped to trip on something over dinner which would lead to a quick resolution of Andreas' disappearance.

The inspector, in less than a week of being assigned this case, had learned much about the Salvaggis. Just in the last forty-eight hours information had been pouring in. His suspicions had been confirmed that Giacomo Salvaggi, his hosts' oldest child, held a leadership position in the *'Ndrangheta,* a crime organization more vicious and more impenetrable by law enforcement than the Sicilian Mafia. He wondered to what degree did Giacomo's involvement in the organization account for his extensive, cash-generating business holdings. Bellin would have loved to pose this question to Calvi who was always ready with an opinion and statistics to back up everything. But there was one thing he feared: that what the government knew about Giacomo was less than a drop of water in a deep well. And he found it amazing that such a relatively young man, Giacomo, had obtained such standing in the province. Maybe what some people said in private was true: that what he lacked in years and life experience he more than made up with his smarts, his shrewdness and viciousness. For one individual who, in less than ten years, had managed to climb "the ladder of success," there had to be more.

Inspector Bellin knew that his department had been working closely with the *Guardia Finanzia* (Finances and Customs Agents), which operated as a paramilitary force in the country. This sector, unlike the local police in the cities and villages, was more resistant to corruption. Much of its brass was assigned from the northern cities, and that made it more difficult to have the family ties and the local influences that bound the *'Ndrangheta* members in their dealings and recruitment practices even tighter than a religious cult.

The briefing he had received the day before was particularly illuminating. One of Giacomo Salvaggi's associates stood out more than others in his mind: a Tunisian man of small stature and deep olive complexion. The man had a thin face, hardly a chin, and his right ear was deformed and protruded unnaturally. While the man's opposing ear was normal in size and shape, it also provided a sharp contrast augmenting the disparity. The report stated that the incident with the ear went back to his teenage years when he was a gang member in Tunis. One evening a rival group cornered him and gave him a vicious beating, then they raped him, and cut off his ear as a final insult and as a reminder whenever he looked in the mirror that he should never, ever, fuck with them. He managed to drag himself home the next morning where his only surviving relative, his grandmother, literally sewed back his ear with needle and thread and nursed him back from the edge of death. After he recovered, he vowed revenge on four of the boys. One by one, within a span of seventy-two hours, they were found in back alleys, dead and mutilated beyond recognition. Then, as soon as the Tunisian authorities were on his tail, the teenager escaped from his village and was smuggled in a crate 170 kilometers across the Mediterranean to Sicily. From there he had managed to live underground in Mazara del Vallo, a tough, southwestern Sicilian city known for having a large Tunisian population and a recognized fishing industry. The young man did odd jobs to survive, including gutting fish at a local plant, but he never worked on the docks. During the summer months he sold cheap trinkets and shabby merchandise to gullible tourists on street corners. When local merchants complained to the police and they swarmed down, his lookout would signal to him and he would wrap his wares in a blanket, heave it over his shoulders and disappear into the crowd. This scene would play out many times during the week. Then he got tired of that lifestyle and promoted himself to selling street drugs. Before long he discovered that he could make more money in the larger cities like Palermo and Cosenza, and his customer base kept growing. It was in Cosenza that he had come to the attention of Giacomo's subordinates.

Bellin learned other facts about the strange little man, besides being in the country illegally. He also knew that he operated from Cosenza, did some work for Giacomo, was a vicious killer and went by the name of Moustafa Bourguiba.

*

The indissoluble bond with Giacomo's group occurred on a crazy, hot day in July. The weather had been unbearably humid. Fires were continuously burning in the higher altitudes, with new fires starting almost on a daily basis. The land was parched; the tall grasses, the trees and other vegetation hadn't seen a drop of water for months. Everything green was wilted. The rivers and creeks were virtual mud holes. It was a time when the municipality had to truck in water to the main square where locals, with buckets and containers, came in to collect their daily allowance. The people who had indoor running water were rationed to no more than two hours every morning. Often, the water only trickled in their bathtubs when they tried to fill them. The problem was that everyone turned on his or her tap at the same time and the water pressure was reduced to a minimum. Some folks even left their waterspouts perpetually open so that they could catch every drop from the moment the authorities turned on the generators. People kept their windows closed and doors shut until the sun went down and, even then, men came out shirtless and the women were braless, in loose-fitting garments with a fan in their hands. Add everything in the mix and you had a hot, dirty, sweaty, sticky, uncomfortable and almost unbearable summer.

It was during one of these sweltering days that Moustafa Bourguiba revealed the content of his character. He was the go-between in a cocaine sale. His two Turkish contacts, of whom Moustafa had become increasingly suspicious during his last large transaction, were to deliver the merchandise inside the garage of a small decrepit building. The upper windows were boarded up and chunks of limestone stucco were missing in some strategic corners. Faded and partially torn posters from ancient political campaigns were still glued to the cement walls, even though the office seekers were long dead or retired. People's washing hung limply from balconies and clotheslines on nearby buildings. Several blocks down the narrow street, after turning the corner, a *gelati* storefront with a few tables on the sidewalk was serving a few stragglers.

This was the old section of Cosenza, an area probably built around the eighth century when the Greeks arrived, and if one had any doubts about the age of the architecture, the stench and the grime on the cobblestones and the façades of the buildings would secure that conviction. It was a place where rats had procreated for hundreds, if not thousands, of generations before the Great Plague. And after the scourge, the rodent population had only grown fatter, larger and bolder in the dingy basements. Moustafa, with his well-placed connections from Mazara del Vallo, had managed to smuggle some three million dollars, street value, of high-grade cocaine into the country.

Giacomo Salvaggi's organization was believed to have funded the purchase. This was the first time Moustafa had arranged a sale with this "family," even though he had known some of its operatives through small deals and through some acquaintances. He was convinced that the family was real and that they were serious. Therefore, he was anxious to please and anticipated more lucrative business deals down the road.

At the appointed time, an old black Citroën with its hood discolored and its paint peeling, a result of nature's abuses near salt water, pulled into the garage. Inside were the driver and another man sitting next to him. The driver made an upward gesture with his head, representing a greeting and recognition of Moustafa. Attila, Gregorio and another short, barrel-chested man with several days of stubble on his face, two missing front teeth and two tiny diamonds in his left ear waited with Moustafa. The two men got out of the car. The driver was a pudgy man with a fat face and the passenger was a lanky, much taller man wearing a forced smile under a serious face. The taller man greeted Moustafa: "*Salam alaikum* (Peace be with you)," followed with, "*Wa-alaikum-as-salam*." Both embraced and kissed three times; tradition expected and demanded no less. Moustafa made a general introduction towards the other three men who were waiting and observing from the sideline.

"My brother, did you bring the goods?" Moustafa asked in a low-key voice.

The lanky man nodded and proceeded towards the rear of the car. Then he fished a key out of his pocket and opened the trunk.

"It's all here, my friend," he said as he pointed inside the car and looked towards Moustafa and then the three buyers. "Do you have the exchange?"

In answer, Attila raised an old, frayed, leather briefcase he was holding, without saying a word. As the thin Arab-Turk moved towards the briefcase, Gregorio spoke.

"First, we'll check the merchandise."

The lanky Arab sniffed and crinkled his prominent nose, staring directly into Gregorio's eyes. Then he took a few steps back towards the opposite side of the car where Moustafa was standing.

The man with the missing teeth approached the trunk of the Citroën, lifted a cover and with a pocketknife punctured one of the numerous bags of white powder. He sniffed it intently, like a dog sniffing another dog's piss on the trunk of a tree. He seemed mildly satisfied. Then he reached for two other bags: one stashed in the back of the trunk and the other towards the bottom of the pile. He punctured the first bag and then the second bag.

Without any outward sign, Moustafa sensed that the Turk's body tensed up. The man took a sample of powder on the tip of his knife and licked it. His tongue went around his mouth a few times as he smacked his lips. No noticeable reaction. Then he repeated the process with the third bag and looked first at Moustafa and then rested his eyes on the lanky man standing next to him.

"It's not what we bargained for," he said. As his eyes opened wider, his face became stern and cold. His body bristled.

"I don't know what you talk about. This stuff best," the Arab said angrily as his foreign accent became more pronounced. Moustafa sensed the man's discomfort and remembered his previous dealings. Then, with his left hand, he swung open his jacket and with murderous intensity his right hand reached into his smooth leather belt. What he found pleased him, even excited him. His fingers found the hilt protruding from his belt and they wrapped themselves around its grooves. To Moustafa it felt like a perfectly poured mold. The *jambiya* seemed to come alive in the pursuit of its singular purpose, a fanatical purpose, like a feral cat genetically hardwired to pounce on scurrying rodents regardless of consequences. The handle, artistically carved from a precious rhino horn, scrupulous in design and detail. The best the Dark Continent could offer. Its ivory, with its yellow tinge, had taken on an almost unearthly glow, as if light was shining from within. To Moustafa, the curved dagger represented tradition, honor and power, and defined him as a man, much more than acreages of land and Armani suits defined the members of the *Camera dei Deputati* (Chamber of Deputies).

Moustafa's priceless possession had been passed down from his grandfather, who had acquired it from a Tunisian businessman. Before that, the story had it that it was passed down from a prince in Yemen. Moustafa believed the story, partially because it had a Salfani handle, named after one of the most famous families that carved the hilt and forged the curved, double-sided blade. Its origin demanded utmost respect. Moustafa felt proud and knew he was worthy of its possession.

He felt confident that the *jambiya's* existence, here and now, was for an honorable purpose, a fulfillment of its best tradition. Then, quicker than a ninja inside the castle wall, he plunged the dagger deep, deep into the Turk's lower abdomen, cocked his wrist upwards and the curved blade traveled unimpeded up to the sternum, like cutting into warm butter. The Turk grimaced in pain, and without making another sound, folded over and dropped to his knees. The warm, distinct, almost nauseating smell from the Turk's bowels wafted up to Moustafa's nostrils making them twitch. The odor was familiar. He had experienced it in Tunisia. He had experienced it in the poor port city of Trapani, in southwest Sicily, where tensions ran high between the locals and the North African community.

Before the Turk's driver had a chance to fully process what was happening and pull out his gun, Attila and the man with missing teeth were on him like two wild boars. They punched and kicked him bloody. Then they beat him some more to a virtual pulp, centimeters from his coffin. Gregorio finally put an end to it. He said he wanted him alive so as to send a message to his masters. And regardless of which option the driver chose, he was a man whose days were limited. If his masters had adulterated the dope without his knowledge he would die because of the botched-up sale; if he had been in cahoots with the other Turk and they had tampered with the merchandise he would also die for self-dealing. His smartest move was to run. Run. But running and hiding would only delay the inevitable and only buy him time until his people caught up. When they found him, he was assured a more pernicious and agonizing execution, not only for the bad deal but also for the trouble he had put them through in finding him.

That night the Citroën was left parked on a small side street, two blocks from the wharf. The Turk's former driver was curled up in the back seat. He had stopped breathing. The fabric in the back seat was soggy with large bloodstains and the car trunk empty of all its contents.

Meanwhile, Moustafa Bourguiba knew that he had taken the first big step. He knew that he had found his new family.

*

The inspector was seated at a place of honor at the Salvaggi table, directly under an ornate crucifix hanging between pictures of the Blessed Mother and the Sacred Heart. He began to tuck his napkin under his chin when Antonia made the sign of the cross and clasped her hands in prayer and intoned:

"Bless all who sit at your table, great Lord of Hosts, and bless those who should be at this table but are missing." She let a loud sob escape her and continued, "Maybe drowned at sea or lost or hurt and unable to find us. My great and wonderful God, bless my lost little boy, my Vita, my baby who never did any harm; well, maybe he did a little, but not enough to deserve being lost or drowned at sea. Merciful Mother of God, let us always remember those who may be lost to us as we partake of this food. Amen."

Bruno Salvaggi had dropped his head into his hands, shaking it. Somehow, it did not look like he was praying. Annalisa was looking at the ceiling, or at least she had rolled her eyes to the ceiling as she respectfully listened to her mother's prayer. The inspector was speechless and, out of habit, or perhaps for protection, made the sign of the cross. He, Bruno and Annalisa joined in a heartfelt Amen, and bent hurriedly over their plates, all of them avoiding each other's eyes for a while.

The inspector had been at the Salvaggi home for almost two hours before sitting down to dinner. Despite being in noticeable vocal anguish, Antonia Salvaggi proved to be a good hostess and an exceptionally good cook. She and Annalisa had prepared antipasti with fresh *crostini di polenta, frittura di melanzane, fiori di zucca ripieni di salsiccia* and a soup of *minestrone di riso e castagne* that the inspector found especially heartwarming on such a miserable night and with his chills. He felt better after the soup but there was still some sort of residual chill in his system that would take time to shake. For the main course, Antonia had announced earlier that she had purchased a fresh rabbit at the town market and planned to make a *coniglio arrosto* with *pappardelle e pomodoro fresco*. The inspector was delighted and flattered. He told her that it wasn't often that he got such special treatment or the opportunity to savor such delicate flavors. He truly enjoyed the dish far better than fowl or pork. It brought back memories of his childhood in Lucca where his mother would sometimes make a rabbit *cacciatore* with potatoes and vegetables. The flashback made him think how much he missed those simple days.

The mother and daughter had cleared the table and finished washing and drying the dishes when Annalisa came back to the dining room to excuse herself. She said that she was going to her room to study for the upcoming university exam that would determine her entrance into the pre-med program. She made it a point to tell her mother to save her some dessert but would skip the coffee. Her father and the inspector had been talking before dinner and during dinner and continued even now that the table was cleared.

Annalisa observed that the inspector was paying very careful attention to her father's story and occasionally would interject with a question or comment, often validating something that her father had said or had done. She decided that on a personal level the inspector was a very likable person. And that the two of them were hitting it off. Then she reconsidered her observation and wondered how big a part the large bottle of Chianti that the inspector brought had to do with it.

Bruno had started by telling the inspector what conditions were like after the war, forgetting that the inspector was probably a few years younger than he, and surely, he also had experienced the matter first hand. Occasionally the inspector would bring Bruno back on track when the topic digressed too far from the investigation.

"It seems that farmers had more than their share of suffering during and after the war," said the inspector.

"The conditions were wretched; no one bought anything, no one sold anything. The situation with farm products was especially dismal. There was no market, period! Mussolini's military adventures practically bankrupted the country. Then the Allies and Germans bombed each other, up and down the peninsula, and crippled the economy. Farm exports fell about forty percent below the depression era," Bruno said painfully.

"But I always thought farmers were self-sufficient, no?" said Bellin.

"Not in those days, rich noblemen held on to the large tracts of good land. What the peasant and small farmer had were small plots and often non-irrigable. You could break your back day and night and still be unable to provide for your family. Land reforms came much later," said Bruno.

"*Insomma, no c'era alternativa* (There was no alternative), you had to go to Germany as a guest worker, like many others?" Bellin asked.

"Exactly! There was no other way to feed a family. People were starving. We lived on potatoes, dried figs, and wild greens, like dandelions."

"Still, it must've been very painful to leave your family, Antonia and Giacomo, and go to a strange land?" asked the inspector sympathetically.

"It was! What made it a little less painful was talking to people who had been there," Bruno said.

"How did you meet these people?" asked the inspector.

"I approached two local men who were back home, on vacation, from their factory jobs in Düsseldorf. They told me about the requirements for working abroad and the sacrifices to be expected. I had also read a local paper advertising '*Lavoro Permanente en la Germania: Benvenite Italiani* (Permanent work in Germany: Italians welcome).' This led me to attend a meeting in Cosenza, sponsored by a labor union that gave people information and answered questions. *Ho imparato molto da loro* (I learned a lot from them)."

"Going to a foreign country, not knowing the customs and language was probably easier then leaving the family, I would think," said the inspector.

"*La decisione e stata davvero dolorosa* (The decision was very painful). I struggled with it a long time. We were still like newlyweds. Giacomo was only a three-year-old baby in 1947. It was also a time we were trying to have another child, without success," Bruno said.

"Did you have problems crossing the borders?" asked Bellin.

"No! That was the easy part. I went from Italy to Switzerland and then to Germany. But within fifteen minutes of traveling in Germany I was astounded, even shocked, at seeing the total devastation of cities and their entire infrastructure. The Allies had had no mercy. Railroad stations, rail lines, bridges, public buildings, all other infrastructure and homes were bombed-out shells that stood out in rows like splintered, rotten teeth. The Allies' bombing raids had produced lots of rubble and many, many young men had been killed in the conflict.

Many had even perished in prison camps due to lack of food and medical attention. Much of the mistreatment and neglect was a deep desire for revenge. I think the victors were giving Hitler's soldiers a taste of their own medicine," said Bruno.

"*Mamma mia!* (My goodness!)," said the inspector. "This must've resulted in a drastic shortage of able-bodied men who could do the heavy lifting and rebuild the country," he observed.

"Yes! There was even more chaos. Hundreds of thousands of displaced persons who were born in other countries found themselves in Germany, usually not by choice. There were Germans who had lived and settled in neighboring countries that were forced out and repatriated to Germany. There were thousands of orphans as a result of rape and liaisons between foreign troops and local women," Bruno added, shaking his head.

"Okay, now it makes sense to me why they needed the guest-workers program," said Bellin. "Also, Germany had the money after receiving a big chunk of the Marshall Plan funds. However, I'm especially curious, how did you survive finding yourself in a place with a different culture and different language?" asked Bellin.

"*Tutto è stato molto difficile* (Everything was extremely difficult). I struggled to communicate in German, a language I found to be extraordinarily difficult. But thank God, after a few days, I joined a small Italian association outside Munich. They helped me navigate through my daily tasks and even taught me 'survival words' and phrases in German. And when I applied for the job at the Central Railroad Station, I was so anxious that only the elation of being hired, after a short meeting with the personnel administrator, composed me," said Bruno.

"Did the railroad provide housing for guest workers?" asked the inspector.

"No way! We were on our own. But it didn't take me long to settle in my job and to acquire some temporary housing in the old quarters, on the outskirts of Munich. This was very convenient because I could walk to work, and from that location they would transport men out to various places. And after five months, when things were becoming routine, I felt that my weekends were being wasted. I had no hobbies, not many friends besides a few acquaintances in the association, I wasn't big on church goings, playing sports or even attending sport events so I decided to look for a part-time job, on Saturdays and Sundays," said Bruno.

"Wow! You were a very ambitious man," said the inspector. "A lesser man would be afraid of the challenge. How did you do it?"

"Well, at first, I scanned the local papers, I checked bulletin boards in the lobbies of municipal buildings and at church entrances, but nothing. Then I decided to advertise myself in the church bulletin that also carried the schedule of masses, special services and events taking place in the parish. I focused on the inquiries and community services page on the back of the bulletin. I noticed that flower shops, funeral homes, grinders, elderly care attendants were most prominent and were assigned a small square box. I discovered that towards the bottom of the page a couple of lines were taken up by parishes looking for donations for this or that cause and several appeals under the 'WANTED' column. They had posted their first name and telephone number. Someone was looking for a used wheelchair, another was seeking a black and white phonograph, still, three others were looking for employment as housekeepers and one as a leather tanner. I thought this would be a good spot for my ad, superimposed in script. My ad was to be very short. I was determined to keep it under the twenty-word limit so that I would pay the minimum price. It would say:

> 'Handyman, can do many odd jobs around your home or work-place. Weekend work only. Honest, reliable, hardworking. Call Bruno at…'

"I had wondered if the hyphenated 'work-place' would be considered one word or two words. Then I decided that if it constituted two words, I would eliminate the 'or' and use a comma in its place. My friend Fabio translated it into German, since he had lived in Munich longer than anyone else that I knew. No sooner had I worked out these intricacies in my mind than I realized I had another problem: that once the ad was translated from Italian to German the word count might again be changed." Bruno stopped talking, realizing that the inspector was probably getting tired.

"And then what? Don't leave me hanging. Did you have any luck with the ad?" asked the inspector.

"The ad came out the following week, pretty much as I had anticipated. I didn't have my own telephone number so I used Faustino's number. Faustino lived in my flat, on the same floor, with four other men who shared the same toilet facilities and kitchenette. The kitchen was rarely used; but for a cup of coffee in the morning and some toast, I often skipped lunch or bought something out. At night, we all chipped in to pay an old German woman to prepare our meals. The poor woman had been seriously disfigured with burns to her face after a bombing raid which killed her whole family and most of her village. She appreciated the little money she made from the émigrés that helped her sustain herself and, having no surviving family of her own, she treated all the foreign workers as her family. As far as the phone was concerned, it was understood that whoever utilized the telephone number in any way would pay a portion of the monthly charges. Then on the second day of the bulletin's publication Faustino had knocked on my door informing me that there was a woman caller asking for me. Her name was Elsa Moretti-Schemitsch.

Chapter 10

Naples Central Station

It had been more than an hour and a half since he was attacked on the train. Lorenzo had returned to his seat shaking. He was beginning to feel a little more composed but couldn't help wondering whether his attacker had survived the fall from the train. But most unsettling was whether he had acted alone. If he survived, Lorenzo prayed that he would never see him again. He knew that he had been lucky but luck didn't last forever. Since the confrontation he was super alert just in case his attacker had an accomplice on board. Slowly, he came to the conclusion that if others were on the train, they would have found him already.

The conductor announced that the next stop was Naples. Aroused, Lorenzo sat up. He didn't remember which one of the five stations within the city limits was closest to the seaport. He vaguely remembered passing the five stops when he accompanied his father for treatment at the Polyclinic in Rome. If he were a betting man, he would put his money on the third. The only way he'd know for sure was to ask a conductor or try to see a sign that would let him know where to get off. Once out of the station he would hop on a bus, ride the five or six kilometers to the port, go through customs and then board the ocean liner. There he would feel reasonably safe. And once on board, he would try to get some seriously needed sleep.

The train was making good time and he would probably have one to two hours before boarding the ship.

He glanced at the watch Annalisa had given him and smiled sadly. He couldn't resist the little watch compartment where their smiling photo was hidden. He looked at her photo and with his finger traced her hairline and chin bone. Then he focused on her lips. Just to see them brought all the emotional and physical sensation he always felt as their lips touched even slightly. His heart was heavy with a feeling of loss, thinking of the hopelessness, that he would never see or touch her again. He would forever only have this photo to transport him back to his love.

Passengers were already either reaching for their carry-ons in the overhead compartments or were retrieving their baggage from the large storage closets near the exit doors. Lorenzo was surprised to see how many travelers had boarded the station at the city's outskirts, maybe tourists coming up the Amalfi Coast and the islands near Sorrento, making connections in Naples and heading north to Rome.

The next city station was also crowded. People were rushing here and there; children being towed by hand and some little ones crying; friends and families waiting for others. Porters were at the ready to assist, especially those who they zeroed in on as potential big tippers – the well dressed, the well groomed and the ones with elegant accessories. Travelers had to be very careful and very alert in this city. Naples had a long-standing reputation for thievery. A large percentage of the population, more than any other big city in Europe, augmented their regular paycheck by moonlighting as criminals.

Lorenzo had placed his luggage between his legs when the train rolled into what seemed to be the central station. He stood up, hunched over and looked through the windows. He couldn't see any signs but all the activity indicated that this was the central terminal.

To make sure, he asked a man waiting in line at the exit door whether this was indeed the central station.

"*Mi scusi, e questa la stazione centrale?*"

"*Si, certo, questa e la stazione.*"

He merged in line behind him. Once on the platform Lorenzo stepped to the side to avoid being shoved. He scanned the terminal. He saw a huge white board up ahead, automated flap-displays spinning round and round and making smacking sounds – time, destination, track numbers – constantly changing. He saw people clustered around the café counters and gift shops. At the opposite end of the station, where natural light filtered through the large, grimy glass portals, he could see the taxi stand. As he walked closer to the exit doors, he felt relieved in seeing the bus depot just across the street. People were lined up next to bus bays and under shelters where they could get a little relief from the hot afternoon sun. Some guzzled down bottles of *San Pellegrino,* others licked melting *gelati*. Many taxi drivers had their passenger door open, trying to lure fares with the same zeal as Arab merchants trying to hook customers at a Moroccan bazaar.

Lorenzo quickly stepped out of the circular doors and maneuvered to avoid the sea of suitcases. He was momentarily blinded by the intense sunlight. As his eyes adjusted, he could see a row of buses in the parking lot, their destinations flashed directly over their windshields. Some drivers smoked outside their buses while some others gave people directions. The fourth bus was the one he wanted. The sign above the driver was conspicuous: *Porto di Napoli*. He knew that the bus driver could not accept cash. But wondered if he had time to purchase his ticket at the stationery stand, twenty yards away, before the bus drove off. He decided to go for it since the line was short. He just hoped that a woman towing two children would stop talking to the attendant. A young couple ahead of him was also becoming impatient. The young woman was swaying back and forth, fidgeting with some cards in her hands. Lorenzo finally got his ticket when another attendant opened a second window. He dashed across the lot towards the bus; the driver was cutting his wheels in an effort to back out of the bay.

He hoped that the bus driver would see him running in his direction and break. No luck. The driver was concentrating on not hitting pedestrians and other parked vehicles, not on last-minute stragglers. Lorenzo slowed down and realized he probably had to wait for the next bus or take a cab. As he looked across the street towards the cabstand he was startled by what he saw. It was the same crazy bastard from a few hours ago. The same guy who had a knife to his back and then tried to stab him. Lorenzo would never forget that face. He thought about stopping the two *carabinieri* that were by the intersection. But what would he tell them and where would the inquiry end? Then Lorenzo started wondering how that *figlio di putana* (son of a bitch) could have gotten here so fast after tumbling off the speeding train. There was only one explanation: he must've gotten to a phone and had a driver pick him up. The assassin was standing next to a light blue Fiat. Someone else was at the wheel. The car was small but the driver seemed to be even smaller in proportion. Maybe it was the assassin's kid and Papa was breaking him into the family business? The driver was wearing a dark cap that slid down over his eyes. He had a thin face from what Lorenzo could see and a darker complexion than his presumed father.

Lorenzo's attacker had his left arm in a makeshift sling and his face appeared battered and bruised. He also seemed to have a slight limp as he moved near the Fiat. Lorenzo studied him intently until his former attacker apparently sensed his gaze. The injured man said something to the driver; the Fiat quickly pulled away. The big guy, in noticeable pain, headed towards Lorenzo.

Meanwhile, the bus going to the seaport had crossed the lot and was waiting behind two other cars on the exit ramp, heading east on route 37. Lorenzo hoped to head it off. He bolted in its direction.

As the bus was prepared to merge, Lorenzo reached the bus's door. His fist pounded in urgency. The bus driver threw up his palms as if saying, "What the hell do you want? This isn't the bus stop." But two college students, who had been rooting Lorenzo on while he was running for the bus, now appealed to the driver. Other passengers, sympathetic with Lorenzo's plight, joined the chorus and started yelling: "*Apri la porta, apri la porta* (Open the door)." Finally, the bus driver relented. The doors swung open. Lorenzo jumped in.

The man behind the wheel gave him a dirty look, told him to wait next to an outdated coin box, adjacent to the driver. The driver inched his way onto the state road. Lorenzo waited for what seemed to be an eternity.

Finally, the driver took his ticket and he sat two seats behind the driver.

Lorenzo saw his pursuer, even with some momentum lost because of his arm sling, bolt up the roadway ramp behind the bus just as the driver accelerated onto route 37. From the bus window he could see the big man with the sling give up his pursuit and stop. He appeared out of breath and indignant, his piercing eyes glued to the bus. His snarling expression indicated that it was a matter of time before he got his hands around Lorenzo's neck, like a chicken to be slaughtered.

As the bus proceeded on the highway the bus driver could not resist a verbal thrashing. He told Lorenzo that it was against the rules to pick up anyone, anywhere, but at designated stops. Lorenzo nodded his head as if acknowledging what he was saying, but he was really focused on the blue Fiat stopping at the edge of the ramp to pick up the man in the sling. The Fiat accelerated towards the bus and soon was only six car lengths behind. Lorenzo walked to the rear. Through the back window he could see the blue Fiat trying to maneuver in front of the other cars. He had to think fast. In minutes, they would head off the bus and coerce the driver to stop. Even if their strategy wasn't to obstruct the road and force the bus to the side, they would surely board the bus at the next stop. The bus route was prominently posted on the wall, behind the hanging straps, and

Lorenzo noticed that the next passenger drop-off was Piazza Dante Alighieri. If that was their plan, he had five minutes at best.

The bus kept a steady pace down the highway until it came to a commercial strip with a traffic light, ready to turn. The bus driver, seeing an opportunity, plowed through the amber light. The Fiat had managed to weave past a few cars. Now, it was the third car behind the bus when it got sandwiched in place at the red light. Before the light turned green, a delivery truck and another vehicle had made a right from a local street and onto route 37 and were now directly behind the bus. This was an opportunity.

Lorenzo saw a cab. He pulled down hard on the emergency cable over the back door, bringing the bus to a screeching stop. The bus driver yelled: "*Che cazzo!* (What the fuck!)"

As the doors swung open Lorenzo went flying out, suitcase in tow. The cab customer had paid his fare and was about to shut the rear cab door when Lorenzo grabbed it and leapt in.

"Take me to pier 11, at the port," he demanded. "I need to board my boat immediately."

The gray-haired taxi driver hesitated, indignant at how this little *stronzo* (asshole) had entered his cab and his tone of voice. Lorenzo realized the affront. He pulled out some cash, several times the regular fare, and threw it on the front seat. The cabbie, Marco Delgato, on the dashboard identification tag, looked at the money. Then, without moving his torso, he turned his head 145 degrees like a ventriloquist's puppet and eyeballed his passenger, still unpersuaded and impassive.

"Please, I need to get there now," Lorenzo said. The cabbie probably thought the kid had some manners after all. His dignity restored, he grabbed the money, shifted gears and sped away.

Behind them, the bus was still immobilized. The light changed. The guy in the sling and his cohort driving the Fiat managed to cut ahead of the three cars by driving in the opposite lane. They were squeezed behind the bus and truck. The Fiat's driver saw another opportunity, and again, accelerated in the opposite lane. He then swung back in to Lorenzo's lane. They were thirty feet behind the taxi.

"Can you step on it?" Lorenzo pleaded, and demanded at the same time.

"It's not going to do you any good if we get pulled over," barked back the cab driver, as he weaved past two vehicles.

The Fiat mauled down a pedestrian too slow to cross and Lorenzo felt a jolt from behind. The Fiat struck the cab's left rear fender. The man in the sling waved a gun out the window to frighten the cabbie to stop. The cab driver screamed profanities, intent on getting to the police station by the pier.

"*Bastardi pazzi!* (Crazy bastards!) What the fuck do they want? Are they after you?" he asked Lorenzo, fuming.

"At this point, I think they're after both of us," Lorenzo said.

The cab driver tried to elude them by quickly turning down a side road. The Fiat went some thirty feet forward, slammed the brakes and, with tires smoking, backed up and, at full speed, headed down their street. At the corner, the cabbie looked in his rear-view mirror and saw the Fiat midway down the street, approaching at maximum speed. Marco, taking advantage of the pursuer's limited field of vision, made a quick left and a quick right down a short cobblestone street. He went through a garage which led him to an even more narrow street where café stands were lined up on the sidewalk and spilled out onto the avenue.

The cabbie looked back and looked around. He was pleased not to see the Fiat anywhere. He was confident. He smiled triumphantly.

"Great job!" Lorenzo said. "I really think you lost those bastards."

"I know Naples like the back of my hand. I lived here all of my forty-seven years. My family goes back hundreds of years," said Marco.

"I see, so the city grid is engraved in your mind," said Lorenzo.

Marco was positively sure that he had given the Fiat the slip, and lost the gun-toting pricks for good. His remaining concern was to avoid running into them coincidentally. And to that end, he knew precisely which back streets to take for the next few miles.

Lorenzo didn't completely share Marco's feelings. He was scared. He felt nauseous. There was a moment he was convinced he was going to get shot. He was going to die. The narrow side streets seemed to squeeze his heart. He was breathing hard. The never-ending turns and alley-like paths driven by the cabbie had been the longest ten minutes of his life.

The cab came out on Via Filiberti, a wide commercial strip with plenty of pedestrian shoppers and a little traffic. He was heading back north, toward the piers, when he happened to glance across the street. He was flabbergasted. The blue Fiat was directly across the street, heading in the opposite direction. Marco wasn't sure if the short driver recognized them, among many identical cabs in this area. He hoped the Fiat would keep driving in the opposite direction. Lorenzo was also aware of their predicament as both men watched their pursuers make a U-turn in the middle of the avenue.

"*Bastardi disgraziata, non si arrende!* (Wretched bastards, they don't give up!)" said Lorenzo.

"*Non ci pensare. Ave un po di fiducia con me.* (Don't think about it. Have a little confidence in me.)," said Marco.

The cab driver veered left, off Via Filiberti, cutting off a tram filled with tourists in the process, and headed towards the industrial area. This was his most thrilling maneuver yet in eluding the sleazy bastards. In a perverse way, he seemed to relish the challenge, especially in this trade zone. The cabbie knew which streets ended abruptly, that a few ran parallel, while most did not, and that some were so small and narrow that people confused them with private driveways. He also knew which ones had potholes larger than craters and which ones connected with the Old Spanish Quarters. Before leading the Fiat into this labyrinth, the cabbie made certain that the Fiat was exactly the right distance behind his cab.

"What are you doing? Do you know where you're going?"

shouted Lorenzo as he felt the cab slowing down and the Fiat gaining on them every second.

"Wanna take the wheel, if you think you can do better?" asked Marco, brushing aside all fear. For Marco escaping from the pursuers was a lesser objective; it was more about fulfillment. He was the professor; they were the students. This was his element. It was his car, his streets, his people and his city. He felt like the thief who broke into wealthy homes, less for the valuables and more for the exhilaration of being able to do it and get away with it.

"Shit! They're almost on us!" blurted Lorenzo, looking back, panicked.

Before Marco could respond a bullet pierced the rear window with a loud popping sound. Lorenzo ducked instinctively. A second bullet seemed to shatter a rear light.

"*Figli di puttana!* (Motherfuckers!)" The cab driver was angry. "They must want you pretty badly. What the hell did you really do to them?"

Before Lorenzo could respond a white box truck with a shiny meat logo on its side came out of a warehouse and was backing up into the street. Marco maneuvered the left wheels of his vehicle over the curb and down the sidewalk, missing the truck by inches. Lorenzo was thrown side to side and bumped his head on the cab ceiling. They could hear the Fiat coming to a screeching halt behind them.

In a flash, the man with the sling was out of the Fiat, waving a pistol and screaming at the truck driver.

"MOVE THIS FUCKING TRUCK! MOVE IT. MOVE IT. NOW! I SWEAR I'LL BLOW YOUR FUCKING HEAD OFF, YOU ASSHOLE!!!"

The cabbie's strategy of racing down the crazy alleyways had gained them time to lose the Fiat for good. Marco crossed two parking lots and proceeded down a very old alleyway which gave him no more than six inches to maneuver. He knew that the pursuers' sense of direction was lost. All they had was trial and error and slim hope.

While the Fiat struggled to extricate itself from the blockage, in minutes, Lorenzo and the cabbie were out of the maze of narrow streets and on the main road along the port. It was an extensive port.

"Well, I think I've earned my money, huh?" the cabbie asked Lorenzo, while slowing down and looking at him in the rear-view mirror.

Lorenzo smiled. "Don't worry I won't ask for a refund."

"Well, you got to give me this much; it was the most exciting ride you ever had, right?"

"I hope it's the most exciting ride I'll ever have! Thank you!" Lorenzo smiled.

He noticed that they were traveling on the Autostrada 56 and were about to get off on Via Giulio Cesare. He could see that from the Bay of Naples one could travel to a multitude of destinations, the signs said it all: Malta, Sardinia, the Island of Ischia, Tunis and wherever else your heart desired. All you needed was a little money.

"Pier 11 should be coming up," Marco told Lorenzo.

"I think I still have some time before boarding," said Lorenzo, looking at his watch.

"I'll drop you off by that information booth," said Marco, pointing to what seemed to Lorenzo to be a closed newspaper stand. This area was less busy. The activity seemed to be further down, in front of the single-level office building, next to the gate, where people were beginning to cluster. In the background was the white ocean liner, very impressive set against the turquoise waters and blue skies, anchored some thirty feet from the harbor. It was immense. Several platforms were set up for ingress and egress. One of the ramps was reserved for baggage and cargo handlers in light blue uniforms. Supply containers and food boxes were stacked on the pier and new shipments were continually arriving. Various types of uniformed men were present. Municipal police and ship security personnel could be seen on deck and patrolling the ground level.

Lorenzo, with his left hand on his suitcase and the other hand pushing open the cab's back door, thanked Marco once more.

Then, out of nowhere, a figure appeared by the cab's partially opened window and pulled something from under his jacket. Because his face came over the cab's roofline Lorenzo couldn't make out what he looked like. One thing was certain: the man's left arm was in a sling. Just before hearing a muffled popping sound Lorenzo saw the extended muzzle, a silencer, glistening under the cold afternoon sun and thought he heard: "End of the line, asshole."

Blood was spurting out of Marco's temple. Lorenzo was momentarily paralyzed from indecision. Should he help Marco or should he flee? His decision became evident as a second gunshot jolted him into action. He jumped out of the cab. His suitcase had absorbed the second shot, clearly intended for him. Another shot sprayed glass shards from one of the cab windows. Lorenzo sprinted around the newspaper stand, using it as a shield. He didn't stop behind the wooden structure but kept running beyond it, along the edge of the pier and next to the pylons, towards the boat ramp, some fifty feet beyond. As he got closer to the uniformed officers he was panting, his face white from fear. He tried to force his breathing into normalcy. Glancing back, he could only see the front section of the cab but the assassin was nowhere in sight. He was not being followed.

The line at the ticket booth moved quickly. He showed his boarding documents including passport, vaccination certificates and travel tickets to the official behind the counter, and from that point proceeded to the gangplank where he again showed the previously stamped documents to another attendant. All along Lorenzo could not help wondering how the assassin was able to make his way out of the old industrial area, the labyrinth as Marco had called it, and get to the pier before him and Marco.

Unbeknownst to Lorenzo, the assassin's partner, Moustafa, had experienced a lot of back alleys in Tunis and had been operating around the Spanish Quarters, the industrial area and the port for several months. He had been renewing old contacts, making new ones and lining up illegal deals with the ultimate aim of expanding Giacomo's territory.

Chapter 11

The Orphanage

Bruno continued the tale of Andreas' adoption in 1947. As he spoke you saw a distant look in his eyes and he was back in Germany, alone, not sure of where he was. The inspector sipped some coffee and took down some notes from time to time, usually after asking a question.

After Bruno had placed the ad in the paper about part-time employment, he was contacted. The telephone conversation he had with Elsa Moretti-Schemitsch left him in an upbeat mood.

The following day, Bruno pedaled some three miles on an old bicycle belonging to his friend Faustino, who kept it in his room and used it to run errands on weekends. Now he was headed north on a fairly warm day with a brilliant sun shining through unblemished white clouds. In the distant sky was an unusual swath of clouds packed as tightly as fish scales, beginning to unravel and disperse at one end. Bruno couldn't remember ever seeing a sky view so unique. He stopped momentarily both to observe the phenomenon and to look at a rudimentary map drawn by one of his co-workers. He felt that he had gone beyond the directions Elsa had given him over the telephone. Since there were no street signs and not many buildings were standing where the name of the street might be carved on its cornerstone, he was left to navigate via landmarks. The old church building, the vegetable store, the public square and the park were his markers. These sites were scribbled in black crayon on the paper he was holding.

Bruno had found all the landmarks except the park. Across the street where the park was supposed to be stood a mountain of rubble. While leaning on his bike, he took out a handkerchief from his back pocket and wiped his forehead. This site didn't make any sense to him. Then he remembered a conversation he had at the railroad yard about local citizens coming together after the war and cleaning up their streets as best they could. This was due to municipal agencies not existing to deal with the problems. Even if some small agency existed it had no heavy machinery available to do anything, thus, the locals had to rely on each other. The local officials, aware of the extremity of the situation and the lack of available resources, gave orders that dumping debris in public parks was an acceptable solution. Also, since factories making common implements like shovels, picks and wheelbarrows were non-operational, people were forced to clean the streets by hand. Women would put on heavy aprons and carry chunks of concrete and fragments of everything else for blocks in order to dump it in public fields or city parks.

Bruno rode his bike a little further from the wreckage. His mind characterized the mountains of rubble as "pyramids of destruction and shame." It was a befitting memorial to the war except that the bodies of the victims had been buried and the blood had washed away.

Finally, he looked down the street and saw it. It was a two-story structure at the outskirts of town. Poplar trees surrounded the front. The landscaping was overgrown and unkempt. There was a large, almost circular driveway, with an island overgrown with shrubs, crawling thorny bushes and tall dry weeds. At one time, Bruno imagined, it was probably decorated with pretty flowers. Both sides of the drive led to a canopied front entrance with double metal doors, each with a small rectangular glass window fortified with thin metal mesh. It might have been a hotel at one time before the war, and later was converted to an orphanage.

The rear right corner of the building was partially damaged from air raids. A deep crevice nearby indicated that the building had been in some pilot's sights and a bomb had been dropped. But why was the rest of the building spared? Was it because the pilot, at the last moment, recognized it as an orphanage? Did providence intervene and cause the bad aim? Or perhaps, the pilot had felt that by flying another few miles, to a more populated area, he could accomplish a lot more with the remaining ordnance on board.

Bruno left his bike leaning against the side of the building and walked to the entrance. He pulled on the right door handle, but it was locked; then he pulled on the left side – also locked. He looked in to see if anyone was standing inside. All he could see was a long hallway, red brick walls, greenish tiles on the floor and two chairs against the wall opposite each other. He was ready to walk around the building when he noticed an inconspicuous round button adjacent to the doorjamb. He pressed it. A sound, like a woodpecker pecking on a tree trunk, vibrated down the hallway. A skinny woman with a bony face, a pronounced nose and thinning hair came out of a nearby room. She was walking briskly and her face had a forced smile, as if caught napping.

"Yes? How can I help you?" she inquired through the glass window.

"My name is Bruno Salvaggi. I'm here to see Fräulein Elsa Schemitsch." He raised his voice to make sure he was heard. She looked him over, up and down, carefully, then she pushed open the door and let him in.

"Please wait here a minute," she said, motioning to the chairs, then stepped back into her office and dialed a number. Bruno could hear the conversation but couldn't grasp the meaning. He only knew some basic expressions in German. A few minutes later she came out of the office.

"Fräulein Schemitsch said she's expecting you. Her office is upstairs at the end of the corridor. Use those stairs." She pointed with an index finger no thicker than a toothpick, and made a zigzag sign to indicate stairs.

As Bruno climbed the stairs, he made several observations. Paint was flaking off in the stairwell; the black wrought iron railing was scratched and chipped, exposing several previous layers of paint underneath. He heard noises coming from the second floor. Children were crying and whimpering. When he reached the top of the landing the children's noises got louder. He walked a few more steps down the corridor where he saw an enormous room through the door's framed glass. One side wall had prison-style bunk beds, while the center area had single metal beds with thin mattresses and practically no space in between. The beds were lined up against the south and north walls. Some were occupied; the majority were empty. The wall opposite the bunk beds had a mini amphitheater, a stark reminder that in better times a piano or organ probably stood in that very location. Bruno imagined a man in a white shirt and a black tux stroking the keyboard while couples waltzed in the center of the room until late at night. Now, a crucifix on the wall had replaced the phantom piano and the piano man.

The upper wall of the amphitheater, where Jesus kept a watchful eye on everyone, was painted a mustard color that had faded with time; the lower half of the wall was painted a washed-out lavender. There was a bulletin board to the side with notes for the caretakers and a list of names, probably of the children. It looked like a docket in the lobby of a courthouse. A chunk of the ceiling plaster had fallen off to the right where the imagined piano once sat. And, except for an older woman wearing a white smock giving some children what appeared to be medication, no other employees were in sight.

At the end of the hall he came to an office. It was nondescript and without designation of title or name. A reception window revealed an old wooden desk on one side of the room and a lot of printed matter stacked on its surface. Hanging from the wall, behind the desk, was a black and white picture of some six people dressed officially and probably taken at some function. Cardboard boxes and wooden crates were piled in the back corner of the room. Seated behind the desk was a woman with streaks of gray hair, dressed modestly and wearing a thick pair of glasses. She was focused on composing a letter. Bruno knocked gently with the back of his knuckle. The woman looked up from her desk and waved him in.

Chapter 12

On the Ocean Liner

Lorenzo waited in line for a while, still traumatized, before his documents were checked and ticket validated. He was vigilant every second, expecting someone to come from behind and shoot him in the head as they had done to Marco, or for the police to haul him away because someone saw him come out of the taxicab. Nothing happened, so he walked to the end of the wharf and strode up the gangplank. As he stepped onto the ship's deck, he saw a small metal plaque screwed on the wall of the vestibule indicating cabin numbers, black lettering on white background. He checked his number on the ticket stub and matched it with the wall plaque, LQ 137, with an arrow pointing downward: left stairs, one flight down. This could only mean that his cabin was practically at sea level and he would feel the seawater slapping against the porthole window. He shrugged; a far cry from first class but then it wasn't his money so he couldn't be choosy. Downstairs, he took a wrong turn and then had to backtrack. His cabin turned out to be at the very end of the hallway, second from last.

His mother always said, "No matter the circumstances, there's always something to be thankful about." Lorenzo pondered the meaning and wondered if it had any application to the moment. The bathrooms were at each end of the hallway. That was good. He wouldn't have to go reeling down the corridor in the middle of the night if he had to heave or use the toilet. That was also good. The other redeeming feature was that he had more privacy than other passengers. This was due to the boat's design. The last three cabins were smaller and had room for only two passengers, and not four like the other rooms he had seen. This last factor was very important because he could be stuck for about two weeks with detestable roommates.

The door was unlocked so Lorenzo pushed it open with his foot. Good. No one else was there. Since he was first to arrive, he would have the pick of the beds. He decided against the bed closest to the porthole, figuring that the motion of the waves might make him nauseous. He dropped his baggage on the other bed, took off his fleece jacket and approached the small sink near his bed. He ran the water, splashed his face a few times, and then dried himself. He wondered who might be his roommate.

His eyes went to the bullet hole in the luggage. It was his father's old suitcase and was making its first and only transatlantic trip, but now that it had a bullet hole in it he would have to dispose of it when he got to America. He bent over and put his finger in the hole. The bullet had not exited the other side so it should be lodged inside somewhere. He unstrapped the suitcase, clicked it open and carefully followed the bullet's trajectory. It had gone through the side of his suitcase, ripped through some of his clothing and some socks and lodged itself in the sole of his best shoes. "Damn!" As he fished out the bullet with his finger, he thought about the incident and came up with a clever line: "Better in your sole than in your soul." He inspected the bullet, a .380 caliber, but couldn't quite determine the type of gun used; maybe an automatic. It felt heavy in his hand and looked like a button mushroom with a short stem. He knew something about firearms because his dad had taken him hunting in the woods ever since he was a kid. He also read the ammunition and pistol magazines that his father bought each year in the city before hunting season. He bounced the squashed piece of lead in his cupped hand a few times then put it in his pocket; it would be his good luck charm.

He sat on the bed hunched over, holding his head between his hands, reflecting on the day and feeling totally exhausted. Three times in the course of six hours he had come close to being maimed if not outright murdered. He was almost gutted on the train, his head nearly blown off in the industrial park and, but for his luggage, he had come close to getting a bullet in his spine. He was ninety-nine percent certain that it was Giacomo who had set everything in motion. The cashier at the train station, the thug on the train and in the Fiat that tailed his bus, and his cab, were either related to Giacomo or on his payroll. One thing he couldn't figure out was how the driver of the blue car was connected. He tried to place the little man behind the wheel. Nothing came to him. Whoever the strange-looking character was, Lorenzo concluded that he was just a novice and not really a danger. The big guy in the sling was his tutor.

He felt a lot safer on the boat, knowing that the port police, customs inspectors and boat security would not allow anyone on board who was not a legitimate ticket holder. Passengers and their luggage were randomly searched for weapons and contraband before boarding. Luckily, he hadn't been one of those searched. Lorenzo was quite certain that most of the police security by now were at the scene of the shooting. And after such a brazen public execution, the two assailants must've fled the city. By now the *carabinieri* were also involved and canvassing the area for witnesses. Lorenzo was sure that no one had seen him running from the cab and darting behind the newsstand. If someone had connected him with the victim he would've been stopped before boarding.

He thought about Marco, the cab driver. The poor man was just an innocent bystander who had planned his day in the morning, made arrangements with his wife for dinner, dropped off his kids at school, scrounged for some fares, and then instantaneously, from nowhere… everything shattered – his plans, his hopes, his dreams, all swirling down the toilet. It was an undignified death, with no warning and no preparation. Life was so fragile and totally unfair. What remained were the ripples of his existence. Then there were the deeds of a scrambled mind, like Andreas, that could have disproportionate ripples of untold consequences. At that moment Lorenzo was overtaken by a sense of guilt for both Andreas and Marco, who would still be around had he not stepped into their lives.

It wasn't long before fatigue overtook him. He briefly dozed off on the bed when he was jarred back awake. Noise came from outside his cabin. His first thought was *carabinieri*. They were coming to arrest him. He opened the door slightly to see a man and woman enter one of the three small rooms down the hall. They were laughing as they struggled to push their ridiculously oversized luggage through the door. Relieved, Lorenzo quietly shut the door.

He had three things on his mind. But because he didn't feel very sociable, he wouldn't act on any of them until his neighbors disappeared into their cabin. First, he wanted to take a piss. Second, he needed a double espresso to stay up. This he could probably get in a lounge on the upper deck. Last, he wanted to take in the panoramic view of the Port of Naples from the upper deck and see if Marco's cab was still parked in the same spot. From there he could also see the passengers that were still in line to board. The problem was that all three of his wishes were overshadowed by a gnawing anxiety concerning the guy that shot Marco and came close to killing him.

Lorenzo found the coffee bar about mid-deck on the second level. While waiting in line for his coffee and croissant, he was surprised to see only a handful of people in the lounge. There was someone sitting on a bar stool at the end of the counter who looked familiar. He was about his own age. An older woman and her husband were in between. Across the room were a couch and several armchairs. Two young girls were sitting on the couch looking at some photos and giggling. And a short, elf-like man was sitting in one of the armchairs. The little man was half hidden by the newspaper he was reading.

After paying, Lorenzo took his purchase and walked towards the rear of the lounge. No sooner had he sat down than the young man who had been sitting at the counter approached him with a wide smile. "*Scusi*, Lorenzo?"

He was tall, heavyset and almost handsome, a former classmate; they had been inseparable friends throughout their school years. They hadn't run into each other since graduating secondary school.

"Giovanni. What the hell are you doing here?" Lorenzo asked as they embraced.

"I could ask the same question," Giovanni replied as he carefully looked over his friend.

"You can look all you want, I haven't changed," said Lorenzo. "It's you who looks like a Hollywood celebrity. In fact, I saw you sitting at the counter but wasn't sure if it was you. You were facing the other way," said Lorenzo.

Giovanni was meticulously dressed. He had on a blue blazer, blue shirt and gray pants.

"There you go, still teasing me just like in school," said Giovanni, flashing his charming smile.

"I was complimenting you. There's a difference."

"So, you're shipping out for America. Got anybody there?"

"My uncle is in New York. He's got work for me with his construction company," Lorenzo said.

"But I thought you wanted to be a civil engineer."

"I did. But that was before my father got sick. I'll have to put that idea on hold for now," said Lorenzo as he gulped down the two sips of espresso and then bit mightily into his croissant.

"Let me get you another one," said Giovanni. Lorenzo, with his mouth full, waved his hand back and forth to indicate no.

"I insist. If you don't want it you can throw it out."

Giovanni walked down to the other end of the counter to order it from the barista. Lorenzo looked around and sensed the dwarf-sized man behind the newspaper looking him over. As the little man in the armchair turned a page of his newspaper Lorenzo spied one side of the man's face. He had a deformed ear. Lorenzo quickly made the mental association and when he did his heart started racing and blood rose to his face. It was the driver of the car at the train station. His passenger was the guy in the sling, the guy who shot at them in the cab. Somehow, he had slipped past security and gotten onto the boat. He wasn't here by coincidence. He was here for a purpose.

Giovanni came back with his coffee. Lorenzo took it and put it on the counter.

"Look, I need to get out of here," he whispered. "I'll explain later."

The two walked out and went up the stairs to the third deck. Lorenzo kept glancing back every few steps; no one was following. He explained quickly to Giovanni that there was a guy sitting in the lounge who wasn't very friendly and who was probably going to try something. They moved on to the fourth level where it was virtually deserted and decided to split up. Giovanni went around one of the ship's funnels and Lorenzo walked along the rail, amidships. He knew that the man in the armchair would follow. As he walked, he saw a metal door ajar with the inscription: "Engineer's Quarters." Inside were heavy-duty electrical wires strung up against the wall, and there were pipes and motors. Everything was painted in white. The rope-like wires and cables came from below, ran across the wall, looped down and connected to two large turbines. Lorenzo looked in. The room was dark except for light coming in from a porthole on the side. He slid his body in like a cat through a grate and left the door ajar. From the porthole he could see if anyone was following him.

It didn't take long. The weasel-like small man came up the stairs. On the platform he rotated his head, first left and then right, as if sniffing for a scent. He wore a dark cap, an unbuttoned overcoat, nylon sweat pants and sneakers. Then, at an unhurried pace, he followed Lorenzo's tracks. When the weasel approached the unlocked door to the engineer's room he paused and reassessed the landscape as if a device in his head started to tick louder. Cautiously, his hand reached for the doorknob when the door flew open with such power and speed that only one with a will to survive could unleash. But for a quick shift of his body, the weasel would have been smashed against the wall. Instead, he lurched backward and to the side, completely avoiding the metal door. Just when his agile body was off balance, he felt a hand, Giovanni's hand, grab the collar of his jacket. Then a second hand was on the back of his trousers. He felt his body being hauled up from the ground and propelled towards the railing, over the railing. His feet were now barely touching the ground. A split second was all he had. He twisted his upper torso and with the agility of a wildcat in mid-air grabbed his enemy's hair with one hand and the other hand reached inside his belt. There, even at such a decisive moment when his assailant had the advantage of balance and power, he found something he could trust. In one smooth, dazzling motion the hand and the hilt were one. Moustafa raised his right hand to the sky and then thrust the *jambiya* downwards with unnatural precision. His adversary's face was slashed from left temple to chin. Then the blade traveled diagonally; from the clavicle bone, across his right breast, ending at his hip bone. The cut was as intended, deep and fatal, exposing his enemy's cheekbone, his gums, his ribcage and bowels.

Lorenzo rushed out of the engineer's room in time to see both men going over the railing. Each determined not to let go of the other. The weasel kept slashing in mid-air as they plunged into the murky waters. The struggle continued underwater. Giovanni, like a pit bull whose jaw had locked onto his victim, held onto the weasel and pummeled him with his right fist. The other man, wielding his weapon like an unmerciful talon, sliced into flesh, arm, leg and torso. The battle continued until their feet touched the murky bottom of the bay.

People witnessing the fall started screaming, some from the ship's deck and others from the wharf. This attracted the attention of uniformed men on the dock. Two officers reacted instinctively. One untied a small motorboat, while the other jumped inside and started the engine. Before long they were at the spot where the two combatants had fallen. When Giovanni's body came up to the surface of the water, they extended him a pole. He grabbed it but was barely conscious. They pulled him on board. Blood was mixed with water; his clothes were torn to shreds. Meanwhile an ambulance with flashing lights rolled onto the dock. Two *tecnico medico di emergenza* got out and hoisted a stretcher from the rear of the ambulance and ran towards the victim.

Lorenzo made double time down the stairwell, then ran in the direction of the bow towards the lower deck where he had boarded. When he stepped on the gangplank a policeman and a crewmember pushed him back. He was told that no one was allowed off the ship because a police investigation was to follow. While no one was let off the ship other passengers were not permitted to board. Rumors were spreading that the ship would be delayed several hours or possibly a day. Lorenzo watched his friend Giovanni placed on the stretcher on shore. An oxygen mask was placed over his mouth and anesthetic dressing was placed over his wounds. Lorenzo tried to make eye contact but Giovanni appeared semi-conscious as his hand reached for his lacerated face. Then they slid the gurney into the back of the ambulance. Seconds later, sirens wailed and the ambulance sped away.

While Giovanni was being taken away a second rescue boat had joined the first, searching the waters for the assailant. One rescue boat kept going around the ocean liner; the other ventured farther out in the gulf but found no sign of the second man. This had been going on for about forty minutes when two frogmen appeared on the pier. Without hesitation they both jumped in the water at the very spot where Giovanni was fished out. When they emerged they were several hundred feet apart. They gave a thumbs-down sign to their superior to indicate that nothing was found.

Lorenzo was convinced that the underwater search was a waste of time. He believed that because the ocean liner was still anchored and there was no turbulence in the water, and its diesel-powered propellers were still turned off, that the attacker had had a perfect opportunity to elude everyone. He could visualize him, swimming like an eel, alongside the pier, undetected, and then leaping onto a remote part of the wharf. He could've also swum around to the starboard side of the ocean liner during the time all heads were focused on the port side where the emergency workers had caused a commotion. Then he could've slithered away almost motionless, effortlessly, as if taking a midsummer swim in a tranquil lake.

After some jurisdictional squabble with customs officials, the *carabinieri* had come on board with some Coast Guard people and had requested that passengers on each level gather in the two lounges. Luckily, the police work was not overwhelming since less than one hundred passengers had boarded out of a capacity of 1700. Also, interviews had not been very extensive. They asked a handful of questions. Each passenger was required to complete an index card with name, contact number and address. There was even an open-ended question pertaining to anything suspicious that was seen. Lorenzo volunteered no more than the minimum information for fear that he would be taken off the boat. The officials realized that some accommodation had to be made between the state police who wanted to do a more thorough and time-consuming investigation and the ocean liner, *The Augustus*, embarking on schedule. However, the several hours of delay were already evident in the change of moods. Passengers who were still waiting to board inside roped-off areas were getting impatient and frustrated; kids were hungry and thirsty, some were crying and tempers were flaring up.

At last, two high-ranking officials, one in a white uniform and the other in a blue uniform, both with stripes on their shoulders, came out of a small station house on the wharf and gave the signal to allow the rest of the passengers to board. Lorenzo thought that someone had reasoned the matter out and brought everyone back to their senses, arguing that this was, after all, an assault and not a murder investigation. And yes, the victim had serious injuries, but he would probably survive the attack. Thus, about two and a half hours later, the rest of the passengers had been processed for boarding, anchors had been pulled up, diesel engines had been fired and the ship's whistle blew.

Chapter 13

Day to Day at the Orphanage

At Bruno's house he told the inspector that Fräulein Schemitsch's maiden name was Moretti, and he was very surprised when he found out that she spoke Italian. She had worked at the Italian Embassy in Berlin prior to the war, where she met and married her husband, Franz Schemitsch, a German national. She told Bruno that after her child, Heidi, was born they moved to Munich and she became an administrative assistant at the orphanage. At that point, her life became permanently rooted in Germany. But still, she managed to visit her family in Turin every year.

During the conversation it quickly became evident to Bruno that Elsa Moretti-Schemitsch was more interested in talking about the orphanage than she was about asking him questions or even talking about herself. She had an incredible passion for the wellbeing of the orphans, her "children," as she referred to them. She saw herself as the gatekeeper, between perdition and salvation, for all these young lives. They were innocents born into a world at a time of tremendous upheaval and chaos; through no fault of their own, they were condemned to a world where the natural parent-child bonds never existed, never would exist with the ones who gave them life. They were like delicate flowers in a field of weeds. Elsa was determined to do all in her power to give each child the love and security that she and the orphanage could maximally provide.

They had talked for some forty-five minutes when Elsa came around to explaining the responsibilities of the position. This was a relief for Bruno since he figured she wouldn't be wasting her time going over the job requirements if she had no intention of hiring him. The core duties, she explained, were general maintenance: some carpentry, basic electrical, masonry, janitorial and even gardening and landscaping. There would also be times when he would be required to drive the truck to pick up supplies or even escort a sick child to the hospital. Bruno assured her that, as a family man, a farmer and a railroad employee he had the skills and even some of the tools to perform the tasks.

Later, Elsa gave him a tour of the grounds. She started with the top floor where the children's largest sleeping quarters were located. Additionally, there were a few offices, supply stations and a small infirmary. Then they visited the first floor where several other assistants had rooms. There was also a games room, kitchen and cafeteria. The children took their meals here twice a day she explained, early morning and early evening. A little further from the cafeteria was a room with games and two small bookshelves in one corner. Here the children were separated into two age groups and would read stories a few times a week. For the older children some schooling took place here as well. There was also a meeting room to accommodate the few relatives that some children had, who visited from time to time.

Then they walked to the basement where a large, rusty, coal-fired steam boiler was located, the electrical system consisting of a panel box with various-size fuses arranged in sequence, a water pump with two large sinks, a cleaning supplies room, and a laundry room where the clean linens were. She also explained that water from the outside well was primarily used to water the vegetable garden, which was quite extensive. The older children did most of the gardening, and the vegetables grown provided much of the orphanage's food needs.

When they finished the tour, they found themselves by the front entrance where Bruno had entered the building. The subject of pay had not come up and he was a bit uncomfortable in asking. Elsa broached the subject indirectly. She told him that much of the work that went on here was God's work. Many on the staff were voluntary workers; others, like herself, were paid less than minimum wage if all the work hours and the extra time were tallied up. Catholic charities provided basic funding to keep the orphanage going. The local government also provided a miniscule amount of the funding but it was never enough. Private contributions also trickled in from time to time, mostly from distant relatives of some of the children. The difference between what was available and what was needed was made up by the efforts of the older children. About seven of the older children, between fourteen and seventeen years old, worked at odd jobs outside the facility and still lived here so they contributed some of their earnings.

Finally, she got to the point.

"Mr. Salvaggi, as I said previously, much of this work is God's work. Times are difficult for everyone. This country, in fact all of Europe, is trying to recover from the Second World War's devastation. Those that have some shelter and one decent meal a day are considered fortunate. But I'm optimistic that things will get better. In the meantime, all must make some sacrifices."

"I would be willing to volunteer some of my time, but I also have a family to support," answered Bruno, in a supplicating manner.

"We'll pay you minimum wages for Saturday and Sunday, eight-hour days," she said. "If you could spare any extra time, voluntarily, it would be profoundly appreciated. I guarantee that you will derive other, incalculable benefits."

"In that case, how could I ever turn it down? I'll volunteer as much time as I can, when I can," Bruno replied.

"I couldn't ask for more than that," Elsa said as they shook hands. "How soon can you start?"

"Tomorrow?" asked Bruno. She nodded her head and smiled. Before she could say anything else, he smiled back at her and added, "Tomorrow will be voluntary."

*

"Herr Bruno", as the staff affectionately called him, became particularly attached to a young, very blond boy after several weeks. The child was almost six years old, big-boned and strong. He appeared to be smiling at Bruno whenever he approached his bed or during meals, when he passed by his table in the cafeteria. Even the attendants and nurses had noticed and were intrigued by the child's reaction, because Andreas was generally unemotional with the other adults and wanted nothing to do with the other children. He never even cried during situations when his peers broke down. But, overall, he was an easy child to manage and his quietness, restraint and independence were of no concern to most of the staff. Bruno interpreted the child's taciturn personality as strength of character.

The staff eventually concluded that the child reacted to Herr Bruno's antics or work accessories, such as when he carried a ladder over his head, red wires strung over his shoulders or his wooden box filled with tools. It was assumed that, to the child, the accessories made Bruno look profoundly different and perhaps funny. Naturally, Bruno, who sorely missed his young son, Giacomo, would play up to the child's reaction. He would lift the ladder over his head and spin it around like a propeller, or he would set the ladder down just to climb up and down for the child's amusement. One time he had a long, yellow electrical cord dangling from his neck. At the end of the cord he had made a loop like a lasso and was attempting to rope Andreas' footboard. All this was going on while standing on the third rung of the ladder, rocking it back and forth as if galloping on a horse. While some children looked on with bewilderment, others giggled. Andreas had the biggest smile on his face. At that instant, unbeknownst to Bruno, Fräulein Schemitsch had walked into the room and was standing near the door. Another few staff members had collected behind her and all were absorbed by the show. The maintenance man and the child were oblivious to the world.

"Bruno," she called out after a few minutes. Bruno turned around to see everyone staring and was somewhat embarrassed. "Surely, if you want to kill yourself there are easier ways of doing it than breaking your neck on the ladder," she said sternly.

"*Scusi, Signora*, but the child seems to love ladders and wires. Perhaps he'll be a fireman when he grows up."

"That's to be seen, so long as you don't kill yourself or kill him in the process."

Chastened and more composed, Bruno came off the ladder, collected his tools and walked away from Andreas, whose hand was still outstretched towards Bruno, his smile beginning to fade.

*

After Antonia made a second pot of espresso coffee, she poured a full cup of the aromatic elixir for the inspector and her husband, followed with a ricotta tart and *biscotti di anice*. Outside, the rain continued and the wind was whipping branches against the house. Annalisa, having smelled the coffee upstairs, came down from her room and, after grabbing a piece of the tart and three *biscotti* on a small plate, went back upstairs with the sweets and a cup of coffee.

*

As often happens, lifetime bonds are forged slowly and over long periods of time. There's no perceptible and singular experience that cements people's lives together, but it does happen. Bruno's attachment to Andreas grew stronger each time he saw him over the course of some seven months. In fact, he became so compulsively preoccupied with this child that he made it a habit to volunteer several hours of work on Wednesday nights, after his regular day job at the railroad. He would finish a few tasks in the basement workshop and then spend the remaining time playing with Andreas.

Bruno had studied an old pre-war map that he acquired from the cook. Initially, his interest had been in the quadrant of the city where he lived, and the new rail lines that had been rerouted through areas of the city that no longer existed. But his analysis of the map led him to find a shortcut to the orphanage. At first, making sense of the map was difficult because entire streets had been cleared of rubble to make way for new construction, and street signs were non-existent. Still, he finally managed to find a shortcut to the orphanage, cutting his travel time to almost half. This new route took him past a vendor that sold coin-sized chocolates and on two occasions he purchased them for Andreas. He often wondered what type of future this child could have if he stayed at the institution. Convinced that the child ought to have a better life, he had some ideas he wanted to express to Fräulein Schemitsch. It took him a few weeks to muster up the courage to make an appointment with the administrator.

On Saturday morning, before starting work, he walked past the infirmary, where several children were recovering from fevers and measles. A new child had been brought in the previous Wednesday and was suffering from serious malnutrition; another was on an IV. One little girl had a broken right leg with a heavy-looking cast. Because it was early and the children were sleeping, all was relatively quiet and no adult was in the room. But he saw several staff members moving briskly in the hallway. As Bruno climbed the steps to the administrator's office, he remembered that he had been in her office only twice during the almost seven months he had been employed there. The first time was when he was hired and the second time, he reframed a window that was rotted from water damage. Unlike that second day, when he had felt that he was there for the purpose of carrying on his employment responsibilities and on invitation, today he felt that he was intruding for his own personal reasons.

He knocked on the door, pushed it open gently and stuck his head in. Fräulein Schemitsch was talking to the spindly, if not gaunt, secretary from the front door area. She was the one who had let him in when he was first interviewed for the job. Her name was Greta. The administrator was not only talking to the secretary but held papers in one hand and a cup of coffee in the other.

"*Guten Morgen,* Bruno," she said as she waved him in.

"*Guten Morgen,*" Bruno repeated, looking at both. The secretary nodded and smiled at Bruno. He wondered if it was for the way he said good morning in German. He smiled back.

"Please come in and have a seat. Would you care for some coffee?" Fräulein Schemitsch asked. Bruno declined the offer by holding up his hands.

"No! But thank you."

She followed the secretary out into the hallway and before shutting the door behind her, she looked at him and said, "Excuse me for two minutes, Bruno. I'll be right with you."

He then spoke with Fräulein Schemitsch for some thirty minutes before he came out of the office. Before she even sat down, and before she could ask him about his family and if he liked the work at the orphanage, he told her that he was interested in knowing about the adoption process. The first few questions were vague and general and structured as if inquiring for a friend or relative. Then, he got more specific, and Andreas' name came up. Bruno learned that there were currently no families interested in adopting Andreas, that the child had some learning disabilities, and that the adoption process was more involved than he realized. For starters, some preliminary screening would be required to determine the type of household the child would be placed in and the family's ability to provide for his welfare. He and his wife, Antonia, would have to be interviewed at the orphanage since they lived in a different country and too far away for anyone at the orphanage to visit. Assuming all went well and the recommendations were favorable, the local magistrate would have to make his own assessment before the proper adoption papers could be signed and issued. He would also need a visa and other papers from the Italian Consulate to permit the child's entry into Italy.

Fräulein Schemitsch told Bruno that she would help him in that regard, if and when they got to that point. She still had contacts with the Italian Embassy in Berlin where she was employed prior to getting married. If all went well, Andreas could be home with Antonia and his other child within three months because it took that long to process everything.

Bruno thanked the administrator profusely and told her that he would immediately contact his wife and make arrangements for her to be here in ten to fifteen days.

That same night Bruno composed a letter to his wife that expressed his excitement and optimism at the prospect of adopting this child.

August 23, 1947

Carisima Antonella,

I hope this letter finds you and little Giacomo well. Things are good here.

As you know, on weekends I've been working at St Mary's Orphanage for the last seven months. During this time, I've had an opportunity to get to know Andreas (the little blond boy I told you about in the two previous letters). He seems to have taken a liking to me. Whenever I'm in the room he responds to me like no other, including the staff. I feel genuine love for this little man.

This morning I inquired of Signora Moretti-Schemitsch, the administrator, about the possibility of adopting him.

She left me hopeful. I left her with not such an unfavorable impression. But, as a first real step, she would like to meet and talk to both of us. Would you like to come?

She also gave me a little background on the child's mother. And this is what I learned: she said that Andreas was born to a hotel employee in Oslo, Norway. This young woman had the misfortune of getting pregnant during the war. The father was a German lieutenant who had promised to marry the girl and take her to Germany when hostilities ended. But, as destiny would have it, he was transferred with his unit to the Northern Front and was killed by a mortar shell soon after the child's birth. Subsequently, the mother's family disowned her because of the illicit affair. So, there you had a young woman with no family, no money and no job in the middle of a war. What could she do? It became obvious she could not provide for the child and gave him up to an orphanage in Oslo. She always believed that a decent family would adopt him and give him the things in life she could not. When the war ended, the Norwegian government repatriated him with many other children back to Germany, to the father's birthplace. The child was moved from place to place until eventually he found his way to St Mary's Orphanage – a truly unbelievable story. Considering the ordeal this child has experienced at such a tender age, anyone with a heart would be moved.

I truly believe that God has special plans for this little boy. Considering that it has been three years since Giacomo's birth and we haven't been blessed with any more children, I believe we are part of that plan. Besides, Andreas could certainly be a great help on the farm and would be good company for Giacomo.

I am enclosing 200 lira for your train fare and travel expenses, assuming that you will be coming. If so, meet me in Milan on September 10th, at my cousin Alberto's house. I will promptly notify him of our intentions.

As far as little Giacomo and the farm animals are concerned, your family could look after them temporarily while you and I looked into this most important matter as soon as possible. I think you will take a strong liking to Andreas as soon as you see him.

If all goes well, he could be living under our roof before Christmas and calling you *Mama* and Giacomo, *fratello* (brother).

Abbracci e baci a tutti
(Hugs and kisses to all),
Bruno

The letter reached Cosenza on Tuesday, August 30th. It had taken seven days for the letter to arrive in Cosenza. But since the postal system did not deliver in remote areas where they lived, and Antonia didn't pick up her mail in town until Friday, her actual receipt was September 3rd. At times, the mail would take weeks to arrive from foreign countries like the US. It often happened that someone would learn of a relative's death maybe months after their loved one was buried.

While Bruno had suggested that Antonia's family care for little Giacomo and their farm animals during her absence, she knew better. Antonia certainly knew that her family could look after Giacomo and that they would be delighted to do so, but the farm animals were a problem. Bruno was not aware that her father had had an accident two days earlier while chopping wood and could not move around. Instead, she would have to ask her neighbors, the Benedettas, to care for the animals. After all, Bruno had known Matteo Benedetta since childhood and each had bartered for the other's labor during harvest time. She did not feel uncomfortable asking them for help. Matteo was very reliable and he knew that they would do the same for his family.

Thus, goaded by the urgency of the letter and the excitement of sharing the good news, Antonia decided to see Matteo and Francesca that same night. But her head was preoccupied with her husband's affection for this child, Andreas. He had mentioned this little boy in his previous letters but this quick movement of events struck her as uncharacteristic of her husband since he had never spoken of adoption before. Maybe God, working in his mysterious ways, had planted the seed in Bruno's mind. Yes, it was God's will! As she walked to her neighbors' house, she became more convinced of that and quietly started reciting the "Our Father," while looking up in a tree and seeing a crucifix formed by the criss-crossed branches. The child was to have a new family, her family. He was to have a new mother, herself. Now she finally understood why the Good Lord had not blessed them with a child of their own flesh and blood for the last three years. They were going to be the parents of a very special, blessed child. The Holy Mother had listened to her prayers and entreaties and answered them. She was going to have another son.

In the end, saving a child from an institution was indeed an act of divine intervention, but her family would also be blessed and Bruno was right. There would be two extra hands during harvest time and someone else to care for the animals.

Antonia considered herself a dutiful wife and a good mother but sometimes stood her ground with Bruno. In this case things were different, it was God's plan, an answer to her many prayers to the Blessed Mother. Since this was God's plan it was a critical matter, and she did not think of crossing Bruno. In the past, even when Bruno showed his temper, she had challenged him and he had yielded. Then, they both cried over their bickering. Slowly, she came to realize that Bruno cared for her deeply. Now, he had insisted on meeting her at Alberto's house because he didn't want her to travel alone in a foreign country; he had taken several days off work which was difficult.

As expected, and without hesitation, Matteo and Francesca jumped at the idea of helping. Matteo went further in accommodating his neighbor by insisting that he escort her on horseback to the train station in Cosenza the day after tomorrow. Antonia spent the following day making preparations. That night she couldn't sleep, partly from being tired and partly from wondering if she had considered and planned for everything. She felt somewhat apprehensive until she purchased the ticket and boarded the train bound for Rome where she would change rails for the express to Milan. Antonia had never traveled so far by herself, but her faith and trust were in the Lord and his Mother. She bid goodbye to Matteo with a peck on the cheek before boarding. Matteo was still waving while he was tying the reins of the horse she had ridden on to the saddle of his own animal.

She found that she could not sleep on the train because of the whistle-blowing and the commotion from passengers getting on and getting off at the various stations. Antonia was in a catatonic state until she saw a black man with a small beaten-up valise walking about the station in Rome. She perked up, as if smelling salts had been passed under her nose. She had known that black people lived in Africa but had never seen one before today. Then she saw him stop a railroad employee to ask directions. The train employee was talking to him and pointing. Evidently, this black man could also speak Italian! As she glanced around for signs indicating the transfer line to Milan, she could not help herself gazing once more in the direction of the African man who was mixing into the crowd but still standing taller than anyone else.

When she arrived at the Milan train station, she received an exceptionally warm welcome from her husband, Bruno, and cousin Alberto. This was Antonia's second visit to Alberto and Veronica's home. The first had been with Bruno on their way back from their honeymoon in Lake Como several years back. Since then Alberto and Veronica had had two children and managed to buy the home they had rented for several years. It was nothing elegant but was in a modest, neat, middle-class community with all the amenities very convenient. As she remembered it the house had a stone patio with roses climbing on one side and geraniums and a variety of other flowers in large ceramic pots. Two balconies faced the street from the upper floor. The first floor was virtually all marble and the upstairs had wide natural planks of wood on the floor like one would expect in a Swiss cottage.

What was important to Alberto was the short distance to his work from his home. He was a second-level clerk with the Department of Justice in the White-Collar Crime Division in the center of the city. From what Bruno had told her, he was instrumental in preparing court calendars and reviewing and filing certain proposed court orders and reviewing related documents. His office was located on the fourth floor so, aside from attorneys with particular inquiries, he rarely interacted with the public.

Veronica and Alberto, during dinner, asked them about their family and the trip, then asked them more questions about what Bruno had disclosed to them over the telephone.

"So, what's with the little boy, a German orphan, you're thinking of adopting?" Alberto asked, not realizing that his cousin would talk for the next ten minutes non-stop about the child.

Finally, Alberto suggested that if they had a few testimonials it would make their case stronger and, since Bruno and Antonia were leaving the next morning, Alberto went upstairs after dinner to prepare three affidavits. Veronica and the children were left alone to entertain the guests.

About an hour and a half later Alberto came down and read them the three documents. One was to be signed by Alberto and his wife before a notary. They would run around the corner and take care of that before dessert. The other two were intended for friends or neighbors who knew them well. In general, the documents praised them for being people of good character, having a tight-knit family, being church members in good standing, farm owners who made contributions to their community, etc. In the documents, Alberto had stressed that they were economically self-sufficient under normal circumstances. It was only in situations as currently existed that Bruno sought work abroad to better his family, such as when the harvest was bad or because of the post-war turmoil. But the family never lacked the necessities of life, even in bad times. Before the summation paragraph, Alberto pointed out that even though Bruno and Antonia had had a sixth-grade education they realized the importance of a higher education and would strive to send their children to secondary schools, at the very least.

Over dessert, while Antonia was showing some pictures of little Giacomo to Veronica and her children, Alberto explained to Bruno that from what he read about Germany, after the Nazis were defeated, the country was in a state of depression, the economy was in shambles and its government and social institutions were very ineffective. The number of displaced children and orphans was overwhelming. Part of the problem was the tens of thousands of children that had been abducted from Poland and other Eastern European countries by the Nazis for the purpose of fulfilling the Third Reich's obsession with "Germanization" and increasing the population. The other part of the problem was the large number of illegitimate children born to German women, often a result of rape by Russian and American occupying forces. These factors had created pressures that allowed for a more lenient adoption process that still existed.

According to Alberto, church and public agencies were often permitted to screen the potential adopting parents without court hearings. Once the agency had interviewed the prospective parents and the child had undergone medical evaluation, and a determination was made that the biological parents were non-existent, then the paperwork was submitted to a magistrate who, as a formality, would sign off on the adoption documents and grant the new parents the right to call their child by their surname.

In Bruno and Antonia's case, Alberto assured them that the opinion of the administrator of the orphanage and its associated doctor would probably be sufficient. He was trying to alleviate their apparent anxiety. The cousin also pointed out that character references and the fact that Bruno worked at the facility, and the staff knew him and they were happy with his work, were bound to be favorable. As a last resort, he could even ask his railroad employer if he would testify on his behalf. But at the end, both of them would come across as qualified parents who could give Andreas the love and care that he would otherwise not receive in an institution. Also, having little Giacomo close in age as a companion to Andreas couldn't hurt.

The newness of Alberto's house, the change of beds and the anxiety about meeting the administrator all were contributing factors to a restless night of little sleep. Bruno and Antonia were up early but didn't want to walk around, fearful that they would make noise and wake up Veronica and Alberto, so they quietly stole some time for each other in the early morning hours when the flesh is often most receptive. It was only when they got a whiff of the cappuccino that they rolled out of bed. By the time they were washed and got down to the kitchen Veronica had prepared each two poached eggs and some toast. Alberto soon joined them.

At 8.45am their cousin dropped them off at the train station. The express was bound for Geneva; there they would transfer for their final destination, Munich. Bruno had been diligent in purchasing tickets the previous day while waiting for his wife's arrival. They avoided the long lines and boarded as soon as the train pulled into the station.

On the train ride through Switzerland, Bruno became a little more talkative and affectionate than usual, perhaps to lessen his wife's anxiety or because of his own nervousness in anticipation of his wife meeting Andreas for the first time. In one instance, while crossing one of numerous tunnels, he actually kissed Antonia on the lips and held her hand, assuring her that everything would be fine. He found comfort in knowing that the orphanage was aware that Andreas had been living in institutions for some four years and no one had come forward to adopt him or even make inquiries; it was a known fact, and not just by the staff, that the older a child got the more difficult it became for an adoption and that, unfortunately, some of the children would be condemned to live at the facility until old enough to live on their own.

On crossing the border into Germany, they had to show their documents at two checkpoints. Bruno knew the process and had his papers ready to avoid any snags. When they got to the Munich station Bruno told Antonia that buses and taxis were limited, or almost non-existent, so they decided to walk the two miles to his rooming house. There they would share a small room. Since the bed was too small to accommodate both of them Bruno had asked the housekeeper for some extra blankets. Then he took the mattress down from the cot, placed it on the floor and arranged the blankets next to the mattress so that they would sleep next to each other.

The following day they were to meet with Fräulein Moretti-Schemitsch and Dr. Reinhold Hoffmeyer, who was associated with the orphanage and visited once a week, unless some children were critically ill.

Antonia had packed her best dress in her suitcase, normally reserved for Sunday Mass, and Bruno took out his well-worn blue suit from his closet. The last time he had worn the suit was at his job interview. They got to the orphanage before the appointment so Bruno showed her around and introduced her to two people on the staff. It wasn't long before Antonia asked if they could be permitted to see Andreas. When Bruno pointed him out from the glass window the boy was still sleeping. Antonia fixed her eyes on him and smiled.

"*Quanto e bello* (How beautiful he is). *Dorme como un angelo*," she told Bruno. "*E piu di quello che mi hai detto* (He is everything and more than what you've told me)." She crossed herself, and thanked the Good Lord.

Chapter 14

Making Difficult Decisions

When they finally arrived at the administrator's office, they were escorted by a staff member to a small side room with six chairs. Three adults were inside. Bruno knew Fräulein Schemitsch and Dr. Hoffmeyer but not the second woman. She was introduced to be from Child Services, a government agency. Dr. Hoffmeyer sat at the end of the table. They seemed to be discussing the condition of the children in the infirmary when Bruno and Antonia walked in. After a quick introduction and some polite small talk about their trip, they were invited to take a seat opposite the administrator and Frau Schneider, the woman from Child Services. Fräulein Schemitsch closed two files and pulled out a new one from the small stack. On its cover, printed in large black letters was the name, Andreas Kortig-Kuhlemann.

"Now that we know each other and why we're here," said the administrator, "I'd like to give you a little background."

Fräulein Moretti-Schemitsch proceeded to tell the other two that Bruno had worked for the orphanage for about seven months and that he had given the facility many hours of voluntary work. That the facility's appearance and much of its efficiency was largely due to

Bruno's efforts and, consequently, the staff were very pleased with his overall performance. Bruno had spoken to her previously about the possibility of adopting Andreas and had brought his wife, Antonia, to visit, in pursuance of that objective. Antonia stood there quietly, fidgeting a little with her hands, occasionally smiling. Bruno knew she did not understand a damn word. The administrator, who spoke Italian, was kind enough to interject, from time to time, and explain what was said in Italian. Bruno, on the other hand, nodded as if he understood. In reality, he understood little, although he did have a sense of the mood and direction of the conversation.

"I understand that you live in Calabria where you have a farm?" asked Frau Schneider, directing her question to Antonia. The administrator translated.

"Yes. We own forty acres there and are essentially self-sufficient," responded Bruno, already feeling defensive and at the same time protective of his wife. "The only time I seek work away from home is after a few years of bad harvest or, as in this case, post-war economic conditions. None of these circumstances are one individual's fault. Currently, I'm working for the Munich rail system, and at other times I've worked as a carpenter. My family has always been provided for even in the worst of times." After nervously spluttering out the words, he cleared his throat.

"How many other family members do you have living with you?" asked the doctor, who seemed to be about sixty years old. He wore glasses and had a precise part in his well-combed but thinning hair. He had a heavy accent. Not German, perhaps Swiss, Bruno thought.

"One child, his name is Giacomo," answered Antonia. "He's three years old. We tried to have another but God hasn't sent us others yet. Maybe it's His will that we're here."

"Assuming that no one has misgivings about adopting this particular child, what could you offer him that he's not receiving in this facility?" asked Frau Schneider.

"We can give him the bonds of a family, love, perhaps more than here and more than the basic necessities of life," Bruno said. "He could grow up, play and share experiences with Giacomo, who is close to his age, and we could provide schooling beyond the elementary level." Bruno finished his answer with a smile, not because he was pleased with his delivery, not because he could top whatever the orphanage could ever do for the child, but because he truly saw in his mind's eye the images of a better future for Andreas.

"Herr Salvaggi, now that you have brought up Andreas' schooling, it is time we disclosed some medical conditions that Andreas has been diagnosed with." While saying this, Dr. Hoffmeyer reached across the table for the file that the administrator had pulled out of the stack and turned it right side to face him and opened it.

"What do you mean, 'medical condition'?" asked Antonia, once Bruno translated this, with concern in her voice and on her face.

"Well," the doctor started, "each child in this facility has undergone a medical examination, and while some have some serious problems, others are in excellent health. Andreas has shown to be a little slower in mental development than some of his peers. However, he doesn't appear to have any negative, distinctive physical conditions, with the exception of some ear infections." The doctor's finger moved down the page as he scanned the handwritten notes. "There's some speech delay that shows up as stuttering, but this doesn't mean that he can't catch up if given enough stimulation. Unfortunately, this orphanage doesn't have the staff and resources to provide what a family could provide on an ongoing basis. Please realize that many of these children have had incredible hardships during their short lives. Many were born in the middle of a war and many of these problems will be transcended." He stopped and looked up at Bruno and then Antonia.

Fräulein Schemitsch felt obligated to clarify, summarizing in one sentence what the doctor had said in a paragraph. "Physically, the child is fine from what we know, it's just that he is not at the level he should be for a child his age."

Bruno moved closer to the edge of his chair, while Antonia was wringing her hands in her lap.

"Does this mean he will never speak or walk right?" asked Antonia with trepidation in her voice, fearful of the answer she might get. Then, when another thought crossed her mind, she inquired further: "Will he be able to take care of himself as he gets older?"

"No, it doesn't mean that," clarified the doctor, while showing a bit of impatience. "Andreas walks already, he speaks with some difficulty but should improve as he gets older. He may not adapt to new situations quickly but he will be able to do what other children do, just a little slower."

"What caused this problem?" asked Bruno, more concerned than inquisitive as he held his hand over his mouth and ran it down to his chin.

"We don't know for sure," the doctor said. "Medicine doesn't have all the answers. Probably hereditary factors at play. Sometimes it could even be a disease the mother acquired while the child was *in utero*."

Then an unbearable silence came over the room as if the reality of the problem dashed everyone's hopes.

Frau Schneider looked at both Bruno and his wife compassionately and finally spoke.

"From what I've been told and have seen during this short period, I will be frank in saying that I would recommend that Andreas be adopted by your family. I believe that life on a farm would be less stressful for the child than living here or in a large city. He is amiable and very strong for his age. But the ultimate decision is yours."

Bruno and Antonia looked at each other in a state of confusion, each hoping that the other's conviction would override everything. Bruno took a deep breath, but neither spoke.

"Let me suggest something," said Fräulein Schemitsch. "Why don't you both take your time and visit with the child today and tomorrow morning? We'll meet back here at three tomorrow to talk it over." Everyone nodded in agreement.

"*Questa e una buona idea* (This is a good idea)," Bruno added.

"*Grazie a tutti voi,*" Antonia followed up. "*Specialmente a lei dottore per la valutazione medica* (Especially to you, Doctor, for the medical evaluation)."

"*Domani torneremo qui, indipendente da como abbiamo deciso* (We'll be back here tomorrow regardless of our decision)," said Bruno, looking at Fräulein Schemitsch to translate.

They didn't waste any time. After leaving the meeting Antonia followed her husband to the basement of the orphanage, to a storage room. Bruno stood on his tiptoes and felt around the upper shelf. Then he brought down something wrapped in brown paper and opened it for his wife to see: a beautiful spinning top painted in a rainbow of colors.

"I got this from a vendor at one of the railroad stations. Do you think the boy will like it?" he asked, flashing back to the time he was a kid playing with a top that was constructed of wood and operated with a string. The one his wife was inspecting was made of a light metal, probably tin.

"It's very pretty," Antonia said, smiling, as she put it in her palm and pressed the rod downwards; she giggled.

They found Andreas in the lunchroom sitting at a remote table with four other children who appeared to be drawing on pieces of cardboard. Bruno spoke a few words with one of the women attendants and then he and Antonia went directly to the child's table. When he saw Bruno, a coy smile came to Andreas' face, but upon seeing Antonia he shyly put his head down. Bruno tousled the child's blond hair and told him he had something for him. Bruno held the brown wrapping before the child and explained that before he gave it to him, he wanted Andreas to meet Antonia. At that point the child raised his head slightly and looked at Antonia suspiciously from the corner of his eye. Antonia tried to touch him but he pulled away. The other children looked at both adults with curiosity. They knew Bruno as the maintenance man but they seemed to wonder if the lady was Andreas' mother or someone related to him.

Bruno coaxed the child to leave the table and walk with them to a playroom down the hallway. Antonia didn't take her eyes off Andreas but let Bruno do the talking since the child felt more at ease with him. In the playroom they were alone. They sat at a wooden table with benches near a window where the sunlight was filtering in. There, Bruno handed him the gift. Andreas quickly unwrapped it in silence. When the sunlight from the window bounced off the toy and a kaleidoscope of colors reflected off the walls, his face lit up. With his finger he traced the brightest color around the toy's circumference and then turned it over, looking at Bruno in puzzlement. Bruno took it. And in halting, broken German, tried to explain how the toy worked. As the top spun on the table a wide smile came to the child's face. Then he started flapping his hands in uncontrolled excitement.

"He really likes it," Bruno whispered to his wife.

After several minutes, unexpectedly, the child turned to Bruno and said,

"*Danke!*"

"*Bitte schön*," Bruno responded.

Antonia had been watching the interaction without interrupting. She was pleasantly surprised at the child's good manners and his endearing smile. Her initial fears and concerns seemed to dissolve. She remembered having a few *biscotti* that she had not eaten on her trip and they were still in her purse. When she gave them to Andreas, he looked at her shyly and didn't accept them until Bruno intervened and passed them on from Antonia to him. He put one in his mouth, smiled, and returned his attention to the spinning top.

The three of them spent much of the afternoon together. It was a beautiful afternoon with a gentle breeze and warm sunshine. They spent a little more time in the games room; Antonia was making some progress playing with Andreas. Then they walked outside and around the facility. Antonia admired the small farm and all the vegetables that were being cultivated. There was even a small patch of flowers growing next to a cypress tree where there was a patch of grass and a weathered wooden bench. Some of the older children were tilling the soil and weeding the plants in one area while, in another section, others were irrigating vegetables with buckets of water being carried back and forth from the well. Antonia told Bruno she was surprised that there was hardly any supervision; yet, the children seemed to be very serious and efficient with their tasks. An older woman did appear sometime later carrying some wooden sticks. She dropped them when Bruno approached to speak with her. Andreas followed him, hand in hand, as he clutched his new toy in the other hand.

At dusk they brought the child back to the facility. Bruno told Andreas that they would be back tomorrow to see him and kissed the child on the forehead as they were leaving. Antonia realized that she was still an unknown factor to the child and merely waved and said, "*Ciao.*" When Bruno and Antonia were about to leave, they turned around and saw Andreas' hand opening and closing in rapid motion as if to say goodbye. The child had a sad look on his face, as his blue eyes were fixed on Bruno. Later, Antonia swore to Bruno that she had seen Andreas' lips moving as if he was whispering, "*Ciao.*"

The next morning, they were up early. They decided to get some coffee and a couple of eggs for breakfast at a little shop that Bruno had stumbled on the second month he worked at the orphanage. It was a very unassuming storefront with two large glass panels and a roll-up awning. As you walked in, there were two tables to the left and a small counter to the right where coffee and some different breakfast items were sold. Except for them, not a soul was in the store. Toward the rear was a deli case with various types of raw pork products and raw chickens. On one side of the store were two shelving units with a variety of dry goods.

Bruno wolfed down his eggs and coffee. Antonia was still nibbling on hers, when he told her he wanted to see if they had anything for lunch in the rear of the store. There, Antonia could see Bruno was having a little problem communicating with the butcher who had served them breakfast. When they ordered breakfast, he seemed to have a nice personality and kind eyes. He had been patient in speaking slowly to Bruno and Antonia that even she understood. Now, the butcher went into a refrigerator and came out with a small tray. Finally, Bruno nodded approval. It wasn't until later that Antonia would learn that her husband had asked for white sausages – *weisswurst* – pretzels and sweet mustard. The problem had been in asking if the butcher had any that were cooked. In addition to the sweet sausages he bought some *knodel* – potato dumplings – a little bottle of Riesling and a fruit drink.

After paying for the breakfast and the wrapped lunch, he came back to the table where Antonia was about finished.

"I got something for us and I got something for Andreas," he said.

"I saw that you almost didn't," she replied.

"I'm not quite the linguist yet, but between basic words and phrases and hand gestures I manage," he said. "It's like being thrown in the middle of the ocean. You utilize any means you can to save yourself."

They were at the orphanage a little before eleven. This time they found Andreas with several other children near the storage shack. The other boys were kicking around a soccer ball on the grass and Andreas was on the sideline, looking around, lost in his thoughts. When the ball came in his direction, he picked it up and held it. One of the older boys came over to retrieve the ball and reprimanded him for not kicking it back. To Bruno and Antonia, he looked confused, as if he didn't understand the game or was totally unmotivated. But, as Bruno approached, his mood changed and he gave Bruno his characteristic wide smile.

The three of them took a walk for several blocks and figured to be back about noon. Bruno explained to Andreas that they were all going to have lunch together, in the grass, under the big cypress tree. The child flashed another smile until Bruno told him that he was going to get a blanket and their lunch from the basement workroom. That he and Antonia should wait there a few minutes. Instantly, the child's mood changed. As Bruno let go of his hand Antonia grabbed it; the child flinched and put his head down, looking away from Antonia. This was the first time she had actually made physical contact. She was surprised at how delicate, smooth and supple the boy's skin was. She remembered having a couple of tiny mints in her pocket that she had taken from the restaurant counter early in the morning. She handed one to Andreas but he just looked at it, not sure if he should take it. Antonia kneeled before him, opened the mint and pointed with her index finger in her open mouth, demonstrating that it was good to eat. Andreas, instead of taking it from her, opened his mouth wide like a fledgling waiting to be fed by its mother. Antonia saw this as a good sign.

The three spent a few hours having lunch on a blanket under the cypress tree. Andreas had a hearty appetite, eating almost everything they gave him and guzzling his fruit drink. The pretzels were his favorite, the potato dumpling didn't go over well and he left it half unfinished. Antonia was reluctant to bite into the *weisswurst* until Bruno explained that they were basically the same as the sausages she made back home. The only difference was that, in addition to pork, there was veal mixed in and stuffed in the casing. It took a small glass of the Riesling to raise her courage. After a few bites, and another small glass of wine, she ate the strange *wurst* and even enjoyed the half dumpling that Andreas had left on the side.

While Bruno and Antonia finished lunch, Andreas was busy collecting pine cones from the nearby evergreens and dropping them on the corner of the blanket. When Bruno saw him peeking from behind a thick bush, he snuck behind another and they started playing peek-a-boo and running behind the bushes; both totally engrossed in each other, laughing, and oblivious to the world. In that instant, Antonia made her decision.

*

They were a few minutes early for the meeting. No one was there except the part-time assistant who wore a uniform that seemed to be a cross between one worn by nurses and the habit worn by nuns. The fashion blending made some sense considering that the Catholic charities ran the place, but Antonia didn't know that and she seemed perplexed. The door to the small office where the conference took place the previous day was open. They were invited to sit and wait. The administrator and Frau Schneider arrived momentarily. They quickly learned that the doctor would not be joining them since he was attending to one of his patients who had had an appendicitis attack, but that he had made his recommendations to the administrator.

The Salvaggis told the two women what they had done with Andreas. He liked pretzels and *weisswurst* but didn't care for *knodel*; that he liked to play hide and seek and peek-a-boo; that he was a little frightened by the activities in the surrounding neighborhood when they went for a walk. Finally, Antonia couldn't resist telling them that Andreas and Bruno were almost inseparable. Then, almost simultaneously, they said that they wanted to proceed with the adoption and they were ready to do whatever was necessary. Antonia reached for her bag under the table and placed it on her lap where she opened it and took out the affidavits that Bruno's cousin had prepared and notarized in Milan, and the one signed by his railroad foreman. The administrator looked at the documents, nodded approval and handed them over to Frau Schneider who also gave them a once-over and placed them in Andreas' file.

Fräulein Schemitsch reminded them that certain documents were also required from the Italian Embassy in Berlin, including a visa for the child, but she would do her best to expedite that part of the process. Additionally, she said that she would recommend, on the basis of interviewing both potential parents and having known Bruno for over seven months, that he was a man of good character and that their family and the farm environment were ideal situations for this child.

When everything was said, Antonia got to ask the final question that was pressing on her mind. "How long will the process take?"

Frau Schneider told her that she could have her paperwork for the magistrate in two weeks and it was hoped that a response from the embassy would take another week or two beyond. The outside time would probably be a month before they could take the child to his new home. They said that for the sake of expediency, it was invaluable that Bruno was in the building to answer any further questions and sign any other document that might be required.

At about four thirty in the afternoon it was over. The two women congratulated them. Bruno and Antonia walked out of the office, arm in arm, feeling relieved, happy and a little sad at the same time, as they were mindful that Antonia was leaving on the six o'clock train for Milan.

Twenty-seven days to the hour, after meeting with Fräulein Moretti-Schemitsch and Frau Schneider, Bruno told Inspector Bellin, Andreas was clutching his hand tightly as they walked along the train platform in the Munich station. They had tickets bound for Milan and one small suitcase containing mostly Andreas' clothing and a few personal belongings, including his spinning top. The visa from the Italian Embassy had arrived (thanks to Moretti-Schemitsch's contacts); the local magistrate in the suburb of Munich had signed the adoption order (the orphanage administrator had given him a glowing report and all the staff members at the facility signed it). And Bruno had prevailed upon his supervisor to give him a week off with the understanding that he would be available on alternating weekends for the next four months.

Inspector Bellin glanced at his watch. It was almost 11pm. Despite the unlimited coffee and sweets consumed, he felt completely exhausted and announced that he should be going. And, if Bruno would be kind enough to finish the story of Andreas Kortig-Kuhlemann and his family's fascinating journey at another time, he would be delighted to hear it. Perhaps it might also assist the investigation. He also invited them as his guests at a nice little restaurant he frequented on the outskirts of Cosenza. Antonia offered that they meet at their house again, but the inspector held firm and it was agreed that he would pick them up at 7pm the day after tomorrow.

Chapter 15

Matteo's Funeral

Lorenzo had arrived in New York Harbor about two weeks after embarking on the ocean liner. Pietro, his youngest uncle, had made many arrangements on his behalf. This included signing a lease for a small apartment. He had been employed at his uncle's construction company several months when he received the dreaded news. It was a telegram delivered at his job site on Monday morning. It was terse and to the point.

> "Lorenzo. Regret to inform. Matteo died.
> Saturday, May 13, 1973, 11.15pm.
> Arrangements for funeral, Tuesday, 9am.
> Francesca and Gabriella by my side.
> Painful time for all. Take courage.
> All our love. Uncle Dominick." (letter follows).

Lorenzo's hands trembled as he read the message on the thin yellow sheet of paper. Then his legs collapsed beneath him and he sat on the front steps of the stick-built home under construction. He reread the telegram. As the trembling subsided a cold shiver took hold. His eyes welled and tears began cascading down his cheeks. His consciousness reached deep into his eighteen years of life with Papa. Then it reached into the future only to see a void. This was permanent, unalterable and unforgivable. He thought about the good times with him; he thought about the fortress that his father was; he thought about Papa's final battle with the disease that claimed him; he thought about his mother and his sister and the pain and grief they were suffering. His dad was like a tent, protecting them. Their tent had just blown away. And it was cold, bone-chilling cold in the middle of the night, in the midst of an unknown desert. His mind was overloaded, confused. He went blank.

Gradually, his thoughts stumbled on guilt and questions came tumbling into his mind. Had he been impetuous? Did he really have to leave his father in that condition? Did he have to be absent from his mother and sister at this point of greatest need? Wasn't there an unspoken bond between them that superseded all else? Had he been selfish in running away to another part of the world? Would he have come to America had it not been for Andreas' life he had extinguished?

Then his psyche traversed guilt and took him to the very essence of life. Was that night in the barn to control, to direct, to pervade the course of his entire existence? If so, where was "free will," when you reacted as you were programmed by your culture? And then, what was left of free will when you accounted for both your nature and your cultural requirements? Dregs, was the answer. The bottom of the flask had nothing left but dregs. Free will in a civil society was nothing short of an illusion.

He folded the telegram along its creases and put it in his shirt pocket.

"Lorenzo, are you alright?" asked Gustav, his foreman, as he stood over him wearing an overflowing tool belt. Gustav saw the emotional turmoil on his face and squatted next to him.

"I just received a telegram. My father died," Lorenzo said, lowering his head.

"My deepest sympathies," said Gustav, showing shared pain in the manner he enunciated the words. "He was sick for some time, wasn't he?" the foreman asked.

"Yeah, he fought a long debilitating battle, but he lost," answered Lorenzo, his voice cracking.

"Your Uncle Pietro was telling me about his poor health on Saturday when he was doing payroll. Your father will be missed."

"Not just because he was my father, but he was a good man," Lorenzo said.

"I have no doubt," Gustav replied. After a moment of quiet, he added, "Are you planning on flying back for the funeral?"

"No. We said our goodbyes before I came here."

"Well, go home. Take a few days off. In fact, take as much time as you need." Gustav spoke in a paternal voice.

"I don't think I should. Besides, I wouldn't know what to do with myself. I think working will help me keep my mind off things."

"Alright, but if you need to take some time, don't hesitate. I know it's difficult, I've been there with both my parents."

"Thank you, I appreciate it."

Gustav put his arm around Lorenzo and pulled him close without saying anything else. Then he stood up and went to the back of his open van searching for something.

*

The letter promised in the telegram came about a week later, four pages of small script on very thin, white, onion skin paper. His sister wrote the letter but his mother, in her own handwriting, had added a few short paragraphs at the end. Lorenzo scanned the letter and read his mother's words first.

Dear Lorenzo,

    Your sister and I miss you dearly, as well as everyone else.

    It's been a trying time for all of us recently. Even though we expected Papa to succumb to his illness, it's still hard to process his departure and to deal with such big emptiness. One of the things that keeps me going is that *our third child* will soon come into the world. And you and Gabriella will soon have a little brother or sister.

    I have received a letter from your Uncle Pietro. He praises your hard work and says you're a quick learner. He even said he cannot believe how fast you're learning English.

    I've asked Gabriella to update you on our situation here, because I've been experiencing some fatigue and nausea. This is a normal condition of late-term pregnancy. Nothing to worry about, I remember having the same symptoms when you and Gabriella were born.

    I'll end here.

    I love you. Stay safe, and take good care of yourself. With all the love a mother can possibly have for a child.

    Mama.

Lorenzo learned that Uncle Dominick had proposed hitching the horses to a wagon and having the casket horse-drawn for the two-mile stretch to the cemetery. He would control the reins and lead the funeral procession that would follow behind. Uncle Dominick had felt that Matteo was entitled to nothing less than what a head of state got when he passed away. He had seen that kind of tribute in the papers and on television when government leaders were brought to their final resting place. However, this idea was short-lived. After managing to pull the wagon out from the rear of the barn and cleaning it, he noticed that one of its wheels was cracked and bounced up and down as it rolled on the hard soil, so the idea of a stately horse-drawn funeral procession was dashed.

Matteo's body was laid out in his bedroom on the second floor of the house on Sunday and Monday. Most of the bedroom furniture was removed to other rooms. Chairs were set up across from the casket. Over the casket, on the wall, hung a crucifix and below that a picture of the Holy Family. Flowers, some in the shape of crosses and others in the shape of hearts, were laid on a table and others overflowed on a blanket on the floor. The aunts had brought over prepared dinners, casseroles and platters that sat on the dining room table for hours, uncovered, with flies swarming around until someone shooed them away.

Father Adano had been called on Sunday afternoon to say a few prayers for Matteo. He had been there for about two hours to pray with the grievers and to overload his plate twice from the food trays set out in the dining room. Before he left, he took Francesca by the hand and walked her into the next room; Uncle Dominick followed.

"Francesca, I know you have plans to have Matteo's wake at home and to have a sermon here and at the cemetery. But it is of the utmost importance to have a Mass in church, in the House of the Good Lord. If not, I cannot join the procession or say Mass at the cemetery," said the priest. "Everyone has an obligation to see Matteo's soul properly depart."

"But, Father, it's such a hardship to bring the body to the church considering the distance. Many relatives and friends are old and might not be able to make the journey," said Francesca, whimpering.

"Perhaps, I could use the truck to take the coffin to church. Having the pall-bearers carry the body for that distance, in this heat, is almost impossible," said Dominick.

"I think it's an excellent idea. The Lord always helps us find a solution."

"I think I can accommodate the three of us in the truck," said Dominick.

"I will not be one of the three. You, Francesca and Gabriella belong together. I will walk with everyone else. My place is in front of the procession," said Father Adano, in no uncertain terms.

*

After the idea of the horse-drawn casket was aborted, Dominick spruced up the truck even though it was twelve years old, was a faded red color, and was not in the best mechanical condition. The hinges on the back panel were also broken. He rectified this problem by placing two wedges of wood behind the casket to prevent any sliding on steep grades or when the truck went over ruts and potholes.

Uncle Dominick managed to convince the relatives that he was going to use the truck. Francesca was too distraught to give it a second thought and assumed that her brother-in-law had Matteo's best interest in mind. The other relatives, because of Dominick's age and his closeness to the deceased, deferred to him.

After all-day and night vigils on Sunday and Monday, the immediate family and closest friends met the next day at 8am at Francesca's home. A black and purple banner had been placed over the front door proclaiming Matteo's death and, to some, Ascension into Heaven. Francesca and her daughter had not slept much for the last two nights and their eyes were red and irritated from frequent weeping over twenty-four hours. Every new visitor that came to express their condolences or say something kind not only released new tears but resumed the weeping of the wife and daughter.

Bruno and Antonia Salvaggi came together on Sunday afternoon to pay their last respects and to temporarily put their differences with the Benedetta's aside. Truly, in their hearts, they came more to avoid criticism from neighbors than out of sadness.

Antonia was dressed in black, from head to toe. She had her black hair in her typical bun, maybe pulled a little tighter than usual. Bruno wore a black suit, white shirt and a skinny blue tie. Antonia brought her bible and rosary and for several hours sat with the other women in a semicircle. They recited passages from the gospels out loud and recited the rosary in a sing-song voice over and over again. When they finished, they took turns kneeling next to the casket and offering up personal prayers. When it was Antonia's turn, she kneeled next to the deceased and hunched over with the bible in her lap like a sparrow burying its head in its feathers on a frigid day. Then she crossed herself three times, for the Heavenly Father, the Son and the Holy Spirit, and said a short prayer. Following, she crossed herself nine times; three times were for each member of the Trinity, to make her invocation more powerful. These actions were followed by a multiple of other prayers, repeatedly, until two women came and took her by the arm. She was still praying and crossing herself as they walked her back to her seat.

Uncle Dominick and his family had gone home to get a few hours of sleep late Monday night and were back by sunlight the next morning. The truck was spiffed up and he had parked it adjacent to the porch so that the pallbearers wouldn't have to walk farther than necessary. At a quarter to eight Dominick rounded up four male family members and instructed them as to what would happen. He also instructed the other mourners present as to procedure. Francesca and Gabriella were to ride in the truck with him and all others were to follow behind. Once the church services were over, the priest, friends and neighbors would follow the casket to the cemetery. After the interment the family members would regroup back at the house for a little pasta and other nourishment, provided again by the aunts.

When it was time, the plain wooden casket was closed, and Francesca and several other women had to be pried away. It seemed that they reinforced each other's misery so that when one started with a passionate cry or painful wail the others would follow. The men tried hard to remain strong and solemn, and whenever emotions seemed to overwhelm them, they would either stare out the window or walk out the room. Despite suppressing their emotions, one could still see their eyes were red and puffy from their personal anguish. Matteo had been well liked and respected by most of the people in the hills.

Four men carried Matteo and his coffin downstairs from the second-floor bedroom at 8.15am. They placed the casket in the bed of the truck. Uncle Dominick adjusted the wooden box directly in the middle, between the two side panels, and then pushed it as far back as possible against the sheet metal, behind the driver's seat. The truck's back panel did not exist since he removed it. So, he remembered to wedge the two triangular blocks of wood behind the coffin to stabilize it from rolling backwards.

As the truck drove away from the house and down the long dirt driveway to the unpaved public road the procession of some thirty-seven people showed some structure and order. At the very end of the line were some great-aunts and uncles and Matteo's godfather, Pasquale, followed by his inseparable mutt, Rudolfo. Whenever the procession stopped for any reason, Rudolfo sat on his hindquarters, at attention as if at a military drill. Despite their advanced age and assorted infirmities, the whole lot of octogenarians had insisted on seeing Matteo to his final resting place and would not hear anything about staying home. Much of their social life consisted of attending funerals when they were not attending Mass. Thus, the men had donned their rediscovered, somewhat wrinkled, black suits from the back of their closets or in trunks that were at least one or possibly two generations behind fashion and certainly before the war. The women's wardrobe was of the same period but neater and cleaner, even though the black dresses had a little more mileage and a few moth holes. This clothing was cleaned and pressed between funerals and held at the ready. The couples traveled arm in arm, holding each other up, while those without spouses relied on their canes.

The two-mile journey to the church piazza moved at a crawl but without drama. They arrived some forty minutes late because of the slow pace and the late morning heat that was quickly becoming oppressive. Many of the men were carrying their jackets draped over their arms or thrown over their shoulders, and everyone was sweating and becoming dehydrated. Without hesitation, once at the piazza, most surrounded the public drinking fountain. Others took refuge on benches and under trees, fanning themselves. Uncle Dominick backed his truck with the precious cargo as close as possible to the church's main entrance and then proceeded inside to get the priest. The priest was nowhere to be seen. Finally, in a side room in back of the church, he found an altar boy who informed Uncle Dominick that Father Adano had waited half an hour and then retreated to the rectory where it was cooler. But he would fetch him immediately.

The funeral High Mass went on until about noon. Afterwards, Matteo's sister read some passages from the Missal, and Uncle Dominick and Gabriella spoke to the congregation. Uncle Dominick reminisced about some lighter moments in their lives when they were growing up. Gabriella told them that Matteo was the best father anyone could ever want and told them how he had read bedside stories to her when she was a little girl, *Pinocchio* in particular. It had taken about two weeks to finish the book and, at the end, her father had presented her with a wooden doll that he had lovingly carved with so much precision that it did look like a real boy. To this day she kept it on her nightstand. She said that she would treasure that doll forever and someday pass it down to her own children. The tenderness of her voice, her innocence, her genuine pain and the image she elicited of her papa spending hours carving Pinocchio for his little girl triggered another flurry of emotions in the church.

As the services and eulogies continued, the pews were gradually filled, not only by family and friends. The worshippers had swelled to more than five times the numbers in the procession. The majority of those present were distant relatives and acquaintances; others were curious spectators. The elderly folks were there as a relief from boredom, to get out of the heat, to see who was still alive or to watch a preview of their own demise. A funeral was the most exciting thing in town and made for good conversation. Everyone felt some cathartic relief that the bell had not tolled for them. And Matteo was leaving them with a lesson: that death was fickle and they should appreciate life intensely.

The tears flowed when Father Adano gave the final blessing, when the pallbearers walked out with the coffin, and when the crowd spilled into the piazza. The well-used and over-used handkerchiefs were worked into snowballs and gripped for support by the cryers' tightened fists.

In the piazza, the crowd became completely and hopelessly disorganized. A structured procession began to take place only when Dominick's truck began moving through the narrow streets. Father Adano was, again, offered a ride in the cab but that meant putting Gabriella out and he, again, opposed the idea. He explained that his place was directly behind the truck, at the head of the procession, and next to the other family members.

By 2pm the procession had traveled about a mile. It was midway up the mountain in the direction of the rural cemetery where a freshly dug grave, near Matteo's dead parents, grandparents, various aunts, uncles and cousins, was waiting to receive him. The cemetery itself dated back to the Middle Ages or maybe further back, to the Dark Ages; it was believed that many victims of the Great Plague had been buried there. Unfortunately, the town records didn't go back very far and the headstones didn't give any clue since they were rain-polished, as smooth as ocean pebbles. Chemical reactions also formed dark gray streaks obliterating names and dates. The entranceway, from the west side, had a large wrought iron gate. A six-foot stone wall separated the north side of the graveyard from the dirt road. It was not possible to enter from the east side or south side because the cemetery property sloped downwards from the mountainside.

Mourners were allowed on Monday through Friday, between 9am and 2pm, and on weekends it was closed, except for one hour after Sunday Morning Mass when Father Adano was in attendance. These were exceptionally good hours for the cemetery workers because, during the last three years, the Provincial Cemetery Workers (PCW) had unionized and had won very favorable terms from the local government. Now they were on strike again and demanded more vacation time. The strike had lasted nine days. During that time no burials took place and caskets were set next to undug plots. Finally, when locals complained of horrendous odors and the health department got involved the strikers got pretty much what they wanted. After the settlement people grumbled that they had better hours than bankers and better pay than doctors.

From the opposite side of the valley, the procession could be seen like a giant black caterpillar undulating along the narrow mountainside, very much like an image from Ingmar Bergman's *The Seventh Seal*. When it came to a precipitous incline a group of stray dogs were seen running into the woods, on the north side of the road, parallel to the procession. At first, many of the mourners saw them but didn't pay much attention to them until Pasquale's mongrel, Rudolfo, started barking uncontrollably at the lot of them. Since he was not on a leash, he broke away from his master in the middle of the procession and darted up the cliff, barking and growling, and then returned to the side of his master. This went on for several minutes until the leader of the stray pack decided to put an end to the annoyance. The leader rushed towards Rudolfo with the other strays following. They all charged, at once, in little Rudolfo's direction. Pasquale picked up the little dog in his arms. Rudolfo, being a cunning and smart dog, accepted his master's protective impulse.

"*Vai via! Vai via!* (Go away! Go away!)" Pasquale shouted, as loud as he could.

"*Scappa!* (Get away from me!) *Che animale disgraziato!* (What a wretched animal!)" another mourner yelled.

"*Che situazione pazza* (What a crazy situation)," a lady told her husband, holding his arm for dear life.

"*Da dove vengono tutti? Vogliono farci a pezzi* (Where did they come from? They want to rip us apart)," Antonia said to Bruno.

The alpha dog jumped on Pasquale, attempting to get at Rudolfo. He bit Pasquale's arm and knocked him to the ground. The other strays barked and displayed their teeth threateningly, circling the other mourners. The women were screaming. The men were shooing the dogs but to no avail. Finally, one dog was kicked in the mid-section and retreated. Another dog was whacked so hard by an elderly man swinging his cane that he toppled over. Pasquale, despite his injuries, held on to Rudolfo steadfastly. Rudolfo remained motionless until the other octogenarians made their way over to see if the dog and his master were dead. Apparently, the commotion and the yelling of the mourners frightened off the strays. They raced away howling.

The screams attracted Uncle Dominick's attention. He responded by slamming on his brakes. Simultaneously, he heard a rumbling sound in the back of the truck, followed by several heavy thuds and an agonizing high-pitched shriek. As he turned to look behind, his face registered shock at what he instinctively knew must've happened. He stepped out, and glanced at the bed of the truck. The casket was missing. Father Adano, standing some five feet behind the rear right fender, was limping on one foot and holding the other with both hands, muttering to himself. His face was contorted in pain. Two men assisted him to the side of the road and sat him down on a large boulder. Meanwhile, other relatives were looking over the edge of the mountainside, aghast at what they were seeing. Some had their hands over their mouths. One elderly aunt and her uncle came over to the passenger side of the truck and attempted to prevent Francesca and Gabriella from getting out, determined to spare them the anguish of going to the edge of the cliff and seeing the grisly sight.

When Uncle Dominick approached the edge of the road, he saw a precipitous drop some thirty feet down. At the bottom, suspended between the trunks of two chestnut trees, was the smashed coffin. The planks of wood at the head of the casket were torn apart. Uncle

Dominick's hands grabbed at his temples as if what he saw was unimaginable. Not only was the upper part of the casket broken apart but his younger brother's torso was hanging out. His arms were dangling in mid-air, his head tilted sideways with mouth open and eyes staring into the sky. His face had the look of terror, like someone whose soul had witnessed the afterlife.

The orderly procession from before was now in total chaos. The pickup truck was parked on a steep grade, in the middle of the road. Behind the truck was the priest, more seriously injured than previously thought. He needed medical attention for what appeared to be a crushed foot, skin excoriated from the middle of his shinbone to his ankle and bleeding profusely. He had pulled his monk's robe up to his knee and was being attended to while sitting on the rock opposite the cliff. A crowd of mourners was gathered near the truck and looked down from the edge of the road. Toward the back of the procession people were trying to assist Pasquale with his injuries. Throngs of grief-stricken people tried to assist others; some guarded against returning dogs with rocks in hand at the ready.

Meanwhile two vehicles traveling in the same direction on the narrow road were patiently waiting behind the procession. The drivers and their passengers were out of their respective cars trying to make sense of what was happening. They saw women crying but didn't know that some were crying because of Matteo's death while others were wailing from the shock of his accidental ejection from his eternal shelter. Children were acting up because they were thirsty, hungry or just uncomfortable, while the hot midday sun beat down on them. Chaos reigned.

Francesca, who had suspected the worst, insisted on leaving the truck and had to be assisted out, slowly.

"*Povero Matteo!* (Poor Matteo!)"

"*Che incidente orribile!* (What a horrible accident!)" she said to her aunt, weeping. "Please help me out of this truck. I need to see Matteo."

"Ouch! What a sharp pain," Francesca exclaimed as Gabriella and her aunt helped her.

"You cannot go to the edge of the cliff. You're in pain, you could get dizzy and fall," said the aunt. "The last thing Matteo would want is any harm to come to this child you're carrying."

"That's right, Mama, just sit there," said Gabriella.

They sat her down next to the priest who had his shoe and sock off while someone was trying to stem the bleeding. Gabriella, overwhelmed by all the events and the accident, was leaning on the side of the truck, sobbing and being comforted by two female cousins.

Uncle Dominick and the pallbearers had gathered around the truck trying to figure out what to do, when a young man from one of the stalled cars, wearing a beret and on leave from the military, suggested that he could run to his home nearby and bring back ropes to pull up the coffin. In the interim, one of the drivers at the end of the procession had offered the priest a ride to the hospital. Father Adano declined. He seized on the moment to show Christian selflessness and to impart a lesson to his flock of what it was like to be a true follower of the humble man from Galilee. He told them that putting Matteo to rest for eternity was more important than tending to his temporal injuries.

Bruno and Antonia Salvaggi had managed to make their way up from midway in the procession to the ledge where the casket had tumbled down the mountainside. Bruno went to speak to Dominick. Antonia craned her neck over the ridge just enough to see Matteo's torso and arms splayed out like a crucifix. She instantly dropped to her knees on the hard dirt and, with rosary in hand, prayed feverishly and loudly.

The young soldier came back quickly as promised. He was sweating profusely, but had several ropes across his neck and shoulder and was carrying a hammer in his right hand. It was decided that, while four men held onto the rope from the road, he would climb down the precipice. Upon reaching his destination he would brace his feet on the tree branches and tie one rope on one side of the casket and then a second rope on the other side. It would then be up to the men wielding the ropes to pull the coffin and corpse up gradually.

The descent went as planned, but the soldier soon realized that with every slight stress he applied against the tree trunk the coffin would slide down a little more precariously. The collective fear from the road was that the casket or corpse would plunge to the very bottom of the mountain. Further complicating the perilous rescue was the soldier's attempt to stuff the body back into the box. It seemed that the more he tried pushing Matteo's torso, head and arms back inside the casket the more resistance he met. This was because the heavy lining inside the coffin had bunched up like tangled-up bed covers. The few mourners near the edge, who were witnessing the rescue, saw this as a sign that Matteo didn't want to go back into the eternal darkness; that he wanted to gaze at the bright sky. Antonia was now joined by a handful of women all genuflecting and praying for Matteo's soul, for a successful rescue or for salvation in general. Father Adano, seemingly oblivious to his own pain and blood loss, blessed them and prayed along.

It was about four o'clock when the soldier and the men yanking on the rope finally got the coffin up on the road. Matteo's head had been forced back in the box but his arms were still extending out over the sides. It wasn't until the top of the coffin was completely pried open and the lining inside readjusted and his eyes closed and his feet pulled down that the soldier and Uncle Dominick were able to align his head and fold his arms over his torso. Then the soldier hammered back the planks on the coffin, as best he could, using the same nails that had been forced out when the casket plummeted down into the trees. This took more time as some nails were completely bent and he had to straighten them out on a rock.

Pasquale refused to let go of Rudolfo, but he was taken to the hospital by one of the Good Samaritans driving a car behind the procession. The vehicle had to turn around on the narrow road. But everyone agreed that, considering Pasquale's age and the depth of the puncture wounds on his leg, he needed to be treated immediately. Some of the relatives had even expressed fear that the dogs might be carrying rabies, which started a new wave of fervent prayers.

The casket was back on the truck and tied down securely. Father Adano was ultimately convinced to ride inside the truck and Gabriella to follow on foot. The makeshift hearse and procession finally arrived at the cemetery about four thirty. As the truck came to a stop by the freshly dug grave, the cemetery supervisor came out of his one-room office building and demanded to speak to Uncle Dominick, alone. The two conversed for some ten minutes before Uncle Dominick came out somewhat perturbed. It turned out that, unless he made an extra payment to the supervisor and the two gravediggers for three hours of overtime, no burial was going to take place. Uncle Dominick tried to explain the incident with the dogs and the accident with the coffin but the supervisor did not care. An accommodation was finally reached when he agreed to pay the three employees for two hours of overtime.

The cemetery prayers were shortened because Father Adano was turning pale due to blood loss from his injured leg, and the interment was expedited. Also, because the gravediggers were still indignant from not receiving full payment for their lost time, they forced the mourners to throw their flowers in the grave instead of allowing each person to go up to the casket. Finally, everyone slowly trickled out of the cemetery.

After dropping Francesca and Gabriella off by their driveway Uncle Dominick took Father Adano to the hospital. It wasn't until 8pm that he rejoined the grieving family at Francesca's house.

Chapter 16

Giacomo's Quest for Control

Giacomo's quest to spread his tentacles and gain increased control of the ever-growing international drug-smuggling and distribution network met with fierce resistance. The Carlo Lozito *'Ndrangheta* family was the biggest impediment. Blood had been shed between the two crime families and was quickly becoming an uncontrollable roller coaster of ever-escalating violence. Lozito was not about to close shop and move on, or even make room in his quarters for an upstart. Negotiating a mutually beneficial arrangement, if it could be done, was the only viable alternative for Giacomo. But Lozito's attitude was that he had staked a claim to the disputed territory first. He had created the market. He had organized it. The connections and distribution network were in place because of his people, and the demand for his merchandise was ever growing. He was the recognized leader by a substantial number of families in the Calabrian organization. And he had underground legitimacy over this new and insatiable industry. No wet-behind-the-ears punk like Giacomo Salvaggi was going to step on his family's toes and maneuver events behind Lozito's back. He was fuming.

Lozito saw his business as being no different from the pharmaceutical industry that traded on the stock market. Like the Pharms with their patents and copyrights, the same rights had vested in Lozito. The principle was the same. The only difference was that the government did not recognize Lozito's rights but Giacomo should, and if he didn't, or refused to, then enforcement was Lozito's obligation and right. He saw Giacomo as too young, too ambitious, too hasty in attempting to grab a large piece of the pie, like a hungry mongrel that comes in from the wild and challenges the alpha dog in his yard for the prime cut of beef. Giacomo Salvaggi had already climbed too far, too fast, without being put in his place, and it was high time to teach him patience. His charm, ingratiating style and professional demeanor were to be brushed aside. Lozito could see through all that for what Giacomo truly was: a pig at the trough. The kid's ambition had to be curtailed, the sooner the better. Thus, he had agreed to meet Giacomo's two lackeys on Lozito's turf, in the city that never sleeps. Giacomo had been warned that if his terms weren't acceptable, all bets were off.

The Boeing 747 landed at Kennedy International at 9pm, June 5th, 1973. The two men carrying duffle bags wore clean-cut and sporting casual, but neat, vacation attire. One was a large, heavy-set man, with a very unusual tattoo on his right forearm, somewhat fading, but still depicting a scene from Hieronymus Bosch's triptych, *The Last Judgment*. The scene was from the lower central panel and was surreal, hellish and scandalous. Death, personified by a black figure with a black hood, was walking and supporting a long pole on his shoulder, like a hunter carrying game. But the game was a naked human being, with legs and wrists bound and suspended from the pole. He was in his fifties and wearing an almond-colored silk shirt, of the best quality. Peeking out from the shirt's sleeve was the tattoo. Although relatively young, the top of his head, like a landing strip, was smooth and shiny. His hair, on the sides and back of his head, was curly and mostly gray. His goatee was salt and pepper, wide and trimmed to perfection. He was a calm man who effused poise and self-assurance. When he spoke, he spoke from the left side of his mouth, a distinctly unique characteristic. His words were controlled and serious.

His gravitas was relieved by an occasional smile from well-defined lips and perfectly set teeth. He had banished fear and learned patience during the multitude of seasons he had walked the Earth, including the time he had spent in the penitentiary twenty-seven years earlier. It was the first week in the prison yard that a violent inmate threatened to make him his bitch when he gouged his eyes out.

The other man was younger, much smaller in stature and of darker complexion. He wore a plain black cap. Both sat in the rear of the plane but in different rows and on opposite aisles. This was for defensive tactical advantages and not to draw attention. The larger man was also convinced that in the eventuality of a crash-landing the passengers in the rear section were more likely to survive. He had read a study in some journal and since forgotten the source but remembered the conclusion.

As the plane's nose turned around and approached the gate, passengers unlatched their seatbelts and jumped in the aisle to retrieve their carry-ons. They had encountered some turbulence while over the Azores and the experience had fomented more anxiety than usual. In addition, family members had been waiting at Kennedy's arrival gate much too long because of the delayed take-off from Rome's Fiumicino Airport. Both men waited patiently while the other passengers hurried to disembark.

They were scheduled to be in New York for three days. No personal time. The trip was strictly for business. They were to first meet with Don Carlo Lozito the following day and, second, resolve another smaller matter that had been simmering for nearly a year. This had to do with the disappearance of their employer's brother.

Giacomo was not as concerned about his adopted brother's disappearance as with the insulting thought that someone had the audacity to harm anything associated with himself. He and Andreas had never been close, despite his parents' plans. Where Andreas was light-skinned and blond, Giacomo had dark skin and hair. Where Andreas was tall and big-boned, Giacomo was compact and lean. Where Andreas was genuinely amiable but slow-witted, Giacomo was pleasant, when it suited him, and a brilliant schemer. One thing he loved was the pristine beauty of the country Andreas came from: Norway. His defective brother had been useful and was abducted without consent. That would now be rectified.

The two men had been given specific instructions as to what to communicate to Don Lozito. They were neither to be confrontational nor overly solicitous. A businesslike and professional approach was expected. Both recognized that Lozito wielded enormous power; he was a no-nonsense type from the old school. Lozito was known to monitor everything, and nothing got past him without his input. He had survived assassination attempts, Justice Department investigations and tax audits but always managed to come out unscathed. He could be described as a dictator without fanfare or state credentials. At the opportune moment, and in the most underhanded and secretive manner, he would unleash his fury on his enemies. Then he would send flowers and condolences to the victims' families, feigning total revulsion for the animals that had performed such despicable acts. He had even been seen holding hands and crying with the mothers and widows at the wakes, promising that if he ever found the *disgraziati* (depraved culprits), he would rip them apart with his bare hands.

Don Lozito, in essence, was a complicated man. On one hand, he was calculating and ruthless; on the other hand, he had a sympathetic and good-hearted side – that is, if he liked you. His mind was sharp, analytical and able, so much so, that if he had dedicated his life to worthy causes the Nobel Laureate Committee would have easily recognized him for his accomplishments. There was only one way of dealing with Don Lozito's split personality: carefully and judiciously.

The tattooed man, Gregorio, proceeded to the baggage claim area while the younger man, Moustafa, with the tiny diamond in his left ear, went outside the arrival terminal to hail a cab. The wide luggage contained two inner boxes. The first was made of soft, light balsam wood and held thirty-six freshly picked and especially selected large purple figs, each with a tiny drop of honey at the very end. The fruit's teardrop shape reminded Gregorio of a young black woman's breasts, firm and sweet. Lozito's cravings were not many, but fresh figs directly from the soil of the old country was definitely one. To Lozito it wasn't just a gastronomical matter but, in his mind, the figs were like an umbilical cord, an attachment to the Calabrian soil. They were necessary for nourishment of the body and to restore the soul's balance.

Inside the same suitcase was another box, much thicker than the first and quite heavy. It was lined with a velvety red cloth puckered and dipped like small craters. Nestled in each cup-shape depression was a solid mahogany ball four inches in diameter and several smaller ones. Each ball had a band of three colors: red, white and green, depicting the colors of the Italian flag. As added elegance, the initials CJL, for Carlo Julius Lozito, were engraved by hand, gold-leaf-filled on both sides of the colored bands. It was Lozito's father who chose the middle name because he had a premonition that his first-born would be worthy of a great leader's name.

Gregorio was never fond of figs; they gave him diarrhea. And *bocci* was a game for old men – a last thrill before the exit door. But his opinion didn't matter; what mattered was a reconciliation, a deal that would ultimately allow Giacomo unfettered access to move his operation north, into the large urban centers of Italy and, within a year, market the nose-candy in Germany, France and beyond.

What Gregorio cared most about was not the gifts he was bearing for Lozito but what was in the secret compartment of the luggage, a .357 Magnum that he had acquired on his last visit to Milan where he frequented the fashion shops for his wardrobe and visited a young fashion model for his pleasure.

The baggage claim area wasn't quite as crowded as he thought it would be, and his singular luggage was the fourth to come off the ramp. He quickly snatched it off the conveyor belt and headed for the exit doors. The guard at the end of the roped-off area made eye contact but didn't stop Gregorio, who nodded his head to acknowledge him and in recognition of his authority. As he went through the sliding doors, he saw that a yellow cab was already waiting some twenty feet to the right. Upon seeing him coming, the driver went to open the trunk. Moustafa was already sitting in the back seat, blending in with the dark gray fabric, almost invisible.

"Where to?" asked the cab driver.

"Woodside." Gregorio leaned forward and handed the driver a card.

"No problem, about twenty minutes or so."

*

He knew the exact location of the hotel: a brick building off Queens Boulevard, minutes before you got onto the Queens Borough Bridge for Manhattan. The building had been a seedy spot for drug dealers and prostitutes but had been renovated under new management in an attempt to attract a more respectable clientele. The cab driver remembered having gotten laid there, in his early twenties, when he picked up a forty-two-year-old divorcee at a local bar. He had reflected back many times on that night and concluded that he had taken full advantage of the mother of three who had spilled her guts after downing a few white vodkas. The things she had said about her husband, who had moved in with a gay guy, were mortifying. That experience had left her shattered. She had tried to regain her self-confidence in the only way she knew. And he had been happy to oblige her.

In his head, the driver estimated the time, calculated his fare, and the anticipated gratuity. He always did this before he turned on his meter. Through the years he had developed a certain knack for being able to size up his passengers and determine, fairly accurately, how they tipped. Ninety percent of the time he would hit it right on the head but these two guys fell into the unpredictable ten percent column. Often, it was a matter of mood. To create the proper mood, he would at times invite conversation, but he sensed that the two men in the back seat weren't receptive to overtures.

Twenty-two minutes later he stopped before the motel, neither plush nor seedy. The large man paid the cabby and gave him a modest tip, neither too much nor too little and certainly not very memorable.

*

Their single room, double bed, was on the third floor, the top floor of the motel and at the opposite end of the management office. Gregorio specifically requested a quiet area from the Indian woman behind the desk. She had a bindi on her forehead and was wearing a sari. He paid in cash for one night and told the woman that they might be around a few days and would pay as they went along. When the clerk placed the room key on the counter-top he tipped her five dollars. She hesitated a second before taking the money and told them to wait a minute. She took back the key she had just placed on the counter and replaced it with another, telling them that the second room might be more suitable. They walked out and made their way around the building to the staircase. The back of the motel had a wrought iron fire escape and faced a dimly-lit parking lot with a handful of trucks and vehicles. Their room's entrance was approachable from a balcony which wrapped around three quarters of the structure.

Gregorio inserted the key in the door lock and pushed it open without going inside. A small light revealed a standard room, clean, but with few amenities. He strained to listen… quiet. Moustafa followed him, with his duffle bag over his shoulder, carrying the luggage. Gregorio stepped aside to let Moustafa in before pulling the key out of the lock and closing the door. Moustafa went to the opposite end of the room, dropped the suitcase on a small round table, threw his duffle bag onto the nearest bed and looked out the window. Gregorio went directly to the bathroom.

He looked out the bathroom window and wondered how far Flushing was from Woodside, where they were. He knew that both communities were in the borough of Queens but wasn't familiar with the geography. Later, he'd go downstairs and ask the clerk for a map. After tomorrow's meeting with Lozito he had one day to accomplish the second objective of his trip. It had to do with Lorenzo Benedetta. His luck would finally run out. Gregorio would see to it that his past efforts and future plans would be erased. His watch would stop, period!

Gregorio mused about death. No one seriously thought about their inevitable end. People put it off as far as possible into the future. When death came, it was always a surprise they never expected. The greeting was always with a look of astonishment on their faces. But Gregorio Bastone would never forget this unavoidable truth. His daily meditation was not inspired by religion or fear. No! For Gregorio it was a form of preparation, much like a Samurai prepared himself for the ultimate act. Where and how it happened were not important. What the meditations provided was an enhanced awareness of his existence and prepared him to stare into eternal darkness. It was this very attitude, this deranged attitude, as some psychotherapists would call it, this fascination with the "when," that often led him to almost feel the exhilaration of suicide. The taking of his own life would allow him control of time and place.

Lorenzo Benedetta had been in the States for almost a year and nothing had happened to him. By now his guard was down. He was well into his routine. And Gregorio had all the information he needed. He knew where the kid worked and where he lived, when he got home and when he slept. His small apartment was on the second floor of a sixteen-unit building a few blocks from Northern

Boulevard in Flushing. He still found it hard to believe that in the span of one day the kid had managed to elude Attila on the train, from Calabria to Naples, and even came close to killing Attila. His luck had continued in the Port of Naples and on the ocean liner with Moustafa. Lorenzo had managed to humiliate Giacomo's two top men. But this time there would be no chases, no cops, no spectators, just the three of them. Time to pay. It would be quiet, clean and fast. And the best place to deal with him was at his apartment, late in the evening, when he was tired after work.

Attila had his reasons for requesting that he be allowed to even the score personally. But Gregorio trumped him because he had met Lozito on a previous occasion and Giacomo felt more confident on several other levels in sending him.

Gregorio's previous meeting with Lozito had been two years earlier on Ocean Boulevard, Palm Beach, Florida. Lozito had a summer home overlooking the Atlantic Ocean; he was a neighbor to some of the biggest wigs in the country. Gregorio had been there as an emissary, one of seven, in an attempt to iron out some differences that had resulted in vicious feuds. In the province of Calabria, Reggio, some 214 people from various families had been slaughtered during turf wars. Lozito's proposed reconciliation had been honored for some time, but events had changed fast in the last few years and the truce was disintegrating. This meeting was to prevent a total breakdown.

This "get-together" was different from the former because it just involved Giacomo's and Lozito's affairs. It was to take place at Lozito's social club in Brooklyn. Gregorio had been briefed that it was a two-story brick building ribbed by iron bars on the front door and windows. The building extended from block to block, from the front to the back of his property. The yard was a long rectangular lot and Lozito had a vegetable garden in the far rear and a *bocce* court toward the front. Stockade fences adorned the two sides and an eight-foot cement wall closed off the rear of the property.

Gregorio woke early the next morning and for some fifteen minutes meditated in bed on his favorite topic: death. Then he splashed some water on his face, went downstairs to grab some coffee and get a map. He brought up a cup of tea for Moustafa with six cubes of sugar wrapped in a napkin and stuffed in his pocket. When he got back to his room Moustafa was lying on his bed, hands behind his head, watching some National Geographic program.

While Moustafa showered, Gregorio studied the map. He was surprised to see how close Lorenzo Benedetta's apartment was to their motel. After the two men finished their morning rituals in the bathroom, they walked a few blocks from the motel to a local diner for breakfast. Gregorio ordered his usual hard-boiled eggs, toast, home fries and black coffee, while Moustafa ordered pancakes and scrambled eggs. Gregorio had always felt that eggs were dirty considering where they came from and what they looked like after the chickens laid them. Only by boiling them did he feel assured that they were sanitized. At home he would take precautions by washing the eggshell and then going as far as dissecting the egg and removing the white string, the chalaza, between the yolk and albumen.

*

Several minutes before noon their taxi pulled up in front of Lozito's social club in the middle of the block, like so many other blocks perpendicular to Myrtle Avenue, Ridgewood. The Avenue was a commercial strip, with shoe stands on the sidewalk, five-and-dime stores, second-rate clothing stores and pizza joints; a working-class neighborhood with dirt under its fingernails. The building was intentionally unpretentious with a brick façade, aluminum siding, gray front door and metal bars over the windows and door. Neither the building's architecture nor the wrought iron bars covering the windows made it look any different from other structures in the neighborhood.

When Gregorio stepped onto the sidewalk the only visible activities were two women crossing at the opposite end of the street, one pushing a baby carriage. Also, a young boy with his back against a parked car, talking to his mom who was leaning out her front window.

Gregorio knocked on the gray door. He could see three black numbers screwed directly into the door panel, "787", and a mail slot just below. So, this was it, he thought. This decrepit little building was the epicenter of hundreds of millions of dollars and an underground army of hundreds, if not thousands, of blood ties and people on payroll. Moustafa waited behind him, holding the valise in one hand and adjusting his cap with the other, when a miniature window, the size of a car visor, slid open. Gregorio identified himself and the door was opened. A handsome man with a thick black moustache and well-proportioned body opened the door. He frisked them in the small foyer. Gregorio's Magnum and Moustafa's knives and valise were confiscated.

"Temporarily," the man assured them.

The man walked over to a small table and searched through the valise. Its contents not arousing suspicion, he closed it and handed it back to Moustafa. Inside, they could see a bar on the left and a large espresso machine in the corner. A skinny bartender was washing glasses and watching a soccer game on a black and white TV, unconcerned by their presence. Opposite the bar were a handful of tables and a single bathroom with a paper plate tacked on the door that read, "His & Hers." Near the tables were two pictures: the Brooklyn Bridge with the New York City skyline, and the other, the Statue of Liberty and New York Harbor. Toward the back of the long room two guys played pool. A few feet from them, an oak staircase led to the second floor. When Gregorio and Moustafa started moving in their direction the two players stopped their game and their eyes followed Gregorio and Moustafa as they walked across the room.

The man who confiscated their gun led them past the two players and answered their inquiring eyes.

"Mr. Lo is expecting them," he said.

To Gregorio and Moustafa he added, "They'll take you up."

Putting their cue sticks down the men moved past the visitors. One led the way; the other one followed from behind. At the top of the stairs the sweet smell of tobacco wafted through the open door. There he was in the flesh, Lozito himself, sitting on the edge of a recliner while puffing copiously on a cigar. He seemed excited about a Brazilian soccer match, the same game the bartender was watching downstairs. On each side of the recliner were two black Dobermans. They cocked their cropped ears and their heads toward the door. Their eyes fixed on the two strangers but didn't move. The dogs were sleek, shiny and very muscular, like black porcelain statues.

"This Pele guy is unbelievable." Lozito was pumped up from the excitement of the goal just scored, pointing at the TV and speaking loudly.

"A one-man show. They need several players just to cover him." Then he turned to face Gregorio. "You like soccer?"

"I watch it when the Italian team plays," Gregorio responded.

"Too bad they're in a different league… little talent." He walked over and turned off the TV.

"It's been a few years, Gregorio. How's everything?"

"Personally, everything is fine. Just fine, Mr. Lozito."

"And our mutual friend, how's he doing?" Gregorio thought about the significance of not mentioning Giacomo's name.

"Mr. Salvaggi? He's also doing well. He sends you his warmest regards and sends you something." He turned to take the case from Moustafa who was holding it out for him when one of the pool players reached over first, took it, placed it on the recliner and snapped it open.

The pool player held the box containing the *bocci* set before his boss.

Lozito picked up one of the larger balls, spun it around, looked at the inscription and then bounced it in his hand.

"Heavy, and very attractive. Too nice to get them dirty," he said. "Especially with my initials. Your boss outdid himself. Tell him the old man was very appreciative."

"Will do," responded Gregorio. "There's something else he thought you might like," continued Gregorio.

The pool player opened the second box revealing the succulent purple fruit.

"Now, your boss must truly know my weakness," he said as he feasted his eyes. "They look mouth-watering. Please try one."

He took the box and put it in front of the two visitors and then passed it to his two bodyguards. Then he took out his handkerchief, opened it and wrapped two of the succulent fruits in it.

"Just had espresso, but I'll save these two for lunch," he said.

Gregorio knew that Lozito didn't trust anyone and would eat the figs only after a few hours had lapsed to see if his men had any reaction. The two of them were like miners' canaries in the tunnel.

"I know your boss put a lot of thought into these generous gifts. But I also know that he's been freelancing; operating independently... outside our rules." Gregorio could see that Lozito's expression had changed.

"Mr. Salvaggi wants to work with you. He wants to cooperate with the organization," answered Gregorio. Moustafa stood to his right, hands clasped over his belt, as if he was assessing the risk.

"His actions belie his words." Lozito punctuated his words with a slow smoke-puff. Then laid his cigar down in a crystal ashtray. "Salvaggi is not a stupid man, he's just driving too fast and too recklessly." Lozito's tone had sharpened. Gregorio noticed he had used his boss's name for the first time.

"Mr. Lozito, our boss wants to work out a mutual agreement with you; a partnership of sorts, something that increases business and is beneficial to both. He's proposing doing all the field work for a 50/50 split." As Gregorio finished saying this, Lozito's face became reddened.

"Salvaggi is smart to realize that he's getting in over his ears. He should also be smart enough to realize he doesn't have what it takes. Yet, he sends you to make a deal." Then he paused. "Why would I need him?"

Clearly, Lozito was getting more cross by the second; inside he was like a pressure cooker. He was seething. A vein on his left temple bulged. Still his exterior remained under control.

"The thinking is, Mr. Lozito, that by joining forces the sky's the limit. There are unlimited markets out there. Mr. Salvaggi has tremendous respect for you, and the last thing he wants is to encroach on your territory. The proposal is just that, a proposal; he's open to other considerations," said Gregorio.

Lozito was listening with head leaning back and lips puckered up. His suspicion was now confirmed: Salvaggi knew that he, Giacomo Salvaggi, was up against a brick wall. His incursion into Naples' and Milan's drug distribution had cost him dearly. His supply chain was largely cut off. He was a wounded animal and ostracized. Most *'Ndrangheta* families, even in their loose association, still viewed Lozito as the final arbiter, the capo. They knew Salvaggi had strayed; he was the black sheep of the "family." They had concluded that it was better to stay with a known entity than someone too young, too brash, too ambitious and untried. Now, Salvaggi had sent his two idiots, hats in hand, to do his bidding because of the cost in blood and treasure for having crossed Carlo Julius Lozito.

"I'll consider Mr. Salvaggi's proposal. And will get back to him. Please tell him how much I appreciated the wonderful gifts."

Then Lozito turned around, petted the Doberman closest to him, went back to the TV and turned on his game. Gregorio and Moustafa were led down the stairs and escorted to the front door where they retrieved their weapons.

Outside the sun was shining brightly and there was more activity on the street. Gregorio felt that very little was accomplished and wondered what kind of counter-proposal, if any, Lozito would make to Giacomo. If nothing else, he was known to be a man of his word and would not sit on whatever decision he arrived at.

The cab was waiting as they had earlier requested. They got in and Gregorio turned back toward the building. He could not fathom how this place could be the epicenter of an empire and was even more puzzled as to why a man like Lozito spent his days there. Maybe it was the same mentality as Warren Buffet who was a billionaire, the second richest man in the world, yet, he lived in the same middle-class house as he did when he was a kid, and walked to the corner to get his paper every morning.

Back at their motel, after a phone call relaying the details of their meeting to Giacomo, they spent the rest of the afternoon relaxing and eating lunch at the diner. Then they hailed a cab on Queens Boulevard and went directly to Lorenzo Benedetta's apartment building. They cased the street, the rear of the building and the stairwell. All was quiet and the premises were very accessible. At the opportune moment, Moustafa picked Lorenzo's lock and the two entered his apartment. They had nearly three hours before the occupant arrived, and Moustafa took the opportunity to have a glass of iced water while Gregorio opted for a cold soda from the refrigerator. The three-hour window would allow them to get back to their motel, pack, relax a bit and come back with enough time to spare for Gregorio to be sitting in the same spot and Moustafa to be behind the door when Lorenzo walked in. Within minutes they would set the record straight, quietly, decisively, and permanently. The kid wouldn't know what hit him until he felt the warm liquid running down his neck. No struggle, no screams, just a few gurgles and then, eternal quietness. Less than an hour later, they would be on board a 747 Alitalia bound for Fiumicino Airport; all flawless and easy, like a walk in the park.

*

They had been back at their hotel room less than thirty minutes when Moustafa noticed a figure running in the parking lot behind the motel. His suspicion aroused, he signaled to his partner. Gregorio pulled out his Magnum. He advanced toward the door, gun in hand and listened for outside movement. Then he positioned himself behind the door while Moustafa slid his body inside the closet, where he had a view of both the windows and door.

Seconds passed in total silence. Then Moustafa noticed a shadow under the door. Before he could signal to his partner, the door was kicked open. A man with a weapon drawn slowly stepped in. Gregorio fired, blasting a hole through the composite door, hitting the intruder in the flank. He collapsed on one knee but still held onto his gun. And like a perfectly orchestrated Hollywood sequence two other men appeared on the fire escape. Seeing their comrade on the ground wounded, they shattered a pane of glass and fired through the window, targeting Gregorio. One bullet found its mark in Gregorio's chest, inches from his heart. Gregorio felt the sting. He felt his shirt soaked by a warm liquid, but didn't go down. Gregorio unloaded five shots toward the window, hitting his assailants, then his legs caved in. The men quickly took cover to the sides of the glass panels. The window shattered into a thousand pieces and one shot blew away half of someone's wrist.

Moustafa, who was observing the exchange of fire, was also waiting for the right opportunity. When another intruder came through the door and popped Gregorio, who was still firing at the window, Moustafa pounced. With the agility of a cobra he grabbed the man's skull with his left hand, as if blessing him during a religious rite, and in a flash sliced from ear to ear and across the trachea. The first attacker with the bloody flank, who was on all fours, saw the exchange and lifted his weapon to fire, but Moustafa proved quicker with an upward thrust, virtually decapitating him. Then he launched himself toward the bathroom, kicked the door closed, yanked a drawer out of the vanity and rammed it through the small bathroom window. By now, two others and the man with the shattered wrist were in the main room; one kicked Gregorio in the face and the other, with a black mustache, shot him point blank in the heart. Gregorio's face, strangely, expressed an uncanny smile as if the mysteries of the universe were finally revealed, and a final sense of satisfaction was experienced.

Then one of the three men turned the knob and pushed open the bathroom door. He saw nothing in the bathroom but a busted window. As he approached to look out, a hand reached from behind the corner of the partially drawn shower curtain and the *jambiya* found its target. In a downward sweep it penetrated clothing, tissue, nerves, cartilage and bone, exposing spine and paralyzing the victim – an agonizing death. Moustafa sensed the second man enter the bathroom and spun his body around to deal with him but lost his balance and slipped on soap scum on the porcelain tub. The man fired twice behind the curtains. The first bullet found a home in Moustafa's temple and the other blew out his elbow bone. The *jambiya* bounced off the rim of the tub and landed on the ceramic tile next to the man's boots. The shooter ripped down the liner and saw a man whose small frame was sliding down the tub wall that was streaked with blood. The small man, whose eyes were blinking non-stop, seemed to be intensely focused on the curved knife as if to will it back into his hand while his body slouched downwards, as if preparing for a bath.

*

A week later Giacomo received a plainly wrapped brown paper package. The sender was from New York, USA. As he sat behind his desk, he untied the string and opened it carefully. Attila was sitting on the couch thumbing through the *Corriere Della Sera*. Beyond the brown wrapping was a box and inside the box was a perfectly sealed black plastic bag. As Giacomo cut across the top of the plastic bag a putrid smell reached his nostrils. He leaned back in his chair as if to move away from the unpleasant odor and emptied the contents of the bag on his desk. Attila, seeing his boss react, moved from the couch to stand next to Giacomo's desk. Lozito, as promised, had kept his word and given his answer. Both men, not saying a word, stared at the two objects on the desk: a human ear with a small diamond earring and a piece of curled skin with a black figure carrying a pole over his shoulder with its naked prey, hands and feet bound around the pole.

Chapter 17

Lorenzo's Horoscope

It is said that cause and effect can literally lead you to the ends of creation. After all, the Big Bang Theory has it that all universal matter was once condensed onto an area smaller than the tip of a pin. Then, boom! When it exploded, the universe as we know it was formed; and from that singular burst of energy all other events flowed, including all real and all imaginary events in the cerebrum of sentient creatures. But in the small sphere of human existence it is imperative to have stop signs at critical points, where we draw the line. "Event relatedness" becomes too numerous and too attenuated for our limited minds to grasp the ripples of the original incident. In fact, great thinkers have said that we can only consider that which is within the orbit of the foreseeable, and all other outcomes outside that orbit, whether major or minor, should be left by the wayside. Applying this principle in a social context, one becomes responsible for his or her actions where there is a natural and continuous sequence of predictable results.

So, the question becomes whether the one who put a vile action into motion, like Giacomo Salvaggi's attempted murder of Lorenzo Benedetta, should still be held responsible when the predictably bad outcome is broken by another intervening act. The intervening actor was Carlo Lozito, who caused much damage to the initiator of the bad act and, in the process, unwittingly saved Lorenzo Benedetta.

In most legal systems any intent to do evil is punishable. But, again, it comes down to the gray area of "event relatedness." Legal systems will break down the concept into smaller components and analyze it from different angles: clear intent, degree of preparation, extent of potential injury, proof beyond a reasonable doubt, etc. Unfortunately, in most cases the perpetrator will walk and his punishment will ultimately not be left to courts but to some cosmic karma, if it exists.

In Lorenzo's mind there wasn't an iota of suspicion that his life could have ended in a matter of seconds when he came home from work, waved to his neighbor across the street, entered his lobby, placed the key in his mail slot, retrieved his mail and walked up twenty-two steps to his second-floor apartment. But for Lozito's universe, colliding with Giacomo Salvaggi's universe, the scene that Gregorio and Moustafa had planned a few hours earlier would have been realized. The two would have, again, entered Lorenzo's sanctuary as if taking a casual walk in the park or nonchalantly entering their mother's kitchen. They would have sat on the intended victim's couch or perhaps around his kitchen table, sipping a cold beer from his refrigerator as if they were honored guests. Then, at a definitive point, they would have heard a key being inserted in the lock, the knob would have turned, and the door would have slammed behind Lorenzo for the last time. Moustafa would have been the appointed agent waiting behind the door, the *jambiya* being less noisy than a silencer. The two men, in synchronized movements would've taken their position; no need for any cue between them. The curved blade would have made a quick, clean, deep cut around the jugular as the victim's body dropped. At first, it would be gently suspended and then slowly laid on the carpeted floor like a new mother putting her infant child to peaceful rest. And perhaps in an alternate universe it did play out with meticulous precision.

Lorenzo did enter at the exact time as he entered every Monday night. He pushed the door to his apartment closed behind him with his boot and flicked on the light switch. Mail in hand, he pulled off his muddy shoes and placed them on a newspaper in the corner. In the kitchen, he turned on the light over the table, placed the mail down, went to the refrigerator for a beer and set it down next to his pile of mail, mostly junk mail and political propaganda. In the midst of the pile he noticed a letter with international markings. It was his mother's handwriting. As he carefully tore open the thin envelope, he pulled out two pages of script. He didn't have to read beyond the first paragraph before he stopped, his head supported on his left elbow and the fingers of his right hand slowly combing through his hair.

August 6th, 1974

My Dearest Lorenzo,

I hope this letter finds you well and sheltered in the midst of the Lord's palm.

At the start I want to announce that I've been blessed with another child, a baby boy, and you with a very handsome and healthy baby brother – Marcello Matteo Benedetta. He was born on the 25th day of July, at 5am, with the rooster's crow. I'm told this is a lucky sign. He weighed 8 pounds, 3 ounces. A large baby at that weight, considering that you were about a pound less when you were born and your sister was even smaller. Everything went as well as possible for both of us. He has beautiful, deep blue eyes and with the most remarkable sparkle as if filled with wonder and amazement. He has a tiny dimple on each cheek. His tiny hands always reach out as if he wants to grasp; maybe a better word is to embrace the universe. His hair is light brown and he has this totally disarming smile like you and your sister had as infants. He gives us much joy at an otherwise sad time, so soon after your father's death. Your papa would have been in absolute bliss to see this precious bundle…

Lorenzo stopped reading the rest of the letter and pondered the words "large baby." Then counted back the months from the middle of August to November of the previous year: about eight and a half months. The child was a little premature but still within the normal gestation period. He had at first believed it was unlikely, although a remote possibility, that anything like this could happen but it was probably true. His father had been too ill to conceive a child around that time. But his mother must have been intimate with him at some point to believe that it was his child. His mind's past denials were giving way to the reality of the events. He had to accept that this "healthy child" with the "remarkable sparkle" in his eyes was most assuredly his half-brother; that unbeknownst to the woman that gave him life, this "precious bundle" was the consequence of a rape.

Lorenzo scanned the rest of the letter and felt an acute headache coming on. He couldn't pinpoint a cause – the cold beer, the exhaustion, the letter's contents? He put his head down over his crossed arms resting on the table and began feeling a smidge dizzy. Maybe it was just lack of food. It occurred to him that he had not eaten since breakfast. He went to the refrigerator and brought back another beer and some leftovers from the previous night: cold chicken and mashed potatoes. As he wolfed down the cold food, he realized that his half-brother was a mixed blessing. Sure, he felt a certain shared happiness with his mother and sister, particularly in the knowledge that the infant was healthy. It was a first step but a promising first step in that the child did not appear to be mentally defective. Still, doubts and questions filled his mind. What if the doctor had been lax and not screened the baby sufficiently? After all, he had not been put on notice of the probabilities of genetic abnormalities. What suspicions would the doctor have in looking deeper and probing further? The underlying assumption had always been that the Benedetta family had had two previous healthy children, and no mental disorders were ever evident in their lineage. Then his mind leaped forward. What if something became noticeably wrong as the child grew older? He knew that some mental defects were latent and expressed themselves during the formative years or even after. Popular magazines were filled with cases of children not being able to walk or talk, incapable of emoting, lacking coordination, and processing information and experiences improperly at various developmental stages.

But what really gnawed at his belly, even more than the child's potential medical conditions, was his inability to tell anyone what he had done. Now, with the birth of this child, how could he turn his mother's joy to pain and sorrow? He had come closest to telling Annalisa on the mountain top, but the animosity between the two families, and his fear of seeing a look of horror and disgust in her eyes, had prevented him. He wasn't sure if he could trust her totally then or now, and their strong connection seemed to be waning. They shared fewer and fewer letters, and those they exchanged spoke less of their future than of the mundane details of their present. It was one thing to disclose the rape that had occurred but it was another to ask her for forgiveness for taking her brother's life. And both matters would unavoidably surface. Some weeks later he had almost confided the incident to his Uncle Pietro but stopped short, fearful of the uncle's disapproval. The first question would be: why did you wait so long? Why didn't you go to the police from the onset? Then the ultimate unanswerable and inexcusable lapse: that his mother could have received immediate medical care when proof of her having been raped was clear and unquestionable.

After devouring his cold chicken and potatoes, and halfway into his second beer, he looked over his other mail and finally returned to reread his mother's letter.

The last page spoke mainly about the Salvaggi family and how Antonia, and to a lesser extent her husband, Bruno, had made several efforts at warming up to her and Gabriella. At first, they had joined the funeral procession. Later in church and on the route to the cemetery, they had been a bit cold and distant towards Matteo's relatives but soon realized that as neighbors, community obligations sometimes trumped anger and even personal animosities. And since death was permanent and a common enemy of all mankind, differences should be set aside and buried with Matteo. At the end of the letter, it was Antonia who told Bruno it was a chance to do God's work and put into practice good Christian charity. Her husband was reminded that the Almighty looked favorably toward a neighbor helping an expectant widow in difficult circumstances. Thus, a day after the funeral they and another neighbor presented themselves, unannounced, at the front door of the Benedettas' house bearing a box of pastries and a large basket of fresh fruit.

Lorenzo wondered if Annalisa had a role in convincing her parents that they should let bygones be bygones.

The Salvaggis tried to give Francesca emotional support and she had reciprocated with warmth and hospitality. They had chatted about various things in the past and about their daughter's acceptance at the University of Bologna where she intended to fulfill her dream of being a doctor. They had briefly discussed "the Americano" and Lorenzo's new life in the USA; they had touched on the misfortune of Andreas and the status of the investigation and even talked, frankly, about Giacomo and some difficulties he was experiencing.

Once Giacomo's name came up in the conversation, Antonia almost defensively offered that he was having some setbacks, mostly involving his business. She explained that the news reports were wrong in naming him as "a suspect" in the probe of several people who had been executed in Naples, presumably business adversaries of their son's. Then, without being asked, she blurted out that the propane explosion at his building supply yard was nothing other than an accident. She was confident that the police would conclude no differently, despite speculation abounding that it was connected to killings in Naples several days before. Francesca and her brother-in-law, Dominick, were momentarily left with their mouths open, but quickly recovered. There was business and there was Business. This was, after all, Calabria.

None but his inner circle knew the truth, which was that Giacomo had ordered revenge killings for the deaths of Gregorio and Moustafa. The Confederates of Lozito's in Naples were the targets of his venom. Giacomo had reacted swiftly and decisively upon learning of the murder of his two top men. The swiftness of his response went against the core of his very nature. In the past, his deliberative calculations with Gregorio proved to be invaluable in realizing his objectives. But Gregorio wasn't around and Giacomo felt humiliated and disrespected, not only on a business level but also on a personal level. The timing and manner of his men's assassination made his stomach churn. Gregorio and Moustafa were merely ambassadors who were working towards a resolution of the two families' differences. A meeting had been pre-arranged, gifts were given in good faith and proposals had been expressed in an amicable attitude and a spirit of negotiation. Their safety should have been inviolate. Lozito had exhibited barbarity, pure and simple. And he probably believed that Giacomo didn't have the *coglioni* (balls) to strike back and to strike back so quickly and so hard. This was Lozito's mistake. Despite having a fraction of Lozito's organization, Giacomo had the advantage of being younger and more energetic, of effectively operating in his backyard, and of being able to adapt to changing circumstances more readily. He visualized himself as fighting guerilla warfare against a more powerful and traditional army. And history had plenty of examples where the underdog succeeded.

Lozito's presentment of civility was just a veneer. He could only understand one thing: force. And Giacomo Salvaggi wasn't taking his *merda* (shit), not now or ever. The thought of sending Attila and several of his best men directly to Lozito's nest to exterminate the cancer at the source had crossed his mind. But it was easier and faster to strike locally. A quick, surgical hit would send an unequivocal message that Giacomo Salvaggi was not a pussy, and would not be intimidated.

*

The other news from Lorenzo's mother was about Annalisa Salvaggi and about Inspector Bellin's efforts in finding Andreas. Annalisa had scored relatively high on her entrance exams and had been accepted in the pre-med program at the University of Bologna in northern Italy. As of the date of the letter she was there for orientation. Bits of information about the university had been shared by Annalisa with Lorenzo in letters he had received: that it was the oldest university in all of Europe, founded in 1088, that the university was a multicultural institution, and that the campus was scattered over a wide geographical area, accommodating about 100,000 students from all over the world. He had also, surreptitiously, corresponded with her through her friend, who was receiving mail on her behalf as they had planned before his departure.

As far as Inspector Bellin was concerned, his mother said that he was adamant about closing the case, despite the passage of over six months from his disappearance and diminishing leads. The police had done everything possible. They had even looked into Andreas' background in their pursuit of abduction theories. It was obvious that interest in the story was diminishing. The local newspapers and even some voices inside the police department were more and more inclined to conclude that the victim had had an unfortunate accident at sea and the fish had consumed his body. A local paper had even sensationalized the story by publishing photos of a bloated, partial body that was washed ashore and claiming that it was Andreas. The police lab later determined it was the remnants of a dog.

Nausea was the prevalent feeling Lorenzo experienced every time word of the investigation reached him, while anxiety was a close second. Images of the Salvaggis' mentally defective son would take control of his mind. He would cry; he would experience feelings of hopelessness and despise himself for killing Andreas, for not protecting his mother, for not telling the truth. He was in an impossible position. He would see himself at the bottom of a very deep pit, with the point of light above becoming dimmer each passing day, and feel that God was walking farther away, forsaking him. Then his mood would turn to anger for being weak. For not being able to surrender to the temptation of suicide, for not being able to kill God within and set himself free of His judgment. The torment of guilt would last until he fell asleep from exhaustion, to re-emerge in his dreams. He was the only person who could put closure to the unassuaged inner torture, perpetual agony of restlessness, and the speculation and wasted resources that the family and community were still expending. He knew that at some point he would have to make it right.

Ironically, while tensions between the two families had somewhat eased and he felt a little relief for his family, he also sensed that in her last two letters something had changed between Annalisa and himself. For whatever reason, or reasons, she had become more distant in the tone of her letters, her expressions of feelings. Was she deliberately trying to distance herself? Was she evolving into something else, somebody different? Was it because she had been too preoccupied and distracted as a result of school pressures? Could it be that Giacomo had influenced her with the suspicions he had about their brother's murder? Finally, his mind went to the most painful supposition: could it be that she had met someone else? She would have much more in common with someone who was also university-bound and who was traveling on the same path and forging fresh bonds. If that was the case, how could he, Lorenzo, compete with this type of daily interaction from over 3,000 miles away? How long could the past teenage experiences endure in a future constantly changing and demanding readjustment and expansion of her cultural values, her thoughts, and with her aspirations always influenced by exposure to a larger world view? She was traveling along a road leading her far away from him. She was entering a world of intelligentsia and he was a day laborer. It was time for him to think of his future, but not now, he was too tired.

He stopped thinking what he considered unthinkable thoughts. He blamed himself for being overly sensitive and suspicious and for being overly disposed to anxiety and fear of loss. The reality was he was lonely. His family, his sweetheart and his life were on the other side of the ocean and he was here alone. He had acquaintances and his uncle but everything had changed. The fact that he had been up some fourteen hours working in the unrelenting summer heat for the last three days didn't help. He always felt totally exhausted. What he wanted more than anything else right now was to sleep; no TV, no shower, no telephone calls, nothing but sleep.

With supreme effort he pulled himself away from the kitchen table, swigged the last drop of his second beer, grabbed a blanket from the closet and slumped on the couch, dirty work clothes and all. No sooner had he arranged the pillows than he started dreaming that he was an old man retired in some far-off place. His life's work, his purpose, his dreams were over. Every muscle in his body ached and hurt, his joints, his back. He tried as hard as possible to recognize the place where he was and the date on the calendar but was unable. One thing was for certain: there was a cemetery nearby and no Annalisa present in his life.

BOOK II

Chapter 18

In the Beginning

Six months earlier, on a Sunday evening, near the time of Andreas Salvaggi's disappearance, Calvi was off duty due to the birth of his child, and Inspector Bellin was stuck at the station house with a witness who was trying to identify a suspect in a line-up. The case was very fresh. It involved two women who were victims of a robbery and murder. As the facts were related to the inspector, it started with the women driving on a secluded road. They came across what appeared to be an accident: a man lying in the middle of the road with a mangled bicycle next to him. He was holding his leg. His pant leg was torn and seemingly bloodied. He appeared to be in agony. When the women stopped to render assistance, he pulled out a gun and demanded their purses. One of the women resisted and was shot; he hit the other with the butt of his pistol. He grabbed their car keys and took off, leaving the beaten and bloodied women by the side of the road. By the time another vehicle drove by, some twenty minutes later, the woman who was shot had lost considerable blood and died in the hospital lobby.

Despite this incident, which had demanded the inspector's attention for most of the late afternoon and early evening, he had one of his men pick up Bruno and his wife, as he had promised on Friday night. Time was of the essence in missing cases and the inspector wanted to learn more about Andreas' adoption. Bruno had clearly narrated the sequence of events that led to the adoption but Bellin was also interested in what happened to the child prior to this, as well as some background on his parents.

The driver was instructed to explain to the Salvaggis that the inspector was delayed due to unforeseen circumstances for which he apologized, but would meet with them shortly. The plainclothes officer had been further directed to take them to Nino's Restaurant, a busy but quaint eatery on a side street off via Garibaldi, located just on the outskirts of the city of Cosenza. The eatery had ample parking around the Tuscan-style building, and outside tables were arranged under green tents for informal gatherings. The inside was a different story. It was more formal, the ambience more delicate and the staff lavished inordinate attention. And like any good capitalist venture, all these amenities were reflected in the tally. Luckily for the inspector, Nino, the proprietor, was also his cousin and blood ties usually had some benefits. But it turned out that Nino was out of town so the inspector had called ahead and spoken to the *maître d'*, requesting his favorite table and giving specific instructions that the Salvaggis be accommodated with a good bottle of wine and the traditional plate of appetizers.

Bellin came through the front door at about 7.30pm. From where he sat, Bruno could see the restaurant management was fawning over the police chief. He was led to their table as the appetizers were being served. He gave them both a hearty handshake and apologized for being late. Then, pointing to the large food tray sitting in the middle of the table and the freshly baked bread, he joked about having to let out his belt another notch, every time he frequented Nino's. Upon sitting down, he conveyed a short story about the restaurant's debut some seven years earlier before the conversation turned more somber.

The inspector noted that his guests were wearing black and were already privately mourning Andreas. When the subject of their son came up, he was tactful and empathetic. He assured them that his department was still very active with their son's case. His assistant and a few officers had, again, combed the coastal waters for any other clues that might have washed up but there was nothing new to report. His office had also tracked down several vehicles with German plates that had been spotted locally but it was heart-wrenching to conclude that, with the possible exception of one vehicle that was still being followed up, the rest of the leads went nowhere. Then, in a very calming manner, almost apologetic for touching raw nerves, he asked Bruno if he would not mind continuing where he left off Friday night. He reminded them, again, that it was not uncommon for a miniscule piece of information to be the key that unraveled the case.

He also asked why the orphanage had contacted him twice after the adoption was completed. Bruno told him that they were checking up on Andreas' welfare and on him, as well, since they considered him not only a co-worker but a friend. The first time they had contacted him, Fräulein Moretti-Schemitsch informed him that a packet of letters from the boy's mother had been delivered by Sonya, his mother's sister. Sonya briefly inquired about the child's welfare and seemed pleased that he had been adopted by a loving couple who lived in Italy. The administrator wanted to forward the packet to him for safekeeping for the child. He was contacted a second time a few months later because distant relatives of Andreas' father had found the man's journals in the wreckage of the family home. Not knowing what to do about the journals the family spoke with some government agencies and were finally referred to the orphanage. The administrator had reminded Bruno that it was their policy to forward any material about a child's past to adoptive parents or to give the material to the child on their eighteenth birthday, if they remained at the orphanage. Bruno remembered thanking the administrator and requesting that the journals be sent to him, promising to discuss their contents with Andreas when he was old enough to understand. Bruno had read the letters and journals several times. What he told the inspector was derived from their contents and filled in with general information Bruno had learned when he worked in Germany.

Bruno picked up the story where he had left off forty-eight hours earlier. He told the inspector that Andreas' arrival into the world, and his early childhood, had been much more difficult than his life at St Mary's Orphanage in Munich or his growing up in Calabria. Much of his hardship had to do with his parents' legacy.

In a way, he said, events affecting the child's father, a military man, were put in place in the early spring of 1940. The circumstances were out of his father's control because the man with the "toothbrush mustache" was calling the shots. This was how Bruno described Adolph Hitler. The dictator had ordered various studies and convened numerous meetings with his top military brass in Berlin to determine the feasibility of invading Denmark and Norway. The Nazi leader's distress was caused by the British becoming excessively involved in the North Sea, especially in the territorial waters off Norway; something had to be done to stop them. He saw London's increased involvement with neutral Norway as an attempt to damage German interests in two critical areas. First, the blockade of sea lanes, which jeopardized access of the Führer's U-boats into the northern Atlantic, and second, the flow of iron ore coming from Sweden through Narvik, a port city in northern Norway, that was at risk. The iron ore was the lifeblood of the Third Reich's war machine and Hitler felt that it was imperative to establish bases there before the British did, under the pretense of saving Norway from the Nazis.

Accordingly, on April 9, 1940 the *Wehrmacht*, all branches of the German defense, were ordered to take part in the invasion of this peaceful neutral country. It started out with a German naval armada, led by one of the most modern and best-equipped cruisers, the *Blücher*, when it left a small port from northern Germany. Tailing the *Blücher* was another handful of warships that made their way across the North Sea and into the mouth of the Oslofjord. The lead ship transported not only naval personnel but also army units and teams of Gestapo agents. They constituted a well-trained fighting machine totaling several thousand soldiers. The other vessels in the procession also carried a substantial number of troops, arsenal and mine-sweeping equipment.

It was about 4.30am, pitch black and foggy. The invaders had a perfect cover. As the armada steamed up the seventy-mile fjord, its primary objective was to dock in the harbor of the Norwegian capital, Oslo. There the troops would swarm onto land like locusts and fan out, capturing and occupying strategically vital interests. Nazi Special Forces were assigned the task of capturing the King and members of Parliament, thus forcing the immediate surrender of the Norwegians. The entire operation was brilliantly calculated; some generals felt that this northern country would fall into their hands like a ripe fruit in late autumn. But there was one glitch. That problem for the Germans started when they ran into a small Norwegian patrol boat that became alarmed when it observed the flotilla in the dark of night. The patrol boat couldn't make out the ships' flags in the pitch black so it sent up flares to illuminate the sky. In that instance, the Germans fired upon it and destroyed it. However, in the commotion the patrol boat had managed to send out a communiqué. The receiver of the communiqué was a proud, crusty, straight-as-a-rail, no-nonsense colonel and veteran of WWI by the name of Biger Eriksen.

This officer was in charge of an old defensive fort at a narrow passage called Dromback some miles up the mouth of the fjord, beyond the destroyed patrol boat but closer to the capital of Oslo. Poor Eriksen had to contend with many drawbacks at his fort. Not least was his age of sixty-five years, subordinates who were very fresh recruits and totally untrained with the fortified cannons, and a shortage of overall manpower. Add to the mix a few other factors to really appreciate Eriksen's anxieties: he hadn't received orders from his superiors, the equipment that he was charged with was over forty years old, its operation was questionable, and his time for decision was imminent.

Yet Colonel Eriksen, laboring under uncorroborated information and enormous stress, had a strong visceral feeling about the events that were unfolding. He concluded that the ships in the flotilla were not allies but enemy warships. And since they had destroyed the patrol boat and killed one of his men, he felt that it was unnecessary to even fire warning shots over their bows. As he stared through his field glasses, he could barely make out the armada swiftly slipping past the fort's armaments. He took a deep breath of the cold morning air and let it out slowly. Now or never, he thought. His men would later corroborate that he was overheard saying, "Either I will be decorated or I will be court-martialed. FIRE!"

Eriksen's military seasoning, timing and luck prevailed. When the first shell was fired out of the heavy and cumbersome cannons, he not only gave the orders but assisted, alongside the cooks who had been awakened, to help man the batteries. The first shell found its way directly in front of the aft mast and penetrated the side of the German warship and exploded in an area containing flammables. Moments later a second shell hit the *Blücher*'s gun turret, not only destroying it but sending large sections overboard and igniting more fires. Eriksen's men were elated, jumping up and down, until they saw the cruiser stubbornly undeterred as it kept moving upstream, past the gun batteries. The defenders, seeing the ship plowing onwards and not realizing the extent of the damage, worked feverishly to fire again. But because of slow reloads and untrained personnel, their chance of doing more damage to the belligerent Nazis had ended.

From his hilltop fortress Colonel Eriksen and some of his officers tried to assess the degree of destruction on board the lead ship. The light from the burning fires allowed for some visibility in the pre-dawn hours. Squinting through his binoculars the colonel could see a lot of commotion on the deck of the *Blücher*. Then, in an attempt to keep up morale in the midst of chaos, the boat's crew began singing:

"*Deutschland, Deutschland, über alles.*" Upon hearing these words, the defenders knew for certain that they had fired on the enemy.

As the *Blücher*'s sirens and emergency warning systems blared in the night, its crew scrambled frantically to try and put out the intense fires created from burning oil and diesel fuel. But the fires were difficult to contain since electricity as well as fire-fighting systems went out. Also, the stench of burning flammables and electrical wires and putrid, suffocating black smoke prevented containment. In the main control room, the steering system was also disabled. But the ship's engineers were able to utilize secondary controls to maneuver the ship upstream until it came in the sights of torpedo batteries, another archaic defensive system, positioned on a small island called Kaholmen. History would later discover that faulty German intelligence had discounted the effectiveness of the cannons and had totally failed to recognize that the antiquated torpedo systems even existed.

One of the first torpedoes found the ship's bulkheads as its mark. They were blown open. More vicious and uncontrolled fires spread to more sections of the ship. The damage was disastrous and water began flooding the decks and the engine rooms. Within moments, chaos and pandemonium were everywhere; all the engines were knocked out, fires reached the mid-ship ammunition hold, the bulkheads between the boiler rooms were ripped apart and caused fuel containers to ignite. To a distant observer, the *Blücher* looked like the epicenter of an elaborate fireworks display on Independence Day.

It didn't take long for the officers on board to realize that the damage was catastrophic and no help was to be had from the rest of the armada, which had concluded that the fjord was mined north of Dromback and turned around. The best the endangered crew could do was to anchor the ship at its current position and make a last-ditch effort to try and contain the fires. The captain even gave orders to fire the boat's torpedoes against the coastal land to avoid exploding onboard. But all this valiant effort was not enough. Around 6am the ship's commander ordered that the limited number of life jackets onboard be distributed only to soldiers, reasoning that navy men were expected to be able to swim. Moments later, hundreds of sailors and soldiers were perched at the edge of the deck like birds on a high wire. They dreaded the inauspicious moment of leaping into the subfreezing waters that were coated with a widespread, thick layer of super-hot burning fuel. Some men were preparing themselves mentally and gauging distance to the nearest islet or to the coast without knowing if they could make it or, if they made it, whether a bullet was waiting for them from the local militia. The less contemplative men were plunging into areas of seemingly clear water, away from the fires. However, as each man broke the water's surface an unintended consequence resulted. The burning oil slick drew closer. And as the soldiers came up for air, the burning fuel attached itself to their clothing and set them ablaze. When they dove deeper into the water to douse the flames and resurfaced for air the process was repeated and their flesh burned again.

Then the bow started sinking. The remaining soldiers and sailors on deck jumped overboard and the screams became intense. Within moments the ship tilted over on its port side and flipped upside down. Like a giant sink drain whose stopper was removed, the freezing water sucked the hulk down some ninety feet and, with it, the troops in the ship's proximity.

At the crack of dawn there was no sign of the *Blücher* on the surface of the fjord. What remained was black oil gurgling up from below, spreading wider and wider. Burning corpses, like lit candles, floated on the black, oily water. Other men who were killed by the explosions or were seriously injured or couldn't swim were overcome by hypothermia and were swallowed by the frigid waters. Some 750 perished but 1,400 men made it to the various small islands or the coastal shore. About a third of these, wet and freezing, many suffering from wounds, burns and hypothermia and unable to fight, staggered to shore, not to a rescue, but to be captured by the Norwegian military.

After being disarmed of shoulder holsters and other weapons, most of the soldiers and sailors were held in a makeshift camp under armed guard until further orders came from the top. For the most part, the Norwegian captors treated them humanely and provided blankets and hot coffee. A few dozen who made it to shore with severe wounds were even brought to several temporary shelters in the area.

"How does this tragedy connect to Andreas' father?" asked Bellin.

"Ahh! You asked at a pivotal moment," said Bruno as he continued.

Amongst those captured was a Lieutenant Hans Dietrich-Kuhlemann. Some would say he had a very lucky day; others that he had a very unfortunate one. It all depended on one's perspective. He had been lucky to swim past a ring of fire when he jumped in the water or, as some of his fellow soldiers would later refer to it, the "scalding cauldron." He had been lucky to have swum in the frigid waters, against the current, and for some 685 feet, despite an injury he had sustained to his left thigh right after the second shell blew out the ship's gun turret. The lieutenant had been unlucky to be in the vicinity of the explosion which had sent pieces of shrapnel in all directions, one piece lodging itself in his left thigh. During those frantic moments the ship's medic did everything he could to mend him. He had removed the three-inch piece of steel that had ripped into his thigh muscles and wedged itself alongside the femur bone. He had treated the injury with a small bottle of antiseptic sulfa powder and bandaged the wound. He couldn't give him any morphine since the pharmaceutical storage room was inaccessible because of the fires.

Lieutenant Kuhlemann was an excellent swimmer who had won awards at various competitions both in Munich and Berlin and was on his way to the nationals before the war. So, while many soldiers and sailors saw the distance from ship to shore as a challenging feat, it wasn't so for the lieutenant. Under normal circumstances, it was no more difficult than a morning's warm-up. He would have refused a life jacket but for the injury he had sustained which put him at a serious disadvantage. Thus, when the commander ordered that all life vests be turned over to the soldiers the lieutenant accepted the offer.

Fortuitously, moments before the cruiser flipped over and the lieutenant and other officers jumped over the railing into the frigid waters, it was the life jacket that saved his life; not because he couldn't kick his injured leg and tread water to stay afloat, even though it was difficult, but because of the incredibly large pools of searing oil that was continuing to spill from the disabled battleship. The toxic swamp of chemicals which fed the fires had a temperature in excess of 300 degrees Fahrenheit and melted flesh upon contact. All around him he saw men burning alive. Their skin was literally melting while they were constrained to stay in place. This was because the thick oil turned to tar after burning and was unforgiving once it got on one's legs and arms. Whenever the swimmer started to tread water his legs would stick together and whenever he took a forward stroke, his arms would stick to his sides. Every attempt to maneuver rendered the soldier tired and hopeless. Exacerbating his plight was the current bringing fresh burning oil to where he was thrashing about. For dozens of young men, the tail end of the night brought only screams, horrendous screams. They knew they would not see the daylight.

The lieutenant had attempted to help a private next to him whose clothes had ignited. He retrieved a two-foot plank of wood floating nearby and managed to sweep burning tar away from the soldier. The soldier was flailing his arms in total panic, and then, probably succumbing to heart failure from fear and the intense cold, ceased moving. The lieutenant then discovered that not only was the plank he was holding on fire but he was enveloped by smoldering black oil and gasoline that had floated next to him. He felt a burning sensation on the side of his rib cage and noticed his life jacket burning. He struggled to remove his life preserver, his army jacket and shirt. Only a tattered undershirt remained to protect his upper body. He glanced around to swim to a clearance but saw what appeared to be a lump of hot lava approaching him. As the lava came closer there was a stench of burning flesh. Then his mind recognized the burning lava as the charred remains of a still smoldering corpse. The sight gave him an adrenaline rush and a sharper awareness of his dire predicament. He took a deep breath and submerged himself several body lengths underwater where he could avoid not only the blazing, viscous oil but the men thrashing about, kicking and struggling. He swam under the murky waters as fast as his numbed, aching and broken body could take him. When he came up for air in the faint moonlight he could see that he had navigated some forty feet beyond the hellish site. But he also found that he was farther from what he thought was the nearest island.

He had two choices: either circle back around the ever-spreading inferno or head for another island farther upstream, on the opposite side of the fjord. He felt that he had a better chance to cover the extra distance and not to get entangled again with the burning detritus and fuel. He had precious little time. His body temperature was dropping below the critical point. Or, maybe it was already there. His lower extremities no longer felt cold or pain. This was a bad sign; some of his systems were probably starting to shut down. He could also be losing more blood from his leg than he knew. The other concern was that his mind might be playing tricks on him. Everything came down to raw survival; this was his existential moment.

As he swung around to propel himself in the direction of the larger island, he could still hear the piercing cries of the hopeless and see silhouettes of heads and arms stroking the waters in the direction of the marshy land and to safety.

He was semi-conscious and felt a sort of paralysis to his extremities when he felt his hands touching river reeds, his legs and feet brushing against silt and finally scraping against rocks. As he staggered up to firmer ground, he saw several Norwegian guards with rifles, towering over some dozen sailors and troops sitting on the ground, giving orders: "*Hendene opp!*" One of the guards pulled him up by his arm and virtually dragged him to the clearing where the others were sitting: "*Bevege, over der!*" The guard pushed the lieutenant to the ground. His lower body was numb, beyond cold, and beyond merely shivering. He could see himself trembling uncontrollably while a severe headache, like brain freeze, was demanding his attention. He thought that his core body temperature had dropped precipitously, when it occurred to him that he was about to die, right here, right now, on this spit of foreign land.

As he slumped to the ground, he recognized a few men who were part of his unit. Some were lying prostrate on the ground, exhausted. Others sitting on rocks or huddled under blankets, physically unable or unwilling to do more than make eye contact, perhaps because they didn't want to expose his rank. Then a lanky teenager, wearing civilian clothes and too young to be in military service, came over and threw him a blanket. As he struggled to wrap himself, he saw blood oozing down his leg and turning the white bandages a crimson color. He felt the burn at his side and craved a shot of morphine. It was more extensive and severe than he had realized while in the water. It stretched from his left armpit down to his waist; at least a second-degree burn, maybe worse. Small patches of tar were still stuck to his side. Where the flesh was exposed it was red and raw. The worst was between his left nipple and the end of his rib cage. The hot oils had burned several inches of his skin and practically exposed three of his ribs. Whatever had anesthetized his body and diminished the pain in the water, whether his brain's emergency responses or the effects of the icy waters, it was now gone. His body registered unbearable, agonizing pain.

The last thing the lieutenant remembered was a loud humming noise approaching on the narrow road some distance behind him. The lanky kid stood next to him again, holding out something. Was it coffee? Did he want him to take it? He couldn't, he was just too exhausted and too cold to reach out. Behind the boy he could see the sun rising, its rays sparkling and bouncing over the frigid fjord waters. Then he closed his eyes and everything went black.

*

Inspector Bellin and Antonia were mesmerized by Bruno's telling of the story. They had only eaten several bites from their appetizers when the waiter came over to tell the inspector that he had a phone call. As he got up, his face seemed to register annoyance. The inspector was led to the bar area. Antonia looked at Bruno with some bewilderment, asking without asking why he had not related these events to her in the past. Bruno shrugged his shoulders, a married man's defense of last resort. Then he told her that all these details were not really important or determinative in their decision to adopt Andreas.

"Were they?" he asked.

"No," answered his wife, "but I would have liked to know the whole story of our son's background."

"Antonia, listen," Bruno said as he took her hands in his, "you have to understand that many of these details were relayed to me during the last few months I was at the orphanage and through information and letters forwarded by the orphanage later. Once the adoption was completed the staff felt that I could have access to Andreas' file from Norway, which was fairly detailed, perhaps because the child's father had a high rank. And much of the text was in Norwegian with occasional addendums in the margins written in German. Fräulein Schemitsch and others had spent some time with me translating and explaining them. His mother's letters and the journals filled in the blanks, and out of curiosity I went to the library to read about the invasion of Norway."

Antonia seemed to accept Bruno's explanation but she still looked resentful when the inspector came back to the table.

"Sorry about that," he said, "just an update from my office; nothing pressing."

He forked onto his salad plate more *soppressata*, *formaggio* and *pepperoncini* and poured Bruno and himself a second glass of wine. Antonia had barely touched her first glass and when the inspector offered to top it off, she held up her hand, indicating she was fine.

Then the inspector, anxious to get back to the story asked, "So, how did the lieutenant get out of his predicament?"

*

When the lieutenant passed out from exhaustion his problems were hardly over. His breathing was shallow, his heart rate was slow, and he had lost considerable blood due to the shrapnel penetrating his thigh. He was also suffering from hypothermia and possibly an onset of infection from the burns to his left side. The Norwegian Royal Guards had arrested a total of thirty-seven Germans who had made it to the same location as the lieutenant. The highest-ranking officer of the Royal Guards, a captain, had experience with people falling into the frigid fjord and knew that time was of the essence in saving a life. Where there was prolonged exposure to cold and the victims were not treated within half an hour the rate of survival was dismal. He now had a handful of enemy soldiers who were seriously injured from burns and who were suffering from severe hypothermia. The responsibility of getting them immediate medical attention lay squarely on his shoulders.

The captain was also keenly aware that the Germans had violated Norwegian laws and were probably an advance invasion force. But the world still saw Norway as a neutral country, without having declared war. Therefore, motivated by humanitarian concerns and international law, which mandated the proper treatment of prisoners of war, he had the officers and a handful of other seriously injured soldiers placed on stretchers and transported on a military truck to Astergarden. This was a beautiful hotel on the waterfront overlooking Oslofjord, several miles from the camp where other German soldiers were being detained. The hotel was located in the town of Asgardstrand some ten minutes away. The captain also knew that after the battleship had shelled the coast some wounded Norwegians had been brought there; it was warm and medical assistance was present.

The hotel was an ultramodern structure for its time, constructed on a hillside with miles of panoramic views of the waterway. The original idea behind the project was to attract northern vacationers, especially people who lived in cities above the Arctic Circle, who craved a little seclusion and warmth during the summer months, and some foreign travelers. It also helped that guests could be in the capital within an hour by either land or water. The road leading to the capital was very picturesque as it snaked along the waterway and was in fairly good condition. The same couldn't be said if you headed south. The cracks, potholes and soft shoulders made it supremely difficult to traverse on rainy days. Still, all types of land vehicles found their way to the hotel's gravel parking area. From the dock, concrete pathways stretched up the hill, for all disembarking pedestrians. The flag of Norway, red with an indigo blue Scandinavian cross outlined in white that extended to the edges of the flag, flew prominently at dockside. A pier ran for some fifty meters into the fjord, and a few boats of various sizes and shapes were moored next to it.

The Norwegian National Guard truck pulled into the gravel lot some eight minutes after the injured troops were loaded. A few hotel workers and a local doctor rushed out to greet the truck and to offer assistance. Five stretchers were unloaded and carried inside the front entrance. Three other soldiers who had various burns and blast injuries made it on their own, while one whose foot had blistered and was missing several toes hobbled on one leg, supported by two bellboys.

At the entranceway, a woman was holding one of the double glass doors open while the other was held open by a chair. Beyond the reception area was a ballroom for various functions and wedding events. The tables and chairs had been stacked on one side of this room, freeing a substantial portion of space for cots and mattresses. One nurse in a blue uniform seemed to be in charge of traffic and directed the stretchers to different corners, after a quick assessment of the injuries. Meanwhile, the male medic and a nurse assistant were at the far end. One was hooking up an IV and the other was applying bandages to a woman's head injury. The front desk receptionist, a young woman in her early twenties, was running about, carrying pillows and blankets.

When the medic evaluated the lieutenant's condition he was still breathing, but his pulse was critically low and his body was trembling violently. As the doctor spoke to him, he went in and out of consciousness. Alerted by the gravity of the symptoms the doctor shouted for one of the nurses. He informed her that this man had to be immediately treated for severe hypothermia; there wasn't a moment to spare. The other problems he had could wait, including the wounds that had coagulated and any potential infection. With the assistance of the receptionist, the nurse and medic moved the lieutenant from the stretcher to a cot and his wet clothing was cut up and removed. He was wrapped in warm blankets and warm water bottles were placed between his thighs, under his armpits and against his feet. His forehead was covered with warm wraps. While the women were doing their best to warm the patient externally, the doctor had mounted an IV which fed him a five percent dextrose solution to warm his core. Before the doctor moved on to another patient, he also requested that two pots of hot water be placed on top of the cast iron radiator, next to the lieutenant's cot, to help with breathing and as a warming agent. The receptionist promptly volunteered to run down to the kitchen and bring back the hot water containers.

It wasn't until the following day that the lieutenant briefly opened his eyes. During the short period he was awake he tried to recall the events of the previous day and especially the time just before blacking out. He had seen the sunrise in the east with brilliant points of light bouncing and skimming over the fjord waters as if thin strings were connected to the bright ball of fire. He also remembered being on a hilltop with men in his regiment and Norwegian Guards pointing rifles in their direction. Now he was inside a large, featureless room with tall, rectangular windows letting in the last glimmer of April twilight. As he shifted his body to make better sense of his surroundings, he felt a sharp pain along his left side and thigh. The pain stunned him and brought him to a standstill. He lay motionless and listened while trying to blink away his drowsiness and fatigue. He saw the IV stuck in his arm and other men on cots.

An angel framed in glowing light was leaning over him. He heard voices, incomprehensible sounds, and feet shuffling in the corner of the large room and beyond the partially opened doors. Convinced that he was a prisoner in some military hospital, he fell back into a deep sleep within minutes.

Later in the day, when the conquering Nazis overran Oslo, with the exception of some limited resistance on the fringes of the city, he would be identified as an officer of the *Wehrmacht*. The lieutenant would also come to understand that after this fateful day his life would change radically.

The German commanding officer, after substantially conquering Oslo, learned the whereabouts of the lieutenant and other injured men. He wanted to transfer all of them to Aker University Hospital, northwest of the capital. This site was taken over by the German army for the sole purpose of caring mostly for wounded officers. However, the German field surgeon in charge of the hospital and responsible for reporting directly to the sector commander had convinced his superiors that the lieutenant and a handful of other soldiers were too weak to be moved. These men required several more days to recuperate and should remain at the hotel under his staff's medical supervision.

By the second day at the Astergarden hotel the lieutenant's breathing, pulse and temperature had noticeably improved and the German army medic felt that the hypothermia was sufficiently under control to permit them to deal with the officer's other problems. So, the lieutenant was put on another IV and given a pint of fresh blood and hemoglobin. The muscle damage from the shrapnel was also attended to. First it was cleaned and disinfected with sulfa powder, and the gash was closed with twenty-seven stitches. The leg was already inflamed and swollen like an overinflated football. Lastly, the medics turned their attention to the burns on the side of his rib cage. The oily tar that had adhered to his skin was dissolved with a solution and cleaned. Antiseptic was applied to the area and overlaid with an ointment. Strips of gauze were wrapped around the injured area, taped and, last, bandages were placed around the lieutenant's entire torso. Infection was the doctor's current concern. Thus, specific orders were given to the nurse to be constantly vigilant and to report any change in the patient's vital signs.

On the day the lieutenant's body was fully treated at Astergarden, the war had been going on for two and a half days and the Nazis kept advancing beyond Oslo. Their warships pummeled cities along the long Norwegian coast and poured out troops. Airborne units jumped out of airplanes to capture airports and strategic sites, and Gestapo agents did what they did best: sabotage and terrorize. On that same morning the Norwegians woke up to a mostly overcast sky and a startling revelation being broadcast over their shortwave radios. The news was also spread by word of mouth in shops, villages and cities from the beaches of Kristiansand in the south to the arctic port city of Narvik in the north. It confirmed many rumors about Hitler's invasion, his violation of the country's neutrality, and the specter of hundreds of thousands of troops marching down Main Street.

After this terrible news, a momentary feeling of sweet vengeance, pride and a surge of morale came over many citizens when they heard that at the very gates of their capital, at Oscarsborg Fortress, a small contingent of Norwegian defenders under the leadership of Colonel Eriksen (who took shit from no one, as some broadcasters put it) had taught the German navy an invaluable lesson. The colonel and a handful of his men had first crippled and then sunk the *Kriegsmarine*, the German navy's most modern and most powerful warship. This patriot had scuttled Hitler's best-laid plans and forced overboard thousands of Nazi soldiers and sailors; the radio reports were understandably exaggerated when announcing that thousands had been killed, maimed or taken as prisoners by the Norwegian Royal Guards. The rumors even had it that the rest of the armada was forced to turn back down the river like fish pursued by piranhas, leaving the impression that they went back to Germany. But in truth, the flotilla's troops disembarked a few miles south of the fortress and, that very afternoon, overran all fortifications and freed the German prisoners.

The rumors and tales were even greater in the country's northern cities and outposts. The misinformation was disseminated there not for purposes of accuracy but to boost morale and mobilize resistance by a disorganized, demoralized and poorly equipped Norwegian defense. But it became more evident that, as the hours and days went by, the various cities along Norway's long western coast, including Bergen, Trondheim and Narvik, were falling into the hands of the *Wehrmacht*. Some resistance was evident, particularly in Narvik where British and French forces had come to the aid of the embattled Norwegians. The British navy had even managed to intercept German boats and destroy a number of them. But regardless of the spotty resistance, the effectiveness of the German air force was crucial in permitting ground advances.

In a matter of weeks, to the dismay of the Norwegians, the French and British forces picked up and left. They were redeployed to the continent to assist against Hitler's campaign, which had started against France and was suspected of starting against England. The incursion into the northern continental countries and France had been so quick and successful for the Germans that manpower was crucial for the Allies in this region. The decision to move the troops south amounted, essentially, to saving France and sacrificing Norway. Thus, within weeks after the French and British pulled out of Norway, the German forces became unstoppable.

Still, areas that were not totally under German control kept reporting on the effectiveness of resistance efforts and on the valor of

Colonel Eriksen. This hero had slapped the face of that madman who stood on podiums in Berlin and Munich and screamed from the top of his lungs until his face turned purple. But what the news media didn't readily mention were the larger consequences of Eriksen's actions in saving King Hakoom of Norway and the Royal Family from being captured by Special Forces of the SS being transported on the *Blücher*. But not for the colonel's actions, this battleship and much of the SS crew would not be resting some 400 feet at the bottom of the Oslofjord.

Chapter 19

Who is Birgit Karlsen?

Several minutes had passed since Bruno finished his narrative of Norway's plight. He kept eating and sipping his wine unhurriedly and as if in deep thought. Inspector Bellin and Antonia suspected that he was trying to recall details of events as they pertained to Lieutenant Kuhlemann when he started wondering aloud:

"How could I have been living near Cosenza all these years without discovering Nino's Restaurant?"

He was enjoying his *antipasto e soppressata* so much that he was almost oblivious to his wife's stare and the inspector's unspoken desire to have him continue with the story. Finally, Bellin refreshed his memory by resetting the stage.

"So, you left us with the Nazis consolidating their grip on Norway and already in control of the capital and Asgardstrand, including the hotel where Lieutenant Kuhlemann had been brought to, while critically injured. And his commander had been convinced that he was too sick to be transported to the Aker Hospital where many soldiers of the Third Reich were being treated. Tell us, how did his convalescence go at the hotel?"

"Well, the commander had given clear and unequivocal orders to his army medic, the hotel supervisor and front desk manager that if anything happened to the wounded troops, specifically any officers, which included Lieutenant Kuhlemann, they would be held responsible and would answer directly to him. His concern was not so much with the Norwegian resistance forcing their way into the facility and harming the injured men, because several guards remained on the compound. His worry was more about potential mistreatment by hotel staff. The tone of the commander's voice couldn't be clearer to the three people he was addressing. When he exited the hotel lobby, acknowledgment of the orders was reflected in the medic's sharp salute. The effect was not lost on the hotel supervisor, an elderly gray-haired man, nor on the front desk manager, a young woman of twenty-two, who had been hired some eleven months earlier."

The young woman's employment had been based on three criteria: that she was attractive; that she could type forty-five words per minute; and that she could speak some German. Without parsing words, the supervisor had told her precisely that, in his second-floor office. She was also expected to be attentive to all guests (not only German-speaking tourists), answer telephone calls and be a general liaison person. Her responsibilities and her compensation would grow accordingly as time went on. Then she remembered the supervisor grabbing his raincoat and walking out of the office while she was still seated. She realized, after considerable time, that he wasn't coming back and went to inquire at the front desk. The attendant told her Mr. Johansen had left word for her. She was expected to start work Monday morning.

Birgit Karlsen was the young woman's name. She had learned German words and phrases from her father, who had worked on merchant ships in German ports and other continental European countries. He even gave her a German language textbook for her twelfth birthday which was marked up in pencil with certain phrases translated into Norwegian. She also had picked up some phrases from the few German tourists who frequented the restaurant where she had worked as a waitress.

Birgit Karlsen was the personification of the modern, young Norwegian woman of her day. She had light brown hair, deep blue eyes, and a fresh, clear face with a high forehead. Her overall physique was not slender but proportionate. She had been very dedicated to her job for most of the year and Mr. Johansen had delegated more and more managerial duties to her. During the last few days, like her countrymen, she was worried about the future of her nation should it fall to the Germans. The fact that she had just been in the presence of a commander of the Third Reich stirred a certain amount of general apprehension and also an unexplained attraction. The man in his gray uniform had given them an order. The fact that there were eight wounded soldiers, the lieutenant and two other officers of lesser rank, plus five privates, who were partly in her care, worried her. She pondered the consequences of disobeying a direct order of the commander, and the result of defiance frightened her.

Besides room and board Birgit's hotel offered many amenities but was far from being equipped as a hospital. It was often described in vacation brochures and on postcards kept on the corner of the front desk as a resort. This time of year, the hotel would normally be half full and, as the weather became progressively more pleasant, it would fill to capacity by mid-summer. In September the crowd trickled slowly away and emptied by December when it shut down for three months of winter. Many "northies," or people from higher latitudes, were repeat vacationers and constituted about sixty percent of reservations. Another thirty percent came from Great Britain or continental Europe, including Germany. Local parlance often referred to tourists from the continent as "southies," who loved the spectacular views and the natural, unspoiled beauty of the Scandinavian countries. Locals and other nationals of foreign countries, including Americans, made up an amalgam of the remaining ten percent. The hotel had some sixty rooms. Three days earlier it had thirty-four rooms occupied and, after word of the invasion spread, all but a dozen or so guests checked out with amazing rapidity. The scene was like rats scampering from an old building being demolished. Sailboats and motorboats left the pier as well.

The swastika symbol flew high on the flagpole at the top of the hill, where the Norwegian flag had been flying the previous day. Overlooking the fjord waters, the Nazi flag was an unmistakable reminder to passing boats that things were not the same. Three soldiers and a sergeant were assigned to the hotel. Two of these men were stationed by the front door. The sergeant and the third private often patrolled the area in a green military Jeep and were the link to headquarters or zone command. Birgit had felt a sense of anxiety even before the commander had spoken to them in the lobby. After he left the grounds, tension was supplanted by fear. She knew she wasn't alone. A sense of heaviness affected everyone around her.

Perhaps it had started earlier in the day when she and the staff heard gunfire exchanged as the German troops came on shore. Word was that a small band of resistance fighters was firing from the woods, but no Nazi casualties resulted as far as anyone knew. The exchange of gunfire had been very limited and sporadic; the *Luftwaffe* (air force) wasn't even called in to shell the forested hillside. Birgit had been frightened for the lives of the young men who had dared to show some resistance. When the German soldiers dispersed in the trees and gave chase, more shots were heard in the distance. This was too painful for her to even think about.

Birgit thought about her father, Bjorn Karlsen, and how he would have dealt with the Nazis on the hotel grounds if he was the hotel supervisor. He was a man in his fifties who was furious when he heard news of Hitler's conquests in Europe. Then, upon hearing that the Nazis had invaded his homeland he went into a rage.

How could they? How could the Germans invade a neutral country that posed no threat to them? A country that was virtually unarmed. What could they conceivably want? Hitler and his cronies had proven to be backstabbers. Publicly, they presented themselves as friends and protectors of their northern neighbors, while secretly they were scheming to subjugate and massacre his people. Birgit could visualize her father turning red with fury as he held up the morning paper. He would pose these questions to no one in particular, pacing around the kitchen.

Bjorn Karlsen was known to be a pleasant man, a man of character. A man who knew who he was and what he wanted out of life. Physically, he was strong and muscular. He was tanned, healthy, and looked more like a Roman gladiator than a Norwegian national. These were the very qualities that her mother, Kristiana, had found attractive. They met at a function organized by the Norwegian Shipowners Association, whose objective was to promote the interests of the Merchant Marine, one of which was to put pressure on the legislature to reduce tariffs on imports. Her mother had worked as a secretary at the association's headquarters in downtown Oslo. One of her job responsibilities was to help put together events every two months. Both of Birgit's parents were familiar with, and proud of, the shipping industry. They were also patriotic Norwegians and had a high regard for their heritage.

Her parents were married over twenty-five years and had two children. Sonya was three years older than Birgit, married with children of her own. Birgit remembered enjoying her family's company when they got together on holidays. But within the last two years things changed. Their father lost his job and Sonya moved to Trondheim. Her sister's move to the north-west coast of Norway was because of her husband's work. He and his family owned a furniture factory there. Although they weren't wealthy, he made a decent living, owned a home and she stayed home with their children.

Birgit's supervisor was now standing at the corner of the front desk, and next to him were the gardener and a bellboy. She was on the phone, telling the caller that the guests they were looking for had checked out earlier and had not given any information about where they intended to go. She distinctly remembered the faces of the two newlyweds. They had been at the resort for three days prior and left hours before the vessel loaded with German troops landed at the dock. She noticed that Mr. Johansen looked annoyed and impatient. As soon as she had the phone away from her ear, before hanging up, he spoke.

"Birgit, no use standing behind the desk waiting for guests to arrive that never will."

Then he nodded towards the gardener and the boy standing next to him, as if saying, "They're waiting for you."

"I want you to transfer the three officers from the ballroom into private rooms at the end of the hall. And make them comfortable. The commander ordered that they get good treatment. Remember? And we certainly don't want him disappointed if he comes back." Then, sarcastically, "I think we may have a couple of rooms to spare. These two gentlemen will assist you."

Birgit wondered why he didn't refer to the bellboy and gardener by their names, Eirik and Arnauld. Perhaps he was too distraught by the presence of Nazi troops and the number of vacancies that would surely continue for some time. She thought that at some point he would have to close the resort and let everybody go, unless the Germans who were now in control had other plans for this place.

"Let's go do what the boss wants," Birgit said.

The men followed her across the lobby into the makeshift hospital ward and past some folding tables stacked with sheets and towels. Then walked past the wounded soldiers, bandaged and with IV tubes sticking out of their arms. She informed her two assistants as to which patients had to be moved, then left. The doors were unlocked to the first three guest rooms. Birgit looked inside, then told the gardener and bellboy to move out unneeded furniture until there remained a bed, nightstand and chair. The larger of the three rooms had a bathroom; the others had to make use of shared facilities down the hall. Her plan was to have the lieutenant, who was the highest-ranking officer, occupy the third room, which was larger and had more amenities, in order to placate the commander and Mr. Johansen.

Birgit was not a nurse, by any means, not by training, nor by any natural affinity toward the profession. However, she was well aware of the serious injuries each soldier faced and wondered why the German commander had pulled out all medical personnel from the resort grounds. Did he expect a bloodbath in the field or many more victims to be taken to Aker Hospital? There wasn't much resistance in the capital and no other incident like the explosions on the *Blücher*. It occurred to her that they were probably moving their medical personnel north where heavier fighting was expected.

Birgit was to keep the patients comfortable and to look after their wellbeing until the Red Cross or an army vehicle came to move them. She had been impressed to take on the role of clinic administrator. She had prepared breakfast for five of the six soldiers from the cafeteria downstairs, requested that the maids assist her in changing the linen on the beds, and had even given each soldier medication that was left by the army medic. Now she found herself directing Eirik and Arnauld as they tried to move one of the first officers off the cot and onto a stretcher while she followed closely, carrying the IV bag and the pole to which it had been hooked. The officer-soldier momentarily opened his eyes when he was placed on the stretcher, looked straight at her, smiled weakly and then faded again, probably from the morphine and other drugs in his system. The steps were repeated with the second lower-ranking officer, who looked like a boy in his early twenties and harmless without his green army uniform. Both were given separate rooms at the start of the long hallway.

Lieutenant Kuhlemann was probably the second most wounded under her care. He was not as seriously injured as one private who had lost a lot of blood from his left arm that was amputated two days earlier. But that was not the private's only problem. Much of his left clavicle bone had been shot off and his chin was missing which had exposed his teeth and gums in a most grotesque manner. Birgit found it difficult to look at his disfigured face. She remembered his condition when he was first brought in and was surprised that he was still breathing. The army medic did everything possible to stitch him up, give him blood to make up the loss and bandage the wounds, but blood was now soaking all the bandages and seemed to be pooling at the end of his stump. It was swollen at the tip and purple closer to the shoulder. She was terrified to even touch him for fear that his heart would completely stop or the pooled blood would burst out of the bandages like an overfilled dam. He was in a coma and had not been able to eat, which probably made him even weaker. For this poor soul the medic couldn't get here fast enough. She would inform the sergeant patrolling the grounds.

Lieutenant Kuhlemann was moved in the same manner as the other officers but, as planned, occupied the last vacant room down the hallway. Not only was the room more spacious but was located in a quieter area; no noises from the front desk or crying sounds from the other patients. At the opposite side of the ballroom, where the lieutenant had been for the last two days, was an older, local woman who had been injured from strafing by the *Luftwaffe* and was constantly crying out in pain, asking for something or other, cursing the German army. Two Norwegian men who had been shot were on cots across from the Nazi soldiers; neither of the two men had military uniforms. Birgit found it ironic, if not surreal, that people from opposing sides, people who were out to kill each other, were in the same room, listening to each other's agony, and she, Birgit Karlsen, was the arbiter and caregiver to both sides. This was not the way it was supposed to be. She wished for a savior who could take her away from this madness.

During his move the lieutenant awoke from the jostling. He was breathing heavily and with some difficulty but was not trembling or even shivering as he had been the last two days. His hypothermia was in remission. And his body temperature was getting close to normal.

As Birgit pulled her hand from his forehead the gardener and bellboy stood around the bed, confused as to why they were attending to this man who had led some of his troops to invade their homeland and even kill their fellow citizens. The gardener may have been thinking to sneak in at night and bash his head in with a sledgehammer. To Birgit his left arm felt warm as she took his pulse. Perhaps an infection was tearing through his body. When she pulled her hand off, he opened his eyes briefly, looked at her and smiled. In an almost inaudible voice, he thanked her in German, calling her "my angel Birgit," in an almost incomprehensible mixture of German and Norwegian. She tried to assure him that he would be alright. She asked Eirick to bring the two pots of steaming water from the lobby and place them on the radiator next to the patient's bed.

The medic didn't arrive until seven o'clock. He came in a regular military truck, with a male nurse, escorted by two Jeeps. The medic was a tall, skinny man, with glasses and a pinched nose slightly askew. No one recognized him as the same doctor who had been there the previous day and no one knew exactly what rank his stripes indicated. The sergeant on duty met them by the front entrance and gave a brisk Nazi salute. Then some words were exchanged and the doctor was escorted to the wounded soldiers across the lobby. He walked from patient to patient and made a mental assessment of each, including the three wounded Norwegian nationals.

"Where are the other three?" he demanded of the sergeant who stood some ten feet away. The sergeant quickly turned toward the hotel supervisor and Birgit, who were huddled a few feet outside the door. Birgit quickly responded that the officers were in separate rooms and, as she walked closer to the sergeant, pointed in the direction of the long hallway.

"On whose orders were they moved?" asked the medic in a tense, angry voice as he moved closer. The effect seemed not intended for the hotel staff as much as it was for the sergeant. He was in charge of the compound and apparently had no idea what was happening.

"We moved them, sir, to make them more comfortable and allow them better rest without noise." Birgit spoke in a submissive voice, hoping that what she said was understood and was viewed as a sensible action. The officer-medic turned abruptly and headed down the hallway.

The medic found two of the three patients in the guest rooms, groggy but responsive. He ordered his nurse assistant to change their IV bottles and their dressings. Without deliberation, the nurse opened a large satchel and started to carry out the order. The medic looked inside the last room and said something inaudible to Birgit. She didn't respond. She was concerned that the lieutenant might have taken a turn for the worse and that the medic might put the blame on her, for having moved him and for not having done more to contain the infection.

Of the eight Germans, only two had not eaten their fish soup that Birgit had specifically requested from the cafeteria. The amputee and the lieutenant were not sufficiently conscious to swallow, even with the assistance of her staff. Both men were living on what was in their bellies from two days earlier, if anything was there, and on the IV fluids since arrival. She had noticed that the lieutenant looked a bit more gaunt than earlier. She was curious to see if the medic would force-feed him somehow, and what he would do about the lieutenant's infection. Birgit lingered near the door and saw the lieutenant's light get turned on. And moved closer to the door to get a better view. The doctor had his bag on the foot of the bed and pulled out a long syringe and a small vile. Probably penicillin, she thought. This was touted as the new miracle drug and from what little she knew was used to counter infections. He administered the medication in the patient's limp left arm. Once that was finished, he proceeded to remove the almost empty IV bottle hanging and replaced it with a new one.

She was startled when the medic unexpectedly called her to come inside the room and help him support the patient. She thought that he was probably going to change the dressing. As she got closer to the headboard she noticed that the lieutenant was still unresponsive. So, she placed her hands under his arms in an attempt to lift him when the medic yelled at her to stop. He was speaking rapidly in German, which she could not understand. He made a motion with his hands that they were to turn the patient on his side. Then the doctor cut through the old bandages and gauze. She could see that the bandages coming off were bloody and that the injured area was raw and oozing pus. This made her feel sick to her stomach, ready to vomit. The medic then requested a pot of clean water and some clean towels. Another moment, she thought, and she would have disgorged her food.

Birgit was back in less than five minutes with clean white towels on her shoulder and her two hands wrapped around a water basin. She was surprised to see that the medic was already cleaning the wound with a cotton cloth from his bag and warm water from a pot on the radiator. He quickly grabbed two of the towels she brought, dipped them in the warm water and finished cleansing the wound. When finished, he applied a yellowish ointment and covered it with gauze and clean bandages around the patient's torso. While the lieutenant was still semi-conscious, his body was repositioned with his head slightly elevated.

The doctor was stressed and overworked. His abruptness and irascibility had less to do with his nature than the pressure of his position. Birgit felt empathy for him, constantly seeing suffering and death. While searching inside his bag, he pointed to the water basin she'd left on the nightstand and motioned for her to place it on the radiator. Finally, he pulled out a jar containing large pills, leaving eight on the nightstand. Birgit was instructed to give the lieutenant one in the morning and one at night. Then the doctor rearranged some contents inside the medical bag, zipped it and headed for the door, presumably to treat the next patient. After taking several steps, he turned around and looked at her while she balanced the water container on the radiator.

"You are forbidden to move these men again. You are not to spare anything for their wellbeing, understand?" She didn't totally understand but she got the gist of it and nodded her head. "*Ja, Doktor.*"

From the hallway the doctor looked into the other two rooms. His nurse assistant was still attending to the second officer. He didn't go inside to assist but headed directly for the ballroom. When he saw Birgit coming out of the lieutenant's room, the medic called her to follow him. Inside the ballroom, he attended to the three privates quickly, almost mechanically, and then turned his attention to the amputee. Birgit was surprised that the medic had left the most critical soldier for last but, within moments, she had her answer. She learned that this soldier's name was Heinz Muller; his cot, his pillow and the area around was a bloody mess. Birgit had mixed feelings about the boy's condition. Seeing him like that, it looked like his medical prognosis was dismal, but she was surprised at his alertness. He responded to the doctor's questions in a very lucid manner. He even attempted to sit up but the doctor asked him to lie down and calm himself.

Birgit was told to sit on the other side of the bed and hold Heinz' good hand. The patient closed his eyes. Her touch seemed to calm Heinz. Meanwhile, the surgeon started to unravel the soaked bandages from his stump. Birgit could swear that as the bandages came off, she saw the medic shaking his head. Then, unexpectedly, as the final layers of bandages were unraveled, coagulated blood and fresh blood from the transfusion ruptured the stitches and exploded like an overfilled water balloon. The medic's jacket was splattered red, making him look like a butcher in a slaughterhouse.

The doctor took a pillowcase and made a makeshift tourniquet, wrapping it tightly above the stump to stop the blood flow. The eighteen-year-old soldier opened his eyes and his face had a grimace expression, revealing his missing chin and exposed gums from under his bandages. The doctor worked quickly and filled a syringe with what seemed to be morphine and injected that in his thigh. In seconds she felt the boy's body relaxing and easing into a slumber. Several uncontrolled jerks of the body followed. He opened his eyes wide and then his breathing ceased. The medic closed his eyelids and pulled the sheet over his face. It took Birgit a while for her brain to process what had just happened and to let go of the young man's delicate pale hand still clasped around hers.

The doctor stood up from the kneeling position next to the cot, stone-faced. He muttered something inaudible and gave out a deep sigh. Then he walked to the sergeant, standing on guard by the lobby's front entrance, and ordered him to place the body in the back of the medical truck. By now, the assistant male nurse came walking down the corridor, down the two steps and across the lobby. Birgit took a deep breath and mustered enough courage to approach the doctor.

"Please check on the three civilians on the other side of the ballroom."

He stared down at her, as if momentarily contemplating the request, shook his head, balked. Almost as if he didn't want to be understood, he spoke quickly, dismissing the idea by telling her something about being forbidden or it was against army regulations. He left telling her to change the dressings and let them rest. Birgit felt that his words and manners were condescending, as if the Norwegian civilians didn't matter.

It was nine thirty when the convoy pulled out of the hotel parking lot. They had finished loading the body on the truck when the officer-medic called Mr. Johansen, who had been keeping himself busy behind the front desk. Again, Johansen was admonished that if the injured men in uniform were harmed, in any way, or even moved, he would be held responsible. Birgit translated the orders but was certain that the officer's stern warnings were directed equally at her. She felt they would have no compunction in shooting anyone that was suspected of not following orders. Mr. Johansen seemed to be shaken. He seemed particularly upset after the medic studied him closely for an uncomfortable minute, as if examining an insect under a microscope. For Johansen the minute seemed to be an eternity. Finally, the pinched-nose medic looked back at Birgit. "Ask the administrator if he's a Jew."

Birgit was surprised at the question and its timing. But her employer didn't need translation; he knew precisely what the medic was asking and the type of man he was.

"Tell him that I am a fifth-generation Norwegian national," he said to Birgit.

She translated, after which the doctor's gaze came off the administrator. He turned around and walked out, followed by his assistant. Mr. Johansen's hands were tightly gripping the corner of the front desk. His look told Birgit that he would do everything possible to assure the safety of these Nazis in the hope that, in several days, he would be rid of all of them when they transferred them to the army hospital.

Mr. Johansen was able to relax a little after the officer-medic left. But the doctor's question had pierced him and he felt humiliated by the look of contempt. He had heard reports of the mistreatment of Jews in Germany and wondered if the bigotry and hatred were being exported to his country.

Birgit prevailed on Mr. Johansen to help her with the three wounded Norwegian civilians who were refused care. Together they changed dressings and fed them dinner. It wasn't until after 10.30pm that they finished. Even at such a late hour the old woman was still crying about this or that. Basically, she just didn't want to be left alone.

Birgit thought about the lieutenant and the eight pills on his nightstand. She decided to cut each pill in half and give the lieutenant half and the other half she would administer to the sickest Norwegian man who had been critically wounded and was also suffering from infection.

Moments later she was in the lieutenant's room. As she held up his head to facilitate his swallowing, he opened his eyes briefly and asked where he was.

"You're in a safe place. You were wounded and now you are getting stronger each day," she said, sounding a little foolish for what she said and how she said it.

"And you're the angel watching over me?" he asked.

"You should drink this and not talk," she responded.

He made an attempt at swallowing the warm water with the pill's chalky taste. After two swallows his head collapsed back onto the pillow. She couldn't hold him up again but was content that he had drunk most of the tea with the medicine. It was the first time he had ingested anything since arriving.

She knew he was an enemy soldier but couldn't believe that he was as evil as her countrymen made the Nazis out to be. Wounded and without a uniform, he seemed to be a helpless young man, and there seemed to be little difference between him and the two Norwegians in the ballroom. She found his bluish-green eyes captivating. He was probably a few years older than her and was strikingly handsome, like the hero in the novel she was reading. She shook herself out of her daydream. She wanted to ask if he wanted some soup or something else from the kitchen but it was too late; he was out again.

Chapter 20

Time Spent Recovering

On the morning of the third day of the invasion the first floor of the Astergarden was functioning more as a hospital ward than a resort hotel. Olaf Johansen called for a staff meeting at ten o'clock. At the end of the meeting he had dismissed all personnel, with the exception of a handful, telling them that the hotel could no longer afford to keep them on the payroll due to disruptions caused by the war. Some of the maids and kitchen help started crying upon receiving the news. But they could see for themselves that business was dismal and Mr. Johansen didn't know the wider implications of the occupation and how it would affect the resort in the future. He assured them that if things got back to normal, they would be rehired. In the meantime, after this whole affair with the wounded was over, he intended to close the resort until further notice. Many of the employees had seen the disruption first hand; just before the German troops came in and occupied the town most of the tourists and guests had vacated the hotel as soon as they possibly could and by any means they could find. The hotel's ten to fifteen percent current occupancy was shrinking even further. This knowledge led them to a rational acceptance of the termination but did not do anything to alleviate the state of emotional upheaval and economic concern on their individual faces.

Before the staff meeting, the morning had started with certain electricity in the air. This was prompted by news that Vidkun Quisling, a Norwegian politician and former defense minister, had been named the functioning Prime Minister by the Nazis. This led some people to speculate that some unity government was in the works and if Norwegian leaders held high positions then they would have leverage against the Nazis. They even hoped that the occupation of their country would not be total and what was happening was a unity government where each party's mutual interest could be recognized. Still some reports contradicted this assessment by pointing out that Quisling was a Nazi sympathizer and traitor and not looking out for his country's best interest. He was primarily motivated by his own selfish gain, even if it meant selling out his homeland.

Mr. Johansen appeared to have had his fill with the injured on the previous night so he asked the bellboy and the gardener, Arnauld, to assist Birgit with the daily care of the patients. She, in turn, asked them to sponge-bathe the soldiers, carefully, and not to exacerbate their injuries in the process. The gardener refused outright. "*Det er en styrer!* (That is disgusting!)" He said he had had enough. His attitude was that they were invading, filthy swine and he would not stoop that low. He had certain Norwegian pride and would not be so humiliated. He felt that while their comrades invaded, raped and killed his people he would not debase himself to intimately touch their flesh and clean their asses.

"I would rather take a pruning knife and slice their throats," he said.

Upon hearing the commotion Mr. Johansen fired him on the spot, telling him that he was not only jeopardizing his own life but everyone else's on the premises; that there was a time to fight and a time to follow. He reminded the gardener that there were soldiers stationed outside the front door and they would not hesitate to shoot any one of them. Still, the gardener wouldn't have any of it. He had worked himself up into such a frenzy that, in a huff, he went to pack his things.

It was the bellboy who suggested that the porter, Sveinn, would probably be willing to assist him in doing the job and went to get him on the south side of the building where he was hosing down some door mats.

After the sponge baths were finished, Birgit fed the patients herring and waffles and warm milk mixed with nuts with the help of two cafeteria workers she had convinced to stay on. Birgit felt that this diet was more palatable for some patients and easier to masticate and ingest, considering their condition.

The injured Norwegian woman refused to have any breakfast. She remained very irascible and knocked the kitchen worker's tray to the ground. Desperate to get rid of her, Mr. Johansen contacted her husband to come and get her in his horse-drawn wagon. He didn't care if the man had to fight off every Nazi on Norwegian soil to get there. She had told the administrator that the place had been a nightmare the last few nights and that if she was going to die, she'd rather do it in her own home. But the reality was that she had recuperated sufficiently and had even eaten a couple of meals since her arrival. Mr. Johansen breathed a sigh of relief. He was glad to see her go. Not only was she an ingrate but had a dangerous tendency to say anything that came to her mind at any time. She expected the world to revolve around her. Better that she go home and annoy her emasculated husband, he thought.

The lieutenant had been one of the last to be fed. Birgit had planned it that way. He had captured her imagination the night before when he was feverish and she was wiping his face with a cloth. In his delirium he had grabbed her hand and squeezed it just enough, as if to tell her that he needed her, that she was his salvation. In that momentary connection she had felt something stirring in her.

She entered his room with a tray containing a bowl of warm

cereal, napkin, spoon and half a glass of warm water with another half pill dissolved in it. She hoped that half the medication was sufficient to fight off any infection in his system and planned on giving him the other half in the evening. She also noted that there were still six and a half pills remaining on the nightstand. The lieutenant seemed to be more alert than ever. He was slightly elevated on two pillows. His face had been shaved and the hair bordering his forehead and around his temples was still wet from the sponge bath. A lock of hair hung haphazardly over his left eye. His face had some color. Birgit was convinced that hypothermia was no longer a problem. When she got closer, he took the initiative and greeted her with a warm smile that caused her cheeks to flush unexpectedly.

"*Guten Morgen, schöner Engel,* I see my guardian angel is still looking after me."

"I can see you're feeling much better," she responded with a small smile.

"Yes, thanks to you, Birgit (he read her name tag), I am feeling much better overall. I was even thinking of getting up except that my side is still quite painful," he said as his right hand moved across his chest to the tender spot.

"Don't! You'll open the wound!" She remembered the admonition about not moving him. "You need to get more bed rest and fortify yourself before you go walking around. I brought you some breakfast to make you stronger," she stated.

Then she placed the tray on the nightstand, put a cloth napkin under his chin, brushed back the lock of hair hanging over his eye and sat on the left side of the bed ready to spoon-feed him when his expression suddenly changed.

"How many others are here from my regiment?" he asked.

"If you mean how many wounded German soldiers are currently here, there are six others besides yourself," she answered. "And the last time I counted there were four others outside the compound who looked pretty healthy," she added.

"If my men are patrolling outside, does that mean that Oslo has fallen?"

"Yes. At this time there's very little resistance according to reports. Even the national troops that brought you here, and their medic that saved your life, escaped north when your troops marched in. I suppose you could feel very proud."

"It doesn't matter what I feel. I'm just one of many soldiers carrying out orders." He looked straight ahead, pensively. His mind was elsewhere when he finally asked, "How many days have I been here?"

"Three days. You were brought here from the river bank by the Norwegian Royal Guards. You were almost frozen to death and bleeding from multiple wounds."

"I suppose the same people that tried to kill me then tried to save me."

"That is our way; my countrymen cannot allow the helpless to die if it can be avoided," she snapped back. "Besides, you would not be in this predicament if you had stayed in your own country," she added.

"And then we would never have met," he quipped back as his facial muscles relaxed and a slight smile formed on his face.

"I think you should eat and get mended so your field medic can have you transported to the army hospital."

"In that case I should go slowly to get better. I like it here."

Birgit, flustered by the way the conversation was proceeding, shoveled a big spoonful of cereal into his mouth before he had time to say anything else. She continued the feeding until a quarter of the bowl was left, at which time he put his hand lightly on hers to indicate, "No more." She put the plate down; then placed her right hand behind his pillow to gently elevate his torso a bit more so that he could take his medication, mindful that his left side was stitched and still raw. When he had swallowed the half glass of water with the medication, she set the pillows back down and pulled the blanket up to his neck.

"What was in the drink?" he asked.

"Too late, you drank it already. Damage is done," she said with a grin.

"Well, if I die make sure my name, Hans Dietrich-Kuhlemann, goes on my gravestone," he whispered, while meeting her eyes directly. Then feeling weak and sore and as if surrendering he said, "Thank you, Birgit," and closed his eyes.

"You're welcome," she responded almost inaudibly, startled by the depth of connection she felt when his eyes held hers.

"It was penicillin, if you must know. Your army medic left it for you." She was unsure if he had heard her before dozing off.

Twice, Hans Dietrich-Kuhlemann had pronounced her name and each time it sounded more melodic. She found it intriguing that a name of French derivation, pronounced with a German accent, could sound so pleasant to her Norwegian ears, or maybe it was just the way he said her name that sang to her heart.

When she left the lieutenant's room only five and a half pills remained on his nightstand. She wanted to double back to the young Norwegian man who had been shot, with the bullet still lodged in his chest. His infection was becoming more life-threatening despite the small dose of penicillin she had given him the night before. She came to the conclusion that half a tablet was insufficient and his body was not responding. It was for that reason she was now carrying a round, white, horse-size pill in her pocket. Regardless of the consequences, she needed to get back to the boy's room and administer the medicine to try to suppress the infection that was spiking the high fever. She hoped that the Germans would evacuate the hotel grounds soon so that they could get him outside assistance. Mr. Johansen could probably contact the local town doctor who would be able to operate and remove the bullet, assuming there were no roadblocks. Now that blood loss was minimized, she hoped to buy him time by suppressing the infection. She also felt that by the time the lieutenant went through the remaining medicines he would probably be transferred to the army facility. In any case, his recuperation was progressing remarkably well. She found herself smiling upon thinking about the lieutenant's smile. She shook her head to clear it as she hurried down the hall. She did not understand her reaction, but could not seem to help it.

*

Nazi control seemed to be getting more pervasive, not just in the capital but even on the hotel grounds. The guards allowed the hotel staff to either stay on the premises or leave and go home after establishing proof of employment and proof that they lived in the community. But they were a bit more inquisitive when it came to the remaining hotel guests who wanted to check out. Mr. Johansen, after getting permission from the sergeant in charge, made arrangements for a truck to come in the afternoon and take a group of guests to the train station. Accordingly, one Dutch family and several Norwegian families that lived in other northern cities were cleared and waited, all clustered by the main entrance with baggage nearby. Separated from the group was an English couple who claimed to be on their honeymoon and were being detained, at the other side of the lobby, near the stairs leading to the downstairs kitchen. A guard stood nearby. They had been waiting there for half an hour and both were getting fidgety. When the sergeant finally came back inside, they were ordered back to their room. The husband protested the decision. He said he needed to leave. He kept waving his travel documents and pleading his case. Then he moved towards the officer to show him. But before he could thrust the passport and visa in his line of sight the sergeant had the barrel of his gun pressing against his forehead. As the safety catch was disengaged the Brit seemed to freeze. His female companion, acting sensibly, pulled him back in the nick of time. Then they picked up their baggage and headed back upstairs. The military suspicion was that British nationals present in Norway were probably connected with British Intelligence. England was already considered an enemy nation by the Nazi high command. Its navy was already attacking and destroying German ships, blockading the North Sea lanes and the North Atlantic waters, and providing armaments and men to fight with the Norwegian resistance in the country's northern ports.

Almost like perfect stage direction, while the English husband and his wife headed back to their room like humiliated grade school students, Arnauld, the gardener, came through the hotel's back door, walked down a narrow corridor and across the lobby. He carried a large bag strapped over his shoulders. As he pushed open the front door he was muttering under his breath. Either he was so worked up about being fired that he was oblivious to the guards or assumed that they knew he was part of the staff, having seen him around for several days, that he kept walking at a fast pace.

"*Achtung!*" shouted one of the guards. Still the gardener kept walking, preoccupied with his own thoughts.

"*Achtung! Sofort stoppen* (Stop immediately)," repeated the guard louder as he dropped to his knees, the rifle cocked against his shoulder, finger on the trigger.

The rifle's metallic engagement elicited a response. Arnauld turned to see the rifle pointed squarely in his direction and the guard's head tilted, looking through the weapon's sight. He dropped his bag from his shoulder to the ground and raised his hands. The tourists still clustered together and waiting for transportation to the railroad held their collective breath, some realizing for the first time the serious nature of their predicament and that they should have evacuated earlier. It obviously didn't matter if you were a local or a tourist; the Nazi occupation was affecting all of them directly. And there was no way their embassy, the Norwegian government or their documents could protect them. They were at the whim and mercy of these barbarians. The tourists felt that the sooner they could be on a boat steaming away from Oslo the better.

While the first soldier's weapon was trained on the gardener, a second soldier walked up to him and swung the butt of his rifle against his face. He went down with teeth and blood splattering from his mouth and a gash across his right cheek. The man in uniform stood over him with bayonet in hand, ready to thrust at the slightest provocation, but the gardener was down, stunned. The guard bent over and recovered the large stuffed bag and started rummaging through it. Shirts, pants, shoes, underwear, shaving paraphernalia were tossed out. The remaining contents were emptied on the ground. No guns or other armaments were found, except a Swiss knife which the soldier confiscated. Then the empty bag was hurled against the prostrate gardener and the soldier walked back towards the hotel entrance.

The shouting brought Birgit out from behind the counter. She ran to the front entrance where she saw the tourists huddled together. She stared incredulously at what they had just witnessed as the soldier walked away from the man on the ground, leaving him still writhing in pain. As she quickly walked the forty feet towards the defeated hulk the guards didn't interfere. When she saw the man's bloodied face, she took off her scarf, rolled it into a wad and knelt next to him, pressing it against his face. The group of tourists could see her speaking briefly with the gardener as he slowly and painfully sat up while pressing the cloth against his face.

When the passenger's transportation arrived, the truck driver rolled into the parking lot close to the front doors. He came down from his cab and showed the nearest guard identification. The soldier who had come a split hair away from taking the gardener's life was now standing over Birgit and the bloody-faced man, ordering him to move on. His belligerency and disdain for the two of them was still palpable in his gestures and the sneer on his face. He made several motions with the point of his bayonet toward the road. Birgit helped her former co-worker to his feet. Then he composed himself as best he could and, still holding the cloth to his face, staggered down the road. His gray, extra-large duffle bag was crumpled in a heap under the afternoon sun and his personal effects were scattering around the parking lot from the gusty breezes blowing in from the cold fjord waters.

Chapter 21

The Affair

The bellboy, the porter and one of the maids had been assigned the full-time role of making the beds and bathing "the unintended guests" for as long as they were there. That was how Mr. Johansen sarcastically referred to the wounded Germans. The handful of employees that remained, after the massive lay-offs, were assigned tasks beyond their normal scope. As a result, hotel services suffered. The beds would be made every other day. The dining room and bar were closed and menus were removed from the tables. The new reality, a "no frills" menu: cereal or an egg for breakfast, a ham or fruit spread sandwich for lunch and a bowl of thick soup and bread for dinner. But the true reason for the new frugality had less to do with the barebones staff than the inability to get deliveries. In less than a week the war had disrupted everything. The butcher didn't slaughter, the farmer didn't ship, and the fishermen didn't go trawling. Who could blame them? Boats were being blown out of the waters, trucks couldn't get past the Nazi roadblocks, and when the occasional brave soul tried to make deliveries soldiers would point a rifle, force him out of the truck and confiscate his goods. This scenario may not have happened often, but all that was needed was one incident for word to spread. So, the general fear that things could get worse convinced the small business owner to hoard the commodity for his own family's use.

By the end of the third day Birgit realized that some of her charges seemed to be recuperating faster than others and passed their time looking through magazines or walking about a little. Soon decisions had to be made. She did not know what would happen to the two young Norwegians once their health was restored. She feared that they might be interrogated and possibly arrested by the Germans for suspicious activities or hostile intent. It was still not clear how their injuries occurred but it was widely believed that they had resisted the occupying forces. The English couple was also a source of anxiety for her. They had approached her on the second floor and begged her to get a letter from them to the British Embassy. She had promised them that she would speak to Olaf Johansen and if there was any assistance he could give them he would.

It was about 6pm when Birgit came to the lieutenant's room, carrying his dinner in a covered tray. The door was open a few inches and she pushed it the rest of the way with her hip. She found him sitting on the side of the bed staring through the window. As she walked into the room his head turned and he smiled, a disarming smile with a perfect set of teeth.

"I was thinking of breaking out and hunting for my own food. Then I realized I have no weapons and can't run very fast so I'd embarrass myself," he said.

"Our healthcare may not be optimal but we don't starve our 'unintended guests.'" She used her boss's line, finding it very appropriate. "I figured you'd be hungry for some real food." She placed the tray down on his nightstand and pulled off the cover. "Hope you like venison stew," she said. "No deliveries are being made and the pantry is running low."

She watched as the lieutenant saw chunks of meat, potatoes, carrots and celery floating in a thick reddish-based liquid. Several pieces of hard crusty bread were resting on a white napkin and a small saucer contained a square piece of cornbread. Also, on the tray was a small flask containing a reddish beverage with a small glass turned upside down over the flask.

"I love venison. It brings me back to a different time in Bavaria when my father used to take me hunting in the Black Forest. You'll find no complaints here."

She saw him wincing as he attempted to rearrange himself on the side of the bed.

"You shouldn't be sitting up like that. Your wounds are still tender." She propped his pillows behind his back as she had other times and helped him swing his legs back on the bed.

"There, isn't that better?" she said, looking for approval. None came.

The lieutenant's eyes locked onto her eyes. He seemed to be enraptured by her soft, sparkling, deep blue eyes. They were probably a window into another realm where madness and war didn't exist. And he seemed to bask in her soul. Birgit sensed it and felt exposed. She wanted to walk away, yet she wanted to be drawn deeper.

Something was stirring inside him like an irrepressible tornado gathering physical and spiritual energy. He yearned to have her near, to caress her face, to hold her close. In this room they were not part of the outside world. The world out there was like another universe, remote. Here, now, this moment was the pinnacle of existence! They were not the lieutenant and the Norwegian girl, they were just Hans and Birgit, young, lonely, frightened, and falling in love.

He reached for her hand – smooth, soft white skin and long delicate fingers. He enveloped her hand in his. She didn't pull away. Their connection was like one breathing in, the other breathing out, in a life-giving exchange. Gently, he placed his other hand in her midsection to bring her closer when a startling noise ripped them apart: glass shattering in the hallway. The clumsy maid had dropped a glass from a dinner tray. Birgit rose from the side of the bed and went to the door. The maid was apologetic while picking up the shards. The lieutenant seemed to listen for a second, as if visualizing all. Then he exhaled loudly, leaned back and tried to compose himself. When she came back, she picked up the fork and the plate of venison. Her heart was still fluttering.

Birgit cut each chunk of the reindeer steak smaller as she fed it to the lieutenant with an occasional spoonful of potatoes and greens. Hans asked her what was troubling her. Then she told him what had transpired earlier in the day when the gardener had been stopped at gunpoint and his personal belongings were searched in the parking lot. She told him of her fear of the guard when she ran to help Arnauld. His eyes widened briefly, because he knew only too well the danger she had placed herself in. Birgit also recounted how Mr. Johansen had fired the man earlier in the morning for insubordination. When he asked why he was fired, she told him the truth. The gardener had refused to do some of the chores he was assigned; specifically, he had objected to treating the invading forces as honored guests.

The lieutenant didn't ask for more specifics, not because it didn't occur to him to ask but because the subject might make her uncomfortable. He suspected why the man was really fired. And he knew that she was caught between different forces: that which demanded patriotism for her country and condemnation of all things German, and whatever feelings he suspected that she had for him.

When she finished recounting that morning's events, in a low but serious and commanding voice, he said, "If anyone mistreats you, I want you to tell me. Do you understand that?" she nodded. "Please, promise me that you will not put yourself in such danger again," he implored, grasping her hands.

Birgit was confused. "What danger, Hans?"

"You must realize that our countries are at war and soldiers live by different rules. You could have been hurt or killed today, *meine Liebe*. You must promise me, please, you must promise me now that you will stay safe until…" Hans did not complete the sentence but his fear and passion were reflected in his eyes.

He let go of her hands and cleared his throat, confused at how much he had come to love this girl. It was not just physical desire, he loved her.

Birgit was equally aroused and bewildered. He was supposed to be the enemy. But she only felt passion. She began to quickly feed Hans to avoid further conversation for the moment, until she could sort her feelings out. It wasn't until the lieutenant had eaten his way through half the dinner when she realized that he hadn't drunk anything.

"You were eating so heartily that I didn't offer you a drink," she said.

"Frankly, I'm enjoying the food and the attention lavished on me so I also didn't think of drinking anything. I was more famished than dehydrated," he responded carefully, his eyes never leaving her face.

"But this is a special drink," she said as she looked toward the small carafe with a skinny glass topping it and sitting in the corner of the tray on the nightstand. "It's a French wine from Bordeaux. I thought you might like it. I heard people from Bavaria produce wine and enjoy drinking it," she added almost shyly.

"Yes, Bordeaux is a very good wine, but I'll drink it under one condition." A broad smile formed on his face, showing a tiny gap between his upper teeth. She found that endearing, too.

"And what condition might that be?" she said coyly.

"That you share it with me," he responded. "But first, hand me that half glass of water by the lamp." He took the water and drank it. "There, now we have two empty glasses," he said as he emptied the decanter in both glasses and handed her one of them.

She hesitated briefly and looked at him, trying to discern his intentions. It was only when he whispered, "Please," that she complied with his request. He grasped his glass a little clumsily and held it close to his chest to avoid spillage.

"To Norway's natural beauty, embodied in the radiance of your face," he said as he made an attempt to stretch out his arm and clink glasses, but his limited mobility prevented him, so she stretched over to touch his glass. Both took a long sip, their faces acknowledging that the liquid was delicious.

"Thank you," she said. "You're very kind considering that your reception was not very hospitable," she added.

"That still doesn't detract from what I saw and what I see," he responded.

She placed her glass down and grabbed his dinner plate to feed him some more when he said, "Thank you, but I'm not feeling hungry anymore, perhaps a little later."

"In that case," she said, putting his plate back on the tray, "I'm going to help the maid with the other patients and come back later to check on you and to give you your medication for the night."

He took a final sip of wine before handing her the glass. Then she readjusted his pillow as he slid farther down under his blankets.

"I promise not to go anywhere until you get back," he said, smiling, as she headed for the door.

Birgit wasn't outside the lieutenant's room for more than a few minutes before finding out that the maid had not made much progress in feeding the other "unintended guests." She had been preoccupied with two of the more seriously wounded and had not gotten to the others. When Birgit went downstairs to the kitchen the cook had lined up four trays of food on a work table that were now barely lukewarm. He had his back turned to her, making a racket scrubbing pots. She took two trays, one in each hand hoping to make it upstairs in one piece. There she would wake the men, if they were sleeping, and place the trays on their lap hoping that they could feed themselves. And then she would come down for the last two dinners. While walking through the makeshift infirmary she could see no improvement with the Norwegian boy. He had not responded to the medication even with the extra dosage she had pilfered for him.

On her second trip to the kitchen, she ran into the maid who was ready to bring up the last two trays. Birgit took her hand and told her that she needed help in changing the boy's bandages before trying to feed him. She appealed to the maid's sense of compassion by emphasizing that his life was in their hands since the German medics had no interest in attending to him. Besides, it was getting late and she wasn't sure if the army surgeons would pay a visit to Astergarden. She imagined scenarios that kept the medics performing surgery through the night because of valiant resistance by her countrymen.

She told the maid that they had to do everything possible to keep the boy alive until tomorrow since Mr. Johansen had contacted the local doctor who had promised to be there the next morning. But that was optimistic. It would come down to whether the Gestapo, at roadblocks or by the front door, would allow him to pass, since the boy was suspected of firing on the Germans. The suspicion had lingered, despite Mr. Johansen and others swearing that he was a local farm boy who was out hunting rabbits and was never part of the local militia or any resistance group. He had simply been in the wrong place and at the wrong time. When the advancing German troops saw him firing his weapon, they assumed the worst and shot him, leaving him for dead in the field. It wasn't until hours later that an elderly villager passing with his mule spotted a blue cloth in the field, approached, found the boy and took him directly to the hotel.

Birgit saw that the maid looked nauseous when they redressed the boy's wound. He had been losing blood since he was brought to Astergarden, perhaps a little less each day. Still, she wondered how much blood could be in his body. How long he could last without a transfusion, without eating anything and with a raging infection. Birgit knew in her heart that he was getting weaker despite what they did. Now they couldn't even get him to swallow water or to take medication. Even the maid wondered how much time was left since his pulse was weak and his breathing shallow. The best they could do was to wipe his boyish face with a wet cloth and maybe try to get some liquids into him again later. Both were saddened when they left his side, heavyhearted in the knowledge that he might not last through the night.

If he did manage to pull through until the next morning, and if the local doctor came and if the doctor was allowed in to see him, could the doctor make a difference at such a late stage? So, there were no real answers for a dying boy.

Birgit didn't get back to the lieutenant's room until an hour and a half later. She was both eager and afraid to go back to him, but she promised to check on him and say goodnight. All the lights were out except one small light in the middle of the hallway and one over the front desk. The maid and cook had left for the night and Mr. Johansen, who occupied a small room on the second floor, was the only staff in the building. Birgit and the maintenance man did not stay in the hotel. They occupied two of several tiny cottages in the rear of the main building. On some weekends or whenever her services were least needed, she would go to her parents' home in a small village some ten miles west of Astergarden.

As she got closer to the lieutenant's room, she could see light coming through the partially closed door shining from a small bulb over the bed. As she walked, she felt her heart racing. She pushed the door a bit more and squeezed in sideways, thinking that he might be asleep. She was surprised to see him looking at a magazine. His food bowl and the two glasses of unfinished wine were in the same place. He stopped reading, looked in her direction and placed the magazine down on the right side of his bed. Her breath caught in her throat; she placed her hand on her chest afraid that he could hear her heartbeat. It was well past the time for lights out as electricity was being rationed. Birgit lit the candle on the nightstand and looked at Hans in the flickering light.

"I see you didn't lie to me," she said, softly looking down at him. "You kept your promise and didn't go anywhere."

"I was afraid I would fall asleep. But I knew you'd keep *your* promise and come back. I forced myself to stay awake for I don't want to miss a moment of time with you." He spoke in a husky voice, looking up at her face, softly lit by the small flame. His words had layers of meaning and she was not really sure what was happening. Birgit knew that she should leave now, but her heart told her she could not leave him, now or ever.

"Would you be interested in some more dinner?" she teasingly asked as she touched the corner of the leftover soup bowl. "I'm willing to go downstairs and warm it up for you."

"Thank you, but I'm not hungry for food. But wine's another matter," he said. "That is, if you care to join me again."

She handed him his glass and then reached for hers, and daringly sat on the edge of his bed. His eyes were large and luminous when she shyly gazed at his face.

"To a continuation of the earlier toast," he said as he held up the glass. Both drank deeply of the purple liquid.

As the lieutenant's glass came away from his mouth a few droplets spilled onto his pajamas. He caught himself. She giggled a bit and placed her hand over her mouth. She felt her mood altered somehow. And felt her body stir when she was near Hans. Her head was far away in a different place, as if she was watching herself.

"That was clumsy of me," he remarked; as she reached to take his glass, her hand grazed his. Their eyes met with the shock of an irresistible spark. She reached for the linen napkin on the tray and tried to absorb the spot on his chest. When she leaned forward; her breasts were centimeters from his face. He seemed to take in a deep breath of her fragrance, while looking at the glow of her hair in the candlelight, framing her face and her full velvety smooth lips. She looked at Hans' powerful frame as if seeing his body for the first time and felt the tension in his body while she dabbed the spilled wine. Her breath came a little faster, her pulse raced; his chiseled face, his penetrating eyes, the wide locks of hair tipping over his forehead and the captivating slow smile were rendering her defenseless. He reached up and placed his hand on her shoulder.

"Hans, I don't think this is a good idea," she whispered. "You're in pain and your sutures may tear."

"I heal fast. Besides, when I see you, there's no feeling of pain," he said, smiling. "Please, let's share this precious moment."

She smiled tenderly and caressed his face.

Then in a moment of madness, he moved his hand from her shoulder to the back of her neck and, gently, pulled her closer until his lips met with hers. She felt his strong body beneath her and she felt her lithe body joyfully surrender her innocence as he entered her in a moment of uncontrollable fire.

An hour later, she gathered herself, gave the lieutenant his medication, they kissed and she made her way to her room in back of the resort. She lay there in the darkness, staring at the stars in wonder. It was true that she had drunk too much wine, yet, she had given herself freely and blissfully to Hans.

Birgit had lost her innocence to her lover, but she was still an innocent in the ways of the world.

Chapter 22

The Gardener's Folly and the Administrator's Problem

When Arnauld was ordered to leave the compound at gunpoint, he was infuriated. Who the hell were these butchers and bastards to come into his country and take everything from him and his people? Nothing was safe, not their land, not their treasure, not their women, not their government or even their dignity. He had been humiliated and treated like a dog in the parking lot. He came inches from being riddled with bullets, and his personal belongings scattered like worthless crap. It would have been better if they had shot him. And it had crossed his mind to force their hand to do just that, but for the overwhelming desire to avenge his people, and regain his dignity. While mulling all these thoughts, with burning hatred for the Nazis, he reached his village only to have his contempt for the Germans refueled when he saw a group of six troopers patrolling on the outskirts of his village – a checkpoint. They checked documents and interrogated friends and neighbors. He made his way through the backyards of his neighbors to reach his home.

At his house his cousin informed him that a small group of resistance fighters was operating from the west Hamsund area, a thick forest of mostly spruce trees up in the hills. When a Nazi convoy was observed by one of their own "eyes and ears" they would strategically position themselves behind rocks on the ragged mountains and attack the troops with sniper fire from above – hit-and-run tactics. They had been successful in taking out dozens of enemy soldiers before they could call in the *Luftwaffe* to strafe the area. But by the time the planes arrived they had disappeared into the woods like shadows. If nothing else the troop convoy would be delayed from moving north in their quest to occupy other towns and cities, and eventually link up with forces coming into the major ports of Bergen and Trondheim on troop carriers. The delaying tactic would give the national forces up north enough time to recruit and mobilize and to blunt the Germans' tactics of sneak attacks in the middle of the night.

That very evening, Arnauld pulled up the floorboards where he had hidden his rifle in order to avert confiscation. He was well aware that having a rifle was a death sentence, but he no longer cared. He flung it over his shoulder, filled a pouch with ammo, tied it to his belt and headed for the forest. He made no effort to conceal his weapon. He rationalized that if he was stopped, he knew that they would kill him, but by God, he would take a few Nazis with him.

He had traveled some twelve miles guided only by moonlight, through back roads, swamps and thick brush, to finally join up with a band of men who held a common view: to kill as many Nazis as possible any way they could.

When he arrived near the camp, he was escorted by one of two lookout men. The organizer and leader was a Norwegian army officer of mid-level rank. He had five of his own men who had separated from their unit a few days before. The gardener didn't recognize anyone from his village but, from a neighboring town, he knew the blacksmith's son whose father had a reputation for being xenophobic, hating anything that was foreign. Arnauld was welcomed as a long-lost family member. What they admired in him was that he had the guts to stand up to the *"Tyske,"* and that he had a rifle. Like them, he was prepared to shed his blood to turn back the enemy from their homeland.

During the night Arnauld slept a few hours before dawn, but his sleep was far from restful. He had a single blanket to wrap around himself but had been uncomfortable and cold. Every time he turned over to make himself a bit more comfortable, rocks seemed to pierce his sides and back. When he wrapped the blanket tighter to keep out the morning freeze another part of his body became exposed. Every time he woke, he cursed the Germans and blamed them for his predicament.

At a quarter to six in the morning he woke up to some commotion. The camp had gotten word that a convoy of Nazis was on the move north and would be traveling on Stasjonsveien, a narrow mountain pass, some twenty minutes from their camp. It was decided that they could engage them at an optimal position, causing a large number of casualties before falling back. Their plan seemed infallible: carry out a quick strike from an ideal location and then disappear into the well-known forest. They knew intimately the rough terrain and saw it as leveling the playing field against the better-armed Germans. In fact, were the Germans to send a party to pursue them in the woods they would be able to position themselves behind the thick brush and trees and pick the enemy off one by one. They would give the Nazi hierarchy a taste of humiliation by using their own technique of surprise and deception. The officer passed around his pack of American cigarettes as a symbol of their solidarity.

By seven o'clock the men were on the high rock ledges with their weapons loaded and positioned. Within ten minutes the convoy of troops was spotted in the officer's field glasses as they were advancing around a turn about half a mile south. The mid-rank officer could see tanks, trucks, horses and troops on foot. The army trucks were divided between the front and rear and probably loaded with supplies, ammunition and packed to the hilt with troops. The tanks and vehicles would be useless in the engagement, especially if snipers could disable the first two vehicles with grenades and block the roadway. Then Arnauld and his group could fall back fast enough that even if the Germans were to try and head them off from both sides of the hills they would fail.

All the men waited patiently with their weapons at the ready thinking that they could at least get off two or three rounds before falling back. As one of the civilian fighters looked around, he saw that many in his group had not shaved or showered for days and a comment was made that the enemy might be able to smell the stench if the wind was blowing southerly. His comrades laughed not so much at the joke but more to release stress and tension.

As the convoy moved closer, the officer admonished his civilian fighters to stay low, motionless, and to make each shot count. And not fire until he gave the order. As the first German truck came within a stone's throw, Arnauld had his sights directly on the green uniform behind the steering wheel. He knew in his heart that he could make the shot, and if the bullet found its way to the driver's head or a vital organ, he would lose control of the truck and it would plunge into the ravine. Arnauld could also see his compatriots targeting individual soldiers marching behind the first and third truck. They were nervous with anticipation, and beads of sweat were forming on their foreheads. Not him; he was thrilled that after taking out the lead driver the other soldiers, who were squeezed under the tarp, would jump out and he could maim or kill about a dozen more.

Moments later, bullets roared and gunpowder billowed in the crisp morning air. A handful of the green uniforms crumbled to the ground, mortally wounded. Others dropped down on their knees or fell prostrate to the ground. By the time a second round of shots was fired the convoy was stirred like an intruded beehive and many uniforms dodged behind defensive positions. Arnauld's first bullet penetrated the driver's windshield, hitting his shoulder and forcing the truck to swerve to the side opposite the ravine. The truck braked and stopped. The few grenades available were hurled and one truck exploded into a fireball. The Norwegian officer gave orders to fall back. Two of the civilian fighters hesitated, wanting to get another shot, but what they saw made them halt. The green tarp on the truck that had swerved to the side flew open simultaneously with another tarp of a rear truck. The snipers saw an elite paramilitary unit leap out, some of them holding onto the collar of barking, growling dogs. The snipers immediately realized that these were track and attack dogs.

The Nazi soldiers that had scrambled for cover pinpointed the direction the shots were coming from and returned fire aggressively. Simultaneously, the Gestapo paramilitary began running toward the mountain, scaling both sides, front and rear, in an attempt to head off the snipers. This elite Special Forces unit was embedded with the *Wehrmacht* to counteract precisely this type of insurgency that had attacked and been effective in the past. The elite division consisted of trained mountaineers who had their teeth cut in the rugged Alps and had seen first-hand action. The headquarters of the Third Reich had anticipated more resistance north of the Arctic Circle, in Norway, and trained these soldiers precisely for those conditions. Within seconds they had reached the snipers' location on top of the mountain ledge. They allowed the dogs just enough time to pick up the scent and to follow the snipers, Norwegian scum, into the thick spruce forest.

As the Special Forces' dogs pulled on their leashes their handlers followed behind. The resistance fighters knew that they were being tracked and doubled their pace until they reached a predetermined area where they planned to surprise their pursuers. Positions were taken behind rocks and dense pine groves. Again, they would inflict casualties on the enemy and fall back. However, the commander of the elite force anticipated the tactic and ordered that two Shepherd dogs be let loose. They were pulling so hard that their masters could not unleash them at first. Once freed and the scent fresh, they bolted in pursuit until the handlers lost sight of them. Then they heard a man screaming and instantaneously, following the scream, two shots rang out. The Gestapo commander expected the two dogs would be sacrificed but, in the process, he learned what he needed to: the direction and distance of the enemy. And that an ambush was waiting. As an experienced soldier in these types of skirmishes he knew that the sequence of fire came from guns trained on would-be targets. He deduced that if the dogs gained on the slowest runners their comrades would appraise the situation, aim and fire. Timing was the key. It was inconceivable that the guns could otherwise be fired in such rapid succession if the enemy was running. He signaled to his men to split into three groups. One was to pursue directly, evasively, and the other two to circle around, cutting off the snipers' lateral escape.

The quarter-mile distance separating the two forces was covered in no time. As the eastern flank of the German force was observed and fired on by the resistance fighters, the front assault team came into view. Meanwhile, the German western flank kept advancing beyond and behind the Norwegians' location in an attempt to decimate them when they retreated. The Norwegian officer sensed that the Germans were closing in on them and gave orders to fall back, but, as they pulled away from their cover, shots seemed to be coming at them from all around and confusion was multiplied by the echoes in the mountains. Norwegian men were being hit and dying all around. The officer had taken a bullet in his temple. Arnauld and a uniformed Norwegian were the only ones lucky enough to make it through the crossfire. The Norwegian soldier stumbled on a tree root and dropped his rifle. Arnauld retrieved the rifle, and because he knew the trails told the other to follow.

He led the uniformed man through an almost impassable cluster of birch trees, up and down hills, and to the side of the fjord cliffs with narrow paths and astounding heights. The views were breathtaking. Finally, at a narrow point, they drank from a stream emanating from the snow-covered peaks, waded across a rivulet, and at last felt less vulnerable, if not safe, from the Nazis. It was then that Arnauld suggested to the Norwegian soldier that he might want to lose his uniform. The soldier wanted to make his way to unoccupied northern cities where he could rejoin national forces. The gardener, Arnauld, was of like mind and was obsessed with one thing and one thing only: to kill the German bastards. But now they both realized that they were exhausted, not just from lack of sleep from the previous night, but because of the ordeal they had just experienced. Arnauld prevailed on the younger man to head across a meadow and past a row of oak and maple trees where there was a boarded-up cottage. There they could climb through a window and rest up until the following day.

The two-room wooden cottage looked like it hadn't been occupied for several years. The windows and doors were boarded up with thick planks. The front door was impossible to open since the cross planks were mounted with bolts and they had no tools. One of the side windows proved to give a bit. The middle board was wobbly and could be pried or coaxed loose by hand, thanks to squirrels that had chewed holes in the eaves which made it sag and allowed rainwater to continuously splatter down the side, including on the window. Arnauld tugged on the boards and the entire window frame rattled. Then, with the soldier's assistance, the window lock popped off, revealing rusty screws that had been anchored in rotten wood. As light flooded the dark room the soldier could see that some old furniture had been left behind when the owners abandoned the property. The young soldier braced himself against the window ledge and the gardener boosted him up until his body was half in and was able to drop down onto the hard floor. Once inside, the soldier helped his companion by pulling him up from his shoulders. He came in headfirst like a pole-vaulter, then the soldier supported his torso until he was right side up and on his feet.

There was one room inside the cottage with a little alcove for a table and chairs and a recess on the opposite side with a door that had served as an inside outhouse. The soldier found an old shirt in a closet and a pair of pants with grease stains and moth-eaten around the cuffs. He shook them out a few times and took off his army uniform and put on the old garments. When he was finally buttoned and tucked in, he rolled up the pant cuffs. All along the gardener was searching for food in the skinny pantry and found a swollen can of beans that he put back. Then he found a large can of sardines that he inspected in the light coming through the window. He was initially concerned with some rust around an exterior corner. But after inspecting the same corner from the inside he concluded that the rust had not penetrated and declared it safe. They split it, taking turns using their fingers as forks. The gardener commented that he had used more energy prying the damn thing open than its salty contents were worth. The few bites left them very thirsty.

The gardener never mentioned to the soldier that he had been in the cabin years before when he started working for Olaf Johansen. At the time, when Johansen's father died, Olaf had inherited the cabin with the land but never used it. He was holding on to it with the intention of building a bed and breakfast some day. It was him, Arnauld, with the truck from the hotel grounds, who had helped his boss move some of the more valuable furniture and furnishings. While working, he had stopped to admire a picture of the coronation of the King that hung on the wall directly in front of the couch where he was now sitting. Mr. Johansen, who had noticed his interest, had taken the framed picture off the wall and handed it to him. Now, as his eyes stared at the square spot where the picture had been, he could still see the faded outline on the wall.

Between fatigue and the dimness of the cabin it didn't take long before the gardener fell asleep on the couch and the soldier on a torn upholstered chair. The gardener was dreaming that he was home; he could hear his mother clanging pots and pans in the background.

His semi-conscious state told him that this whole business with the Germans was just a bad dream, that it would be gone when he awoke.

A vicious growling noise jarred him awake from his dream. As his senses brought him back to reality, again, he listened for the growling sound, hearing nothing for a few seconds. He wondered if the sounds had been part of his dream. Thoroughly awake, he heard it again. His first thought: racoons. But racoons were nocturnal creatures and his senses told him it was late morning. He strolled over to the window to peek, only to be met, face to face, with a dog jumping towards the window; teeth bared, growling. The beast came inches from ripping Arnauld's face off, but for the animal losing his balance and tumbling backwards. He was startled and momentarily paralyzed after hearing a thud and a yelp.

Arnauld made eye contact with the sleeping soldier who was now awake from the commotion.

As he looked out the window, again, the dog had disappeared. He scanned past the trees, across the field of high grasses swaying in the gentle breeze and finally his eyes came to rest near a group of boulders flanking the narrow dirt road beyond. His body froze. He could see them clearly: black boots, red army band with the hated broken cross and two of them holding Lugers in their hands. The others had military rifles over their shoulders.

"Damn Nazis!" Arnauld hissed as both the gardener and the soldier rushed for their weapons positioned against the couch. Their weapons cocked and ready, they crossed the room to look through the slit in the front door. Then Arnauld hurriedly went to the opposite side of the cottage and peeked through that window. He counted seven Gestapo troops. They could hear one of the soldiers yelling something in German.

"I think they're telling us to come out," said the young Norwegian, standing next to Arnauld, who seemed, oddly, to be chewing his tongue on one side of his mouth, as if contemplating the offer.

"Yeah, that would be easier for them to force us to kneel before them; to lick their boots and put a bullet through our skulls," Arnauld said angrily.

His naïve friend asked hopefully, "Maybe they'll take us prisoners."

"Not a chance. This is personal to them. Not only did we kill their comrades but we eluded them and put them through the extra trouble of finding us."

Both men cocked their weapons, each peeking out of opposite slits of the cabin. The gardener scoped the closest Nazi by the road and calculated that, depending on the actual distance and wind velocity, he had a chance to take him down. He had always prided himself at being a good marksman and this would be his true test. The Gestapo were standing like statues at the edge of the road, looking down towards the cottage, almost daring him to unload his weapon. They felt smug from that distance. The gardener was poised, his breathing under control, and his sight squarely on the German's chest. Then, still not satisfied with the anticipated trajectory, he adjusted a few centimeters, directly on the man's heart.

The shot echoed through the valley, birds fluttered their wings and took flight, small game darted under bushes and the Germans dropped to the ground for cover. Except one son-of-a-bitch, daring Arnauld, still standing in the same spot. But before the gardener had time to doubt the precision of his shot, the Nazi's knees buckled and he fell head first several feet down the slope. A feeling of elation came over the gardener. He knew that he had just changed attitudes and gained respect. A cornered animal, sure, but he still was not bagged.

The fusillade against the exterior of the cabin came instantaneously. A pane of glass shattered, wood splintered from the corners of the eve and the door rattled. The gardener fell to the floor. The Norwegian soldier took cover behind the recliner. A German soldier crept through the high grasses and managed to get close enough to the cottage to fling a grenade against it. The explosion took down a corner of the house, sent debris flying and sparked a fire to a pile of dry leaves adjacent to the structure. The gardener, unharmed but shaken, crawled on all fours to the window. He knew he had no reasonable chance of scoring a hit, but in defiance, he fired off three rounds haphazardly. Fire was consuming their shelter, smoke billowing and filling their lungs. A charred rafter crashed down on the young Norwegian's head, knocking him down. He had a huge gash on his head. The gardener pushed the burning wood away from his unconscious companion. He was bleeding profusely. And Arnauld's eyes were burning and tearing. His vision was blurred. He groped his way to the exploded corner of the cabin, feeling around for his rifle, when he saw the Norwegian's clothing on fire. It was too late to do anything for the poor fellow, even if he could.

Nothing mattered to Arnauld anymore except getting oxygen into his lungs. He felt his only chance was to run through the fire and head towards the opening that had been created by the blast. He staggered out into the grass, shirt on fire, his face charred and his lungs laboring violently for air. It took him several moments to become oriented and make sense of the long shadows. As Arnauld collapsed to his knees and looked up, he was surrounded by several Gestapo troops. The sun was glimmering behind their heads. The one who appeared to be the leader took a few steps towards him, grabbed him by his hair and spit in his face. Arnauld sprung to his feet like a rabid animal and lunged for his neck. Another uniformed man took a step closer, lifted his Luger and shot the gardener point blank between his eyes.

The SS troops were very interested in exterminating any remaining vermin connected to the resistance group. Accordingly, suspecting that the two men were somehow connected with the ownership of the cottage, they rummaged through anything that wasn't burned for clues, including the dresser and cabinet drawers. In the back of one drawer they found several photographs of King Haakon and of the Johansen family. They talked to the nearest neighbors, inquired about the owner of the cottage, and went through the gardener's wallet meticulously. The Norwegian soldier's body was burned, along with any identification, but the gardener's home address and his place of employment were clearly revealed.

Two hours later, armed with the information and driving a confiscated vehicle, the SS men burst into the gardener's home and demanded to know who lived there and where they were. The gardener's cousin told them that it was just him and his aunt. When they asked about Arnauld, the gardener, he said he didn't live there anymore. When they asked about his involvement with the resistance, he denied any knowledge of that as well. Then the SS leader walked to the mantel, picked up a photo, stared at it, placed it down and walked back to the man being interrogated and shot him in the head. Upon hearing shots, the old woman came up from the cellar. Without querying her, the officer concluded she wasn't worth their time. They shot her as well, and left her dead next to her nephew.

*

That night Birgit got little sleep. It was late when she left the lieutenant's room and even later when she got to bed. Now that her head was clearer, she was surprised by how quickly she had succumbed to the lieutenant's charms and sweet words. He had promised her many things during the time they were together and especially after they made love. He was going to come back after the war and marry her. Then take her back to Munich, if she would have him. She still felt his hand interlaced with hers and she smiled, content with the promises she heard. He assured her that she would like Bavaria. He painted beautiful pictures in her mind. And with his easy smile and confident outlook, she believed everything he said.

The next morning, she was up early and feeding him breakfast. She knew that he loved her and she believed him again when he said he would always protect her from harm.

Shortly after, the commandeered vehicle of the SS troops pulled as close as possible to the front door, and came to an abrupt stop, but without smashing through it. With cultivated swagger and unmitigated resolve, the SS leader came out of the vehicle, adjusted his uniform, and strutted towards the front door. The army privates stationed by the door, almost on cue, gave the Nazi salute and the leader walked through the double doors followed by his five cohorts. The army sergeant in the lobby stood to attention and saluted when he entered. He immediately demanded to know where the administrator of the complex, Olaf Johansen, was. The question was directed not only to the sergeant but also to Birgit, who was at her desk typing. She stood up and walked closer to the counter as everyone expected her to give the answer. Her first thought was to be evasive and to protect her employer, but she realized that the sergeant knew that he was in the building and in a matter of time would find him anyway.

"He's upstairs in his office," she answered, tilting her head towards the narrow stairs to the right.

No sooner had she answered than two SS agents sprinted up the stairs and bolted into his office. They demanded that he go with them. No questions asked, no answers given. One had a pistol to his spine to force his pace and assure cooperation. When they got to the lower lobby he was shoved toward the desk. The SS leader was walking around in the ballroom and checking on the wounded soldiers while the army sergeant tailed behind. When he saw the plump man with gray hair and spectacles by the front desk he turned quickly and headed in his direction.

Beads of sweat were beginning to form on Olaf Johansen's face. He suspected some sort of trumped-up charge growing out of the army medic's suspicions two days earlier, or perhaps they were blaming him for Private Heinz' death due to some lack of attention. The medic's words that he would be held responsible for any harm to the men resonated in his mind. But that was ludicrous; after all, he was not a medical doctor and couldn't be expected to save someone who came to his hotel mortally injured. Now the SS officer approached him, with gloves in hand and urgency in step and demeanor.

"Olaf Johansen, I expect clear and direct answers from you," he said with earnestness in his voice. "Are you the proprietor of a cottage on Thurmond Road?"

Johansen answered in the affirmative, unsure as to why these questions were being posed.

"What is your connection with Arnauld Garben?" he demanded.

"He was the gardener here until recently," Olaf answered, a bit tremulous.

"We have evidence to believe that you and the gardener have been conspiring against the German forces," the officer stated with conviction.

"No, I have not done such a thing," he muttered. The SS man, not satisfied with the answer, slapped him across the face with his gloves.

"You conspire against the German forces to support a worthless monarchy!" he screamed as he walked slowly around him, looking him over as if inspecting a museum relic under glass. The administrator could feel beads of sweat accumulating and dripping down his back and from his armpits. Then the most dreaded of all questions came. Olaf dreaded it because he had heard rumors of the mistreatment of minorities on the continent.

"Are you a Jew?"

Johansen had a knot in his throat and could barely speak.

"My father was Norwegian and so was his father," he managed to get out.

"And your mother, what was she?" The SS officer persisted with his probe.

It crossed his mind to lie but if they demanded to see his birth certificate or make the slightest inquiry of anyone else that he knew he would probably be shot.

"My mother is dead. She was Jewish but I was brought up Lutheran, like my father." He tried to steady his voice.

"Fine, drop your trousers," he barked.

"What?" he responded with incredulity. The administrator's astonishment was reflected not only in his voice but in his facial expression. But in a split second, he realized where the interrogation was going: he wanted proof of circumcision which, to his unhinged mind, would establish "Jewishness" since Norwegians did not subscribe to the practice of circumcision of newborn children.

"You heard correctly!" the SS officer asserted oppressively as another of his men stepped up and put a gun inches from Olaf's temple.

Birgit, still standing behind the front counter, was paralyzed with fear for her employer and wanted to intercede but was unsure what she could say to appease the hyenas. When Johansen, with hands trembling, started unbuckling his belt she turned to face the back wall. It was then that a strong, commanding, yet familiar voice boomed from the end of the lobby.

"What seems to be the problem, *Haupttruppführer?*" The voice was confident and firm.

Birgit turned around to see the lieutenant standing erect, with no noticeable evidence of injury and cutting a commanding figure even in his robe.

"Lieutenant!" The SS officer clicked his heels, came to attention and gave a Hitler salute with his right arm raised forty-five degrees. There was no need to follow the rank with "Sir" since it was considered superfluous in military protocol.

The SS officer recognized Lieutenant Kuhlemann not only from Munich, but they also had been passengers on the *Blücher* when it went down. The *Waffen SS* represented a special unit with a special mission at the inception of hostilities: to arrest the Norwegian King and the existing legislature if they did not cooperate in ceding power to the Nazi invaders and, if they resisted, they had orders to deal with them harshly. But because the King had managed to escape their planned capture, they were reassigned to mop up operations, particularly of resistance groups. This was the very reason they had been embedded in the army convoy when it was attacked.

"The evidence points to this man being part of the resistance and supporting hostilities against the German forces," he answered, with a certain disdain in his voice that could be interpreted as either contempt for the army lieutenant for intervening in his investigation or contempt for Johansen.

"What evidence do you have?" asked the lieutenant, with a certain rigidity in his voice.

"We have proof that his house was occupied by resistance fighters who killed members of our forces and that at least one of the enemies was employed as a gardener by this man." He pointed to Johansen who was quietly shaking his head at the accusations. Then he continued, "There is also strong evidence that this man and his family are staunch supporters of the monarchy."

"The cottage was my father's and was boarded up for years. As to the gardener's employment, he was terminated yesterday for disobedience," answered the administrator, his voice quavering as he looked at the lieutenant for salvation.

"I can vouch for Mr. Johansen that he's been here, on the hotel grounds, for weeks," responded Birgit. But no sooner had she spoken than she remembered that this was only partially true. Olaf had also been at their other hotel complex in the north.

"I've been here four days and I've not seen or heard any activity that would arouse suspicion and can confirm that the gardener was fired for insubordination. Officer, I don't believe there's anything further for you to investigate here," concluded the lieutenant. The SS officer hesitated for a brief second, his face flustered with indignation, then tensed his jawbone and gave a quick salute. He walked out, with his underlings following.

The relief in the room was palpable. No sooner had Birgit taken a deep breath than she saw the pain of the injuries etched on Hans' face, now that the moment of crisis had passed. She darted around the counter to his side. He placed his arm around her shoulder as a crutch and they walked back to his room.

Chapter 23

The Lieutenant's Transfer to Aker Hospital

The lieutenant's wounds were bleeding through his bandages again and his burns were turning into scar tissue. Birgit managed to change his dressing alone. He had surprised everyone by journeying from his bed, across the room, down the hallway, negotiating steps and crossing the lobby. He certainly left everyone with the impression that, despite his injuries and being in pajamas, he still had a commanding presence. In that moment when he stood up to the SS officer, Mr. Johansen was probably even more pleased than Birgit. But in that short exchange, Birgit had seen a man with a far more complex personality then she had imagined. Soon after Birgit left his room he had fallen asleep and had not awakened until evening when dinner was served.

About the same time the maid was serving supper, a medic truck pulled into the gravel parking lot. The driver and the man next to him looked like regular German soldiers when they handed the sergeant in charge of the grounds a note. The note was signed by the army commander and a doctor, authorizing the transfer of the seven wounded German soldiers to Aker Hospital in the north-east part of the capital. The two signatories had obviously decided that their men at Astergarden had recovered sufficiently to withstand a forty-minute journey over some bumpy dirt roads.

Birgit had expected this to happen but not this soon and not without prior notice. She spoke to the sergeant briefly and he had confirmed the decision from headquarters. Not only the wounded, but all hotel guests, had to vacate within seventy-two hours. When she saw the stretchers being taken off the truck and carried inside, the reality became more acute and she went straight to the lieutenant's room to inform him. As she opened his door the evening light was still filtering through his window. The lieutenant was awake and sitting on his bed.

"A medic truck came in a short time ago. They're making preparations for you and your men to be moved to the Aker Hospital," she said, with sadness on her face and disappointment in her tone.

"We all knew this was coming," he said, in a somewhat melancholy tone. He reached for her silky, soft hand with its tiny little fingers. Her hand in his seemed child-like. He ached in needing to protect and cherish her, yet with the knowledge that he must leave. He saw that she was about to break down and start crying. "Please come visit me. I need you. I'll make sure they'll allow you."

"Did you mean what you said last night?" she asked haltingly, fearful of the answer.

"Of course I meant it! When the war is over, sooner if I can, I will come back for you and we'll be together. You'll finally get to see how beautiful Bavaria is and Munich's countryside. There is nothing, nothing, that will come between us. I am coming back for you." He pulled her closer by her arm, kissed her on the lips and held her close.

"I love you," he whispered in her ear. Birgit felt an intense connection and believed, truly believed, what he said. She felt the sincerity in his kiss and the comfort of his arms around her.

"And I love you," she whispered back. He stroked her sweetly scented hair as it brushed against his chin. And she pressed her head against his chest as he caressed her face. They stayed like that for a few minutes until they heard the soldiers coming down the hallway. One voice, sounding like the sergeant's, was telling the others that these two rooms were occupied by officers. They stopped at the door's threshold, saw the lieutenant, and saluted. Birgit busied herself with the medicine tray, preparing to remove the few items from the room. The hotel's sergeant stepped forward to explain to the lieutenant the orders from the command center requiring the transfer of all the wounded soldiers to the military hospital. He handed the document to the lieutenant who nodded approvingly without saying anything.

The two soldiers came in and placed the stretcher parallel to the bed, holding it firmly. All of a sudden, the room seemed to be overcrowded. Birgit pulled off the bedcovers and, with the aid of the sergeant, helped the lieutenant shift his body slowly to the edge of the bed, feet first and then torso. She could see him wincing from pain but, thankfully, his new bandages were not bloodstained. With a concerted effort the lieutenant's body was swung from the edge of the bed onto the stretcher. Then Birgit went around and placed the bedcover over him, tucking it in on his sides. The sergeant took notice and smirked slightly. Birgit and Hans made eye contact; she took his hand and squeezed it as he was being carried out.

As Birgit followed the men down the hallway she could see Mr. Johansen standing and observing from the side of the front doors. He must have figured out, or been told by now, that not only the injured troops, but all, including the stationed guards, were pulling out. In Birgit's mind he was probably elated to see the bunch of them leave, especially after the indignities he had endured the last five days.

When all the patients were loaded, the truck turned in the yard with its small escort. The sergeant and the four troops under his command followed in the two Jeeps. Birgit, who had followed the soldiers outside, was staring in the direction of the moving convoy.

The vehicles descended towards the shoreline where they would turn right to go back up the hill and onto the main road. She started to raise her arm to wave but halfway up caught herself, realizing that Hans couldn't possibly see her from his vantage point and that no one else who saw her would understand why she was waving at the enemy.

She spent the night in her bed twisting and turning, finding it impossible to get any rest. Her thoughts went first to the lieutenant's promises and then to concerns about his recovery, then about the war, then about her job and the closing of the hotel resort. She remembered Mr. Johansen prepared the remaining employees and told them that he had no option but to close the facility. That the war was proving to be devastating to the hotel and the entire tourist industry. Now there were only three rooms occupied by guests. One family didn't want to go back to Bergen because of heavy fighting in their part of the city. Another couple was attempting to make arrangements for transportation by boat to take them south on the fjord, but because of what had transpired earlier in the week with the *Blücher* and German battleships and troop carriers and minesweepers, the faring of passengers was virtually suspended. Then there was the English couple, who had been interrogated by the Germans as possible spies and were told to remain in their quarters until further notice. Their situation seemed to be unresolved. Clearly, if they could find a way of leaving for England, they would surely opt for it now that Nazi guards were no longer present. Finally, there was the young wounded Norwegian whose health, miraculously, seemed to be improving despite no doctor attending him. Birgit liked to believe that the double dose of penicillin she had given him had finally made the difference. But there had been no contact with his family or any plans for his departure. Birgit assumed that in several days, when he got stronger, he would try to leave under his own power.

It wasn't until late morning when she finally fell asleep from pure exhaustion, only to be awakened a short time later by a torrential downpour. She rose to close her window as the shutters were rattling, the drapes were flapping back and forth, and rainwater was splattering off the windowsill. For the most part, she had learned to live with unpredictable weather in Oslo. During the course of a day it could be sunny and warm one minute and rainy and cold the next. The skies would darken instantly and then just as fast clear up and provide a brilliant illumination. Tourists from the continent would often remark on how dazzling and immense the large northern sky was, but there were no more tourists. This typical weather pattern might go on several times a day, especially in the late spring and early summer. In other seasons snow was another factor mixed into the equation. This dismal weather perfectly suited her mood.

No sooner had she closed the window than she heard a knocking on her door. As she angled her head from the closed window, she could see Mr. Johansen under a large black umbrella holding a handbag, standing by the door. She pulled her robe together and knotted the cloth belt. When she opened the door, he folded his umbrella, shook it and stepped inside the foyer. He knew her well enough to consider hellos superfluous and she knew him well enough to know that when something was bothering him, he would get right to the point – and he did. He told her that she was to take charge of the hotel while he was traveling to see family sixty miles north. While there, he would stay at the company's second resort. As he explained it, people were fleeing from the Germans in the south and fighting was still going on north of the capital. People were migrating north to join other family members and were using the other resort as a stopover. Then he got angrier, thinking about the panic and confusion resulting from the German invasion. Whatever the goddamn reason, he said, the northern resort was doing substantially better than here at Astergarden. Above all there were no Nazis, as of now, to scare everyone away.

As Mr. Johansen was telling her this, he noticed that his umbrella was dripping on her floor. He took several steps back and placed the umbrella inside a large potted plant and leaned the handle against the wall. Then he continued to tell her what he had learned.

"The bastards are strangling the city. It's been less than a week and already there's a food shortage. They've seized the local radio stations. They've seized the newspaper offices and they keep spewing propaganda that it's futile to resist. This morning they announced that to even criticize the occupation is illegal and subjects one to arrest and jail. If you have a firearm that you have not surrendered, when you're caught with it, you will be executed." His face turned purple with anger.

"How extensive is the fighting?" Birgit asked.

"What fighting? Our military was caught napping. But who expected that those goose-stepping bastards would attack a neutral country?" He ran his left hand across his bald crown and down the nape of his stocky neck.

"I've heard that there are various pockets of resistance, especially in the suburbs and the woods," she added, as if to give him a modicum of hope.

"This city is lost. It's lost. They've even outlawed all political parties and activities where people could organize against them. The only political party tolerated by the Nazis is the one headed by Quisling and he's an ass-kisser, a bigger Nazi than them," he said with contempt.

"If there's any hope it's up north where the British and French gave some assistance and the Norwegian military had a little more time to organize. But let's not delude ourselves. There are, or will be, about 400,000 Germans on Norwegian soil, commanded by Nikolaus Von Falkenhorst who set up his general staff, I've been told, in the new Royal Norwegian Automobile Association Hotel, several blocks from the city center. On the same day that Norway was occupied by the Germans, this bastard had German troops show up, in their uniforms, in the hotel lobby and announce that they were taking it over for their purposes." Mr. Johansen was shaking his head as if finding the whole episode unreal.

"When will you be coming back?" she asked.

"I'm not," he answered curtly. "This is what I came to talk to you about. I want you to take responsibility for shutting this place down in a week. I've already notified the carpenter to come and board up the place. Remind the few remaining guests that they have to vacate within three days. I would not be surprised if they sent another Gestapo team to come and check. The utility systems will also be shut down. The four remaining employees, as well as yourself, are to be issued final severance pay. After, the only people that will be left are you and the caretaker. If you're planning on staying beyond the following week, I have no problem, but none of the buildings will have utilities, you know that?"

"In that case I may stay a little beyond next week or until I get an apartment and new employment in the city, if I can. I really don't want to return home, unless I have to." Birgit was disconcerted.

"I understand," Johansen said, and gave her a brief hug. Then he turned and retrieved his umbrella from the potted plant. "We'll talk next week," he said as he reached for the doorknob, but before exiting he turned back. "Nobody knows what will happen with the Germans in control but if the north hotel stays occupied, we might need your services there... we'll talk." She closed the door behind him as he struggled to open his umbrella against the wind and rain.

Her thoughts raced back to Hans. She tried to understand the anger and hatred that was expressed by not only Mr. Johansen but most of her country. They seemed to blame all the Germans for what was taking place but to her the lieutenant was different. She remembered what he had said about being a soldier and following orders. Hans was kind and brave; he had no choice but to follow orders, she told herself. Still, questions flooded her mind. Was he a mere cog in a wheel? Who was ultimately responsible for the misery and death brought on by the war? Was it that horrible little man, Hitler, and his cronies, who started the war. Was it the German people that put them in power and supported their policies? Was it the Allies that caused the war by putting the German people in an unbearable dilemma after WWI? Or, was it even something more elusive like an aggressive nature in the hearts of mankind that needed to be expressed every so often? Birgit found the whole subject overwhelming and exhausting and could not think about it any longer.

Chapter 24

Closing Astergarden and Birgit's Visit to Aker Hospital

It was a crisp mid-April morning. The seagulls were gliding about near the pier looking for clams or fish that may have washed ashore from the previous night. As Birgit looked out her window she could see the grounds of Astergarden virtually desolate, no one wandering about and no one embarking or disembarking by ferry. The caretaker's boat was the only one moored by the dock. Transportation on the waterways and land was haphazard at best and checkpoints were established at various main arteries. Confusion and chaos were understatements. The war was wrecking the country. Daily, there were reports of brutality and arrests. It had been the fourth day since the *Wehrmacht* had taken the lieutenant to the hospital and three days since Birgit had bid Mr. Johansen goodbye. She welcomed how the lieutenant kept intruding in her mind many times during the course of each day, and with his image came the promises he had made, the intimacy they had shared, and the hopes for the future they had discussed.

She knew that he had been taken to Aker Hospital. And she knew where it was, having been there twice. The last time she remembered being in the emergency room was with her mother, who had convinced everyone that her injuries were from a tumble down the cellar stairs. Although, no one really believed her – beaten women were not that unusual – and they went along with the story to save her more embarrassment. The poor woman had been admitted with bruises on her body and a broken jaw that had swelled up to the size of a lemon. It took three months for the trauma and discoloration to disappear. All along, she lied to her family members, her neighbors, and probably to herself. She had even lied about the events to Birgit and her sister. She lied to protect her two daughters, because she was embarrassed, because she felt she deserved it and blamed herself. Whatever the true reason, she couldn't leave, always hoping that things would get better. Besides, she had nowhere to go. But things never got better despite her father's repeated apologies when he sobered up.

It had all started when her father lost his job with the Merchant Marine. It hadn't taken him long to slide into depression and then to take up drinking as his main occupation. And when he got drunk, he got angry about every imaginable thing that his wife did, whether what she did was right or wrong. According to him, she was lazy, stupid and the reason why he drank. The daughters were not immune to his bouts of drunken rage. Sonya was lucky to have moved out when she married. That was two months after their father had become unemployed. Birgit tolerated the abuses for another three months after her sister's wedding. Then, when she became employed at Astergarden and was allowed to occupy the tiny cottage behind the hotel, Mr. Johansen made it very clear that there was a trade-off. She was expected to be on standby twenty-four hours a day for anything unexpected. Fortunately, after putting in her regular hours, emergencies happened rarely.

*

The resort resident-guests had been advised that the facilities would close within a week. This information had been relayed to the occupants the same morning that Birgit had had the conversation with the administrator. Within two days, the Norwegian boy, still with the bullet in his shoulder, left under his own power. He told Birgit and Lars, the caretaker, that he was looking up a friend in town who would help him get to Bergen where he would get medical care. The English couple had paid the caretaker dearly to elude German patrols and take them by boat to Dromback. From there they expected to get transportation to the Swedish border. Their thinking was that since Sweden was not involved in the war, they could travel through it and across to Copenhagen in Denmark and then find a way to get to London with the assistance of some contacts. Also, on the weekend, two carpenters had arrived in a wagon drawn by two horses, loaded with plywood and tools. The French couple had persuaded the carpenters, after they boarded up the main building, to take them to the French Embassy. Sure, tensions were high between France and Germany but diplomats always found a way, and they felt much safer with their own kind.

The only people remaining in the hotel were the family from the north, who occupied two rooms on the second floor, and a cook and housekeeper from the local village who came to work each morning. The family's youngest child had gotten ill with high fever and diarrhea so they had decided to stay a while longer. They told Birgit that if their child felt better in a day or two, they had arrangements with Lars, the caretaker, to take them by boat to Oslo Harbor. They felt that since they had all their documents in place, even if the Germans stopped them they would be seen as a family unit with a sick child and be permitted passage by rail to the north. At least that's what they hoped.

It was mid-afternoon on Saturday and the housekeeper was laying white sheets over the lobby furniture. Birgit was organizing and storing financial documents and guest records in the safe behind the counter when the telephone rang. This was the second time it had rung today. As she stood up from her kneeling position and went to answer the telephone on the desk she wondered if it was Mr. Johansen, who had told her that he would be in contact. The switchboard operator from the central station spoke first, then connected her with the caller's line.

Her eyes lit up when she heard her name called. The voice was strong yet mellifluous. A smile crept over her face as the lieutenant continued speaking softly. Perhaps, she thought, he didn't want to disturb other patients in the hospital. She said his name to reassure herself that it was him. She asked about his condition, and he asked how she was doing. Birgit told him things were not the same at Astergarden since he had left and that the resort was shutting down for lack of business. She asked him in which section of the sprawling facility he was. The lieutenant informed her that he was in the south quadrant of Aker Hospital, some forty kilometers northeast of Oslo. He didn't know that she knew where it was. Soon after he apologized; he had to cut the conversation short since other people were waiting behind him for their turn to use the telephone. She told him that she wanted to come visit, and asked if tomorrow would be good. The lieutenant joked about going skiing in the mountains but, in fact, he wasn't going anywhere for at least another week. Finally, he told her that he would request the hospital's front desk to permit her entry without the usual delays. Before saying goodbye, his last whispered words were that he missed her. "And I you," she said softly as she placed the receiver gently in its cradle.

The next morning, on Sunday, she met up with the English couple by the front entrance. The caretaker had walked down from his small apartment, which was two units away from Birgit's, and was helping them carry their luggage down to the pier, preparing to board his fourteen-foot motorized boat. The day was bright and clear, the dark green waters were relatively calm, but there was a chill in the air. Mr. and Mrs. Sutherland were noticeably tense, worried that they would probably be stopped and interrogated again before they reached their destination. Very little activity was currently on the waterway. An occasional fishing boat or German navy ship could be seen moving rapidly, flying the German flag and the Nazi banner. The guards' last orders to the Sutherlands had been to remain in their rooms until further notice but, for whatever reason, the Germans had pulled out of the resort compound and not followed up with them. What were they to do, wait there forever?

Mr. Sutherland felt a little more optimistic about reaching the Swedish border without harassment. The border wasn't very far from southern Oslo. Apparently, the information he had gotten from his shortwave radio, as well as from the carpenters and the caretaker, was that the German navy was again allowing small boat navigation on the fjord. The general understanding of fishermen and ferry boat captains was that even though British destroyers could be sighted along the western coast of the country, they had not attempted to enter Oslofjord. The obvious reason was not because the British were afraid of the few German battleships but because of the *Luftwaffe*, the air force. German headquarters had come to the conclusion that the locals relied on their small vessels as indispensable transportation. They had seen maps with numerous islands, some quite large, with inhabitants living there not only during the summer months but throughout the year. Movement on the waterways was crucial since roads and cars on the islands were lacking and bridges didn't exist. Restoring this type of transportation was also in keeping with the greater scheme of Nazi propaganda. German headquarters wanted Norwegians to believe that their enemy was the British and that they were there merely to protect their national interest.

Birgit felt a little anxiety not only for the Sutherlands but also for herself. She had decided early in the morning, soon after awakening the caretaker, that she wanted to hitch a ride with the Sutherlands. Once arrangements were made, she spent the next hour preparing. She tried on and rejected most of her outfits. Standing in front of a full-length mirror, she finally decided to choose a white ruffled blouse with a full-length, light blue pleated skirt. She also took her black sweater and the round tin container that was sitting on her small table, in a pretty wrapping. The night before, she had managed to find scarce ingredients and bake some cookies in the hotel kitchen, then filled the container to bring to the lieutenant.

The carpenters were expected to arrive in less than an hour, bringing new supplies. They were to bring more materials to complete boarding up the compound, in accordance with Mr. Johansen's instructions. Her last conversation with them had been that after they unloaded the supplies, one of them would take her by wagon north to the Bygdoy Peninsula. But then she changed her mind. She had concluded that by the time they arrived and unloaded their supplies it would probably be another few hours and she didn't want to wait. Besides, if the carpenter drove her to Bygdoy she would have to take an electric tram to the city center and then another bus to Aker Hospital. Why go through all that? Lars could drop her off at the dock near the Old City Fortress, after he let off the Sutherlands in Drobak. She felt bad changing her plans at the last minute and had even tried to contact the carpenters by telephone. Then remembered they didn't have one, so she did the next best thing and left a note posted by the front entrance. Surely, they would see it there.

As she made her way down the hummock and toward the pier, she wore half heels and carried the gift. She figured Lars had started the engine since smoke was billowing about. On the starboard side the name of the boat was carefully scribed: *Half a Dream*. Mrs. Sutherland was sitting in the boat with a kerchief over her head, and her husband and the caretaker were talking on the platform. A fairly large piece of luggage was lying a few feet from Mr. Sutherland. Birgit felt sorry for Mrs. Sutherland, who seemed to be very reserved and was extremely accommodating to her husband's wishes. Birgit wondered if her husband's obvious control did not spill over into their relationship to a point where he was physically abusive. One thing was certain: his wife was not very happy and the unhappiness went further back than their impending difficulties with the Nazis. As she approached the caretaker, who was facing her, he announced that Birgit had arrived. Mr. Sutherland turned around, smiled and greeted her. Then he picked up his luggage and swung it into the boat's hull. The caretaker took Birgit's hand and helped her into the boat. Once Mr. Sutherland was settled, Lars untied the boat's ropes from the clasps and threw them inside. As the boat cast off, the water began to shift it sideways. Lars pushed the boat away from the piling and jumped in. When his feet landed on the deck the boat rocked even more wildly, bringing the conversation between the two women to an abrupt halt. From close up, Birgit could see that the wife had been crying. She thought, maybe it was an issue that had surfaced earlier and was still festering.

As the dock receded in the distance, they could see the hillock with the various buildings behind the main hotel. The Norwegian flag had been lowered and the German flag towered in its place since the Nazis took control of the towns and cities along the waterways. Mr. Johansen had thought about hoisting the Norwegian flag in defiance when the army evacuated but was afraid that it would be seen from the sea and he would probably pay the ultimate price, so nothing was done. As Lars steered around an outcrop of rocks, a high wake slapped against the small boat, giving everyone a roller coaster ride. Mrs. Sutherland made a shrill sound and then threw up her breakfast. The turbulence in the water was caused by a fast-moving German patrol boat. Blue navy uniforms were visible on deck and two of its crew looked towards the caretaker's boat but didn't turn around or slow down in an attempt to board *Half a Dream*.

As Lars maneuvered his boat up the fjord, he was consciously staying close to the eastern shore in order to avoid any more German boats. Oscarsborg Fortress was on the right, and they could see the German army unloading boxes of supplies from cargo ships that were then carried to the old cadet house and the warehouses. The Nazis' early morning military maneuvers were being conducted further in towards the center of the island, an area known as "the horseshoe" that seemed to envelop the island's largest building. Hundreds of uniformed men stood in formation like rows of corn. Farther out, towards the shoreline, tall oak trees formed a cordon around the center of activity. Despite the trees the passengers on *Half A Dream* could see through some sparsely vegetated areas.

The garrison had been bombed by *Luftwaffe* planes almost two weeks earlier and taken over. Soon after, it was occupied by the German *Wehrmacht* and there was also some presence of the *Kriegsmarine*. But neither Lars nor Birgit could explain to the others why the Norwegian flag was still flying side by side with the German flag. With time, they would learn that it was due to Colonel Eriksen's conditional surrender after the Germans bombed the hell out of the island. During a lull in the bombing he realized that the situation was futile, especially when the Germans threatened to restart shelling not only Oscarsborg and Kalhomene Island, but the nearby city of Drobak on the west side of the fjord. Thus, one aspect of the negotiations had been a request that the Norwegian flag keep flying for several weeks. The German officer sitting across the table was so impressed by the fighting spirit of Eriksen and his men that he felt that his wish should be honored. Thus, the Norwegian flag remained flying for some time.

As *Half a Dream* made its way towards Drobak the passengers could see a multitude of small islets, some no larger than the dorsal of a humpback, at a distance. Some were rocky with sparse vegetation and uninhabited. Still others were adorned with small homes. The size of the homes was dictated by the local government. They were either painted or in stucco, with some half-dozen colors acceptable, no others. The yellows, the reds and blues made the mountainside of Drobak very visually appealing to the seafaring passengers.

Lars and the Sutherlands had decided that instead of dropping them off by the city's central dock, where chances of being stopped and questioned were likely, he would leave them at a more remote area. From there they could walk through some brush until they came to a road that would eventually connect with a central plaza. Once they reached the main square on foot, they would blend in with other people and should be able to catch a taxi or a bus ride. Their aim was the town of Marker, which was the last town before the Swedish border.

When Birgit and Lars bid the Sutherlands farewell they wondered if there was something true about the Nazi suspicion that they could be British agents. From the husband's coolness and his knowledge of Sweden, Birgit concluded that he might be a spy, but not Mrs. Sutherland. She might be serving as a cover and not even be his spouse.

When Lars maneuvered the boat into Oslo Bay a flurry of activity could be seen on shore. Small groups of Nazi soldiers in green uniforms were patrolling the shoreline; sailors in navy blue were doing routine work on boats. As Lars' boat got closer to shore, a soldier was motioning from the dock to turn around and head for pier 6. He complied. That was where passenger credentials were being checked. Lars explained to the officer who they were and where Birgit was going. After their credentials were checked they were permitted on shore. Lars told Birgit he would remain in this area until she made her way back from the hospital, later in the day.

With the Sutherlands on her mind, Birgit walked the five blocks towards the central station where she could board tram number 607 for Aker Hospital. She was surprised to see how normal everything looked. The street vendors, the merchants and open markets seemed to be functioning as usual, despite armed guards on street corners. The outdoor cafés and bars went about their business, but perhaps not as crowded as before the occupation. Perhaps the merchants were still in denial or felt that whoever was in charge they still had to support their families. Birgit wondered if there were other reasons that the degree of dislocation occurring in other parts of the country had not impacted Oslo proper. But she had the nagging feeling that things might get worse before they got better.

It wasn't until she was half a block from the National Theatre, which was close to the Storting, the parliamentary building, that her mind grasped the scale and reach of the occupation. Right there, in the middle of a small park with green grass and trees, offering a welcoming reprieve on a summer afternoon, was the setting for groups of uniformed men with several trucks lined parallel to each other. The freight on the vehicles was what appeared to be confiscated items, particularly radios, some phonograph sets and even telegraph paraphernalia. All types and sizes of radio: table radios, ham and shortwave, tube amplifiers, turntables and even consoles. People had talked about decrees having been set in motion against Jews. And they were the first people who had to give up their means of communication and information. Soon after, this was followed by the demand for rosters from synagogues and other organizations. And once those lists were collected the names on passports and other documents were stamped with a large letter "J."

At an opposite corner was a short line of Oslo residents turning in their armaments, which were thrown on top of a military canvas spread on the ground. As good citizens, they had wrapped their weapons, guns, rifles and powder pistols in cloth or newspapers and handed them over just below a large billboard with the proclamation: "Surrender Firearms Here." Another sign, twenty paces farther, announced something more ominous in large bold letters: "*Verboten:* Ownership of Firearms. Subject to Imprisonment or Death."

Birgit made her way on the opposite side of the street and walked along Henrik Ibsen Avenue for another short block where she expected to pick up the electric tram and then connect with the bus taking her to Aker Hospital. She wondered to what degree Hans had recovered. She was anxious to see him and wondered if he still felt for her the same way she felt for him. Birgit knew that he was not part of this madness of war. Sure, he was an officer. Sure, he wore a uniform. And he had probably killed people, but she was absolutely convinced that his spirit was pure as he had declared to her that he couldn't wait for the war to end.

She snapped out of her trance when she turned the corner and saw her bus stop at a distance. The tram was already boarding passengers. There were two passengers about to climb on before the bus would leave. She didn't know how long a wait for the next tram was and only had seconds to catch this one. She made a diagonal dash to the other side of the street, over cobblestones and over a barricade. Her heels made balancing on the cobblestones unstable.

When she made eye contact with the bus driver, she knew she was safe. He was holding the door open. She thanked him for waiting, paid her fare in kroner and waited for the driver to issue a transfer ticket. When she glanced to the rear for a good seat, she noticed that the bus was less than a third full. She sat on one of the faded yellow wicker seats, three rows behind the driver. It was upsetting for her to see that on all major intersections soldiers in green uniforms patrolled either in pairs or in small groups.

In less than twenty minutes the tram dropped her off at the connecting point. There she boarded the regular bus that would take her directly to the hospital. Three other passengers had transferred with her; Birgit had struck up a conversation with an older woman who was visiting her brother in the psychiatric unit, a group of brick houses that stood adjacent to the regular hospital. In a relatively short time, the woman had managed to pour out her soul. What Birgit learned from the woman was heartbreaking and frightening. At first, she dismissed it as political propaganda and tried to calm her, but the woman offered detailed facts and first-hand knowledge. Her distress was over the Nazis' treatment of people with mental problems. The Nazis, she kept repeating, wanted to empty all psychiatric wards which were, according to them, nothing more than "swamps in need of draining." They said the resources that went to the mentally deficient should be allocated to more worthy causes. Birgit tried again to ease her anxieties by telling her that no civilized country had ever treated less fortunate people in such a manner. Besides, Germany was a Christian country and the Pope would never permit such destruction of human lives. All men and women were made in the image of God and that, regardless of one's ability, there was an inherently human spirit inside everyone.

The two women fell silent for a while. The older woman, sadly, must've thought the young girl was naïve and without life experience to be able to believe that bad things could not happen. Birgit wondered if what this grandmother was relating could possibly be true. As she looked out the bus window, farms and plateaus and mountains came into view, with an occasional group of farmhouses. But her mind was not on the natural beauty of the countryside but on the lieutenant. She could not fathom that Hans could do any of the things this woman was predicting. Even if others could sink to such a degenerate level, he was different. She could tell from his kindness, not only from the pictures he had painted about his home back in Germany but in the way he had held her that night and caressed her face and made love to her. He had even intervened on behalf of Mr. Johansen and had sided with her and against the SS officer. She knew, with every fiber of her being, that he was a good man and she also believed that they would someday be living in Bavaria together.

As the bus went through the municipality of Baerum and traveled northwest they could see reddish brick buildings and barrack-style structures at a distance. Birgit knew it wasn't Aker Hospital because it was a fairly new edifice, built in a neoclassical style, with functionality being the architect's objective. The six stories had numerous double windows with criss-crossed bars; behind it were very tall pine trees serving as a backdrop and beyond that, mountains. A tall flagpost stood towards the right side of the three-sectional edifice.

"You know what that building is?" asked the old woman as she pointed to the structure.

"It looks like a government building," Birgit answered.

"You're partially right. They call it Grini Prison. It was built as a women's prison but has already been taken over by these Nazi devils," she said.

"For what purpose, administrative offices?" asked Birgit.

"Oh, I'm sure they have offices in there but they're also stuffing every cell with political prisoners and anyone accused of being a resistance fighter. Maybe they'll bring back public executions, who knows? And who knows what kind of horrors are already taking place there."

As the bus looped around to merge with a main road heading towards Aker Hospital, Grini Prison came closer into view. The women could see men lined up in front of the building on roll call, dressed in dark shirts and black caps and gray pants. Two military men in crisp gray uniforms and black boots stood before the lines of men and were talking with what seemed to be a supervisor.

"How can they have so many prisoners in such a short time since the occupation?' asked Birgit.

"Government leaders, academicians, resistance fighters, Jews… it's not hard to collect them when you have several hundred thousand Nazi troops spread across the country from Kristiansand to Narvik. You don't want to know how many they've already killed and buried."

There was a profound bitterness that this woman harbored against Germans. Her emotional response to the invasion seemed to go beyond the norm. It bordered on insanity. Birgit could only remember the gardener, who had reacted almost hysterically and had lost his life as a result. She could only guess that this woman had suffered more than she let on. She tried to think of something to say to compose her before she might lash out at some German soldier and get shot.

"This will come to an end. A negotiated peace settlement is probably being worked out as we speak," Birgit said, astonishing herself at how little these words consoled even herself.

"It'll come to an end alright, after they subjugate or kill everyone else," the woman mumbled gloomily.

After driving on a winding dirt road that seemed to go full circle around the building, the bus was finally nearing the hospital checkpoint. An impressive oak tree stood like a sentinel at the end of the curve and seemed to be taller than the buildings. The bus inched closer to the guardhouse. Personnel inside the house were not in uniform. Two soldiers were standing guard by the gate, rifles at the ready. When the driver cut the ignition and opened the doors, both soldiers hopped on the bus. One entered from the front and the other from the rear door. No greeting. No smiles. Their only request was for documents. The soldier in the rear could be seen thoroughly questioning two young men in their early thirties, believing that they were traveling together. They weren't. One turned out to be a doctor; the other was visiting his mother in the non-military wing of the hospital.

Birgit was asked what her purpose was for being there. She told him that she was visiting a friend, a member of the German military. She was asked to name the individual. She gave the lieutenant's full name. Upon hearing the name, the interrogation stopped and she was handed back her documents and told to proceed. The soldier moved to the next passenger who handed him identification. But before perusing the papers, he turned to Birgit and said that the lieutenant could be found on the third floor.

Birgit stepped down from the bus. She walked alongside the bus trying to make eye contact with her new acquaintance, to wave goodbye. But the older woman was preoccupied with shuffling through her big purse for something, perhaps her identification. She briefly glanced down at her. Birgit saw an expression of absolute disgust on her face. She may have overheard Birgit say that she was visiting "a friend, a member of the German military." As Birgit walked down the circular road, past the quoin of the hospital building, she saw the main entrance. Across the entrance were a few ambulances with red-cross markings and three army vehicles. One of the vehicles, being driven by a soldier, came to a stop. Another man was standing by the door where she expected more questioning but nothing was demanded of her. She gave a courteous smile and walked inside. Sitting behind a long wooden desk was an official-looking man wearing a grayish uniform and spectacles. She didn't recognize what, if any, branch of the German services he represented. The chair next to him was empty, although a stack of papers and some type of journal were neatly organized in the middle of the desk. The gray uniform looked up at her. As she approached, he continued to scratch his left eyebrow. A long stare from head to toe followed. Then his eyes came to rest on the package she carried.

"*Guten Morgen!* What can I do for you?" he asked as he took a very long and deep breath. Birgit wasn't sure if the reaction was one of exasperation from work or whether the fragrance of the cookies she carried elicited the response.

"I'm Birgit Karlsen and I'm here to see Lieutenant Kuhlemann," she responded. He turned a page in the journal and slid down his index finger until he got to the right spot.

"Yes. I see a notation. He's expecting you. The lieutenant is in room 318. Use the main stairs to the left," he pointed.

She walked across the tiled lobby, past the stairwell doors, and stepped onto the concrete landing. Her heart was suddenly racing. She had not seen the lieutenant for about a week and wondered how he looked and whether his condition had markedly improved under the care of army doctors. When she arrived on the third floor, she saw a nurse dart into one room and then another, carrying some medications and what appeared to be a bedpan. She wanted to ask where Lieutenant Hans Dietrich-Kuhlemann was located but decided to muster her courage and find it on her own. The rooms, according to the sign on the wall, were in descending order starting with 315–301. *Must be at the end of the wing*, she thought, and from what she could see the rooms were furnished with two and four beds.

Not all the beds were occupied by young men with battle injuries. Next to room 312 was a lounge. She was about to walk past it, when she took a step back and focused inside. A man in a robe sat in a chair intently reading a book. She craned her neck past the door and softly inquired, "Hans?"

The man closed the book and looked up. His eyes brightened and his face glowed with a smile. "Birgit. I didn't expect you this early," he said as he rose from his chair and moved toward her without a trace of discomfort from his injuries.

"I hope I didn't disappoint you," she said as they moved closer to embrace.

"You could never disappoint me," he whispered as they held each other tightly, with his face buried in her silky-smooth hair. He kissed her gently on her neck, just below her ear. Then their lips met, as if to water after a parched spell. At some point he realized she was holding something in her hand, behind his back.

"Maybe you want to put that down?" he asked.

"It's something for you," she said.

"No package, even with all the treasures of the world, could be more welcome than you," he said as he took the present, set it down on a small table and opened it.

"I remember you liked them at the hotel," she said.

"Chocolate with hazelnuts, my favorite," he said as he inspected the goodies in the open tin. Then he selected the biggest and best.

"Let's share the first one," he said, offering her a bite. She bit into it gracefully like a baby rabbit munching on tender leaves. Then he took a bite, exaggerating delight on his face and making her laugh. He laughed with her as their eyes locked, their yearning swelled and the doors to their souls opened. And while the heart's tempo accelerated, the lieutenant seemed transfixed by the radiance on her face and the sparkle in her eyes.

"I have something for you also," he said as he took a step towards the night stand and retrieved the book he had been reading, *The*

Works of Keats, and opened it to a book marker and pulled out a folded sheet of white paper.

"This is for you," he said, handing it to her. "I wanted to get you flowers but flowers are hard to come by these days, and besides, flowers die much too fast. This will last forever."

She opened the sheet of paper and saw three short poems that he had penned in German and read them slowly.

"They're beautiful," she said, with wonder. "They express both tenderness and power." No sooner had she finished saying that than a tear ran down her face and she started sniffling. The lieutenant pulled out a handkerchief from his breast pocket and dabbed her cheek. Then he kissed her at the very spot where the tear had trickled.

They spent a good deal of time holding hands and making small talk. Then she asked to see how his wounds were healing and he obliged, feeling pleased that his body had mended so well and so soon. Scars and reddishness remained in the most severe areas but he no longer felt pain and discomfort. He told her that two doctors had examined him early yesterday and that both had given him clearance to resume his official duties within seventy-two hours. But that same evening, he had received transfer orders to a base in Trondheim. He explained that in this northern city there was fighting going on with British and French forces that had arrived under the pretense of helping the Norwegian resistance but, as he explained it, they had their own military ambitions for establishing bases in northern territories.

Hans promised her that the first opportunity he had to get a military leave, probably before six months, he would come back to see her. He assured her, further, that what he had promised her about taking her to Germany was real. He shared a dream with her: that the war was over and they were living together in Bavaria raising a family. She listened delightedly and intently. She whole-heartedly believed the picture he was painting and, with eyes closed, she wanted to plunge into that life.

When the nurse informed them that lunch was being served and visiting hours were over, Hans promised that he would write to her often and would look forward to seeing her around October. Then he accompanied her down the stairs to the first floor, held her tightly and kissed her by the stairway before she walked across the lobby, past the clerk's desk and out the front entrance.

It was on her way home that Birgit came face to face with a new reality about the war. As she was walking from the tram stop near the National Theatre to the dockside, where Lars would be waiting, she saw a truck full of what appeared to be detainees or prisoners being unloaded next to a police station. The men were led into a makeshift fenced area guarded by Nazi soldiers. Later, she would learn that the German *Reichskommissar*, Josef Terboven, had taken increasing control of the state police and they had started to weed out any potential "sympathizers" of the resistance movement, as well as Jewish "troublemakers."

Birgit was appalled by what she saw. Mr. Johansen, dressed in a suit and tie but disheveled, was being pushed with the butt of a rifle into the detention area. She feared he was to be interrogated or worse. She tried approaching the enclosure to talk directly to Mr. Johansen, who had seen her, but she was met with the bark of an order not to come closer. The guard had his hand on his holster and seemed ready to use it. Birgit immediately stopped; she remembered Hans' warning. The guard kept motioning to her to keep walking. As she did, she shouted to Mr. Johansen that she would contact his family and try to help.

At the dock, the caretaker had kept his promise and waited with *Half a Dream*. She could not understand why Mr. Johansen would be treated so harshly. He wasn't a politically active man and he was not involved with any underground movement. The Germans had probably made a mistake. After she contacted his family, and they intervened, things would be cleared up and Mr. Johansen would be released. This prospect made her feel a little less apprehensive. While the boat was making its way down the fjord to Astergarden, her mind went back to the night when Mr. Johansen was almost arrested in the lobby. It had been the lieutenant who had saved him at that critical moment. She wondered if this detention was somehow related to that episode. She recalled the SS officer questioning his religion, almost as if being Jewish was a crime.

They arrived at the hotel just before five in the afternoon. It had turned into an unusually warm day for this time of year. She went straight to the phone in the lobby to contact Mr. Johansen's brother but was unable to reach him. She decided to keep trying. If there was no answer, by morning she would try to contact the lieutenant. She hoped he could intervene and have Mr. Johansen released. Birgit had also called the northern resort office to inform them of Mr. Johansen's arrest. As far as they knew, he had gone to the city center to see a bank manager and pick up some supplies. He had not been seen since 8am that morning.

The next morning, Birgit still had not been able to contact her boss's brother. She tried frantically to reach the lieutenant at the hospital but after innumerable questions and holds she was told that the lieutenant had been discharged and was reassigned. No further information could be provided. It wasn't until 2pm that the operator connected her with Mr. Johansen's brother. Rolf Johansen sounded disconcerted about the whole matter but tried to reassure her that the family was aware of his arrest and was working with a lawyer and some officials in the Quisling Political Party to have him released. He thanked her for her concern and would inform her as soon as his brother was freed.

Chapter 25

Birgit's Pregnancy and Turbulent Times

It was the end of June and almost three months since the Germans had invaded Norway. Throughout the country there was a scarcity of basics. This was particularly acute in urban areas. Not only did Norway have to accommodate some 400,000 German troops but in some areas, with their infrastructure bombed by the *Luftwaffe*, it was difficult to move commodities. And the war took a toll on the nation's former trading partners, impacting both import and export businesses. Supplies of food, coffee, tea and tobacco became harder and harder to find. Luckily, the Norwegian spirit proved to be one of resilience and adaptability; people started growing their own food, keeping livestock in their backyards and turned more to fishing and hunting. In the urban areas public parks were sectioned off so locals could grow basic foods.

Birgit had seen the Astergarden hotel and resort go from a prosperous and busy tourist destination to a boarded-up, barren and dreary place. The vegetation around the complex was growing wild and the manicured grassy knolls were taken over by tall weeds. The telephone service had been disconnected several days after the last guests had departed, and the day after that the electricity and heat were shut down. The stockroom supplies had been transferred to the northern hotel on the Bygdoy Peninsula, and there was no further reason for Birgit to enter the main building. Lars, the caretaker, who had been on the payroll until two weeks after Mr. Johansen disappeared was also terminated. But after the employment checks stopped coming, he and Birgit were still allowed to stay at their respective cottages. During the ordeal they became friends. As a former co-worker, he came to visit with Birgit from time to time since, as he put it, they were the "last holdouts" on the large property.

Birgit had spoken to Rolf on a few occasions and he, like Mr. Johansen, assured her that she could stay as long as she wanted. His words were, "better to have someone on the premises than leaving it totally abandoned." He was apologetic for having all the utilities shut down since everything was linked to a main system. So Birgit made the best of a bad situation. She bought some candles and found old oil lamps in the storeroom. She planted a small vegetable garden on the side of her apartment and carried water in buckets for irrigation. She found a part-time job at a small private Lutheran school that had reopened a week after the occupation. She worked there every other day, walking the three miles going and returning. At the school, she doubled up as secretary in the morning and as a cleaning woman in the afternoon. This put a little money in her pocket, barely enough to subsist.

Her mother had asked her to come back home. For a time, Birgit seriously considered it but finally decided that it was better to be on her own, especially since she and her father didn't agree on many things. Her mother interpreted her reluctance to come home as being due to the abuses her father had subjected everyone to. But the true reason was that her family would never approve of her future plans. They would disown her outright if they knew the truth.

What she had not disclosed to her mother, or anyone for that matter, was that she was in love with a German officer and at some future date intended to follow him to Bavaria. For her father this would constitute treason. That she was unwed and pregnant as a result of their treasonous relationship was unspeakable, a subject she knew was unthinkable to reveal to anyone in her family. Troubling, but exhilarating at the same time, was that Birgit began to notice all the symptoms of pregnancy. Not only had she missed her period but she was exhibiting all the other telltale signs of life inside her. Her breasts were unusually tender; fatigue and nausea were exactly the symptoms as described by some of her friends who had had children.

In coming to the conclusion that she was pregnant, she took comfort in Hans' promise that he would take care of her and that they would get married. She imagined a happy home and his parents, unlike her own, welcoming her and their baby. Since her future husband was formally trained as an architect, she envisioned a pretty home. Sometimes her imagination took her down to the smallest details of the kitchen, bathroom, bedroom, and the garden full of flowers and with a fountain. Whenever she caught herself and realized that her projections were getting ahead of her life, she fell back on her conviction that there was no reason why those plans couldn't happen. They were clear and tangible to her. Trust was at the root of it all and there was no reason not to trust Hans. He was an honorable man and was probably liked and respected not only in the military but in their future hometown in Bavaria.

Birgit had received one written correspondence from Hans since his reassignment near the battlefront on the outskirts of Trondheim. He wrote that he had cherished the few hours they had spent together at the hospital. That whenever he had a free moment, his mind pictured her beautiful face. He studied and impressed her features, in detail, in his mind as well as in his heart. The simple sincerity with which he wrote captured his rapture, his tenderness and his dream for their future, more romantic than any forced rhyme of poetry could ever be.

There was also some news about his present everyday encounters. He told her that he had unexpectedly met an old friend from his hometown during a few days of fierce battles against the British and Poles in the northern towns. His friend's name was Heinrich and he was also an officer. Heinrich had gotten married two years earlier to a girl whose family Hans was acquainted with. He had told Heinrich all about Birgit and how they had met at the Astergarden and how she had literally saved his life. Even without medical training, he told Heinrich, she had more talent than most physicians. They both concluded that, some day, the two women would definitely get along together and would turn out to be good friends.

Heinrich had received his education to become a schoolteacher and intended to pursue his profession when he left the military. His ultimate goal was to earn a chair at a university. However, he had no illusion that that was going to happen soon, since he needed to publish some research papers before being taken seriously. Then Hans went on to describe him as a very thoughtful and patient man, a necessary characteristic when dealing with students, especially some of the more "gifted" students that required more patience.

Hans had signed off with "love and yearning, HDK." She pondered the words and wanted to pick up a pen and tell Hans that she suspected that she was pregnant. However, because the news might be too premature, she felt that it might be better if she waited to reveal the secret in a future correspondence or to tell him personally.

A few days later, feeling certain that she was expecting, Birgit had an overwhelming desire to tell someone. She contacted her sister, Sonya, via the school office phone. The principal was coming in late so Birgit gave into her urge. She knew that her sister could be trusted to keep a secret. They had shared many secrets when they were younger. Sonya's first question was, "Who is the father?" Birgit wanted so much to say his name. She enjoyed the very sound of it but stopped herself. She knew that his German name and his position in the enemy army would be too much for Sonya to accept. It would remove the joy from the news Birgit had just confided. She simply told Sonya it was no one she knew. He is a handsome (she stressed the word) man, from Oslo, who adores her and she adores him, and they have plans to marry in the near future. She was clearly overflowing with anticipation and Sonya knew not to press her further. Sonya wished Birgit more happiness and love than any sister could ever hope for and said that she could not wait to meet her handsome prince. In the meantime, if she could do anything, she (the baby's auntie) would always be there for them. At that point, she heard her sister weeping over the phone. Sonya waited a few seconds for Birgit to compose herself, and then said without being asked, "Don't worry, it'll be our secret until you're ready to tell them," referring to their mom and dad.

Chapter 26

Lieutenant Kuhlemann on Leave

It was Tuesday, late September 1940, when the sky changed from a pleasantly calm and sunny afternoon to cloudy and, finally, to a celestial brilliance as if the lines of a power station had been turned on in a single room. Then, the north country sky, a sky like no other on the planet, unleashed its fury like an angry Thor slamming down his hammer. What followed was thunder, lightning and a torrential downpour. Birgit rushed from the kitchen to close the window and as she happened to glance down the dirt road lined with skinny birch trees and fog, a figure seemed to be approaching. At first, she thought it was the caretaker who she hadn't seen in several weeks. But as the figure came closer, she could see a German uniform and the man was carrying something. Her heart leapt forward like a sprinter at the start line when the gun went off. Her heart knew what her eyes could not see. She ran out the door and down the dirt road, wind and cold rain slamming in her face. The distant figure caught sight of her and tore down the road as if outrunning the bulls of Pamplona. Both sopping wet and oblivious to the unmerciful sky, they crashed into each other's arms. They remained in the middle of the road, two blurry figures melded together like inseparable magnets, heart to heart and lips to lips.

Hans' arrival was a total surprise since she expected him the following day. He explained that the convoy had made excellent time, and many soldiers were anxious to catch an early transport from Oslo back to Germany to visit family. He had decided to spend the short leave with her and had written home, telling his parents of his plans. At that moment she wanted to burst out and tell him that she was expecting but then contained herself, figuring that there would be a more appropriate time. Then she berated herself for having waited over five months before disclosing that he was going to be a father. Hans had not so much as suspected, since she was hardly showing. And the little weight she had gained was practically unnoticeable.

Birgit went to the dresser to get dry clothes. While she spoke, he listened carefully to the sweetness of her voice; inhaled deeply the essence of her scent. As they were pulling off wet clothes, he saw the curvature of her body silhouetted against the window. A perfect form. Far more beautiful than how she came into his dreams.

"I can't get my hands on you fast enough to love you," he blurted out.

She smiled. Both eager to have the gift that was each other.

A few hours later, the violent storm outside the bedroom window subsided. Two robes, compliments of the Astergarden Hotel, were lying on a chair next to the window. The two of them were totally spent as they unwrapped each other tenderly and cuddled.

Lying on his side, Hans was stroking Birgit's hair, then he kissed her gently on her forehead. They looked deeply into each other's eyes.

"I've been lying here quietly, enraptured by your beauty, by your gracefulness. I'm thinking, how can I possibly express how much in love I am with you? Only to realize that words and poetry are so inadequate," he said.

She whispered in his ear, "I will always love you, Hans. My faith in you is total, heart and soul."

He caressed her soft, warm body, as if to say, "and I will always be there for you." When his hand came to rest on her stomach, Birgit took her own hand and placed it over his, holding both hands motionless on her belly.

"Listen!" she said. "Do you feel anything?"

He stayed there listening carefully for a few moments before he felt movement inside her, and then suspected, looking like a child after solving a complicated puzzle. His face lit up in disbelief.

"You're pregnant?" he asked. Then he paused, like a boxer who had been sucker-punched, stunned by the conclusion he had drawn. A smile filled his face.

"Yes, I'm sorry for not telling you in my letters. I just didn't want you to worry excessively or distract you from your responsibilities. I thought it would be better telling you personally," she said.

"So that means you're about five, six months along? By January we'll be parents." He was still smiling and seemed unable to contain his happiness. "Wow! I'm going to be a father. A baby born on Norwegian soil."

She was looking at him admiringly and thinking that he would make a wonderful father, when Hans' mood changed before her eyes. His smile disappeared and he became more serious.

"But you can't manage on your own here. It's going to get more difficult for you by the week, if not by the day," he said with much concern.

"I'll be fine," she said. "Besides, Lars, the caretaker, stops by weekly and my mother and father are only half an hour away." She was trying to alleviate his concern but knew full well that her parents would wash their hands of her as soon as they learned that she was having a child out of wedlock. That the child's father was German was enough for her father to disown her forever, even move him to violence.

"But I thought your relationship with them was strained?" he said.

"Yes, but in an emergency, they would probably help." She was trying to reassure Hans. He seemed pensive and unconvinced.

"I've heard that the German government is in the process of setting up birthing homes for military personnel's spouses and girlfriends, right here," he said. "The program started in Germany and is organized within the *Schutzstaffel, SS*. They call it the *Lebensborn* program and they take serious responsibility for the welfare of a serviceman's family. The very same program is being expanded in other countries like Norway. I believe the facilities supporting the program should be up and running, right here in Oslo, by the early part of the New Year. As an army officer, I'm sure I can get you signed up and quickly admitted when the time comes. Then all your medical care and other needs will be provided. I'll feel a lot better knowing you're safe, and cared for by German doctors," he said, finding the idea comforting.

"It seems too good to be true," Birgit responded.

"There may be some standard requirements such as a preliminary examination of you and the baby and proof that you are of pure Norwegian blood. I don't see these matters as being obstacles. I will sign the proper papers acknowledging that I'm the father and the child will bear my surname, Kuhlemann." He took her hands in his, looked at her and a smile returned.

"What if these birthing homes are not set up in time for when I'm due?" she asked.

"The *Schutzstaffel* is very efficient. If they say the facilities will be up and running at the beginning of the year they will be. Who knows? You might be one of the first in the unit, but even assuming the *Lebensborn* facilities are not opened or staffed, I will have you admitted to the military hospital with the intent to transfer you there at the earliest opportunity. I will inquire further about it, and initiate the process before returning to my unit in Trondheim, okay?"

"Thank you for caring so much," she said.

"You and this baby are not alone, you're my family," he said as he ran his hand gently over her tummy and kissed her above her navel.

The rain outside had stopped but in its place an October coldness had become apparent. Birgit snuggled deeper into Hans' robe, feeling for the first time in her life that she was safe and protected. It was a good feeling. There was a man here, a good man, that she could love completely and without the slightest reservation. The fact that he was a German officer might be repugnant to her family but if they truly knew him, as she did, they would someday learn to accept and even admire him as a rare human being.

The lieutenant's ten-day leave went fast. She was obsessed with remembering every moment they spent together and what they did. That first night was the first time they had had real time to themselves, unhurried and unpreoccupied with the military, her work or other people's demands. She had cooked a simple meal and they had shared a bottle of German wine that had been salvaged from the cellar of the Astergarden prior to shutting down. They had made incredible love and spent the remainder of the night in each other's arms, in total bliss. The only time they had separated from each other was at about three in the morning when they had decided to eat almost the entire box of chocolates that he had brought her as a present. And it wasn't until six in the morning that they fell asleep and then slept late.

They had taken walks in the woods, arm in arm, and even though it was chilly they didn't feel it. Whenever the sun penetrated through the branches and made dancing patterns and dapple images on the ground Hans said it was a celebration intended for them. But despite his joking, she was impressed with her man's knowledge of the flora and fauna. He had even discovered some large white mushrooms growing along the base of a tree and picked them and cooked them and they had turned out to be amazingly delicious. On Thursday he had gotten up early, before Birgit, and ventured into the forest to set a trap and in the evening, they went back to discover he had caught a hare which he cooked over an open fire.

One day she arrived from school to see that Hans had cleared the grounds around the cottage and along the road and cut and stacked several cords of wood for the fireplace. Their immediate surroundings looked almost as pretty as they had been in April when Astergarden was in full bloom and operating. The following day he located an old fishing rod in one of the sheds and went to the fjord and, using some bugs as bait, caught a bucketful of fish. When Lars, the caretaker, stopped by unexpectedly the day after, Birgit introduced them and they took a liking to each other. And when the caretaker went home that afternoon, he carried home a bucket three-quarters full of fish.

The caretaker, not wanting to be outdone by Hans' generosity, offered him the keys to his boat which was still moored at the Astergarden pier. This was in case Hans wanted to try other fishing spots or visit some of the other islands. The next morning Hans took him up on his offer when he helped Birgit down the hill, assisted her onto the boat and headed south, together, to Filert. It was a quaint little town and they walked around, visiting several small shops that were, surprisingly, still open so late in the season. In a snack shop they bought lunch and the lieutenant treated her to ice cream, saying that expectant mothers always craved ice cream and that he wanted to satisfy the craving while he could. By early afternoon they passed a small jewelry shop with a few teddy bears holding and displaying trinkets in the window. Hans bought her a small heart pendant that was, according to the old saleswoman, forged in the area. On the way out, he asked the merchant if she could sell him the red teddy bear in the window. At first, she said it wasn't for sale until he pointed to Birgit. When he told the saleswoman it was for the baby, she finally relented.

On the seventh day of his leave, while Birgit was at the school, he took Lars' boat north of Oslo. There he visited military headquarters and inquired about assistance for the women of military men who were expecting. He had been directed to another office, a separate building from headquarters, where he was instructed to fill out papers detailing his own background, his meeting and relationship with Birgit, her characteristics and the date she expected to give birth. Much of the information pertaining to his mate was unknown to him, especially questions relating to any Jewish blood in her family and inquiries going back to her grandparents and whether there had been any discernible diseases and other negative traits in her bloodline. The lieutenant was about to complete the questions in accordance with what the SS office wanted to hear but decided against providing misinformation. Instead, he asked the official if he could have his fiancée complete certain sections and return the documents.

He was informed that his own completed paperwork and acknowledgements would be on file and was advised that Birgit present herself and her paperwork at least thirty days prior to the date she expected to give birth. At such time she would also be expected to undergo thorough medical examinations. When the infant was born, he or she would also undergo examination for "hereditary purity." And, assuming all went as expected, the *Lebensborn* home would provide their total care, medical and financial, until the family was ready to be on their own. The lieutenant was also informed that several of these birthing homes were expected to open at the same time and that he could have his fiancée stay at their preferred location.

When Hans discussed his experience at the SS Office for Servicemen's Family Welfare, Birgit felt a certain disquiet in her belly. The program she had come to rely on during the last ten days did not seem very accommodating. If they truly wanted to help soldiers' families, why create so many hurdles? Why probe so deeply into their backgrounds? Why did it matter if there had been a Jewish relative some generations back or even if there was one now? She did not express half the concerns she had to Hans because he was convinced that there was no better alternative.

They spent the last evening of the lieutenant's leave quietly at home, holding each other and enjoying each other's company by the fireplace. They rededicated each to the other and pledged their love. They even talked about marriage during his next leave when they imagined themselves to be the parents of a beautiful child. A small wedding could quickly be arranged with perhaps a dozen or so people at the Lutheran Chapel in Oslo. He named a few army friends he wished to have as guests, and she wanted to invite her sister and some of her own close friends. She would extend the invitation to her parents but didn't think they would attend, especially if they found out her husband was a Nazi army officer. As for the two of them, all that mattered was that they loved each other. When the war was over, they planned on retaking their vows in Hans' hometown in Bavaria, and to have a large party.

With those images in mind and bodies entwined, slumber overtook them. The next morning, with strengthened bonds, they embraced tightly and separated tearfully. She watched Hans disappear beyond the skinny birch trees, in the seemingly same fog that had brought him, now it had returned to take him away.

Chapter 27

Birgit at the Lebensborn Home

The New Year was two days old. A brutally cold week had ushered in 1941. The snow that had fallen the previous day was encrusted with a layer of ice. Despite the occupation force's reputation for efficiency and punctuality the public transportation system ran sporadically, if at all. The country had been substantially pacified with the exception of small skirmishes along the Swedish border, where patriots would come across and sabotage German assets. Attacks were assisted or funded by the Norwegian government in exile with the blessing of the British government. The occupying forces, however, were not dislodged and every corner of the north country was trampled by German boots. The majority of the native inhabitants, lacking any other alternative, settled into their predicament and tried to make the best of a bad situation.

Birgit had been to the Office for Servicemen's Family Welfare that ran the *Lebensborn* homes two weeks after Hans left. She had discussed her situation with one staff official who immediately located the file initiated by Lieutenant Hans Kuhlemann, the child's father. He told Birgit he remembered the lieutenant well. She completed and submitted all the paperwork required. She had been examined, probed, and felt, by two male doctors in white jackets and had been left on the examination table. She could see them chatting with a uniformed official in the hallway. That same official took her into another room and questioned her about her ancestry, her bloodline and the type of work engaged in by her family. As she spoke, a female secretary sitting next to the official took shorthand notes. The entire exam and interview had taken over six hours and Birgit left with the address of the *Lebensborn* home and with the understanding that she was to present herself on the seventh day of January. By then, her pregnancy would be almost at term or near term.

The *Schutzstaffel*, headed by Wilhelm Rediess, had been busy locating and confiscating properties for the program they were assigned to administer. They had a handful of hotels, villas and buildings that had been targeted for conversion and renovation; some were in Oslo and others in major cities along the coast, about ten sites in all. At least two facilities were scheduled to officially open in March, with planned celebrations and the personal appearance and inspection by Heinrich Himmler himself, the founder of the *Lebensborn* program. However, one home in Trondheim and another one on the outskirts of Oslo, that which Birgit was to occupy, would be functioning ahead of schedule and receiving their final touches.

Birgit was nervous and scared when she found herself standing in front of the Godthaab *Lebensborn* home on the seventh day of January. As she pushed open the wrought iron gate with the SS symbol soldered onto it, she noticed that the building was meticulously clean, having been painted and upgraded recently. The evergreen bushes were neatly trimmed, the patches of grass cropping out from under the canvas of melting snow were cut neatly, and the parking lot and walkways had been shoveled and were totally clear of snow. While no precipitation was in the air there was a blistering coldness and she felt it on her face and legs. This prompted her to wrap her long woolen coat tighter over her swollen belly. She thought about the German doctor she had last seen in October who had advised her to present herself on the seventh day of the New Year because she'd be very close to term by then. She didn't know who else to turn to so she followed his advice as best she could, including diet and rest. She wondered how long she'd be here. For all she knew she could be settling in for several weeks before the onset of serious labor and contractions. Her mother once told her that she was in labor with her sister, very late in term, for twenty-four hours before she was born. She hoped that her own labor was a lot shorter.

As she stepped across the porch and reached for the doorknob a young woman in a crisp white nurse's uniform, sweater and white cap opened the door for her. When she saw her, she smiled and opened the door wider.

"*Guten Morgen! Herzlich willkommen* (Good morning and a warm welcome). You must be Birgit Karlsen, we've been expecting you," said the nurse.

"Yes, thank you," Birgit said, smiling back.

"Please wait a moment, I'll get you a chair," said the nurse, who came back very promptly with a wheelchair and sat her down.

"Don't you worry about anything, you are in the best maternity facility available anywhere."

'I don't doubt it. Hans Kuhlemann, the baby's father, had already assured me of that," said Birgit.

Birgit was wheeled to a private room, completely furnished, and was helped out of the chair and coat. Relieved, she was motioned to the twin-sized bed where she lay down gratefully. The nurse helped her take off her shoes. Rest was what she needed, according to the nurse, and she did feel drowsy since she had been traveling and on her feet for several hours.

It was a warm and comfortable room with wide floorboards and large windows whose curtains were partially drawn. She preferred her cottage of course, and the thought of not being able to go back saddened her. She had lost it forever. Rolf had requested that the caretaker board up all the smaller buildings at Astergarden as soon as Birgit moved out to have her child; to her, the order to board up all the buildings represented the end of another chapter in her life. It wasn't that she harbored any hard feelings towards Rolf; he had extended himself as far as possible during his brother's absence. But she did sense that Rolf's attitude had changed since learning that she was pregnant out of wedlock. He probably wanted no part of the scandal that might develop, which could have potential consequences with his hotel and ancillary businesses in Bygdoy and in downtown Oslo.

Rolf's brother, Olaf Johansen, had been missing for months now. His family's attempts to try to locate him via the German consulate's military attaché led nowhere. Later, the attorney they hired tracked and questioned all the people Mr. Johansen had come in contact with during the week prior to his disappearance. They even returned to the police station for information. This inquiry proved futile, nothing panned out. He was never found. The bits and pieces of information they had been able to put together supported their suspicions that he had been transported to Germany, held as a prisoner.

A kick from her unborn baby brought her mind to her own circumstances. She would have her baby and take some time recuperating here, in Godthaab. The staff had assured her that she could stay for a lengthy period, if she needed to, or wanted to, and they seemed very kind and hospitable so far.

Her mind kept wandering from Olaf's disappearance, to the present moment in the birthing home and, with relief, to her lieutenant. She knew that Hans Kuhlemann was committed to her and the child in every possible way. They had charted a future together. He provided her with moral support and financial assistance as best he could from where he was stationed. She had received his last letter a week before and his love was unquestionable. In a few weeks the child's birth would solidify their lives even more. She expected to receive his first letter at Godthaab in about five days; she had furnished him with the name and address of this new *Lebensborn* home where she was staying.

The small financial support he provided her, after losing her school job, was a godsend. The school administration had fired staff a few months earlier because student attendance was low and funding had suffered considerably. Staff reduction was an unfortunate result of all the disruption caused by the war. But in Birgit's case, there was even more reason to let her go. She was thought to have given aid and comfort to the enemy. She had heard the rumors about the illegitimate bastard she carried and that the father was an enemy German soldier with whom she had voluntarily had sex. They branded her a *tyskerhore* (a German whore) and a traitor to all Norwegians. In a way, some people said she was lucky that the staff and parents didn't take matters into their own hands by punishing her more severely, even wringing her neck, instead of just terminating her employment.

Her memory of the last day in school brought tears to her eyes. In the school supply room, she had overheard co-workers say that even her own mother and father disowned her because of her morally reprehensible actions. This was another rumor because of the strained relation with her parents, predating the German invasion. She remembered fighting back, defending the lieutenant, but they had succeeded in breaking her down. She was left alone, curled up on the cold concrete floor, sobbing.

In reliving that painful scene, she dozed off. When she awoke in her bed, she realized that she had been napping for about two hours. It was still daylight. She looked out from the side of the curtain and saw rays of sunlight shimmering off the frozen snow, while trees drooped down to the ground from the weight of the icicles. On the flagpole clanked a Nazi SS banner. Next to her bed was a glass of juice, three cookies, two pills and a two-page form requesting updated information. The first page consisted of basic questions: the name of the doctor she had last seen and questions regarding symptoms of her pregnancy. The second page pertained to the child's father, such as his name, his current rank, the base where he was currently stationed and a large blank area requiring details of their future plans with the child. She scanned the two sheets of paper but felt too exhausted and nauseous to do anything with them and placed them back on the stand.

*

Birgit had been at the *Lebensborn* home for a little over a week and was beginning to feel at ease. She felt she was well treated. She had been examined the day after arriving and was assured that all was going well for both her and the baby. She had befriended a couple of expectant mothers in the building, managed to learn some of the staff names and had been taken on a tour of the building. The sewing room, the kitchen, dining area were well equipped. The recreation room had a section for movies and two tables where the expectant mothers could play cards and other games. A medical and nursing unit that originally consisted of three separate rooms, but recently had its walls knocked down, opened into one large area. Along a small wall were shelves of pharmaceuticals, gauze, various medical equipment and numerous products for women. Upstairs were the recovery area and the postpartum boarding rooms where women could stay up to six months beyond the birthing day.

There was only one woman in the entire facility, a nineteen-year-old, who had given birth. She had been in recovery for three days before she was moved to her more permanent quarters. Birgit had spoken to her on two occasions, and the young mother had said that the medical staff had thoroughly examined and tested her newborn for all sorts of potential defects and diseases. She was afraid, as well as everyone else, that because the baby was born slightly premature, it might have medical issues. But upon examination was found to be in perfect health. The nurses cared for him in the neonatal area while she recovered in the privacy of her room.

What the young mother said next left Birgit almost speechless.

"I don't know if you heard, but I decided to give up my child for adoption," said the young woman.

"You gave your child up for adoption?" Birgit repeated, wanting confirmation of what she heard.

"Yes, they gave me every assurance that the child would be cared for as good as any mother could expect."

"Are you comfortable with your decision?" asked Birgit, trying not to sound judgmental.

"They told me the baby would be adopted by a good German family. They would meet all of the child's needs, financial and otherwise. Besides, the adoptive parents would undergo rigorous background checks and interviews before the matter was finalized," said the young mother.

She also told Birgit how she met the German father, during the time she worked in a military mess hall. Birgit listened, quietly and attentively, while the young mother divulged sensitive aspects of her affair.

Later, their conversation digressed to the reception that was planned for Saturday, which was only two days away. A reception was being held for a group of high-ranking SS officers. The building's lower level, which opened to a large terrace at the rear, was being prepared. A large concrete room was also converted and decorated. Tables had been moved and colorful tablecloths had been spread; ribbons, balloons and welcome posters had been set up. The officials inspecting Godthaab were intent on using it as a model for other *Lebensborn* homes in various Norwegian cities. A new medical doctor and an architect were also going to be present.

The architect was known for his design of German architectural features, such as the farmhouse look and preferred construction of *Lebensborn* homes away from the city's noise, stress and unhealthy conditions. His preference was to start with a "clean canvas," an empty lot, and on that lot create something splendid. The new structure had to provide privacy, and at the same time exhibit large balconies to offer panoramic views into the garden and beyond, preferably mountain peaks. His underlying thinking was to construct an organic whole where man, house and surroundings formed a harmonious unit. Where there were restrictions, such as converting an existing structure, as was the case with Godthaab, the interior space had to emphasize comfort for the mother and functionality for the staff. It was this view that led him to eliminate three rooms and to create one open unit for the doctor and nurses. "Think in terms of natural light, fresh air and beautiful views from balconies that would be decorated with lots of plants and flowers," he would say.

While discussing the party, the expected attendees, and the young mother's future, Birgit couldn't help but feel a twinge of sadness for this girl who had a need to give up her baby for adoption. She had considered an abortion but was morally troubled with the idea, she said. More importantly, the Germans had declared all abortions illegal and no doctor would be willing to perform them. Instead, since privacy of her pregnancy and birth could be assured and assistance was available, she had decided to follow the path prescribed by the Godthaab staff: have the child in an advanced facility and give it up for adoption. She, also, planned to leave the Godthaab home and attempt to get her job back at the army base. The staff assured her that they would do everything possible to get her position restored.

Birgit spent the next two days in her room. Although she felt energized, a sense of anxiety had taken possession of her. The student nurses not only brought her meals but visited her room frequently, realizing that she was very near to term. During the afternoon she tried to read a book but the child's movements inside her made her uncomfortable, whether she was standing, sitting or lying down. The staff were preoccupied with final preparations for the party and most of the activity was concentrated in the lobby and at the bottom of a wide staircase that led to the lower level.

At about five o'clock some vehicles had arrived and she could see from her window that important people were looking around the Godthaab facility, often escorted by others of equal rank. Most were middle-aged men. A handful of them had taken a tour of the building and she could hear talking outside her door, wondering if they would come inside, but they didn't. She had also noticed a group of student nurses arriving a little later when large platters of food and drinks were made available. Some had student uniforms and others didn't. Then two musicians began playing a violin and an accordion and the mood got jollier and louder. The laughter of men and women wafted up to her room. The music, the laughter and dancing didn't subside until late in the evening. Birgit fell asleep for several hours, until awakened by the slamming of car doors.

At the window Birgit could see several SS officers climbing up the side staircase from the lower level. Chauffeurs, in uniforms, were either waiting next to a Mercedes or holding the passenger side doors open. A young woman, arms laced around the neck of one officer, kissed him and laughed loudly as she bid him goodnight. Another officer was assisted by two women who braced him up under each arm and escorted him to his car. After some minutes the doors of the vehicles slammed shut and four cars with the SS officers and a few civilians pulled away. The lead vehicle and rear vehicle carried military guards equipped with machine guns.

Finally, the building quieted. The small clock in the room said almost 4am. She decided to go to the bathroom before trying to get a little more sleep. Morning light would soon arrive. In the bathroom, as she sat up, strong cramps started. She wasn't sure if they were labor or prelabor discomfort. Her face became flustered. She chided herself to calm down since it was probably stress or anxiety. Slowly, she got to her feet and walked back to bed. She sat on the edge and tried to get back under the blankets. After several minutes, an unusual rumble in her belly quieted down. She lay on her side and closed her eyes.

Chapter 28

A Child is Born

A young girl, no older than fifteen, came into her room with a breakfast tray. She greeted Birgit and asked how she felt. Before she could answer, Birgit sensed a sudden wetness between her thighs. Panic came to her face. The young girl, seeing the patient's reaction, asked again, this time with an edge of panic in her voice.

"Is everything alright?"

"I think my water broke. Can you please get the head nurse?"

The young girl, more alarmed than Birgit, placed her tray down and rushed out the door, down the hallway. Moments later Birgit was being wheeled into the medical section.

In late afternoon she gave birth to a seven-pounds fourteen-ounce baby boy. Some of the staff must've thought the child would have the required traits to represent the second generation of the Third Reich. Birgit was in labor for seven and a half hours and was exhausted. She fell asleep after delivery. Within the hour she had been taken to the recovery room and the infant was brought to a neonatal unit for a thorough examination and screening. The visual and reflex examination had satisfied the doctor. There was nothing obviously wrong. The nurse had him on the table and was taking external measurements. She checked every square inch: his length, his head size, hands and feet, eyes, ears and genitals. She realized that his blue-gray eyes and blond hair were perfect attributes, which pleased her, and she made notations on her medical chart.

The nurse had seen situations where she had previously worked, at the *Lebensborn* home in Steinhöring, where the outcome was not so joyful. Obvious defects such as a cleft lip, a clubfoot, being severely underweight or evidence that the infant had suffered in the womb from lack of oxygen or other possible mental condition would condemn the infant to a fatal injection. She had even seen a most perfect baby put to death because of the doctor's gross negligence in the use of medical instruments. The official report, however, would always indicate "stillborn." Here, from all preliminary assessments, the child had been born without complications and from good stock. As she made her other required entries on the medical forms, she saw on the opposite page that the father was a lieutenant in the *Wehrmacht*. A little notation towards the bottom of the page, almost like a footnote, expressed his intention of a "continued association" with the mother. She smiled. This meant to her that the child would be brought up by a family with unwavering beliefs in the fatherland. The Führer's goals of increasing the "Aryan stock" would be furthered, not only in this instance, but also as a result of the organized events that she was so good at. The party from the night before was an example of her ingenuity. She surmised that at least half a dozen children would be born thanks to her. She felt content. Godthaab was not even officially opened, yet, conception of Aryan stock at a promising scale had already started. Her work and dedication to the program would, sooner or later, be recognized. This *Lebensborn* home, where she diligently worked, would serve as a model and would help shape all other birthing homes that would mushroom across the northern country's Aryan landscape.

The nurse also felt a sense of satisfaction in knowing that the very first child born at this facility, in her care, would be a gift to the fatherland. The child was born from the seed of an accomplished and much decorated SS officer, during a one-night affair with a young and fertile Norwegian woman. She couldn't think of two purer specimens. The young mother had made the best decision to give the child up for adoption. She and her small staff had taken pains to convince the mother to proceed with the adoption as an unselfish act. They had shown her a black and white documentary film touting the selflessness of giving up a child for adoption. The film showed a financially well-to-do German family treating the child with love and kindness and offering every possible amenity anyone, anywhere could desire. The documentary showed the child from birth through his eighteenth birthday; at every major event, whether a birthday, picnic, graduation or competitive event, he was shown being successful and laughing and in perfect health and smiling with an unblemished set of teeth. The inspirational background music coincided with the boy's accomplishments and ended with the boy and some of his peers grown up, dressed in meticulous uniforms.

The nurse's thoughts came back to this Birgit Karlsen's child. The doctor would want to perform some other routine tests on him before he would be reunited with his mother. In situations where a German officer was receptive to forming a family unit with the mother and child, no form of dissuasion was promoted. It was assumed that the father's military career had permeated his being; that his core beliefs would be passed on to the mother if she wasn't already proselytized. The guidelines, in this case, were the same as when a married officer's wife entered a *Lebensborn* home in Germany seeking assistance during pregnancy. The nurse realized early in her career that there were some other perks to being a ranking officer with a family unit. In at least two instances, she recalled children that had been born slightly imperfect who were given the benefit of the doubt and permitted to live. One child had been born with a clubfoot and another, a girl, was born with two different-colored eyes. Yes, from time to time, exceptions were made due to the rank of the father, the acquaintance with the doctor, or even in moments when the doctor or nurse experienced a rare moment of compassion or as some of her co-workers called it, "weakness."

*

It was Monday morning, two days after her delivery, and Birgit still felt sore and weak. Her future path seemed bleak at least until Hans left the military. She found herself somewhat depressed and couldn't understand why. It was at this moment that the young woman credited for having the first birth at Godthaab peeked in her door. She came in with a forced smile on her face. Birgit could immediately read her deeper torment, as she came in to give her a hug and congratulate her. She brought her a gift, a single flower in a skinny cylindrical vase, which she placed on Birgit's nightstand. Then she told Birgit that she was moving out that same day. All arrangements had been made and papers were signed for her baby's adoption. She was going back home, hoping to resume her previous work and life. According to her, choices were limited for a young woman, with limited skills, in a wartime economy. Birgit saw for the first time how confused and scared the girl was. She didn't have the strength of character to take an alternate path. She gave Birgit her address and asked her to look her up when she had an opportunity. She kissed her on the forehead and was gone before Birgit could give her any words of hope. Birgit thought how fortunate she was with this child, to have such a wonderful, loving and respected man in their future.

Late that same morning, Birgit envisioned walking through the fields and farms of Bavaria with her husband, Hans. He carried their giggling child on his shoulders. She had also managed to wash herself and was walking around a little when she received a letter. One of the nurse assistants had delivered it to her room. The letter was dated as of the previous Tuesday and the return name and address was not that of Hans Kuhlemann but of his friend, Heinrich. She remembered the lieutenant speaking very highly of him. She looked the envelope over, carefully, for any clues and saw a brown streak of dirt on the opposite side of her address, indicating that it had been dropped and wiped clean. She opened it with some fear and trepidation but refused to give in to panic. The calligraphy was a bit difficult to decipher. And, immediately she realized Heinrich was finding it difficult to express his thoughts.

January 23, 1941

Dear Birgit,

My name is Heinrich. Hans and I have been good friends since childhood.

He spoke of you often. He confided to me about your future plans in getting married. He said you were the purpose of his existence. And the ten days you spent together during his leave was the most remarkable time of his life. Whenever I saw him smiling in the barracks, I knew he was thinking of you, and of being a father, to a most perfect child – an extension of you, Birgit.

Please be strong!

What I am about to say has caused me profound grief. But the pain and grief you will experience will be unimaginable.

I am sorry, but Hans has passed away. A soldier next to him stepped on a landmine. He was brought to base camp. Heroic efforts were made to save his life. Unfortunately, he succumbed to his injuries the following day. He is interred in the German military cemetery in Trondheim. During his last moments he called out your name, "Birgit, Birgit." He absolutely adored you. He wanted you and the child to go on living.

  I do not purport to know the answer to why God allows such incredibly cruel events to happen. But sometimes, ten days well spent together will have to suffice for a lifetime.
  Please let me know if I can be of any help, in any way.

Heinrich
PS: Hans' memory will forever be etched in the hearts of the people who loved him.

She sat on the bed in shock; her eyes stared out of the window without registering anything. Soon after, she started screaming in painful anguish. She gulped air but felt unable to breathe. As her mind eased back into her body, she crumbled the letter; tears streamed down her face like an open faucet, while yanking her hair so hard that clusters of hair were entangled in her fingers. Her body, devoid of feeling, slid down from the bed to the wooden floor. She pounded the floor with so much rage that her fists were scraped and bloody. Shattered, physically and emotionally, she visualized her life ripped to shreds. All was rendered meaningless: her future, her plans, her very existence. She refused to visualize Hans' death, even when he called her name in his final moments. Her body felt lifeless. How could God be so merciless? Heinrich had written that it was Hans' wish for her to go on. But how could she? Why would she want to go on? How could she even provide for her newborn? She kept asking herself these questions, with hands trembling and wetness draining from her nose, eyes, saturating her blouse.
  Only a few hours earlier she was giving thanks to God that she was not in the awful predicament of the girl who'd given up her baby. But now she felt she was in a worse crisis. She felt like she was in an open sea, on a raft, without oars. She even pictured flinging herself overboard or going crazy, being placed in an insane asylum. She could not see a future without Hans, there was only blackness. Her despair quickly turned into unstoppable screams. The cries brought

two nurse-assistants running into her room. They found her folded into a fetal position and sobbing uncontrollably.

Birgit was inconsolable. She felt isolated, empty and hopeless. She had cared for and loved Hans without reservation. She had placed her fate, her hopes and dreams in his care and he was dead. She ached with the need to hold him, to speak to him, to kiss him for the last time.

But she would never have that opportunity. According to Heinrich he was buried in a German cemetery. Perhaps not far from the military base. Maybe she could go there and be close to him, close to his spirit. Yes, she would bring him flowers and sit next to his grave and ask him how, or even why, she should go on without him.

How would she care for their child alone? With another stab of sadness, she realized Hans had never seen their child. He would have been so proud of his beautiful son. Together they would give him every opportunity in life. What could she alone give him? Without Hans their future seemed bleak. How could she provide for the child when she couldn't provide for herself? She couldn't go back to her past; there was no job to go back to, there was no roof over her head to go back to. Her parents had disowned her. The community condemned her for falling in love with a German. What did the future hold for her and her child besides hopelessness and despair? The young woman with the flower floated back to her mind. Was it possible that she had made the right decision, albeit heart-wrenching, but a right one, by giving her infant away for adoption? Perhaps he could be adopted by a "good German family," a Bavarian family. Was adoption her baby's only chance, with another father who would love and cherish him for the gift he was, and provide him with all she could not?

Chapter 29

Trying to Pick Up the Pieces

Birgit was despondent for days. Once she started thinking about giving her child up for adoption, the staff began to persuade her relentlessly. They wanted the child placed for adoption through the *Lebensborn* Placement Services. They told her how the child would benefit. They reminded her of her young age, her future children, her new life to come. She was told that adoptions occurred often in the *Lebensborn* homes. In Germany, where the head nurse had worked in a similar facility, mothers saw the benefit of adoptions in over ninety percent of the cases. The head nurse even told her that she knew of no case that she was involved in that didn't work out. Birgit saw no future for herself, so how then, with her and her baby? How could she even hold any type of employment while caring for the infant? Birgit was physically, emotionally and spiritually vulnerable, so the staff began the paperwork for adoption.

It took Birgit eight days after giving birth and one telephone call to her sister in Bergen before relinquishing all her parental rights to Godthaab. Her sister knew that her pregnancy was out of wedlock, and whenever they talked, she was given lukewarm support. All along, Sonya had assumed that it was a Norwegian man who had fathered the child. And Birgit never disclosed that her lover was a German. She also didn't want to tell Sonya that her baby had been put up for adoption. Instead, she told her sister that complications had arisen and the child was stillborn. The lie to Sonya engendered sympathy and Birgit was offered a home until she found herself on more firm ground.

The day after her fateful decision she found herself standing at a bus stop with her bedraggled luggage, heading for Oslo city center, with a token stipend in her pocket given to her by the *Lebensborn* office. For two and a half days, through bombed-out areas, miserable weather and generally oppressive conditions, she numbly traveled by bus and train, directly from Oslo to Trondheim. It had not been easy locating Lieutenant Hans Kuhlemann's burial plot on her own. Her search finally took her to the German base. There she presented proof that the lieutenant was the father of her child and related the circumstances of the birth and the surrender of their baby to a German placement service. Hearing the story, one of the base officers escorted her to the exact location of the burial. The grave was freshly dug, like many others, and even though many had German crosses marking the graves, no inscriptions had yet been carved on Hans' lonely plot. The soldier had to refer to a cemetery map to identify the exact site.

Small and wretched was how she probably looked in the misty cemetery. She had been kneeling on the frozen fresh dirt for more than an hour. The soldier had smoked several cigarettes and was getting impatient as he looked at her from a distance. She had placed a bouquet of flowers diagonally in front of the blank cross and seemed to be conversing with the lieutenant, sometimes speaking excitedly and other times weeping aloud. Then she would caress the cross as if gently stroking his face. Large snowflakes began falling from the sky, as if the gods had been moved by her agony and were also shedding tears. The soldier took it as an opportunity to walk up to her and take her by the arm, telling her it was time to go. Birgit walked and kept looking back at the grave. The soldier could hear, over and over, in a low voice: "Goodbye, my love. Goodbye, my love."

In the following days, she found herself living in one room, on the side of her sister's house. For several weeks, she was greatly depressed. It wasn't until her brother-in-law used his connections that she was able to secure a part-time job at a telephone company's switchboard office. The money she made, she turned over to her sister and brother-in-law, hardly enough to defray her living expenses, but the job gave her a modicum of dignity and self-worth.

By the following summer, she had managed to have her work hours doubled and she had applied for a transfer to the Oslo regional office. There she leased a small two-room apartment and continued working until the summer of 1945, when the Allies finally defeated Germany and all German forces were withdrawn from Norway.

The Nazis were gone. But loathing of everything connected with them still lingered with Norwegians. During the occupation, acrimony towards the Germans had reached such intensity that the Norwegian government in exile had warned that anyone cooperating with the invaders would be dealt with *severely* after the war. And the promise was kept. This attitude resulted in numerous trials and executions for so-called "traitors of Norway," including the death of Quisling before a firing squad.

As to others, such as the women who had fraternized with the enemy, things were not much better. Several weeks after the war was officially declared to be over, Birgit was walking on a city street one afternoon when a seemingly crazed woman screamed from the other side of the street and ran towards her.

"*Hore! Tyskerhore!* (Whore! German whore!)," she kept screaming until other women and a few men surrounded her. The woman's rage seemed to puff her graying mane like an arched cat hissing, ready to pounce. Birgit recognized her as a former co-worker from school who knew that she had gotten pregnant out of wedlock, but what

Birgit couldn't fathom was how she knew that her baby's father had been a German officer. The screaming woman swung her purse at her. Birgit raised her hands across her face to protect herself. At that point another woman pushed her to the ground. Others joined in the name-calling and physical attacks. Several of the gathered men mocked her with cruel laughter. One middle-aged man with a scar on his forehead and a scowl on his face, who may have been a resistance fighter, made his way past the people surrounding her, looked at her icily and, with contempt, spat on her. As Birgit lay on her side on the concrete, with head down and arms over her head for protection, someone grabbed her by the collar of her blouse and yanked it, ripping garment and buttons until she had nothing but her brassiere. The attacks continued until a policeman blew his whistle but, before they scattered, the graying woman twisted her hand around Birgit's hair and pulled out a clump. Then, choking and having difficulty breathing, Birgit was taken away. Tears streamed down her dirty face. The policeman could see scrapes on her face and welts over her right eye.

A short time later, another policeman was holding her firmly under her arm and escorting her into the police station. There she was thrown with others in a jail cell. A few women had had their heads shaved. Birgit wasn't sure if it was the doing of the matrons in the jailhouse or some mob that had besieged them. Another woman who was sitting on the floor in the corner was rocking back and forth and picking strands of hair from her head and rapidly and repeatedly knitting through them. She had been attacked and someone with a nail had carved the Nazi swastika on her forehead.

The trials didn't take place for weeks and the women lived together in crammed, putrid cells during the duration. They had little food. Birgit's head was shaved. One or several eyewitnesses came forward to testify that each of the detained women had given aid and comfort to the enemy. Not only had they been German sluts but some bore Nazi offspring. During Birgit's trial two women came forward. The woman who had attacked her in the street testified that the defendant was morally corrupt and that she had not only fornicated with the enemy but had produced at least one little bastard from her union. Cat calls and howls followed from the spectators. The other witness that came forward was the caretaker's wife. Birgit had met her on one or two occasions when business was flourishing at Astergarden, but never after the German invasion. And because of the limited contact with her, Birgit could only conclude that the caretaker had confided to his wife about the lieutenant and that she had reacted angrily. Even a community group stirred emotions and created a frenzy that resulted in accusations that would not normally occur. The group's spokesperson had sworn that she had seen German soldiers come and go from her home and, later, with the "genetically bad" seed inside her, saw her belly swell up like a watermelon.

After the trial she was sentenced to eighteen months in an internment camp on Hovedoya Island. When the police transported her and the other few women who also had their heads shaved, they placed the internees in the back of an open truck. As the truck deliberately drove down the main avenue toward the pier where a boat was waiting, people gathered on the sides of the road jeering and taunting them and calling them names. They flung eggs, rotten fruit and cabbages at them, and the girl with the Nazi symbol on her forehead was hit directly on her face. A couple of teenage boys ran alongside the truck and one threw a stick with dog excrement stuck at its end. When the truck paused, they mocked the prisoners with a Nazi salute.

Birgit spent the better part of six months in the internment camp doing menial jobs, getting poor food and often being mistreated by the guards. One particularly vulgar guard raped her repeatedly until he was transferred, but she never complained. Feeling helpless and worthless, she retreated further into her own world. Her sister had written to her on one occasion and even tried to visit her until her husband got word of her intention and absolutely prohibited her from making the trip. He told Sonya that Birgit found herself where she was because these were the consequences of her actions and she had to pay the price. One evening, Birgit unsuccessfully tried to commit suicide by hanging herself, leaving her brain damaged. Two days later she was transferred to the insane asylum.

Birgit's child, Andreas, had been relocated to the *Lebensborn* home in Steinhöring, just outside of Munich, Germany. This occurred during the time Birgit lived in Bergen with her sister. Andreas was placed in Steinhöring with the hope he would be adopted by an SS family. He never was. He was one of the few residents too often overlooked while other infants found new families. While other babies were smiling and cooing, Andreas remained strangely withdrawn and silent. He stayed at the Munich *Lebensborn* home for over four years. When the Allied forces pushed deeper into Germany in the spring of 1945, the SS disbanded the *Lebensborn* project, closed down the homes, transferred the children to other facilities and burned all records and files with respect to Himmler's program. Andreas was turned over to St Mary's Orphanage, a Catholic adoption center, where Bruno Salvaggi, a migrant Italian worker, would meet him for the first time at the age of six, in the summer of 1947.

Epilogue

Bruno Salvaggi and his wife had shared everything they knew about their adopted son and his parents' ill-fated relationship. Much of what they recounted to the police inspector came from talking to people at the orphanage, from the child's files, father's diary and even from outside sources. The police inspector kept the case of Andreas Kuhlemann-Salvaggi's disappearance open for two years. From time to time a new tip would turn up and his department would follow up, only to be disappointed again. When the inspector retired and there was a shift in personnel the case file was officially closed. The file was extensive and filled a large cardboard box in the basement of the Provincial Police Headquarters; written on the corner of the box, next to cause of death: "Accidental Drowning (Unresolved)." His assistant, Calvi, had worked his way up the ladder and moved into Bellin's office. He was there for eighteen years until he got a political appointment in the capital serving as a liaison to the Minister of the Interior. When their party lost the election, he became Chief of Staff to the Mayor of Cosenza.

It had taken Lorenzo forty years to come to a decision about how to set his tortured soul at ease. He was tired of the nightmares, though infrequent. When they did happen, he would still wake in the middle of the night drenched in sweat. Instead of fading like an old photograph, the images had become sharper. He made a final decision to not take his secret with him to the grave. He waited until his mother, Bruno and Antonia had passed away. He had no wish to be the source of additional pain for any of them.

Now, maybe, perhaps maybe, he would find some redemption. As Lorenzo stepped down from his plane at Leonardo da Vinci International Airport and walked on the tarmac, it was a poignant reminder that he had not stepped foot on Italian soil for almost four decades. Things had changed in Europe. The Iron Curtain had come down. The European Common Market had taken shape with more integration of its economies, its military might and its scientific aspirations. Any discovery by the European Space Agency was applauded from Portugal to the Caucasus and beyond the North Sea. The psyche of humanity had changed; his had changed as well.

Lorenzo's and Annalisa's feelings toward each other had virtually faded to an occasional Christmas card. They came to the realization that there was no future together. He had toiled for ten years in the construction industry. Then attended Fordham University, graduating in the top five percent of his class, with a degree in psychology. In June of 1984, three months after graduating, he was standing in front of a high school class introducing the work of Sigmund Freud. He met his wife, Loretta, the following year at a pre-school conference. She had sat next to him and seemed nervous and disoriented. Once they started talking, she admitted that she had "big shoes to fill" in taking over Mr. Moreno's Spanish classes after his retirement. Lorenzo befriended her, introduced her to other teachers and they had had lunch together. The following week they were assigned to supervise study hall. Two weeks later, they went apple picking upstate. And, after one year, in late summer, they got married.

Both continued to work the next five years, intensively committed to their students during the day and to after school programs until the early evening. When they got home it was a strict routine. Kick off your shoes, open the back door, let the dog out and throw all the pillows off the couch. Then they would lie next to each other and recover mentally and physically for half an hour. Fridays were their time to forget the world and enjoy each other. Lorenzo swore he knew which Friday their child had been conceived.

While in Rome, he tried to stay focused. He had prepared as best he could, but knew too well that the legal system could be distorted and often produced unexpected results, especially when factoring in a jury's emotions. He had asked his sister to prick her finger and provide a droplet of blood, when she came to visit in New York. It was for the doctor to screen for family diseases, while the fetus was in Loretta's womb, he had told her. Another time, while his little brother visited, he had recovered a bloodstained tissue after Marcello shaved and nicked himself. Like a forensic scientist he had placed the samples in plastic bags and labeled them with name, date and relationship. His own blood was also drawn and labeled when he delivered the samples to the lab.

The results were not astounding. In fact, they were what he had surmised almost forty years earlier. His little brother, or more accurately, half-brother, was the product of a misdeed; his very existence represented an act of rape. If not for that criminal act, his little brother would've never come into the world. Lorenzo was worried about Marcello's reaction. "Why," he would ask, "did you wait so long to disclose what you had known?" And, "Why did you choose to disclose it now? Who does it help?" There would be pain, unquestionable pain, but his conviction was unwavering. His mother went to her grave without knowing. His sister and brother would know the truth. In turn, he would be unshackled from a lifetime of torment. Regardless, changing his mind was no longer an option; events were in motion.

The letters had been forwarded a week before by a personal carrier. The content was deliberately vague but expressed a sense of urgency. "A family matter would be revealed that might have serious and irreversible consequences for all of us." Other people would also be there. But no names were mentioned. Both his sister and half-brother had called him upon receipt of the handwritten letter but he had refused to disclose anything further, merely saying that it was of the utmost importance that they show up in La Pera. All their questions would be answered on that day and at that hour.

Their childhood home had been boarded up since their mother, Francesca, had passed away some seven years earlier. It wasn't until recently that they had discussed selling it. And that was another reason Lorenzo wanted a resolution to past matters. Because, upon transferring title, there would be a loss of control of the land, including evidence. It was agreed that his half-brother, who was a physics professor in Bologna, would fly to Rome. And since Gabriella lived with her husband and two children in Rome, they would meet there. From Rome they would fly together to Lamezia Airport and catch a taxi to La Pera.

Calvi, who had spent a lot of time on the case as Inspector Bellin's young assistant, was now of retirement age. When Lorenzo composed his letter, he tried to picture Calvi with gray hair, perhaps a little senile. But when the envelope arrived on Calvi's desk, his mind proved as sharp as ever; he recollected all the details of the case. And, even though just Lorenzo's name and return address appeared on the envelope and his unlisted telephone number didn't appear anywhere in the letter, Calvi had surprisingly called Lorenzo that same evening. He had been cordial on the phone. Ironically, he talked as if connecting with an old friend after many years. Was it genuine or was it just police training? Lorenzo wondered. He asked how he had been and even offered his belated sympathies on his mother's death. Calvi said that he remembered the case quite well when Lorenzo alluded to having some information. Even though Calvi was not directly involved with those types of crimes anymore, he still felt obligated to possibly put closure to that case. Besides, he believed he owed it to his former mentor, Inspector Bellin, to see the case through.

Lorenzo was ambivalent about the final letter. He had hesitated even in the post office. Should he, or shouldn't he, send it out? He wanted to confront all the issues at once, yet felt that maybe the events could play themselves out without this fourth correspondence. He knew that men like Giacomo could rip your heart out without batting an eyebrow, but could also appreciate a man who finally had the fortitude to come clean. Lorenzo had been told that he had mellowed somewhat in his old age. His anger and his ruthlessness had diminished with time, like the sharp edges of a stone in a stream. But Lorenzo had difficulty picturing him to be anything else than what he had been four decades earlier: aggressive, plotting, vengeful and reticent. The only difference was probably his waistline and his gray hair. Lorenzo also knew that his parents, Bruno and Antonia Salvaggi, had passed on and that Annalisa was still practicing medicine. He wasn't sure where. He had virtually lost contact with Annalisa while he was studying at the university. But, he thought, she would definitely like to know about Andreas. So, the thought of her gave him the surge of energy to drop the envelope in the mail shoot.

Campisi and Figli Excavation Company had to be hired for the entire day. Lorenzo had pre-paid part of the charges in advance to be assured that they would show up. One backhoe and one operator was what he had requested. Instead, the company insisted on having two men at the site. "Safety reasons," the company manager had stated, particularly on mountainous terrain. Then there was the problem in transporting the equipment on a trailer over narrow, winding roads. "Take it or leave it!" was their attitude. He took it, but insisted that the equipment and men be on his family's old farm no later than eleven in the morning.

Lorenzo arrived in Cosenza by train that same morning. He had grabbed a double shot of espresso and a croissant before jumping in a taxi. From the passenger side he could see the sky was an unusual turquoise color, perhaps a reflection off the Tyrrhenian waters. The old section of the city was the same – gritty and old. But the new sector imposed a cosmopolitan attitude – new and elegant storefronts, well-paved streets and new bridges. The ride on the outskirts brought him past new shopping centers with fashionable shops, internationally recognized brands. Large apartment buildings were everywhere, constructed and under construction. The driver informed him that they were low-income units, occupied primarily by the elderly and newlyweds. As they came to the mountain roads, Lorenzo remembered how they zigzagged except that they were now paved and perhaps a bit wider.

It was close to ten when he arrived. He told the cab driver that there was no need to take him up the very long driveway; that he would walk. He paid, grabbed his jacket and his soft leather case and hopped out. As the car struggled to turn around, Lorenzo paused on the side and took a long deep breath. The air felt uncommon. He looked around, taking everything in, as he made his way up the winding driveway to the house that was still out of sight. Trees and bushes had grown out of control. Weeds and algae had stifled a small pond. Small frogs were hopping about, under and over rotting leaves. The old vineyard, once neat rows of lush green, was now full of brown grasses and desiccated vines. The house was still the concrete box he remembered, but the white paint was discolored and stains of green and brown streamed from its roof. Windows and doors were boarded. A section of the loggia had partially collapsed into what had been the animal stall. Lorenzo walked around the property and stopped by the old shade to inspect rusty tools and implements once used by his father. A rose bush he had planted as a child had disappeared; rocks that had been piled as a tombstone to his dog were still there but scattered.

With intense dread he walked down toward the old barn. Tall grasses and weeds had reclaimed the dirt path, making it impossible to distinguish where it had been years past. A corner of the barn remained standing, with loosely hanging boards and supported by a nail or two. The tandoor, the outdoor brick and clay oven, was nonexistent. In its place was a pile of dark stones on the ground and some rusted metal grids partially buried in the dirt. The big oak tree, which seemed to have existed as an eternal landmark, was now reduced to a rotted stump with splinters. A skinny branch, several feet tall, shot up from the stump as if forcing its way upwards toward the heavens. Lorenzo interpreted that as a sign of rebirth and, perhaps, personal redemption. Clusters of other trees had grown in the vicinity. Then he tried to find the exact location he was looking for.

He had narrowed the search visually to a 15x15-feet-square area. Then he marked off the spot by walking around and gouging the ground with a stick. He had barely finished when he heard his name called out from the far end of the driveway, behind the house. He hollered back, hoping that they had heard as he hurried up the incline towards the voice. The excavators had arrived. He could hear clanking. They were unchaining the backhoe from the trailer parked on the side of the street. It took them a while to climb the sloping driveway with the equipment, fearing that the machine could roll backwards. Some thirty minutes later they had positioned the backhoe on the periphery of the square he had marked off and brought picks and shovels and even a ladder.

His siblings and the inspector arrived almost simultaneously. He greeted his brother and sister with warm hugs, inquired about their families and their trip, and they started talking about the impression the property made on them when they first set sight on it.

The inspector arrived in a Ford sedan. The driver wore a police uniform, and his blue and gray cap could be seen in the back seat. The inspector looked them over while the car came to a halt. He tried to picture Lorenzo from memory. Behind the closed windows he raised his hand courteously as if to say hello. When his car door swung open his eyes came to rest on Lorenzo.

"Good morning, Inspector. I'm Lorenzo Benedetta, the man who spoke with you on the telephone." Both men kept a comfortable distance. Neither made an attempt to move closer or shake the other's hand.

"I remember your voice," Calvi replied. "But I confess your face eludes me."

"This is my sister, Gabriella, and my younger brother, Marcello." They both nodded while uttering a perfunctory hello.

To Lorenzo, Inspector Calvi had the same profile. His face was still thin and elongated and had got droopy due to gravity's subtle but pernicious workings. He tried to walk as if he still had a bounce in his step but one could easily tell that he had spent time in a sedentary role. His belt was a notch too tight, an attempt to rein in the extra territory, but despite his obvious discomfort his belly still jiggled as he moved around. His short thick hair from days gone by had not only thinned out where you saw his pink scalp but had also receded. What remained of any noticeable hair was deep behind his neck, and it was puffy and long.

The inspector took a hard look around the property, obviously abandoned for years. He saw the two men and the backhoe digging further below from where they were standing.

"So, you decided it's time to sell?" He wasn't directing his comment to anyone in particular.

Gabriella responded. "Since Mother died a few years ago we had been discussing it but weren't serious until recently."

"I suppose there comes a time for everything." He pointed. "I see your workers are sprucing it up already." His face was turned and his eyes were lingering in the direction of the old barn.

"There's something down there I want to show you," answered Lorenzo as another car, a white Mercedes, slowly made its way up the driveway and in their direction. Lorenzo felt a little queasier than when the inspector arrived. He had no doubt that Giacomo was behind the tinted windows, sitting in the back seat.

"That's probably Mr. Salvaggi. I asked him to be here also," he said. His sister and brother looked perplexed as to what their older brother had planned.

The driver maneuvered the white car over a flat grassy area and came to stop parallel to the inspector's car. The inspector saw the elderly man's shadow in the back seat. He took a few steps towards the car and reached over and squeezed open the door handle. He looked in as the paunchy man slid his body down toward the open door.

"Good morning, Giacomo," said the inspector, addressing him by his first name.

"Nice to see you, Inspector," he said. The policeman extended his arm to shake his hand. Giacomo's left hand reached across his chest and grasped the inspector's four fingers, his right arm limp and dangling on his side from a stroke, years earlier. Then Calvi introduced the Benedettas, who were standing next to each other. One by one Giacomo gave a slight nod, as acknowledgement.

"So, you're the American," he said, directing his comment to Lorenzo. "You've been away for quite some time."

"About forty years," responded Lorenzo, not sure where Giacomo was going with his comments. But his driver reminded Lorenzo of a secret service man for state officials and was probably packing a sidearm in the shoulder of his well-tailored suit. The driver had stepped outside his car and, from behind his shades, was looking towards the excavators who were yelling something.

"I think those men are trying to get someone's attention," he said in a crisp voice, directed at his boss. The timbre seemed out of sync with his demeanor and good looks.

"I think they found something we should all see," responded Lorenzo as he started walking to his right. The excavator's agitation fueled their pace. Lorenzo's sister and half-brother followed him. The inspector, not as sprightly as the other three, ambled behind. The policeman followed closely behind the inspector. He was now in full uniform, wearing his cap and a pistol in his holster. Giacomo hadn't moved from his spot but had shifted his body and thrown his neck back as if looking over a wall. He was focused on the small line of people walking briskly down the incline. His chauffeur, who doubled as a bodyguard, came around the car and gripped Giacomo's good arm and slowly followed the others' tracks through the high grass. Every twenty or thirty feet his guide allowed him to stop and rest and catch his breath.

Lorenzo and his siblings saw that the tractor operator had stopped the engine and had climbed out of the cab. He was puffing vigorously on a cigarette and staring into the large square hole that was dug some four or five feet below the surface. Claw marks from his tractor could be seen around the walls. His assistant stood nearby, holding a shovel from the middle of its handle. They turned towards the two men and the woman briskly approaching. Then the three looked into the crater with their mouths open.

Gabriella was first to react. "Is that a human leg?"

"You'll have a better view from this side," said the machine operator.

Gabriella and Marcello walked around to the better vantage point. From there they could see a partially disinterred rib cage and human head. Pieces of rotted clothing were still hanging onto the skeleton. Its mouth was frozen open; only empty cavities remained where his eyes and nose had been.

"Who could it be?" mumbled the younger brother, seemingly very puzzled. Lorenzo leaned against the tractor as dream-like images flashed in his mind's eye. Wetness formed on his face and forehead and he felt drips rolling from his armpits. A wave of nausea was taking control.

The inspector and the uniformed officer arrived and looked down in the large grave. As the officer walked around the hole the inspector stood still, observing first Lorenzo and then the others. His right hand rubbed the stubble on his face until Giacomo arrived, then he moved closer to the tractor and nearer to Lorenzo.

Giacomo, out of breath and supported by his man, stood there chewing his tongue.

"You want us to dig it up completely?" asked the operator, while looking towards Lorenzo and the inspector.

"No. No need for that, we'll get forensics on it." He motioned to the officer who acknowledged his order and headed up the hill to the car radio.

"Why bury a body here?" asked Marcello. "Any idea who it is, Inspector?"

"I put him there," responded Lorenzo.

"What are you saying?" Gabriella asked sharply.

"I found him in the barn raping our mother. I reacted without thinking and I killed him." Lorenzo's heart was hammering. He felt bile flooding his body at the enormity of his confession. There was no turning back now. There was no sugar-coating it. His life would change forever and so would the lives of everyone else standing around. But he had rehearsed in his mind exactly what had happened. He was determined to give a full account. He was convinced that telling the truth, the entire truth as it had unfolded, might finally unshackle him. It didn't matter if he was condemned to prison for life. There he would finally be free.

"Who was it?" the inspector asked demurely, trying to get confirmation of what he already knew and making public all the pieces of the puzzle.

"Andreas. It's the remains of Andreas Salvaggi," said Lorenzo, his gaze locked on to the inspector and not being able to muster the fortitude to make eye contact with the others as he said it.

"You son of a bitch," mumbled Giacomo as he impetuously shifted his broken body around, almost losing his balance. "I knew it. I knew it from the beginning you were responsible. So many things pointed in your direction." He was pointing at Lorenzo with his arthritic index finger. "You have no idea how much pain and grief you've caused." Giacomo's face had turned red as he stabbed the dirt with his cane. His bodyguard steadied him from his paralyzed arm and, like an attack dog, stood at his side ready to carry out his orders.

"Let's all calm down," said the inspector with an air of authority. "I assure you everything will be sorted out."

"He was like an innocent child. Andreas didn't have an ounce of malice in his body. He couldn't harm anyone, least of all force himself on your mother." As Giacomo stressed his point, he kept looking in the pit, as if defending his brother would somehow resurrect him.

"Yes, he had disabilities but he still raped our mother." He looked up at his sister and brother. Gabriella was crying and being consoled by her younger brother. It tore Lorenzo's heart even more to say what he was about to say but there was no turning back. His brother had a right to know. He, Lorenzo, had waited long enough.

"And his blood runs through my brother's veins." As the words came out Lorenzo felt a weight lift off his chest, a certain catharsis, an emotional and psychological cleansing. Marcello was aghast, numb, astonished and speechless by the revelation.

"Lorenzo, what are you saying?" snapped his sister.

"I'm so sorry. There never seemed to be a right time. I never wanted to hurt you two. Before today, I never had the strength." Lorenzo, who had felt a catharsis a moment earlier, now felt totally drained, empty and alone.

His brother, still stunned from the disclosure, like one who finds himself on the ground after being stricken by a bolt of lightning, inquired further.

"Let me get this straight," he said, visibly shaking. "Are you saying this (pointing at the body) is my father?" Haltingly, he repeated the words.

Lorenzo hesitated a moment, barely able to look at Gabriella and Marcello; tears flowing down his face, crushed by remorse, he nodded softly, "Yes."

*

Within an hour a police forensics unit had swept onto the scene. They had secured the area. They removed the remains in special containers to a police lab in Cosenza. Lorenzo was taken into custody. His passport was confiscated. Then he pled not guilty before a magistrate and bail was set for 350,000 euros. His counsel, a prominent criminal attorney, had been referred by a New York City firm that had offices in Rome and Milan. He spent two and a half days in jail before Gabriella and his wife, Loretta, who had arrived in Cosenza the day following his incarceration, managed to raise the funds and get him released pending trial.

His younger brother, distressed, confused and shaken from the revelation had opted to go back to Bologna, telling Gabriella that he needed time and space to sort things out. Undeniably, tensions remained between Marcello and Lorenzo. The younger brother believed that, assuming the story was true, he didn't understand why Lorenzo had to use deadly force on a feeble-minded man. Marcello even thought that the "act" could've been without malice. Besides, Lorenzo didn't have to conceal the facts from him for forty years. Marcello was also deeply disturbed that since his father had been feeble-minded, what did that mean for his own children?

"He is uncommunicative and angry," was the way Gabriella put it, when Lorenzo asked how Marcello was doing. She too was trying to understand the tragic events. She was also bothered by another dimension of the incident which involved their mother. That she had gone to her grave not knowing that the life she had carried in her belly for nine months, and the infant she had raised as a single mother, was the seed of another man, not her beloved husband. Gabriella also pondered whether their mother, Francesca, had suspected something when she told Gabriella that certain characteristics of the child were "uniquely his own." Unlike herself and Lorenzo, Marcello's speech and physical development had accelerated beyond the norm; he always had an uncanny ability to absorb and retain information. As Lorenzo listened, his sister told him that she now found something else eerie that their mother had said: that it was almost as if Marcello's spirit had been constrained far too long and was finally free and uninhibited.

"What do you think she meant by that?" asked Lorenzo, looking at Gabriella for a response.

"Whether Mom suspected anything or not, the love she had for the child was pure and unblemished, and certainly no less than she had for us," said Gabriella.

*

When the prosecution sent bone fragments to Sardinia for DNA analysis, Lorenzo's counsel had arranged with the state prosecutor's office to have his own expert, from an independent lab, be present. Blood samples had been provided by the three siblings. The results corroborated Lorenzo's story. He and Gabriella were the offspring of one father and their younger brother of another, Andreas Salvaggi. They were relieved to be informed of the results, since the lawyer was prepared to have a court order signed to have Francesca's body exhumed and to have her DNA analyzed as well.

The scientific findings forced the state to release the body for a proper burial. This was six weeks after Lorenzo had been taken into custody. Andreas Salvaggi was finally at rest in a mahogany casket. The family had grieved in Giacomo's parlor for two days and buried him on the third day next to his parents, Bruno and Antonia Salvaggi. Annalisa had been instrumental in facilitating the attendance of Gabriella and Marcello. She had explained to her brother, Giacomo, over various conversations, that Gabriella was innocent and her younger brother was more than innocent in the entire matter. In fact, Marcello was their nephew and they should treat him as no less than that. Giacomo took a while to come around but finally made amends with Gabriella, and even put any ill will aside, when he hugged his nephew at the cemetery.

Lorenzo's trial lasted four days. The case piqued the nation's interest and was carried by all major news sources as a bizarre human-interest story. Giacomo and his family attended court each day. He listened attentively to all the evidence, occasionally exhaling loudly or shaking his head, not so much because the evidence was incredible but because it was painful. Annalisa, who sat next to him, kept her eyes on Lorenzo and her nephew, who was sitting just behind the defendant, next to his sister. DNA and other forensic evidence were introduced. Lorenzo was allowed to take the stand and tell his story, which came across as very credible, until Calvi took the stand.

The former inspector injected a new premise. Yes, the defendant's actions could be considered self-defense even when one defends another, such as a family member, from harm, but maybe it had been a consensual relationship. This attack had been blunted when Gabriella testified that her mother had suffered a serious head wound, multiple lacerations and bruises from head to toe. She also testified that her mother had previously been unconscious and then dazed. When she saw her mother in the house, all the signs indicated injuries from a struggle. It was certainly not some casual or consensual fling and to suggest otherwise was a smear on a good woman's honor and integrity.

The jury took forty-five minutes to come back with a verdict of not guilty. But little celebration took place. Lorenzo sat in the front pew, crying on his wife's shoulder. His younger brother, Marcello, started walking out with Annalisa and behind Giacomo and the bodyguard. Midway to the front entrance, he paused, and returned to the first pew where Lorenzo was sitting. Seeing the pain on Lorenzo's face, he put his arm around his brother's shoulder as they walked out together.

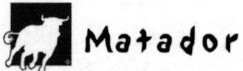

For exclusive discounts on Matador titles,
sign up to our occasional newsletter at
troubador.co.uk/bookshop